THE OPERA SINGER

by

Keith M. Costain

Produced by:

FriesenPress
Suite 300 – 852 Fort Street
Victoria, BC, Canada V8W 1H8

www.friesenpress.com

Distributed to the trade by The Ingram Book Company

For Vera, my beloved wife, without whose constant encouragement this book would not have been written.

"Collar the Lot."
Winston Churchill on the internment of
German-speaking European refugees in
Britain.

CHAPTER ONE

Vigorous pedaling of child-sized Cowley Roadster with small wooden steering wheel, once-red tubular bent plywood body faded now to dappled pink. Sky cloudless blue. Sun hot on my skin, on the plywood of the sporty car bowling along. Small square black-railed gardens of tall slender seaside houses drunk with scent of wallflower and rose. Sea mirror-calm, salty tang and flower aroma drugging the bypedaler. These are what come to mind about that morning when, in childhood trance, time and all things linear faded into the present moment, I was wakened by death.

I was nine – so long ago – another world, another century. It was 1942 – a crucial year in the World War my students now equate with Kaiser, Queen Victoria, Napoleon marching – flags flying, drums beating – in confident folly on Moscow.

It was a Saturday. Free of school I was "driving" the car my father had salvaged – sanding off rust, fixing the pedals, soaking every moving part in oil – a superb if second-hand Christmas present. Generous of Pop – who struggled to work on an ancient bike – to give me a car in a war.

I was in love with that car, unaware that when it was new and red it had been Toby Wood's whose father was rich enough to buy him something grander when he abandoned the Cowley to frost and rain in the grounds of the family house – second largest in a neighborhood of large houses. When he grew older (he never grew up) Toby drove his snazzy MG over a cliff ("failed to negotiate the corner," said the paper as if he were trying to mediate a dispute at his father's factory) and much of his father's wealth went to nurses and technicians and machines to keep him breathing for forty more years. But that was long after the war – long after he punched me on the nose making it bleed lavishly and I went home howling in pain thinking it was broken and Pop in his oily overalls marched over to "do" the posh, elegant Mr. Wood and came home with a big bag of pears and a bunch of grapes.

The day I met with killing, pedaling my car in a dream along the brief promenade empty of people save for the sentries at one end guarding the estate of the largest house in the neighborhood (the one next to Toby's) where a Nazi diplomatic grandee, his wife and teen-aged daughter were shut away "for the duration" – that day I was startled by a strange commotion in the sky. I looked up, leaning back in my wooden driver's seat with the green and yellow floral cushion put there by Ma for comfort but was blinded by sunlight.

The sound above – a harsh insistent chattering – commanded attention. I wriggled out of the car and, shading my eyes, looked up to where the sound seemed to be. At last I saw two smallish aircraft high in the sky chasing each other the way I'd seen hawks go after sparrows, the sparrow dodging the hawk by sudden turns, rapid dives, steep climbs, frantic bursts of speed. Sometimes the sparrowplane became the hawkplane only to revert to sparrowhood when the other gained an advantage of height or position. From what I had seen on the newsreel on Saturdays at the *Plaza* children's matinee I knew it was battle I was watching.

I had no sense of danger. It was like seeing a movie in technicolor with scents as well as sounds and picture. I wondered why the sentries guarding the Important Nazi had started to shout at me. I didn't associate the duel in the sky with death – the news shown to children didn't deal with death. Crashing planes, yes – that was exciting – but not death. The pilots always cheerfully bailed out and floated gently to earth like dandelion seeds to be welcomed by admiring farm-workers as they coolly produced pipes and tobacco tins and asked for a light. Leaping from a 'plane into the empty sky was all in a day's work to them. We didn't see the pictures of raging German peasants nailing wounded pilots to the fertile earth with pitchforks or bodies hurtling when carefully packed 'chutes failed to open.

I had no idea the pilots up above me were trying to kill each other because one was a Luftwaffe officer off-course but still ready for Spitfires and the other a refugee from Poland burning to kill as many Germans as came his way.

The Isle-of-Man wasn't like Germany and Poland. The Manx didn't destroy each other's houses and murder their occupants and burn their crops no matter how much or how often they felt like it. There was occasional house-breaking but that's not the same thing – at least it wasn't then. There was plenty of poaching, but killing only of game and poultry, cattle, pigs, sheep and assorted vermin. The days of Viking raiders, violent brandy smugglers, Illiam Dhone's doomed rising against Charles II were long past and, unlike in Ulster, stayed that way.

So I stood and looked up at the climbing, diving aircraft in wonder while the English sentries yelled from the distance, ordered not to leave their sentry-boxes except to march the distance between them once every fifteen minutes. I wondered why Herr and Frau Nazi hadn't figured this out. Why, after dark, between sentry marches, they hadn't climbed the high stone wall surrounding the estate and run off with their daughter. I didn't know then that at dusk a sergeant led a roving band around the wall to disappoint such attempts and keep the sentries awake. They would also raise the alarm should a rescuing U-boat surface at night in the bay. So far as I'm aware none ever did and the Germans, with nowhere to go, stayed on their sequestered estate till Hitler shot himself and the thousand-year Reich died in its childhood.

I watched the 'planes in the sky for what now I suppose must have been no more than a few minutes though it seemed much longer at the time. Then one spiraled toward the sea, its tail missing – falling … twisting …

falling … smash-splash! A geyser of white spray rose and fell like salt rain then, after scant turbulence the sea was mirror-calm as if nothing had happened. A subject for Brueghel.

I had seen the roundels on the fuselage of the falling plane and expected a parachute with a pipe-smoking pilot to drift down like a dandelion seed. But there was only the German 'plane streaking away. I was shocked. The Spitfire pilot must be hurt badly. His fall had been a long one. He had been swallowed by the sea with no-one to help. All the sentries did was yell at me. I decided to do something heroically helpful to save the pilot but couldn't think what so pretended I had not seen what I had seen and went back to playing, racing my roadster round the block we lived on 'till I was hungry.

"Did you hear?" said Pop just in for lunch. "One o' those Polish f'las shot down in the bay this morning. Herman got away." Pop had been raked with machine-gun fire at Ypres which hadn't improved his temper but he called Germans collectively nothing more abusive than "Herman." Just "Herman the German."

"What happened to the pilot?" Ma asked.

"Dead," said Pop, "another damn Spitfire lost. Air-Sea Rescue's out there looking for the pieces."

"I saw it, I saw everything" I told them feeling superior.

"Oh Lord!" Ma looked horrified. "You could have been killed! That's the last time you go out on your own! I told you not to give him that car! There's a war on!"

"I heard," said Pop, adding "He's making it up."

He took refuge in the *Daily Express*. On occasions of storm he sheltered in the outside toilet where spiders crawled over your bare bum. For brief squalls the *Daily Express* sufficed.

"A spitfire's down in the bay! A dogfight in broad daylight! The war's getting awful close."

The bearer of this superfluous news was the neighbor from the house on the right of ours, Mrs. Corkill, known to us simply as Bessie. She was a tall, large-breasted woman imposing as an operatic Brunhilde, someone you could never ignore. Her long graying glistening hair was brushed back tightly from her forehead and imprisoned in a bun. She was overbearing, her voice loud, bossy, truculent – as if she was always in a fight and had to defend herself. She wore glasses that made her eyes seem big and sinister. She was nosy, aggressive and at heart the soul of kindness. She rubbed Ma and Pop – Pop especially – the wrong way by telling them how to run their lives and bring up their children. She bragged about a superior niece in England who had done all the right things despite a meager education – married a wealthy foreigner, had twins and lived in luxury in Bolton. Bessie drove Pop wild by dropping in while we were eating.

"She does it on purpose – waits 'till we've started then walks in. Thinks she can come in here large as life like we're the bussy caffy (bus station café) – stands there watching – goes on about what we're eating – puts me off me dinner – tell her!"

"You tell her," said Ma. "She's lonely. Willy hardly ever speaks to her. She likes to talk."

"Likes the sound of her own fog-horn voice. Willy couldn't get a word in edgewise – gave up years ago. Why's she always here at mealtimes?"

"She knows you'll be home. She's fond of you."

"I'm not fond of her – you tell her."

"Tell her yourself. And she's always wanted children – so she likes to see Erik and Carlo."

Carlo wasn't old enough to have formed any firm views about Bessie – he was only three – but I found her rough attentions annoying. She didn't know how to be gentle with children the way Ma did. She was always roughing up my hair, telling me off, laughing a loud mirthless laugh after cracking jokes I didn't get. Nature knew a thing or two in denying her children. When I was an adult we became good friends but as a child I found her as much a trial as Pop whom she loved, as she confessed four decades later when Pop and Willie were both dead and Ma was clinging to life by her brittle fingernails at Ballacashin Old Folks' Home with the palm trees round it.

"The pilot come down in the sea on his parachute and it drownded him out there," said Bessie dramatically, indicating the bay by a quick jerk of her head.

"Erik saw it all," said Pop who seemed to have changed his mind about me making the story up. "There was no parachute. F'la didn't get out. Shot to bits most like. They'll be dredging him up – looking for'm with a net or a sieve."

"Ernest!" Ma wasn't having graphic talk in her living room.

"He was drownded by his parachute," said Bessie aggressively, "I heard."

"You heard wrong. Crashed. No parachute," Pop declared.

"Perhaps Erik was mistaken," said Ma to keep the peace. "Perhaps there was a parachute and Erik didn't see it."

"There wasn't," I said. "How would *she* know, she wasn't there."

"Don't you talk about your Auntie Bessie like that," said Ma, "and don't call her 'she' – *"she's the cat's mother."*

Ma was fearful of being talked about in the neighborhood as "soft" – an indulgent parent who let her children wrangle with grown-ups instead of observing a respectful silence.

6

"Well, she was'n there and I was and there was'n any parachute – you don't believe me ask the soldiers minding the Nazis – they saw the whole thing and there was'n any parachute and she is'n me auntie either."

This passionate utterance left me breathless. Bessie turned red all over from contradiction – from a child!

"You going to let that kid stand there and give me a mouthful?" Bessie demanded of Ma and Pop. "You let that kid talk back like that he'll be talking back to you."

"He does and I'll clout him," said Pop.

"You'll do no such thing," said Ma.

"Who says?"

"I do. There'll be no violence in this house."

"We'll see about that," said Pop banging his fist on the table so the crockery jumped, determined on violence as long as Bessie occupied his living-room.

Having fomented discord in our house Bessie withdrew to the silence of her own, there to taunt the unspeaking asthmatic Willy for not being with Monty in the desert fighting Rommel.

CHAPTER TWO

CHILD OF AN AGE BEFORE TELEVISION, UNACQUAINTED AS YET WITH History, unenlightened by Ma, Pop, Bessie, neighbors, relatives, schoolteachers – all of whom knew different – I took the realities of my daily life to be the normal state of things everywhere. It seemed unremarkable to me when I was ten that my town – Ramsey, Isle-of-Man – should be divided, the people living south of the harbor (our side) going freely about their daily lives while those north of it, along the Mooragh Park sea-front, were imprisoned behind barbed wire.

On the Mooragh side of the harbor men had been herded into seaside hotels and boarding houses surrounded by double ten-foot-high barbed wire fences guarded by armed soldiers. They had been locked away like our neighborhood Nazi but not in such comfortable quarters. I didn't ask why this was so – whether it was fair or a good practical thing to do. It was a simple fact of life, a given, like my Uncle Sidney's over-fondness for drink or our Cumberland terrier Milby's incontinence on carpets when wildly excited, which he was easily and often.

The men imprisoned behind those fences were "enemy aliens." On our side of town people were neither enemy nor alien though some were decidedly peculiar. I supposed "the prisoners" as they were also called must be criminals – people you couldn't trust for a minute. When they were moved about outside the Camp, in small groups out for a walk or in long columns marching to see the "pictures," they were carefully guarded. *Marching*, though, isn't the right word. That is no doubt what the guards wanted them to do but the prisoners shuffled slovenly along just to be awkward. Admittedly they had plenty to be awkward about.

They were guided to the *Cinema* – the generic name of the town's other more down-at-heel movie house. Unlike the upscale *Plaza* it didn't have an effusive manager dressed rather like Noel Cowerd to greet you at the door rubbing his hands together as he did so like a Manx Uriah Heep. His affected upper class English was inevitably sabotaged by his Northern vowels. He wore a toupee on his egg-bald head, which caused Pop to refer to him as "the man with the patent-leather hair."

Our neighboring Nazi wasn't taken to the *Cinema* or anywhere else as far as I knew but he had his wife and child with him and an estate to walk about in wearing his well-tailored suits while the prisoners, separated from their families, shabbily dressed, living three or more to a room needed their outings now and then to cheer them up. Bessie thought they were mollycoddled.

"Keep'm locked up!" she declared nodding vigorously to indicate the strength of her feelings. "Taking'm to the pictures! They'll be coming to Sunday dinner next. Letting'm work on farms! All they'll be doin' is lyin' about in barns! With them about the place farmers' wives, daughters, land-girls – we all know what they'll be up to and it in't farming."

When I asked what farmers' wives and daughters and land-girls would get up to that wasn't farming she told me to shut up and not listen to other people's conversations.

"The ones land-girls better watch out for is farmers," said Pop from behind the *Daily Express*, provoking Ma every time he said it.

The Ramsey of those days would seem now, in contrast with the vicious Russian version, to be part of some relatively benevolent gulag (if that isn't a contradiction) – part of a national network of towns housing prisoners of war. To my ten-year-old self its peculiar partition seemed natural. It felt most unnatural when, the war over, Carlo and I walked with Ma and Pop over the swing bridge that crossed the harbor to the north promenade free now of entangling wire and the "internees" it had enclosed. It took gradual mental re-adjustment for me to see the town as a whole instead of two adjacent settlements, one penitentiary, the harbor between.

I wasn't old enough to be able to make comparisons between now and the way the town was before the war. Ma and Pop never spoke of the time when a fleet of ships (later repainted gray and summoned to Dunkirk) with black hulls, white superstructures and red and black funnels ferried Lancashire's tens of thousands to enjoy beaches now deserted and, it was said, mined to blow up any unwise sea-borne Germans who should come our way.

Soldiers, sailors, airmen and women, wire, prisoners, gray naval ships anchored off shore, barrage balloons drifting above like bloated kites or whales of the air, 'planes overhead (except when crashing), tense talk of air-raids we never actually experienced despite hysteric sirens – these and more were matters of routine.

When the war ended and life returned to "normal" the world for me turned upside down. The thousands of military personnel and prisoners, the ships, the 'planes vanished as if by magic. We looked out on empty horizons. There was an unaccustomed silence after so many years of noise; there was unfamiliar light after years of blackout. Street lamps shone freely, we flicked electric switches instead of the matches that lit the gas mantles, the oil lamps or the candles of war. Ugly blackout curtains came down. Carlo's red Mickey Mouse gasmask was good only to frighten really little kids with. Normality took some getting used to.

But to return to the prisoners. Some people in the town had a low opinion of them. After all they talked to each other in foreign languages which was evidence enough of their hostility to Britain especially since they could speak English when they felt like it. They were dangerous fascists, some believed, and deserved to be interned.

"Ugh!" said Bessie with a theatrical shudder, "they're dirty – they're enough to make your flesh creep." Her face was scrunched in horrified disgust as if she had blundered into a rat's nest.

"Who are they?" I asked her.

"Foreigners," she said. "Dirty foreigners" as if that said it all.

"What's a foreigner?" I asked.

"Someone as doesn't use soap and won't speak English and'd gut yer like a herrin' in a dark alley and think nothin' to it. They've all got knives – sharp knives as they'd stick in yer and twist sure as eggs is eggs."

"Is that why the guards have guns?"

"Course it is. They'd all run back to Hitler if we let'm"

"How?"

"They'd steal the fishermen's boats and sail'm over to Germany, that's how."

"Wouldn't our navy ships stop them?"

"By day they'd have the nets over the side…they'd pretend they were decent Manx fisher folk…they'd sneak off by night like the thieving murderers they are."

I was so impressed by Bessie's grasp of prisoner mentality and insight into their plans that I hurried to tell Pop about it.

"Don't take any notice of her," he said, "she's barmy."

If I took the wartime town to be normal I also found living in a house full of strangers to be nothing out of the ordinary. I have Ma to blame for that.

Ma's father, an enterprising Lancastrian, had "made and lost three fortunes" according to family lore the veracity of which I couldn't test since Grandfather Wellman had fecklessly died before even my elder brother Ronald was born. Grandma Wellman was inaccessible, elderly, possibly ill, somewhere in England so I couldn't verify family history with her either. However, if Ma had had a moneyed background growing up that would explain her sense of being "Middle Class." Why she married Pop, a penniless Manxman with only a worker's weekly wage to support us all it's hard to say. It must have been for love since Ma was incurably romantic. Maybe also it was because of Pop's skill and popularity as a ballroom dancer (he won prizes for it) though he never danced another step after he married Ma nor ever again wore the smart Fred Astaire evening dress, with tails, featured in the photographs of his dapper dancing days.

Whatever the cause Ma's hankering for bourgeois respectability made her persuade Pop into leasing a very large house the rent for which must have stretched his limited means. He complied because, as he often said, "all I want is a quiet life." If I'd been riddled with bullets at Ypres when I was eighteen I'd want a quiet life too.

So they moved into *Rosetree Villa* just after Ronald was born and stayed there for the rest of their married life. In the Sixties the elderly widow who owned the house died and Ma (Pop had died too by this time) was offered the place for a pittance and bought it but couldn't manage it on her own and had to sell it again. It's still there, run down, seedy, impossible to reconcile with the house I remember. It won't be long before the wreckers move in to make space for another of the new, enormously expensive luxury apartment houses being built over the old neighborhood. Ma would have loved one.

It was the size of our house that attracted official attention at the beginning of the war. The authorities declared that it was "too big" for Ma, Pop, Carlo, Ronald and me. In any case Ronald had already left to train to fight the Germans (there would later be my sister Rachel but she arrived to celebrate the peace and thus had no influence on government calculations in 1940).

Men from the housing authority assessed all the houses on the Island. They viewed the three storeys, seven bedrooms, two large sitting rooms and dining room of our Victorian dwelling – all in addition to our family living quarters – and found that we occupied too much space. They sent people "from across" to share it with us. These people were, to use the phrase of the time, "billeted on" us – like an occupying power if, on the whole, more agreeable.

Our lodgers were pilots and navigators based at the nearby Jurby and Andreas air stations who brought their wives with them. There were also a few homesick English soldiers whose flat feet, defective eyesight or advancing years rendered them unfit for invasions, long marches, the heat of Burma or of battle. They guarded the prisoners and yearned for the wives and families left, by official fiat, to be bombed in Liverpool, Manchester, Birmingham, London and elsewhere. They were looked down upon by the airmen as a sort of military peasant. Also in the house from time to time were mysterious English civilians in baggy suits, wide-brimmed hats and long trench coats looking like the Gestapo or mafia hit men in movies of the Chicago thirties. They contributed mysteriously to "the war effort" though no one seemed to know how. All of these people paid Ma rent, which made her feel and pronounce herself retroactively justified in prodding Pop to take a house he couldn't really afford.

"See?" she said triumphantly, "see?"

"No," said Pop, "I don't."

In the late 1940s, flush (so to speak) from her wartime experience, Ma turned the place into a seaside boarding house despite its one ancient bathroom and single inside Edwardian toilet with overhead cistern and long wooden-handled chain. Constipation and bladder infection thrived there for the next twenty-five years until holiday-makers went to Spain instead.

The transient war-time occupants of our house were known collectively as "the lodgers." If they stayed long enough we took to using their actual names instead of room numbers in family conversation but most were not there for more than a few months. Some were moved about by military fiat; others simply went to work and never came back. After watching that *Spitfire* crash I understood. The pilots and navigators and bomb-aimers and gunners would leave on their bicycles for the town bus station in late afternoon. There they would take the Air Force bus to Jurby or Andreas airfields from which they would fly off to bomb Germany or attack German aircraft to protect the bombers, and then they would return to us as if from the night shift at a factory. Or not.

Death came to us in telegrams.

Ma had to comfort weeping women – at least they seemed like women to me but many had married while still in their teens and had not long been out of school. One I remember especially – an impressively ancient seventeen-year-old. She came from somewhere called Saskatchewan, the place where I would later live and work for nearly thirty years but which then sounded to me like a sneeze and was as remote as the moon. She had never before strayed from the confines of her small prairie town and now she was on the other side of the world, her boy-husband of twenty the co-pilot of a bomber much sought-after by German flak. Every time he left for "work" she feared he wouldn't return. One gray morning he didn't. The Post Office youth in the pill-box hat riding his official red bike came two weeks later to bring her the routine sympathies of the War Office. She was, it seemed, a widow before her eighteenth birthday.

She fell head-first into despair. She wouldn't eat or even get out of bed. Ma became frantic. After another two weeks had gone by the Post Office boy with the pill-box hat clamped to the side of his head returned with another telegram. *Husband not dead stop Husband alive stop Prisoner in Germany stop.* I can still see the young Saskatchewan wife racing down the stairs from her bedroom shrieking "He's alive! He's alive!"

We never did learn which of the two telegrams was the more accurate.

Ma was surrogate mother, social worker, landlady, cook, psychotherapist, cleaner, whatever was demanded. Pop may have aspired to a quiet life but he was living with the wrong wife in the wrong house in the wrong century for that. Ma insisted from time to time that he "have a word with" young husbands whose wives complained to her in confidence or that he aim a "talking to" at one of the flat-footed dyspeptic army guards consoling himself for his medical frailty and enforced bachelorhood by making generous offers to wives whose husbands were away on training courses. Pop, sent on a number of such delicate missions, hated the role of moral cop, especially in relation to people who paid his wife rent and ended up discussing over a map and a diplomatic drink with the offender the best way to win the war quickly.

Whenever he could he retreated to the half-acre he rented from Joe Broom (spelling rendered down from *Brougham)* the butcher who was never seen anywhere without his stained shapeless brown felt hat. He wore it in his shop – it was reported that he even wore it in bed with the (despite the war) expensively perfumed, beautifully made up, remarkably nubile and much younger Mrs. Broom who married him for his money Bessie said as though stating a fact, "A slender woman like her…imagine!…in bed with Joe Broom and him weighing a ton and only wearing that hat! Frighten anybody on a dark night! Like sleeping with a bull! A whale! He'd crush a body ter death!"

Bessie made remarks like this when Ma said I was safely out of earshot and I was hiding behind the sofa.

Pop always defended Joe Broom whenever Bessie felt inclined to have a go at his reputation because he loved the garden he had hacked out of the wilderness of weeds Joe had rented to him for a nominal fee. It was there that Pop grew the potatoes, carrots, onions, peas, Brussels sprouts, rhubarb, gooseberries and strawberries that we ate in season. It was there Pop built two pens – one for hens (Leghorns and Rhode Island Reds) the other for ducks – so that we had fresh eggs and poultry to eat in spite of war and rules and rationing and occasional massacres by fascist rodents. Pop even indulged a secret passion for flowers which, after the war, became an obsession. His cross-bred carnations and exotic gladioli (grown now in a greenhouse) were legendary on Ballacray Road.

Pop's original garden (after the war Joe Broom rented him part of a small field where he created an even bigger and better one) is now covered by the asphalt parking lot of a row of condominiums just as the mud lane over-arched by tree branches creating a leafy tunnel, a place where we found thrushes nests, and the pond from which we scooped up tadpoles to keep in jam-jars have been replaced by expensive dwelling boxes in rustic brick arranged in crescents each house with a small neat lawn, a small brown rustic wishing well and a green gnome in a tall pointed red hat.

Ma became more reconciled to Pop's garden absences when he started taking there the various miscreants she selected for him to advise either on how to treat their wives or how not to treat the wives of fellow-lodgers. Pop provided spade-therapy for many over the years as they all dug together for Victory.

CHAPTER THREE

POP'S FAMILY, ON HIS FATHER'S SIDE, WAS, AS HE TOLD EVERYONE HE met for the first time, of Viking extraction, which is why he wanted to christen his first-born Ragnald. Ma said "over my dead body" but settled for Ronald. Pop was born in Colby near Castletown, the Island's ancient Capital. In a Geography published when Pop was a child his birth-place is described as "a picturesque hamlet in a glen in the parish of Kirk Arbory."

Pop's brother Sidney and his sisters Emmeline and Agatha had migrated to Douglas, the new (since 1869) Capital of the Island and seat of insular power boasting that Viking institution Tynwald (the Manx Parliament) and that English intrusion the Lieutenant Governor's mansion. When my cousin George's wife became the Governor's private secretary there was such windy pride swelling the family sails that Pop, his Norse blood surging, said disgustedly that he was glad he'd left the lot of them to dwell in the north where the air was pure. "Sour grapes," said Ma.

Why Pop didn't get along with Sidney, Emmeline and Agatha we never knew. I asked Ma who said, "Ask your father." When I took her advice he chanted his mantra, "Because all I want is a quiet life," I hadn't seen signs that my paternal aunts and uncle were especially obstreperous or obnoxious. Even when he was drunk Uncle Sidney was quiet about it. "He gets tired easily" Aunty Avril would say whenever he staggered genteelly from a room unobtrusively displacing furniture, sending an occasional *objet* to the carpeted floor.

Perhaps Pop felt like the odd one out in his family since his brother and sisters had all "married money" or made quite a lot of it. They lived that comfortable white-collar bourgeois life of which Ma felt deprived by her erratic father's uncertain business sense and her husband's peculiar satisfaction in driving a sooty Victorian locomotive for the Isle-of-Man Railway Company.

Pop's collar was defiantly blue. Like his father before him he was a senior driver for the Railway Company, the only member of his generation in the family to come home after a day's work industrially dirty in a Catherine Cookson, D.H. Lawrence sort of way. He was as dusty with coal, as damp with spilled black oil as any miner and as much in need of that tin bath before the kitchen fire (the lodgers in more or less constant occupation of the one bathroom).

He piloted a smoke and soot spewing steam locomotive built in the year of Queen Victoria's Jubilee. When I was ten the narrow gauge railway on which it ran covered most of the Island. It stretched out from Douglas to Ramsey in the north, Castletown and Port Erin in the south and to Peel on the west coast. An equally ancient electric railway followed the coast-line from Douglas to Ramsey. It is still there but only a few miles of steam railway track and some rolling stock remain – a Nineteenth Century curiosity popular with tourists, railway buffs and producers of sentimental movies about leprechaun Ireland.

During the war the railway was as busy as it had been in its heyday carrying soldiers, airmen and women, naval personnel, prisoners and civilians. Among the latter from time to time were Ma, Carlo and me going to stay for occasional long weekends in Douglas visiting Ma's sister, my Aunty Doreen, and calling on Pop's family, which he didn't seem to mind despite his own refusal to visit any of them. We took the train rather than the more convenient Isle-of-Man Road Services bus which went past our door because Pop received free rail passes for his family from time to time.

I looked forward to our visits to the Island's capital as if we were traveling from some remote Highland glen to London instead of only a few miles to a small city.

Those were a long few miles. We began by walking the two miles or so to the railway station, lugging luggage. We could, of course, have taken a taxi, had there been one to take and had we been able to afford it. We could also have caught the town bus if the town had had one to catch. Of necessity we walked and lugged.

Then we had to wait for the train. It puffed its leisurely way to Douglas on a roundabout route stopping at every station, some informal "halts" and whenever a stray flock of sheep, herd of cows, the odd horse or goat took to grazing alongside the track uninhibited by the engine's shrieking stream whistle. The engine always rested, sighing in steam, at the great junction of St. John's where the lines from Peel and Ramsey converged. Down the steep hill above St. John's – *Slieu Whallian* – suspected witches, we were told, were once rolled in spiked barrels. If they survived the descent they were judged to have done so by witchcraft and put to death in horrible ways. If they were found dead in the barrel they were pronounced innocent. "Irish logic," said Pop shifting the blame. "Men's logic," said Ma, shifting it back.

Bessie wouldn't have stood a chance in those days.

Once in Douglas we caught a yellow city double-decker bus to take us the two miles or so to Auntie Doreen's house.

"Wipe yer feet and come in," she would say, "and don't muck up t'furniture as I've just polished, don't play with the ornaments, don't touch the piano, keep yer fingers outa't'lectric sockets we don't want yer 'air on end and yer face all blue, 'ang yer coats up don't leave'm lyin' all over t'place, watch yer don't step on't dog and don't tease 'im or 'e'll bite yer, put that humbrella down yer can't open it in 'ere it's not a parachute….."

Aunty Doreen dropping and picking up aitches at random ran through an impressive checklist of don'ts. Then she would draw breath and say

"Yer must be fair clemmed after t'journey. 'Ere's some Cornish pasties and jam tarts just out't oven. Eat up!" She was older than Ma, her Lancashire speech little modified by Island influences.

Her pasties were the best I've ever tasted. The jam tarts weren't bad either.

Her only son, my cousin Herbert was, like my brother Ronald, away in England being trained to kill. Aunty Doreen doted on Herbert whose personality was not improved by her daily assurance that he could do no wrong. But Aunty Doreen's doting was strictly limited; she had a keen eye for wrongdoing in Carlo and I. However, her house was a large one and she allowed us to spend our weekends at the top of it playing with Herbert's old toys, out of the way while she and Ma caught up on gossip, especially as it related to their younger brother, my Uncle Walter, whose wife, Effie, it was whispered, slept with sailors while her husband was in uniform somewhere in the Middle East. After the war Walter caused a scandal by initiating a divorce – the first person in either Ma or Pop's family ever to take this dire and oh so publicly shameful step.

Aunty Doreen's husband, called Herbert like his son, was denied half his name by general consent. He was "Bert" to all who knew him. He had a clock and watch-mending business. He always seemed glad to see us. We were something of a relief from his termagent wife, who, when they were alone, treated him like a mildly senile elderly relative, lecturing him on everything from the right and proper way to butter his toast to the cleaning of his shoes and the tying of his tie. She stood in their vestibule every morning brushing his suit all over before opening the outer door to launch him spic, span, dustless and stray-threadless upon the day.

"She didn't love him," Ma told me in confidence years later.

This had been obvious to everyone. I wondered why my aunt had made this loveless marriage. Maybe the answer lies in that photograph of Ma and Pop's wedding party where a younger, slenderer version of Aunty

Doreen, wearing a hat like an inverted bucket, stares sourly at the camera through the thick lenses of her glasses. She envied Ma her good looks, her wedding to the handsome man Pop undoubtedly was in those days, she wanted to be married like everyone else and seized upon the inoffensive Herbert who had never said "boo!" to any advancing goose. He could afford to keep her in the style her father had accustomed her to in his days of wine and roses. This in turn enabled her to patronize Ma.

Uncle Bert had inherited his house from his mother. It was as big as ours but much better maintained and more expensively furnished. He and Aunty Doreen lived in it free of military lodgers. There were no airfields in the immediate Douglas vicinity and only part of the City – the extensive promenade well away from Uncle Bert's neighborhood – was used as a camp for prisoners. They "put up" occasional visitors in the form of government officials as their contribution to the downfall of Hitler and the Axis Powers while they prayed that their son would never see battle. He never did but after the atomic bomb modified their view of the war he was sent to keep the Japanese in order. He told us that he did this by threatening to kill them if they didn't obey him. I personally doubted that my cousin would have had the nerve to be so aggressive. In any case he worked in an office as a kind of military clerk.

"I couldn't be doin' wi'em all underfoot," Aunty Doreen would say – not about the Japanese but our lodgers as if through some flaw of character Ma had brought them all flocking to our house. "T'ouse must be a pig's breakfast dawn till dusk."

Unlike Ma, the stone floor of whose ancient kitchen was a minefield of unwashed pots and other dishes filled with cold water to "steep," Aunty Doreen was one of those pathologically house-proud women who, when everything has been washed, dusted and polished, got down to scrubbing the tiled front steps and the concrete garden path. I wondered how she kept herself from flicking a light duster over the flowers.

The first member of Pop's family we called upon during these Douglas visits was Aunty Emmeline, an excessive Barbara Cartland sort of woman, over made-up, clad in flowing bright flowery draperies, her hair dyed blonde, rings with glistening stones on every finger, long ear-rings a-dangle. She exuded strong perfumes and strong opinions on everything. She could out-Bessie Bessie.

Her house was full of ornamental glass. There were gold-framed wall mirrors in all directions – oval, rectangular, circular, square, even a small star-shaped one with colored stones set in each of its spikes. The newel posts of the staircase glittered with small inlaid squares of mirror-glass; there were cabinets with glass doors their glass shelves displaying glass ornaments in colors spanning the rainbow. Glass knick-knacks stood or hung in every room. When she served us afternoon tea there were cut crystal bowls of various sizes in evidence. We half-expected a crystal teapot instead of the shiny silver one that was actually used. Emmeline did have a pair of glass slippers. We imagined her drinking champagne from them. Emmeline's house resembled the nest of a large flock of demented magpies and as children Carlo and I thought it was a wonder of nature. We wanted to see and handle everything – especially my aunt's little colored glass animals.

As we grew older we grew more sarcastic referring to Emmeline's house as "the Crystal Palace," making jokes about people living in glass houses, wondering why Emmeline hadn't grown taller since she lived under glass, etc.. We wondered how Emmeline could afford to indulge her obsession on Uncle Alex's wages as a bus inspector. Perhaps the money they had inherited from his second cousin explained it. The legacy was said to have been substantial.

Aunty Emmeline had been married for many years but was childless so she was indulgent to us after laying down rules for the handling of her glass gewgaws. When we came calling she fed us large quantities of homemade fruitcake in quality on a par with Aunty Doreen's Cornish pasties. Rationing didn't seem to affect Aunty Emmeline's baking in any way.

After the war, when Emmeline was close to fifty she went to see her doctor, concerned by an alarmingly rapid weight-gain. Upon examining her carefully the doctor, shaking his head in disbelief but unable to deny the facts, told her she was pregnant. She was horrified, declared it was ana-tomically impossible, but the doctor stuck to his findings. Subsequent test results backed him up. Emmeline sought a second opinion but the result was the same. "Madame, you are with child," said the specialist who had a taste for florid rhetoric. Shock waves ran through the family. It had been accepted with certain hushed innuendoes that my mild and somewhat effeminate Uncle Alex was impotent so, the virgin-birth theory discarded with giggles, narrowed family eyes focused on the gentlemanly bachelor Mr. Arthur (we never knew whether this name was his first or last) who had lodged with Alex and Emmeline for twenty years. Inferences were drawn, judgments passed. Emmeline retaliated by refusing to see us any more. We were cruelly separated from her fruitcake. How prescient, we said, were our ironies about living in glass houses. Now we knew – or thought we knew – how Emmeline really financed her mania for glass.

Before our visiting days ended she never once asked about or made criti-cal observations upon Pop. Ma took care never to mention him. It was as if he didn't exist. It was the same when we visited Uncle Sidney and Aunty Agatha. They were kind to Ma, to us, but were silent where Pop was concerned. Whatever the immediate reasons may have been it is dif-ficult for people who live in sophisticated cities to take an interest in the unenlightened who don't. To ask a resident of Douglas to ponder long about a brother who had sought exile in provincial Ramsey would be like asking a Torontonian to spare a thought for a relative perversely dwelling in Moose Jaw and professing to enjoy it – worse, to prefer it.

❖

Our visits to Aunty Agatha were as low-key as our visits to Aunty Emmeline were colorful. Agatha was the sober eldest in her family. Emmeline had been the pampered rather frivolous youngest. Agatha's was the largest house of all my relatives but was as drab as Emmeline's was sparkling. It was all dark embossed wallpaper, heavy velvet curtains, mahogany furniture. Pictures of bugling stags in misty Scottish glens adorned the walls along with portraits of Queen Victoria scowling like Aunty Doreen from under her bucket hat at Ma's wedding. I remember ebony elephants making their ponderous way across mantle-shelves, dusty aspidistras standing guard in brass pots from Benares. Unlike Emmeline and Doreen's houses there were legal book-cases stacked with books. Aunty Agatha and Uncle Frank were "great readers" it was said – in a sad, pitying tone as if the crucial word was "bleeders."

Agatha was a highly intelligent woman whose life, when she wasn't reading, was devoted to domestic routine though without Doreen's cleaning mania. It was her daughter-in-law who caused such collective breast-swelling by becoming the Governor's private secretary thereby attending many a jeweled soiree about which she was eagerly questioned whenever she met Emmeline shopping in Strand Street, Douglas's center of commerce. Agatha was very fond of her daughter-in-law but never asked her about her work. She was much more interested in discussing the books they both read.

Uncle Frank was as domestically unassertive as all my uncles. "Eunuchs" Pop once called them, provoking Ma to outrage.

"What's a Yoou-nuck?" I asked.

"Now look what you've done!" said Ma.

"It's an Arctic deer," said Pop.

"What's Arctic?" I asked. Pop didn't answer.

Uncle Frank was something of an intellectual – a man who, born later, would have studied at universities, acquired degrees, become a Professor. Astronomy was the great passion of his life. He wrote a weekly column on the subject for a Liverpool newspaper. Whenever we visited he would take me to the top floor of the three-storeyed house where he had set up an observatory in a spare bedroom and show me his telescope and explain how it worked. He told me that if I looked through it directly at the sun my eye would fry in its socket. It was all right to look at the moon and the stars – they didn't give off heat. Of stars, meteors, comets, suns and moons (these latter two plurals amazing me) he talked incessantly in private. He showed me the thick treatise he had written on the astronomical significance of the Manx three-legged heraldic symbol. It had to do with the planets, the ancient Egyptians and Hindus – even Hitler's swastika.

I understood little of what he said but found his eager enthusiasm infectious. I also found it hard to reconcile this loquacious student of the heavens with the man who sat silent and shy in company, furtively consulting the watch on a long chain that he kept in a pocket of his waistcoat. While his wife conversed with callers he would tiptoe from the room and head for the stairs as soon as he felt he had paid his debt to social custom.

His only son, my cousin George, like his father worked for the Douglas Municipal Planning Department. He was about Ronald's age and the first in the family to attend university and get a degree. He resembled his father temperamentally as well as professionally. He was more excited by an engineering scale drawing than almost anything else. When his wife dressed him up and took him to evening events at Government House he held forth on drains, sewage systems, traffic and its patterns to anyone who would listen. He died when he was sixty after falling down an open manhole his attention absorbed by a blueprint for road alteration at a dangerous intersection.

There was a story in the family that at the beginning of the war Uncle Frank was nearly arrested as a possible spy. A neighbor had reported that he was hiding scientific equipment in his attic. Uncle Frank was visited by gray-faced police in civilian clothes, so the story goes, and had a hard time of it persuading them that he wasn't going to use his telescope to help the Luftwaffe. Had he not managed to ease official fears I might have witnessed my uncle peering at me from behind the wire of the Mooragh Camp. I certainly would have if his name had been Braun, Schmidt or Grunwald.

CHAPTER FOUR

Many of the prisoners behind the wire were indeed interned because of their German origin even though a large number were Jews Hitler would have gassed and burned had they remained within his reach. In 1940 with the English army cornered at Dunkirk and in danger of capture by the Germans, when it was feared that Britain itself would soon be invaded, the jittery powers-that-be in England decided that people of German origin posed a danger. They might respond as one to some mystic call from the Rhein maidens, some emanation from the Schwartzwald or the Vienna Woods and become instant Nazis spying and sabotaging for Fatherland and Fuehrer. Better play it safe, thought the government – lock 'em up, lock 'em all up with Mosley's Black Shirts and others of dubious ilk. They weren't "us"; they were "alien."

So why wasn't Mrs. Hochheimer, with a German name and an Austrian, like Hitler, sent to join the other "alien" women at their internment camp at the south end of the Island? She dwelt freely among us speaking her Teutonic *Englisch,* happily distributing her sweet ration to the neighborhood children all through the war, secure in her ownership and occupancy of a four-storeyed hotel-sized sea-front house. Further, not a single soldier, pilot, navigator, bomb-aimer nor wife to the same was sent to share it with her though the house was half again as big as ours.

Don't misunderstand. No one wanted to see her marched off. She was a charming old lady. She laughed a lot, was friendly and much liked not least because she dressed like the Edwardian dowager she was. Her large-brimmed be-feathered hats, her long elegant gowns, her boas and blouses with ruffled sleeves, her parasol, were secretly admired in a world gone gray, practical and khaki-drab. She seemed an exiled, aged, but still vigorous member of a faded European aristocratic house. But unlike the Nazi on his borrowed estate or many a German-speaking exile in England she did not even suffer house arrest. Why not?

When I asked Uncle Sidney he could only suggest that perhaps Mrs. Hochheimer had friends in high places. Perhaps she had a lot of money. "Money always talks," said Uncle Sidney suddenly yelling "whoa there!" swinging the wheel to avoid an imaginary pigeon. He was the only one in our family at that time to own a car and was driving us all to the Douglas railway station after one of our weekend visits. His car was another anomaly. How could he run it in time of war when others had succumbed to the severe rationing and taken their dusty rusty bicycles out of their garages? "Money," said Pop when I asked him, "talks." This talking money was new to me as I told Pop.

"You'll get used to it," he said, "in time."

When I asked Bessie what she thought of Mrs. Hochheimer's freedom in spite of her name, accent, *jas* and *neins,* she said "She's a spy. They should stick her behind barbed wire. Don't eat her sweets – they're poisoned."

"How do you know she's a spy?" I asked, having already survived whole bags of Mrs. Hochheimer's candies.

"She's a German isn't she? She's got a big house on the sea-front hasn't she? She'll be up on the top floor with a telescope looking for ships, sending secret messages to the Nazis. I bet her house is full of spying gear. She'll be on the short-wave radio to Hitler every night jabbering away in German when we're all in bed."

The more Bessie talked like this the more she convinced herself that her fictions were realities.

I could not see the elderly Mrs. Hochheimer, sprightly though she was for her age, laboring up and down eight flights of stairs in her Edwardian finery to garner and transmit news for Hitler about the details of maritime traffic in the Irish Sea. From what I'd seen of Hitler on newsreel footage he didn't seem the sort of person Mrs. Hochheimer would care to know let alone spy for. Uncouth bawling, yelling, sweating, spitting, wildly gesticulating men with Charlie Chaplin moustaches would not, I surmised, be Mrs. Hochheimer's glass of schnapps though of course at the time I wouldn't have put it like that. I just felt then that Hitler and Mrs. Hochheimer were not suited, wouldn't get on. When I told Bessie so she looked at me over her glasses and slowly shook her head.

Mrs. Hochheimer wasn't the only anomaly in our neighborhood. A few doors down from her lived Andrew Qualtrough, like her, elderly and rattling around alone in a house as big. Though the owner of a large house Andy Qualtrough – known to us as *Quilty* – dressed like a "street person" as we have taken to calling the destitute. While petite Mrs. Hochheimer stepped out arrayed like Queen Mary, Quilty, tall, cadaverous, watery eyes glaring, thin hair plastered to a long narrow head, slunk around in an ancient stained macintosh buttoned to the neck whatever the season, speaking to no-one. To a modern cop he would look the very model of a flasher.

I remember him plodding to town with an empty string shopping bag and plodding back with a few groceries in it. No one seemed to know anything about him so speculation stood in for fact.

"He's a miser," Bessie told me. "He's got money hidden all over that big house of his. There's so much of it he can't remember where he's put the half of it. He's like a squirrel with nuts. I'd help him find it right enough! I'd soon sniff it out."

"He's a poor soul," said Mrs. Corcoran, our neighbor on the other side from Bessie and as kindly as Bessie was rough. "He's eccentric. He's all alone with no-one to do for him."

Mrs. Corcoran's chief delight was to "do for" Mr. Corcoran, a fierce-looking red-faced placid man who worked for Joe Broom the butcher. He reveled in his wife's domestic care but died of a heart attack at fifty, leaving her devastated, lamenting that she hadn't done enough for him. "He did love his beef," she said as if defending herself in court.

"He died a happy fella," said Pop reassuringly as they walked away from the gravesite on the day of the funeral.

"You think so? I do hope so," she said.

"Nothing you can do about it now, is there?" Bessie considered the cold water of realism the best treatment for over-heated grief and looked surprised at Pop's "bloody hell Bessie!"

"Eccentric!" snorted Bessie when I quoted Mrs. Corcoran's view of Quilty. "He's no more eccentric than I am. He's a loony! He belongs in the loony bin. He's as crazy as a coot. He's cuckoo – do-lally. You don't know what he might do next."

What he eventually did – though this was a few years after the war – was to nearly burn down the neighborhood. One day, smoke began to issue from Quilty's house, just a few wisps at first and then great choking clouds of it. The fire brigade arrived, water was poured on to and into the house, the blackening windows of which began to crack and then burst from the heat within. The entire neighborhood turned out to watch. I had never seen a house fire before and this was no small instance. It was feared the flames would rip through the whole block of houses so that Mrs. Hochheimer's place (owned, since her death, by her son) and others would all go. If the fire leapt the back lane ours would too. We might have The Great Fire of Ramsey in the making, which would have a place in the history books.

I was more exhilarated than frightened as I stood watching Quilty's house being gutted. Suddenly there was a figure at a still-intact ground floor back window – a dark shape shrouded in smoke. It was Quilty frantically trying to get out. He vanished suddenly as the ground floor fell into the basement. What was left of Quilty, cremated alive, was sifted from the embers once they had cooled. The shell of his sturdily built house remained to be refashioned into luxury apartments, the first of many such.

It turned out that Quilty was not the fabulously wealthy man of Bessie's imagination. He died intestate so only the necessary officials knew how much he had been worth but it was rumored that his income had been modest.

Bessie, of course, knew better. "What a waste," she said. "All his money was burned in the fire. He didn't trust banks so he hid away untold thousands and look where that got him." Cash to ash.

At the Coroner's inquest it was established that for years Quilty had steadily filled his house with newspapers and flammable rubbish. He seemed incapable of ever throwing anything away. It was surmised that he had absent-mindedly dropped a lighted match or a lit candle and the whole combustible mess had gone up like a Guy Fawkes bonfire.

One would have thought that given the war-time need for housing on the Island and considering Quilty's mental state, the government might have gently pried him loose from his property and placed him in a Home. After vigorously cleaning and re-painting the house they could then have moved the Air Force into it. The government didn't do so. Mrs. Hochheimer, Quilty and also the sisters Quayle were left in sole possession of their large sea-front properties while Ma and Pop and many like them were turned into innkeepers.

The sisters Quayle, even when I was ten, seemed to me to be characters out of a book. There were four of them, all spinsters (as the word then was), all dressed like Mrs. Hochheimer though in darker colors. Unlike Mrs. Hochheimer they were reclusive, rarely appearing in public, communicating with the outside world on daily matters by means of servants who had been with the family many years. When, occasionally, they ventured forth they did so in a black 1919 Rolls Royce car. They had a chauffeur in a gray uniform and black riding boots who entranced the local children by taking this spotless car out of its garage once a week for a superfluous wash and polish. I was impressed by the car's white canvas top, well-upholstered red leather seats, and huge chromium-plated headlights. When the Misses Quayle were all seated in it in their finery it looked like a carriage from fairyland. The princesses in it acknowledged us with delicate regal flutterings of lace-gloved hands and scattered sixpences. How they obtained their petrol was as much a mystery as how Uncle Sidney procured his. Money talking again, I supposed. Their sixpences certainly spoke to us.

After the war, when the last Miss Quayle had a stroke and was taken to a nursing home, the house was turned into a hotel. There being no heirs the family furniture was sold at auction and one of my souvenirs of the past is the little hand-bell the ancient maid discreetly rang to summon her employers to their meals.

I amused myself picturing those delicate ladies beset with unwanted Air Force and Army lodgers. What would they have done if, like our's, their house had become a billet? Hidden for the duration in their private quarters, fearing the license of the soldiery? Acted as genteel hostesses offering little glasses of pre-war sherry from the cellars…afternoon tea? Would the servants have coped or walked out? No one will ever know. What I remember best about the Misses Quayle is the sight of them carefully stowed with their parasols aboard the Rolls as they set out on a sunny summer's afternoon riding in state to the countryside at a dignified twenty miles an hour, figures from the Victorian past still living and breathing amongst us.

The Victorian past had been summoned back by the war. I was living in anomalous times. Steam and horsepower, because of the scarcity of petrol, acquired a new lease on life. Pop's Victorian locomotive didn't seem so out of place when corn was cut and threshed by steam, when roads were made and mended by giant lumbering steam-driven traction engines.

Even as modern science and technology created ever more ingenious machines for the armed forces, farmers were putting away their tractors and reverting to the horse-drawn plough. Instead of trucks or vans horse-drawn carts delivered most goods though the grocer sent his supplies by means of a boy on a bicycle with an enormous basket at the front and another at the back. The chimney sweep also arrived on a bike, his brushes fastened on somehow.

It was a time for the revival of dinosaurs. The baker's van was a fragrant ancient box-shaped contraption pulled by a horse – a vehicle that Hardy's Jude would have no trouble recognizing. One farmer delivered milk in a fast-moving tilted horse-drawn float, a veritable sports car among carts. Fish arrived on a flat rectangular cart with narrow sideboards to prevent them from slithering off. The rag-and-bone man of Dickens's day was still with us – the recycler of his time. The old clothes and bits of scrap metal he collected were thrown on to his cart. Strictly-rationed coal came in dirty bags stacked on a long, heavy, rectangular cart black with dust, pulled by a blinkered weary old horse, fuelled by oats in a nose-bag. Brewers' drays and farm ploughs were pulled by Clydesdales throughout the working year. Manure for the garden was readily obtained from the roads. Pop had me out there with a shovel and bucket at every steaming opportunity.

The few who owned cars had to put them away until the war ended. They walked or cycled like the rest of us although there were exceptions. In addition to my Uncle Sidney and the sisters Quayle there was Bridget Callow's father.

The Callows lived four doors down from us. Bridget's father was a civilian with a government job, which required him to use his car and, rare still, have a telephone installed in his house. Everyone wanted to go to Bridget's birthday parties (held despite the rationing) since her father allowed her guests briefly to sit in his car and pretend to speak into his telephone. The last time I went to Bridget's birthday party, like the other children I became over-excited. Unlike the other children, I seized Bridget's skipping rope to treat the company to an exhibition of my skipping skills then popularly thought to be confined to girls.

"Careful," Bridget's father warned, too late. The rope caught in the dining-room chandelier, tearing it from the ceiling. Aunty Emmeline would have despaired at the sight of so much shattered crystal. I was sent home in disgrace, an outcast, all the other children watching from a bay window as Mr. Callow stood on his front doorstep and bellowed that Pop could expect a bill for the damage. But the bill never came. Soon after the party Mr. Callow was arrested for embezzlement. If money talked it could also tattle. The Callow's house was rented out and the little family simply disappeared.

Apart from the historic survivals caused by war I had personal connections with the Victorians through my grandparents (three of whom were dead) and, of course Ma, Pop, their brothers and sisters, all of whom were born in the late 1890's or the first four years of the Twentieth Century. I have spent half of my life teaching Victorian Literature and History. For my students the Victorians are as imaginary as the characters in their novels but for me they are the elder generation of my family or people like the ageing Mrs. O'Hallaran who Ma visited.

She lived in a gloomy aspidistra-begirt front sitting room into which her large bed had been dragged. Though there appeared to be nothing physically wrong with her she led the sickbed life of a pale Victorian poetic heroine among bottles of colored liquids said to be medicinal. She had gone to bed one night and declined to get up ever again. She died in a room smelling of camphor one rainy day when no one came to visit.

CHAPTER FIVE

THE HOUSES OF MRS. HOCHHEIMER, QUILTY AND THE MISSES QUAYLE faced the sea whereas ours was in a row behind them with land between. We were fronted by North Barrule, the most northerly of the central chain of what we were pleased to call mountains (the highest, Snaefell, rises to 2034 feet above sea level) that provide the Isle-of-Man with a heather and peat-sheathed backbone. From this spare highland region streams and rivers run through lush glens down to the sea.

The foothills of North Barrule are partly wooded. When I was ten there were ruined crofts or "tholtans" on open land above and beyond the woods where poor hill farmers once forced a precarious living from meager soil. They hacked through tough sod, they picked and stacked tons of stones from their land and hauled more from the seashore to build their thatch-roofed cottages, their barns and pig styes. The still-standing dry stone walls round the fields they dug out of stubborn mountainside are testimony to their doomed determination. The land was marginal, the crofts isolated; wind, rain and mist often enveloped them and when I was ten many of the fields of those precarious farms had been reclaimed by wild grass, heather, gorse and tough little blaeberry bushes. In the Nineteenth Century the withdrawal by the Crown of the ancient rights of sheep pasturage and the advent of cheap corn helped to put an end to these crofts, one by one. Stone ruins stood in windswept desolation. Old rain-warped sun-dried weather-beaten doors creaked on rusted hinges as the sad wind blew. Only sheep flourished there when I was ten and immune to pathos.

It is hard in these days of child abduction, molestation and murder to believe that responsible parents would allow ten-year-olds to roam such a wide area without an accompanying adult. But in spite of the war those were more innocent times. As long as children played together in groups and as long as those groups contained older children parents contented themselves by issuing lengthy, unheeded lists of warnings. The darkest consequences of such freedom were skinned knees and minor cuts and bruises. Bones were occasionally broken and children confined to home but restrictions didn't last.

The lowest wooded slopes of North Barrule's foothill region belonged, like the timber, to the government. Public footpaths zigzagged up the sides of *Lhergy Frissel* (the Gaelic name of part of the area). They rise to what Jane Austen would have called the "eminence" from which in 1847 Prince Albert, leaving the Queen moored in Ramsey Bay on the Royal Yacht, viewed the flat plain of the north of the island. There being no dignitaries about early that morning the Prince was guided to the spot by a local barber. The "Albert Tower" was built there to commemorate the Royal ascent. It stands today, a solitary Victorian pseudo-medieval structure in need of a castle.

It was in this region one dark December night in 1942 that I went on my first Commando raid of the war.

It was close to Christmas and we had no Christmas tree probably because of wartime restrictions on the use of wood. Every aspect of daily life was regulated including the cutting of trees. The woods above our house were patrolled, especially at night, to prevent anyone from helping themselves to their contents.

Certain bored alien-guarding soldiers billeted with us and with other families near at hand regarded this situation as a military challenge. They formed a strike-force which gathered in our kitchen round the ancient gas-lamp-surmounted, black-leaded kitchen range (circa 1885) with a coal fire burning in its grate. They consulted Pop who agreed with their plan. He persuaded a hesitant, dubious Ma to dress me up warmly for a winter sortie.

"You will look after him, won't you? You'll make sure he's all right? You'll bring him back safely won't you?" Ma questioned fearfully as we all moved down the hallway to the front door past the battered umbrella stand with its oval mirror and place for shoes.

I had no idea where I was being taken that frosty December night when I would normally be in bed but the fact that I seemed to be the guest of a squad of soldiers and that those soldiers were going out on some martial exercise or other made me very excited. Carlo wanted to come too but Pop said he was too little and anyway it was past his bed-time and Ma had to pick him up because he started to stamp about, roaring "I not ickle. I big. I eat my toat!"

Carlo regularly threatened to eat his coat but he never did.

I was quite delirious when we were outside and the squad leader, a sergeant, said to me: "Now remember yer on a ride (raid). A Commando ride. Y'ave ter foller orders. Y'ave ter keep yer 'ead darn. Enemy sees us . . . well 's all owver. Unnerstan?"

I said I did. Maybe the Germans had landed at last though if they had why didn't the soldiers have their rifles with them? Maybe we were going on a spying mission. Perhaps I'd get a chance to make up for my not helping the pilot of that crashing Spitfire who came to me in nightmares where I saw him struggling in panic to get out of his sunken aircraft the bubbles streaming from his mouth as he screamed in silence, his face turning blue, his eyes racing madly about in his head.

We marched along in the frosty air, our breath visible. The sergeant said we had to get off the road. We had to advance on the *Lhergy Frissel* woods secretly through the fields belonging to Joe Broom the butcher who fattened cattle in them. After we had clambered over a hedge the cattle currently residing in Joe Broom's fields came at a trot to examine us whereupon my eagerness to spy on invading Germans vanished. I was scared stiff by the steers that came milling round. I sniveled that I wanted to go home. I struggled hard to avoid crying, wiping my running nose on the sleeve of my coat.

"Yer not goin' ter bawl over a few cows are yer?' said the sergeant, shining his large flashlight on me as I whimpered. "They're 'armless," said the sergeant.

"No they're not," I said. "They're not cows they're bullocks. They'll stick their horns in you or knock you down and stamp on you if they feel like it." They had quick tempers like Pop though I didn't say so.

"Ah," said our London-born sergeant who before he was 'called up' had got no nearer the country than Smithfield Market. "Well, 'en" he said, 'let's be movin' on smartish," briskly backing away from the curious snorting animals with smoke coming from their wide fleshy nostrils.

"Don't run," I said, recovering a little now that I was in a position to advise our platoon leader, "or they'll charge at us."

"Easy does it 'en," said the sergeant continuing to back away but more slowly from the inquisitive cattle and advising everyone else to do the same.

Our leisurely progress in reverse ended abruptly when one of the steers bellowed and ran at us. We turned and fled toward the woods making so much noise that had any tree patrol or invading Germans been near we would have been caught or shot at once. We experienced the sort of fiasco that occurs in actual battle when planning is wrecked by ignorance or chance as the Gods smile their ironic smiles, wink at each other and sip Olympian tea.

We spent some time in a dry drainage ditch recuperating from the chase. I had never before been pursued across a field in pitch dark on a freezing December night by a steer with sharp horns, a mean disposition and a temper shorter than Pop's. Neither had the men around me. None of us realized how fast we could run 'till we were put to the test. We needed time to calm down, get our breath back, steady our nerves for the assault on the wood above us. It was only now that I learned for sure that our objective was the wood and not invading Germans. I was told that we had come out to steal a Christmas tree from under the noses of the woodland patrol.

"We're goin' ter liberi' one," said the sergeant.

He said we had to avoid the zigzag paths and climb straight up through the undergrowth to some place near the top of the wood. We crossed a narrow road and cautiously made our way up the steep hillside. We pushed through dead bracken which crackled as we stepped on it. It could cut your hand open like a knife if you weren't careful as I had learned to my cost.

"Ow!! Christ!!! SSSHHHHH" pierced the frigid air as the platoon became acquainted with the properties of dead bracken stalks.

Suddenly a light reached out toward us fingering the trees and bushes and we dropped silently into wet leaf-mould. The quickly-suppressed noises we had been making had alerted the official patrol. We lay face down hugging the ground. I was certain we had been seen, expecting every moment to be hauled upright and officially inspected. But the light, after wavering near us, moved on. We heard men on the path above exchange muffled opinions about what they had heard but their voices faded as they went down toward the road we had crossed. We stayed where we were for a few minutes then stood up brushing the wet dead leaves from our clothes. The sergeant whispered to us all to be more careful, not to speak or call out even if we were cut or bruised. He told us not to step on dead twigs and to watch out for low branches. There would be more where that patrol came from he said.

After what seemed to me a long climb we entered a stand of holly trees. The platoon produced sharp bayonets and began to cut holly branches to decorate our house. The sergeant put a stop to that. He reminded the men that we had come to get a Christmas tree. Once we had one then we could cut some holly. "First fings first. Di'n't they tell yer that in trining?"

"Where's a spirit a fuckin' Christmas?" asked one rebelliously. "Wha's Christmas wivout 'olly?"

"What's it wivout a tree?" countered the sergeant. "When yer find a tree yer can 'ave yer 'olly so look smart."

The soldiers reluctantly dropped their holly branches and fanned out to look for a suitable tree. The moon emerged from thick cloud.

"Oy! What you bastards think yer up to?"

Occupied with the search for the tree we hadn't seen the patrol return. Now the light of powerful torches lit us up more clearly than the silvery moonlight.

"You lot come 'ere!" yelled officialdom from the path.

Our sergeant was mortified. Leading his platoon into enemy-held territory he had neglected to post a lookout, distracted by the conflicting claims of holly and Christmas tree. We were about to be captured with our objective unmet. We would be led down the path through the woods in disgrace. The sergeant and his men would be "put on a charge" the sergeant told me later. He could lose his stripes for this.

"This way!" I shouted excitedly to the sergeant, "I know a place to hide!"

"All o' yer foller the kid!" yelled the sergeant.

I led them all across the hillside as fast as the undergrowth would permit but a ten-year-old couldn't move fast enough in that terrain so the sergeant, a tall and muscular man, picked me up and ran where I directed. The other soldiers followed. The patrol yelled at us again to stop and "come back 'ere!" and when we didn't they came after us shouting and cursing as they stumbled into rabbit holes, tripped over fallen branches, or were slashed by bracken. I directed the sergeant to a small dank cave, the entrance of which was covered with brambles and fern. We all crowded in hurriedly getting badly scratched by thorns in the process. We waited, nervously silent, holding our breaths as much as possible after our mad dash. Our pursuers came close but they ran on down into the woods below the cave and the racket they were making grew fainter and fainter then ceased. Not to be caught napping again the sergeant sent out two scouts to make sure the coast was clear.

We didn't dare to return to the stand of holly trees but we didn't need to. Near the cave, in a little clearing, stood a Christmas tree about seven feet tall, its branches perfectly balanced. Soon the men who had brought axes were chopping it down. I was exhilarated. We had our tree!

In these green days I find the chopping down of trees to garnish a few days of celebration a questionable practice but when I was ten I had no such scruples. I'd have chopped the tree down myself if I'd been given the axe.

I showed the soldiers a roundabout way out of the woods in case the patrol was waiting for us further up the road we had initially crossed after leaving the field of bullying bullocks. We went by a circuitous route down into Ballure Glen and made our way along a narrow path by the stream that flowed through it. There was moonlight enough to show us the way ahead and there were dense trees near at hand into which we could fade if the patrol showed up again. We couldn't follow the glen to the seashore which would have been the best route to take since the entrance to the glen was stopped up with barbed wire so after following the stream for a while we cut across it at a shallow point where there were stepping stones. Then we followed a path that led us to the main road from Ramsey to Douglas. After that it was an easy walk to our house. The two soldiers carrying the tree horizontally were relieved to be walking on solid pavement.

Pop was pleased with our prize, placing it upright in a deep bucket of heavy stones and sand. Ma tied festive red tissue paper around the bucket. It was the most beautiful Christmas tree I had ever seen, especially when it was covered in the pre-war tinsel and delicate coloured glass ornaments which Ma hung on it. Carlo liked it so much when he came to see it next morning that he pulled the tree over trying to reach one of the ornaments on an upper branch. A verbal gale from Pop made him bawl loudly. Pop had to add more heavy stones to keep the tree in place while Ma swept up the broken glass.

The soldiers of the expeditionary force, as they called themselves, had been treated with brandy Pop had acquired somewhere and while they drank it they gave Ma an exaggerated account of our adventures, lamenting the abandoned holly. After listening to their tales she said "If I'd known what you were getting Erik into I'd never have let him go with you."

"If 'e anta gone wiv' us we'd all a been nabbed," said the sergeant. "'E 'ad a plice fer us all ter 'ide."

The solders lifted their glasses and wished me good health.

The evening's events evidently over-excited me since I dreamed of being tossed on the horns of angry steers, of seeing Germans exploding on the beach as they stepped on mines, of Spitfires crashing into our house as choirs sang a carol called "Good King Wence's Last Look Out." It was a relief to wake to a normal day in time of war.

CHAPTER SIX

My military career ended that night. The Christmas Tree Caper was one of a kind. I played at war informally with other children but it wasn't like going off on a raid in winter in the black of night with real soldiers even if they were only prison guards a real enemy would have easily routed. That foray was more exciting than kids' games especially since it was my cave that had saved us all from capture.

For kids' games St. Mary's ancient churchyard was a favorite spot. St. Mary's was a very old chapel used occasionally by the Church of England congregation of St. Paul's down on the "free" side of the harbor. Ma and Pop had taken to sending me to this latter church on Sundays with pious Miss Quirk, another neighbor, to elevate the moral and spiritual tone of my life while they and Carlo, evidently not in need of such elevation, stayed at home for a *lie in*.

Miss Quirk was kindly but embarrassing. She was descended from those women Matthew Arnold observed dropping as though shot in the center aisle of the church in homage to the High Altar before entering their pew. Miss Quirk also crossed herself lavishly while down on the tiled floor and mumbled an incantation before rising unsteadily and proceeding to her seat. She encouraged me to follow suit but I hung back when she was on her knees so that she wouldn't see me blush crimson, mortified at the spectacle she was creating, trying to pretend I had no idea who she was.

She was a favorite of the High Church Vicar who had been poisoned at the well of the Oxford Movement and went in for ecclesiastical theatrics.

I tried to get out of these Sunday excursions. I alleged in language consistent with my age at the time that the Vicar (who wore a biretta and dressed like an Italian Monsignor en route to a Papal High Mass) was a crypto-Catholic tyrant (his housekeeper said so) and that his squad of tweed-clad spinster Sunday school teachers were so many harpies but Ma and Pop were unimpressed. Spiritual medicine which tasted that bad must be good, they reasoned. Bessie shared their view.

"You go off to church and give your mother a bit of peace," she said.

"Why can Carlo stay home?" I asked. "He doesn't give anybody any peace."

"I ickle," said Carlo.

The games we played in St. Mary's churchyard all involved weapons. We had home-made catapults, toy pistols and toy rifles, make-believe grenades (large stones lobbed by hand or smaller ones launched by catapult) and used them in battles with imaginary Germans, or in games of cops and robbers or cowboys and Indians. The anomaly of grenades and the tin helmets we had received from Santa in the latter two games bothered us as little as it bothered our parents giving us war toys for Christmas. The fact that we "killed" one another with relish in a Christian churchyard, leap-frogging over titled grave-stones, jumping off the flat tops of tombs, their wealthy occupants' names erased by two centuries of wind, frost, rain and small boys didn't strike us as *sacrilegious*. We didn't know what the word meant so when the apoplectic Vicar caught us grave-hopping and used it to describe our conduct we listened but took no notice. After he had turned, purple-faced from chiding us, to go into the chapel we shot him with an imaginary volley from the top of a tomb and went back to hunting each other down.

We had no idea that this little church was built on the site of an ancient Keill – a sort of Celtic chapel – nor that Martha and Elizabeth Fricker are buried in its grounds, their sisters the wives of Coleridge, Southey and the poet Lovel. We were unaware that in 1760 a victory over French privateers in a sea-battle off the coast at Jurby had been celebrated here. We had as yet no acquaintance with History, no idea how history-making were our own times. We simply frolicked in the graveyard imagining it an ageless field of battle and defied the Vicar.

Girls joined in these games acting as nurses tending boys bruised by stones or with knees bloodied by some rough grave surface. Bridget Callow (before her father's arrest) came with her friend, Elsie Smith, both wearing replicas of nurses' uniforms that they had been given for Christmas. Elsie Smith was a year older than the rest of us though in the same class at school. She was mentally lazy but physically precocious, not entirely satisfied with applying bandages (rags from her mother's rag bag). She offered to show us hers if we'd show her ours. We hadn't a clue what she was talking about until she tried to wrestle David Quiggin out of his pants to bandage a delicate wound.

"Gerroff!!!" he yelled in terror. "Bloody ger-off!!!"

Bridget Callow was told she couldn't play with us any more if she brought her friend with her. When we were teenagers and our notions had changed we lusted after the now finely sculpted Elsie Smith who by that time had acquired considerable popularity with the Air Force officer cadets training at the post-war Jurby Airport. Elsie ignored our drooling admiration, our eager stares as she swayed by in high heels on the arm of her current conquest. We assured one another of the inevitable result. We rejoiced that Elsie Smith would get her come-uppance, that it was only a matter of time before she found herself pregnant and had a baby out of wedlock. Then she would be a pariah. She'd pay the price for haughtily ignoring us, dismissing us as "kids." She'd pay the price all right. Elsie, however, remained as childless as a virgin and married a naïve South African millionaire who thought she was one.

Another favored venue for our war-like games was, of course, the wood above Ballure Glen into which I had led the soldiers after we had hidden in the cave the night of the Christmas tree adventure. I knew of the cave because I had played in the area so often. In the wood we became primitive Amazon tribes living off the land, attacking each other with ferns pulled from the ground and stripped of their fronds. They became *boomerangs* after Billy Teare, who was uncommonly studious for his age, heard one described in a BBC radio talk about aborigines and then looked it up in his father's *Encyclopaedia Britannica*. Fern stalks could be dangerous weapons when thrown with force. One hit Billy Teare just above his left eye and the doctor said it was pure luck he wasn't blinded. We were made to promise never to throw these missiles at each other again. We sullenly promised but were soon happily boomeranging each other, once more indifferent to Billy Teare's left eye and the fact that aborigines didn't live anywhere near the Amazon. They did if we said they did.

During our tribal wars we took time out for meals. I dug up turnips from a field just below the woods and took apples from a tree that hung over the wall surrounding what Mrs. Agnes B. Trelawney (an English woman who had come to the Island upon her husband's retirement from the Indian Civil Service) called her *Casa*. To make sure everyone knew she lived in a *Casa* she renamed the house Casa Bianca. The former owners, people called Blake, had called the house *Dunroamin*. Mrs. Trelawney said such a name was so vulgar that when she thought of it she shuddered until she couldn't catch her breath. She went on to say that it told you all you needed to know about the Blakean social roots and educational level. "Origins," said Mrs. Trelawney as if fresh from reading Darwin, "are everything. I'm not a snob but origins are *it.*"

We ate Mrs. Trelawney's apples just as they came. The turnips we peeled with a penknife, cut into chunks and then, oblivious to infection, boiled the chunks in a rusty can over a small fire made from dead wood. That we were forbidden to either possess or use matches and that lighting fires in the wood was illegal, only added spice to the feast.

The group of children I played these games with thought of itself as a gang. Occasionally other gangs would roam into our territory and the fighting with fern boomerangs became intense. Sometimes we drove the invaders away but at other times we had to retreat to save ourselves from capture and humiliating punishments. Under the cover of bracken and trees we retreated secretly toward the town reservoir, a place declared off-limits by our parents after a child evacuated to the Island for safety from the London bombing climbed the fence, fell into the water and drowned. I can remember staring into the dark stone-colored waters wondering what it would feel like to drown. That London child, like my downed spitfire pilot, would have had his lungs fill with water instead of air, would have choked and gagged and thrashed about till he died. I shivered while I thought such things. The reservoir was so deep you couldn't see the bottom, only your own reflection in the water. Had Ma and Pop known that I had been up there they would have been as apoplectic as the Vicar.

As it was, the only uproar concerning the reservoir that I recall, happened the day I followed an English Flight Lieutenant, his wife and five-year-old son, who went for a walk in that direction. I was bored, I wanted to go for a family walk too but with Pop at work and Ma far too busy to take me, I tagged along with the Flight Lieutenant and his little family. The airman, to my surprise, did not appreciate my presence. He told me several times to go home and stop following them. I told him I knew the area and could guide him and his wife and little boy to places he may never have heard of. He said "Listen you little shit: bugger off or else. . ." I was shocked that an adult would use such language especially to someone else's child. I continued to follow at what I thought was a discreet distance. The Flight Lieutenant strode angrily back to me and slapped me violently across the face. Of course, I ran home more shocked by the man's brutality than any actual pain. Pop would never dream of hitting someone else's child and never across the face. This officer gave me a very bad impression of the English.

Ma was upset by what had happened. When he came home from work she sent Pop to confront the errant pilot who was billeted with a neighbor. The defiant airman took a Lord of the Manor tone with Pop. Pop in response issued loud peasant threats of bodily harm if the man ever touched his child again, and then came home to give me what he called "a good hiding" for provoking the situation in the first place. I was as outraged at the injustice as I was when Toby Wood, so much bigger and older than me, punched me on the nose without warning or cause. The man had given me a very bad impression of the rich. The least I expected on this occasion was that Pop would knock the English officer into one of those piles of manure smoking on the main road.

Not content with sending me to church every Sunday Ma asked the Vicar to let me sing in the church choir. This would entail morning attendance at Matins, my presence at Evensong and, with Sunday school in the afternoon would ensure that I spent every Sunday locked up in gloomy buildings smelling of dust, damp, and dying flowers, under the authority of pale, dusty church people with bad teeth and halitosis, their clothes smelling of moth balls, their skin like old parchment. I would be deprived of fresh air, open spaces, natural greenery. I would be unable to play. My wings would be severely clipped.

"I won't go!" I said in a temper. "I won't sing in the choir and you can't make me!"

"You're going and that's that" said Pop, adding "and I *can* make you go Sonny Jim, never you fear."

"But why do I have to?

"Because I said so," said Pop.

Pop preferred finality when dealing with his children. He wasn't about to reason with me or negotiate. He frequently said, the tone of his voice as wistful as that of one looking back at the customs of a lost golden age, "children should be seen and not heard."

"Why?" I would ask.

"Because I said so," Pop replied.

I tried a different approach. "I can't sing and I can't read the music in the hymn book. I don't know music."

"We'll let the Vicar be the judge of that."

When Ma took me to see him the Vicar was not overjoyed. The prospect of having me in his choir – me, one of those stone-throwing, impudent urchins who desecrated the graves of St. Mary's chapel – such a prospect made him frown with ecclesiastical displeasure. He received us in his library, its dark shelves full of dusty, thick, heavy tomes on Dogma and Church History struggling their way from floor to ceiling. It had the look of a wizard's lair. I imagined the Vicar in here of an evening in candlelit gloom, sticking pins into clay models of obstreperous parishioners or entertaining the Devil himself to brandy and cigars, negotiating contracts for souls.

The Vicar said he "felt it his duty" to describe my violent games in St. Mary's graveyard, to recount at some length his distress at the same, especially in view of Miss Quirk's noble attempts to bring me to the Risen Christ. He opined that I would not be likely to accept such discipline as membership in the choir entailed. Ma said she was shocked – she had no idea I had become so depraved – but wasn't membership in the choir under the Vicar's restless eye just what I needed *to calm me down?*

"I'll speak to his father," she added ominously, offering the Vicar what she considered an iron-clad guarantee of my future good conduct.

"But the boy doesn't seem to want to join the choir," the Vicar observed, correctly interpreting my restlessness in my seat.

"His father and I think it would be good for him," said Ma," especially after what you have just told me. If his father had been here he'd have said the same."

"I can't sing," I said, breaking into the conversation with what I hoped would be a clinching fact. "I don't know Music."

"Neither does half the choir," said the Vicar with a pale, autumnal smile immediately extinguished.

It must have been obvious to him that joining the choir was the last thing I wanted to do, so, much to Ma's relief, he said, "Send the lad along on Wednesday evening to choir practice. I'll have the choirmaster try him out."

I was appalled. Not only would all of my Sundays be taken up but I would have to lose my Wednesday nights to choir practices. I had not yet met the adjective "sadistic" but if I had I would have said that on this occasion Ma and Pop had earned it.

I was admitted to the choir after singing with it at that Wednesday choir practice. The choirmaster, Sammy Beckett, a local newsagent, stood in front of me and bent an ear as I sang with the rest.

"You'll do," he said without enthusiasm, "you're no worse than the rest."

Thus began what I feared would be a prison term. I would be locked behind the barbed wire of strict routine. Half the weekend would be occupied by Church services and Sunday school which, since the rest of the week was taken up by day school, left only Saturdays for play. The only advantage I could see was that the new arrangement released me from the obligation to attend Sunday matins with Miss Quirk.

"So you've joined the choir," she said admiringly as if I had done so under her influence. "I'm very proud of you," she added.

With only Saturdays left for play I became dejected, listless, bitter, taunting little Carlo until one day, in an infantile rage, he raised the toy house brush that he used to "help" Ma with the house cleaning and smashed it down on my head. The lights went out. I sagged unconscious to the floor. Ma, horrified, summoned the Doctor who mumbled something about *concussion* and *bed rest* and wrote out a prescription for a vile bitter red liquid in a large bottle before hurrying off no doubt for a few gins and a quick game of golf with the Navy. When I had recovered Ma sent me back to church and the choir as if they hadn't been responsible for the gash on my head and the other one to my spirit.

I was pleasantly surprised, however, to find that the choir offered freedoms of its own – its own kind of opportunities for larking about. There were the loud, surprisingly varied farting noises timed to echo through the nave in the interval between the Vicar's solemnly and theatrically announced text and his actually beginning his sermon. There was the deliberate singing out of tune to enrage Sammy Beckett. There were the paper aeroplanes launched across the chancel at hushed holy moments in the Service. There were the simulated faintings when a purple-cassocked white-surpliced boy suddenly held his head, moaned faintly (but not too faintly) and sagged slowly to the floor trickling down the carved wooden choir stall to the consternation of a gullible congregation.

These recreations could not, of course, be enjoyed every week. The Vicar, having shaken the hands of departing parishioners, would rush in a rage to berate any boy who had not sped out of the back door of the church's robing room. We let a week or two go by until the Vicar's guard was down before striking again. The odd boy deemed beyond reform was expelled from the choir and left the church skipping for joy but nothing I did caused this to happen to me. When I got out of line the Vicar had a word with Pop. Pop either threatened or administered a "good hiding" according to his current mood. Punishment was carried out in the back yard. Pop's work-hardened hand across my bottom. Despite her antipathy to violence Ma would keep out of the way till it was over and then, as I sniveled at the indignity as much as the pain, reward me for my sufferings with a piece of cake. Mixed messages were not uncommon in my family.

The Sunday acts of sabotage were fun in themselves but I found that the choir opened another and more interesting avenue to play which was the more enjoyable for being unexpected. On Saturdays from time to time Sammy Beckett, who was also a scout master, organized a contest evidently popular with scout troops. The choirboys assembled at the church early and we were given an objective miles away on the lower slopes of North Barrule. The objective was usually a ruined farmhouse which we had to find with the aid of a map. The idea was not only to locate the ruin but enter it without being caught by one of the defenders who had already been sent off to occupy it. This was more like the war games I preferred to play and more than anything else reconciled me to the choir.

The Vicar would have fainted had he watched the secular pitched battles with the defenders that frequently ensued up there on the mountain where swallows nested in the worm-eaten rafters of ruined barns, and curlews swept across the landscape with their haunting cries.

CHAPTER SEVEN

FROM TIME TO TIME, THE CHILDREN I PLAYED WITH WERE IMPRISONED by parents in a jailing mood. On such occasions Ma's standing order was "come back home to play with Carlo." But Carlo and I usually quarreled and since he had knocked me out with his little house brush I mistrusted his temper and the strength of his chubby arms. Photographs of that time show him constantly aggrieved, glowering at the camera, his matted hair on end looking like a miniature savage – a sort of Manx pygmy, his blow-pipe and poisoned darts replaced by a toy bucket and spade that could be used as weapons.

So instead of going back home to play with Carlo I used to wander off on my own, as on the day I followed the violent Flight Lieutenant. I would meander along the river in Ballure Glen or ramble with Milby through the woods or up beyond them to the old ruined crofts where the silence (when they were not being invaded by militant choirboys) was so intense it pressed on the ear like a constriction. Only the doleful cry of a curlew or the delighted yelps of the dog after a rat or a rabbit relieved it.

In Ballure Glen fish sped about in deep pools along the river bed in a great hurry despite the narrow boundaries of their world. Pop said they were trout and that you could catch them by tickling them. You let your fingers gently caress the fish and when it was duly mesmerized you snatched it out of the water. When I wandered alone in the glen I lay on flat rocks above pools and tried this out but as soon as my shadow fell on the water the fish raced for cover under stones. I concluded that Pop, to use one of his favorite expressions, had been *talking through the back of his head.*

I once asked him what he meant by this expression. He said "It's what you do most of the time – talk nonsense."

If Pop thought that catching fish by caressing them made sense then my experience along the river banks showed how fallible he was. The notion that one's parents don't know everything comes as a bit of a shock. I was quite prepared to see Bessie in this light but Pop, who read the *Daily Express,* ought to know better than believe folk tales about how to catch trout with your hands. I doubted that he had ever tried it.

"There's an art to it," he said when I told him it couldn't be done. "It's all in the touch – light as the bee on the flower, the feather on the grass." Pop could wax poetic when he felt like it.

"Don't you ever go to those pools again!" Ma ordered in a raised voice. "You'll fall in – that's what you'll do – you'll fall in and drown yourself – then what'll you say when you're all wet and dead?"

When I was in the mood and the weather was fine I would head for the uplands above the Glen and pass near the spot where Old Pete's cottage used to stand. All that was left of it when I was a child was a stone cistern that caught and held water seeping underground from the hills above. But Old Pete was still talked about like a figure out of legend, which in a way he was. "Old Pete" was a character in a novel by the Manx novelist Hall Caine, based on John Kennish whose cottage it was that once stood near where I walked. "Old Pete" was evidently more "real" than the man on whom he was modeled. Many talked of "Old Pete" but few of John Kennish.

I would have liked to ask him if you could, in fact, catch a trout by tickling it. If so, I felt sure he would have been the one to show me how to do it.

John Kennish was one of the last of the Gaelic-speaking cottars who at one time formed the bulk of the native Manx population. His cottage, a photograph of which I found in an old junk shop, didn't look much different from its Eighteenth Century ancestors.

It had a thatched roof, the thatch held in place by ropes crossing the roof from side to side and from end to end at measured intervals and tied to wooden pegs set in the upper walls and both gables. Dorothy Wordsworth, who stopped at Ballure overnight on her tour of the Island, noted that at that time these ropes were made of straw. The walls of Old Pete's cottage were made of rough stone plastered over, the plaster uneven and in need of a new coat of whitewash. Ivy and wild roses climbing the walls made the place look picturesque. Without them the cottage would have looked run-down and shabby. A large bucket hung from a narrow metal rod driven into the upper wall near the door. An old watering can rested on a slate bench beneath it. A graveyard jumble of ancient wooden farm implements lay on the grass in front of the door.

The windows were few and narrow so the interior with its flag-stoned floor must have been dark which, perhaps, is why "Old Pete" himself is sitting outside in the sun, tilted back on a battered kitchen chair in a manner Ma would disapprove of, reading a newspaper. Or maybe pretending to for the photographer's benefit. The postcard is the sort of genre picture that was popular with holiday-makers.

I wished "Old Pete" was still alive (at that time I had no idea of his fictional nature) so that when I had no one to play with I could visit him in his quaint house. I had no grandfathers extant and felt sure he would have been the sort of grandfatherly person with the time and willingness to tell a child about the past. He could have taught me to speak Manx Gaelic, which in my day was not on the school curriculum, the English government determined to stamp out that sort of divisive pre-literate tribal nonsense. Even Pop had only a few expressions in Manx which he unveiled with an awkward flourish when he'd had a pint too many. "Shoh slaynt!" he'd declare, raising his glass to a fellow drinker. "Kyn-as-ta-shiu?" he'd ask. "Ah well, trae dy liooar," he'd mutter in the embarrassed silence he had created.

For my generation Gaelic survived mainly in place names – names like that of the area of town in which I lived: Ballure – *Bal-y-Ure* or "place of the yew tree;" or others like *Cronk-ny-Iree-Laa* "hill of the rising sun," the *curragh* or the *"marsh"* or in the titles of saccharine verses about the Island – titles like *Mannin veg Villish Veen* which sounds fine but means "Dear, Sweet Little Man" (as in "Isle-of).

"Old Pete," his cottage and way of life, had vanished off the face of the earth and I could only imagine him as I watched the water running into his cistern under what was, by then, an empty field with the imperial yellow gorse advancing.

"Old Pete" wasn't the only mythic figure in my childhood world: people who transcended History, who wouldn't have been anomalies in Homer's time. There was, for instance, the old man I thought of when I was a bit older as "the blind prophet." He was somebody's extremely old grandfather and belonged to a family that kept a dairy in the town. Ma sent me there when our milk supply ran low, carrying a large jug with a beaded lace-like cover over it to keep out flies.

I went reluctantly since the "prophet" scared the pants off me even though he was harmless. At the dairy, as in a bad dream, I had to walk down a long, cool, creepy corridor and turn a corner where the man I feared sat cross-legged on a raised stone dais in a clean white-washed chamber. He was very old with hair like God's – long, white, flowing down over his shoulders. Like God he also had a long white beard. His sightless eyes resembled some of the marbles I played games with in gutters. They were a milky opaque blue, always wide open, staring at nothing. To make matters worse the old man never spoke – perhaps couldn't. As soon as I turned the corner in that corridor and saw him there, all I wanted to do was leg it.

The fact that I didn't was due to a girl of about my own age or perhaps a bit younger. She guided the old man I took to be her grandfather as he scooped milk up in a ladle from a metal churn by his side and poured it into my jug, which I was glad the girl was holding. The girl, who took the money and handed back the change, was for me a kind of tenuous insurance against any harm this strange, blind, silent figure might be meditating. He made me think of dangerous Old Testament celebrities (like Isaac's father, Abraham, with that sharp knife in his hand) into whose company I was forced by those determined Sunday school teachers I disliked.

I was fearful, too, of the exceptionally tall shepherd who trudged past our house followed by two sheep dogs every Saturday on his way into town. Despite his advancing years he walked stiffly upright from his stone house in the valley behind North Barrule on a round trip of at least twelve miles over steep hills. What disturbed me most was his height. He was a giant – as tall as a modern basketball player, approaching seven feet. His size, his robust vigor, his long shepherd's crook, his wild flashing eyes and his thick black beard streaked with grey scared me as if a figure out of the tales of the brothers Grimm had stepped off the page and strode towards me down BallaCray Road. Even his tweed hat, shaped like an upturned plant pot had something sinister about it like the headgear of an evil high priest.

His manner I thought ominous. He never smiled at anyone but glowered as he tramped along, his dogs at his heels, talking to himself. I suppose if I spent much of my life alone with sheep and a couple of border collies out on the slopes of a mountain in all weathers and all seasons I might glower and talk to myself too. But when I was ten the wild eyes, the black beard, the fixed scowl, the audible monologue of that passing giant sent me racing indoors much to Pop's amusement when he discovered the cause.

"He's a quare f'la," said Pop, "but there's no harm in 'm. And he's got the moolah."

"What he's got," said Bessie "is the *Evil Eye.*"

"What's the *Evil Eye?*" I asked, giving the phrase Bessie's dramatic emphasis.

"It's like the *Evil Tongue,*" said Pop. "Bessie'd make a good match for 'm."

"You won't be saying that when he gives Erik the look and the Buggane comes at 'm."

"What's the Buggane?" I asked nervously.

"A huge ghostie," said Bessie, "that lives on the mountain and comes howlin' to yer winder in storm in the wild of the night. He can take his big head off and throw it at yer."

"You're talking through the back of yours," said Pop.

"You won't be jokin' when that shepherd comes by and Erik's missin' from his warm bed," said Bessie, "taken up to the frozen peat bogs and thrown off a cliff in the dark."

"Don't you worry son," said Pop, "she's making it all up. The peat bogs aren't frozen and there's no cliffs up at them anyway. Stop frightening the child Bessie."

I was frightened anyway. Whenever I saw the shepherd coming along our road I ran away. Pop might poo-poo Bessie's warning but I wasn't about to be snatched from my warm bed by the Buggane just for looking at the shepherd the wrong way.

It's interesting to note how context changes so many things. After the war when the shepherd took to driving into town in his newly-acquired army surplus jeep with his collies in the back he was de-mystified. He became a man of the modern mechanical world, a farmer without magical powers, no more in league with the spirits than Ma was.

Willy Kneen was in league with spirits of a different sort. He wouldn't have frightened a soul. He belonged to comedy, not Gothic nightmare, a mixture of Sancho Panza and Don Quixote. He was the eternal peasant though in fact he owned his own farm and was said to be wealthy. He delivered vegetables once a week, coming to us last on his route. He was always offered a cup of tea and a piece of Ma's seed cake – the latter when rationing permitted. He liked to rest at our house before his long journey home. He always arrived drunk.

Drunkenness Ma deplored in general but tolerated in people like Uncle Sidney, Pop – as long as he didn't make a habit of it – and Willy Kneen. He was an intelligent well-read man whose daughters all became academics though you'd never suspect it from looking at him since he always seemed to be wearing someone else's cast-off, worn out clothes. He didn't look as if he had three ha'pennies to rub together, to use a favorite phrase of Pop's.

"He looks like he's robbed a scarecrow," Bessie would say. Willy was of the earth, but when he was drunk he was inclined to tell anyone who cared to listen of his detailed plans for reforming the "howl hoorish world, yussir." Rather than dismiss him as a nut Ma liked to hear what he had to say and while he was saying it I was sent to feed the horse that drew his vegetable cart some of its master's left-over carrots.

Willie cracked jokes in a slightly slurred voice, which made me laugh. Bessie called him a "tipsy boor" but that was because he chose to have his tea and cake with Ma and not with her. In any case she wouldn't have listened to his schemes for world change but, rather, have rattled on non-stop about local scandals, real or invented. Ma, however, who never heard anyone else talk for long about ideas liked to listen and ask the odd question, while out on the street I stood feeding Willie's patient old horse which, while chewing carrots, dropped huge piles of steaming dung and peed hot, highly odoriferous Niagaras. I was amazed that one horse could produce such a quantity of sewage. I wondered how horses – mares like this one especially – could do this in public without warning, apology or any sign of embarrassment. I should have asked Willie but I was embarrassed.

No account of the mythic figures of my youth would be complete without the "little people" at the opposite extreme from the giant. The little people were said to be everywhere but especially at the bottom of the garden, as the Ramsey poet T.E. Brown famously declared. The Reverend Brown was responsible for such deathless lines as:

> Old Manx is waning,
> She's dying in the tholtan. Lift the latch,
> Enter, and kneel beside the bed, and catch
> The sweet long sighs, to which the clew
> Trembles, and asks their one interpreter in you.

I had a hard time imagining fairies at the bottom of our garden – as distinct from Pop's allotment – since it was about fifteen feet square. I concluded they must live with the Woods family and other wealthy people with estates. But there were the undomesticated sort who dwelt in field and forest, mountain glen and seashore to which everyone had access (as far as war-time regulations permitted). When I was on my own in such places I both hoped and feared to meet one of the little people. I kept a sharp eye open for toadstools under which they were said to live. One would not want to squash fairies with a Gulliver foot.

The fairies seemed to have a particular liking for Foxdale in the center of the Island, and for the south where Pop came from. In that region there is the Ballalona Bridge – otherwise known as the Fairy Bridge, crossed by the road that leads from Douglas to the Airport at Ronaldsway. The fairies, like New York mobsters or Norse trolls, demand "respect" so woe betide anyone crossing their bridge who doesn't call out "Good day little people, we wish you well." My sister, Rachel, has a fund of tales about healthy, but skeptical English tourists who scoffed at fairy lore, refused to wish the fairies well and were soon afterward found maimed or dead in their hotel rooms, the doors locked from the inside, the police without a clue.

When we were running about on hillsides and in graveyards, playing our warlike games neither I, nor my friends gave a thought to the fairies. We could have crushed battalions of them like ants as we raced and roared about. But when I took solitary walks they came into my mind, yet however much I wanted to see them they remained stubbornly invisible. Harry Kennish declared in the playground at school that he often saw them at twilight but Harry was "under the doctor" for some mental problem so no one took anything he said seriously. There were some very old people who claimed to have seen them. They said they always left milk and food out for them at night that was always gone in the morning. They refused to believe that cats were responsible.

The fairies faded away with the Manx language itself. They certainly were not compatible with the Second World War, the horrors of which were so much nastier than anything the little people might have cooked up for the disrespectful.

I grew up at a momentous time in history, yet in contact with an older, rural Celtic past, the elements of which went back into the mists the great God, Mannanin-mac-Lir, futilely casts about his Isle to hide and protect it from strangers.

CHAPTER EIGHT

WHEN I WAS TEN, OF COURSE, I SPENT THE BULK OF MY TIME IN DAY school. I didn't actively dislike it – I didn't take illicit days off, like Brian McQueen or some of the fishermen's boys who, despite the law, were out hauling nets on their family's small coastal fishing boats from an early age. I did not, like them, become well-known to the School Board Inspector, a tall, unsmiling, white-faced, black-clad, forbidding figure by the name of Jenkins, fearsome to children as a bad-tempered policeman. But when I try to recall the people and practices of Ninian Elementary School – named for the Celtic saint – my memory is more fitful than it is about many other elements of my childhood. I used to go into a sort of trance as soon as I walked past the school's big wrought iron gates. I would have preferred to stay away and play.

Pop brought reality to bear one day by giving me a "talking to" about school – a subject he had never broached before. "Teacher says you aren't working hard enough...says you could do a lot better, you could. Says you're a sharp f'la but you're dreaming the time away there like you do here at home."

I was genuinely shocked. I wasn't conscious of living in a dreamy state either at home or at school. I did whatever I was told to do, not without grumbling, and thought no more about it. I wasn't concerned about marks. I didn't see why I should be overly worried if mine were low. Pop said they were "too low" but I really didn't know what that meant any more than he did. He was passing on the message of a school report and was disturbed by its note of criticism, its assertion that I wasn't living up to expectations even if those expectations weren't initially his. After all he hadn't done very well at school himself

"It's because you got your mind on that f'la at the Camp – always let'n it run after him instead of thinkin' of anything else."

This had become a familiar accusation after all the commotion. If I seemed distracted it was because I had Jakob on my mind. It couldn't be anything else for Pop.

"Jakob, his name is Jakob Weiss…you know what he's called." I pronounced the name Y*akob Vice* as Jakob had taught me whereas Pop, if he used the name at all, insisted on "Jay-cob Wise." And always added "an' he's not wise neither. He's a damn nuisance."

Jakob, unforgettable Jakob, was one of the most important influences on me in childhood as will appear, but if I was dreamy at school it wasn't his fault though Pop was inclined to blame him for everything I did that seemed to him wayward. In reality, when I was a little older and attending Ramsey Grammar School, it was his influence, after I had turned some developmental corner, that set me rising toward the top of the class from somewhere near the bottom. This rise, ironically, disturbed Pop. Perhaps he saw his dead fortune-making-and-losing father-in-law suddenly resurrected in me and feared I would not lead a quiet life.

The school building was a large, gray-bricked two-storied oblong factory of a place surrounded by tall, black-painted sharp-pointed wrought iron railings set in concrete on top of a low wall. Those railings put me in mind of an ogre's spears and I often wondered how it would feel to be impaled on one. For six hours a day and five days a week I was imprisoned behind them with only our concrete exercise yard to play in during fifteen minute breaks morning and afternoon (we all went home for lunch). There was one yard for the girls and one for the boys with a ten-foot wall between them. There was a door in this high wall but it was always kept locked. The place was brick and concrete functional – not a blade of grass, not a flower, there was nothing to tickle the fancy – not even a statue of old St. Ninian himself. Mr. Gradgrind of Stone Lodge would have felt quite at home here. He would have relished the smell of blackboard chalk that hung in the dark corridors.

In those corridors and elsewhere inside the school there was a great deal of rough wood. The floors were reminiscent of an old warehouse. They were made of knotted timbers that despite years of polish still sent splinters into the knees of any child who collided with them. The classrooms were sided with smoother wood stained a light brown. There were very large, square panes of glass framed above the wood so that whatever transpired within was visible to any adult standing outside. The Headmaster or his deputy, like factory inspectors checking the product, could often be seen peering through the glass while a lesson was in progress. This procedure unnerved the laboring teachers as it was no doubt intended to do. Both the Head and his Deputy relished the pleasures of authority, one of which is to keep subordinates apprehensive – "on their toes" they would have said.

Every day began with Morning Assembly. Each class – minus those of us still dawdling to school – would file into the large Assembly Hall on the second floor of the school building. Assembly itself was usually conducted by Mrs. Gelling, the Deputy Head, who led us in the singing of a hymn, the saying of prayers, and then issued announcements of public interest or necessity, often concerning the wearing of gas masks, and what to do and where to go in case of an air raid. She stood at a lectern on a raised dais with the staff behind her in a wide semi-circle. She wore her gray hair braided into wheels on either side of her head. She favored lyle stockings and always wore a thick green tweed jacket and skirt, covered during Assembly by a faded academic gown. Above and behind her hung a large framed photographic portrait of a man in a mortar board whom I took to be a relative of hers owing to a certain resemblance but was, in fact, the poet T. E. Brown, already mentioned. He was popular in late Victorian England and thus feted in the prosaic town where he had lived, unfamiliar as it was with poets and good poetry.

Mrs. Gelling was beset by the conviction that if she were not Manx and a woman she would be Head of the school, a conviction which the Reverend Thomas Edward, dangling in his frame overhead might have queried in his bluff Victorian way. Mrs. Gelling had been to Oxford: the Head had graduated from London University. Clearly something was wrong when the latter was preferred to the former institution. The bitterness Mrs. Gelling felt about this injustice spilled into her prayers so that when she besought God to cloak us all in lowliness and humility she uttered the words through clenched teeth.

She would not have been uttering them at all were it not for the Head's disability which prevented him from taking Assembly much of the time.

Cyril Bentley, the Headmaster, was an Englishman, a *come-over,* pronounced locally the way Mexicans say *gringo.* He was one of those left by the War Office to his civilian occupation because he had already paid his dues. He had fought, like Pop, in the First World War but where Pop was raked with bullets, Cyril had been smothered by gas. He was a very tall, imposing, blue-pinstriped man, his forceful build and manner subverted by a constant wheeze and a frequent racking cough that doubled him over. He would be reading the riot act to a delinquent such as I, late to school once too often, in the approved Headmasterly way, only to be ambushed by violent spasms. His helplessness before them made him less fearsome than he would have seemed otherwise, despite the canings he administered when he recovered.

"I'm doing this for your own good, boy" he would say, laying on a bit too vigorously when perhaps his mind strayed to the Germans who had gassed him.

Afterwards boys nursed their swollen hands or sat tenderly on the wooden seats of their desks. Girls, of course, were never punished in this way though Mrs. Gelling would have flogged them with vigor had the law allowed.

Parents of caned schoolboys didn't complain. "You must have done something to deserve it," they told their smarting offspring if they whimpered a protest. "Anyway, they would add, "he was gassed in the last war. You've got to make allowances." And, by and large, their smarting sons, who would never have admitted it, did.

Cyril attempted Assembly now and then but was usually defeated by his ruined chest. As he handed the ceremony over to Mrs. Gelling she treated us all to her martyred expression before picking up where he had left off.

Miss Greene was quite a different sort of person. She was a lax disciplinarian but knew how to rouse the imaginations of torpid students like me. She was the class teacher I remember best. Like the others she taught us all the subjects on the curriculum as if we were in a one-room schoolhouse but as hers was the school's senior class she was the school's senior teacher. After her class students either left school altogether or went to the Grammar School. What I remember best about her classes are the Friday afternoons when she turned to Literature.

Or "stories" as she tended to call it. On Friday afternoons she read to us from Victorian imaginative tales – of knights and damosels, of Ivanhoe, Rebecca and Rowena; of Lorna and the Doones; of Norwegian whalers hunting the narwhal with hand-held harpoons in steep icy seas; of Captain Nemo in his submarine or Passepartout floating under a balloon; of Musketeers all for one and one for all; of Monte Cristo and its Count; of the Scarlet Pimpernel (initially misheard as "Pimple") and prisoners in the Bastille ("this school's like that Barsteel Miss," said someone who was told to be quiet); of Mowgli in the Indian jungle; of Lost Worlds; lost tribes, dangerous journeys along steaming African rivers, of forbidden rites in dangerous places and, more domestically, stories of Peter Pan, Alice in a rabbit hole, goblins at a market, a wealthy well-dressed frog with a manor house and a car as posh and polished as the Rolls of the sisters Quayle.

The whole class sat rapt as Miss Greene read in her pleasant, soothing voice, taking us all away from the physical drabness of the school, away from historical dates, arithmetic formulae, geographic data, the Minotaur labyrinths of grammar, away from the very real dangers of a world at war, to imagined lands where freedom ruled, where excess was colorful and not a sin, where audacity thrived and was called "heroism," where those who suffered deserved to and, paradoxically, where many were killed but nobody really got hurt since these stories were another form of play parallel to our games in the woods. Only Brian McQueen and scions of certain illiterate fishermen – boys like Ronnie Skillicorn, with his dirty face and ready fists, missed these Friday afternoons.

Where only a very few would want to miss these classes of Miss Greene everyone would have loved to be excused from Harry Clegg's. Harry was a fifty-year-old ex-army drill instructor, now the school's one and only PT (Physical Training) teacher. Since the school lacked a gym Harry's classes were held in the Assembly Hall. There the boys stripped to their underwear (in those days at that school, children did not have special outfits for physical exercise) before being put through a series of taxing routines like recruits at boot camp. Some boys had only tattered underwear, gray with age and infrequent washing. A few had no underwear at all. Such boys were allowed to keep their dignity intact and their short pants on.

The girls also exercised in their underwear, but in a separate classroom on the ground floor where they were directed by Miss Nancy Appleton-Williams, an elephantine lady draped in the bemedalled brown tent of a Girl Guide leader, who was said to have perverse tastes and who came in part-time "to keep the gells from getting sorft."

She told the "gells" what to do and then watched them do it. Had she tried to lead by example she would have died of the strain. Trim, fit Harry Clegg, by contrast, hopped, skipped, jumped and ran on the spot with us, roaring for speed: "Faster! Faster! Faster!" he yelled, calling us namby pamby weaklings who'd have trouble finding our own arses. Teachers would come out of adjacent classrooms to ask him to dampen his megaphone delivery and to refrain from coarse language. After each such request he'd shout louder and increase the thunder by having us all race round the Assembly Hall – the part I liked best. Then we'd stop for the static exercises that murdered sinew and muscle.

"Arms above your heads!" he'd shout. "Reach for the sky! Streeeeeeetch!! Hold it!! Hold it!! Don't put those arms down!! Now . . . keep your arms up and slowly. . . slowly . . . slowly . . . knees full bend! SLOWLY YOU DEAF DAFT BUGGERS!!!"

Harry's war cries provoked frequent complaint.

"What can I do?" asked the Head between gasps for breath, "there's a war on."

"The man's an ignorant oaf, I agree," said Mrs. Gelling, "but what can I do? I'm not the Head, more's the pity. My hands are tied. I'd make changes if I could but there it is – I'm merely the Deputy – the humble Deputy."

How did I, a ten-year-old, know all this? I knew what I observed but I learned much more when I returned to teach at St. Ninian's when I was twenty-one, an Education student on his first teaching practice. Some of those who had taught me were still there and loved to gossip to one of their own.

The only other man on the staff beside the Head and Harry Clegg was Arthur Ohallaran, a distant relative of the Mrs. Ohallaran Ma knew, who spent the last few years of her life in bed because she ceased to see any point in getting up, getting dressed, living in the world.

Arthur had been turned down for military service on a variety of medical grounds. He became embittered, constantly defending his holding a civilian job in time of war even though no one criticized his doing so. Worse, since the rest of the teachers (with the above exceptions) were middle-aged women – all the younger ones being away in uniform – Arthur felt that to be placed in their company was an insult added to an injury, especially after even the Home Guard and the ARP politely refused his services too once they had scrutinized his medical record.

Arthur took out his frustrations on the children in his class. Parents complained. Cyril Bentley summoned him to his office where he gasped and wheezed his way through a lecture on classroom etiquette. Arthur felt even more ill-used than ever after this. Matters came to a boil on the day he called Mrs. Gelling an "interfering oul' bitch" and promised to "punch her in the guts and kick her in the arse" if he ever caught her spying on him through his classroom window again. He ranted, he raved. Teachers left adjacent classrooms to see what all the noise was about. Help was summoned. Eventually Arthur was taken away by two strong policemen who subdued him only with great difficulty. We heard later that he had been delivered to the Island's only mental hospital "for observation" like a curious specimen dragged up in one of the nets of Skillicorn pere.

Oddly enough once he decided that he was a casualty of war Arthur felt a lot better. He sympathized with the victims of shell-shock and until the peace the hospital found him useful things to do in helping them to recover. When the war ended Arthur was so horrified at his prospective return to "normal" life that he climbed up on to the hospital roof and promised to jump, until the Medical Director said he could stay as long as he liked. He liked the idea so much that he remained there till he died, forty-five years later.

Apart from the children I played with or sang with in the choir, I don't remember much about the others, at least not individually. I have been away too long and too much time has elapsed. I have a photograph of my class taken when I was eight or nine, I can't remember which, and I can only recognize three of the girls and two of the boys. The rest might as well be strangers.

I can say that the children I went to school with belonged to certain broad categories. There were the kids from the oldest part of the town, on the south side just off the harbor around St. Paul's church where then there were narrow streets and lanes ill-lit by gaslight. In that area in those days there were white-washed cottages with tiny latticed windows, some with bull's eye glass that must have been two-hundred years old. They formed a sort of fishing village within the town. Some of the area's inhabitants were manual laborers, more were fishermen or merchant seamen; all were poor.

This was a part of town that Ma, Bessie and many others in neighborhoods like ours deplored as a "slum" though it had character. The town lost a vital link with its past by tearing down this area long after the war to build a drab shopping center and expensive but ill-designed apartments for retired refugees from the English tax laws.

The children from this part of town that I went to school with had a rough upbringing in families making a bare and dangerous living from the sea. Drinking and violence were features of daily life there as was the penury that sent some of the children to school poorly clothed, poorly fed, ready, like Ronnie Skillicorn, for a fight in the playground at the slightest pretext. The police, the School Board Inspector, the doctor, the district nurse – even the Fire Brigade – were frequent, often unwelcome, visitors in that area of town.

Then there were the children of families like mine that considered themselves "respectable." Most of these children were the sons and daughters of the working and small shopkeeper classes – the wealthy, like Toby's father, sent their offspring to exclusive private schools. The differences between the "respectable" families and those who lived in the poorer part of town were partly economic but, more importantly, attitudinal. By modern standards Ma and Pop and many like them were poor – better off than the fishermen though not by very much. But they had steady jobs, a regular weekly wage and they aspired to a secure middle-class status for their children in the world they hoped lay beyond the war. They valued education even when they had had little of it themselves.

In time these children by and large satisfied their parents' social ambitions by becoming officers in the army, navy and air force, schoolteachers, nurses, doctors, managers, scientists, college professors. They left the Island for England, Australia, New Zealand, Africa, the United States, Canada and elsewhere. Their parents endured their absence since they were "bettering themselves" though in my own case, Pop would rather I had bettered myself quietly on the Island. A job in a local bank rather than a university education in England and the United States and a professorship in Canada, was his notion of social improvement. On the other hand he was quite happy when my brother, Ronald, decided to stay in the army where in the fullness of time he became a Lieutenant Colonel. Pop retained an affection for the army despite his traumatic battlefield experience.

There were a couple of anomalous children in the school who didn't fit into any of the local slots because they were refugees, victims of Nazi invasion, driven from their homes to seek refuge in Mannanin's protective mists and fogs. They were exotics; they stood out. Jan Kosinski was from Poland. His parents had somehow evaded the Germans and brought him to England. He achieved a dubious fame in the school by depositing bright yellow turds in the playground lavatory which the rest of us, quite new to such a phenomenon, eagerly studied after he emerged one day without pulling the chain. We speculated about the peculiarities of the Polish gut or diet, we asked Jan embarrassing questions which he tried to answer in his heavily-accented English – another source of interest to us.

Then there was Pierre Lamontagne whose parents had taken him from the Channel Islands one step ahead of the German invaders. Pierre spoke perfect English though French was his native tongue. He regretted, he said, that he was unable to tell us what a Nazi looked like, much to our disappointment. He described in detail the adventurous journey in a small fishing boat, which brought him and his family to the south coast of England in stormy weather. Only Ronnie Skillicorn was unimpressed. He said his Dad made such journeys year-round and thought nothing of it even though he couldn't swim a stroke. He reckoned that Pierre should have stayed put and thrown hand grenades at the Germans. That would have been what he, Ronnie, and his intrepid, un-swimming, generally inebriated Dad would have done. Pierre knocked him down, thereby establishing himself in our affections especially since, when Ronnie leapt up to attack him, he knocked him down again.

Life is odd, though. Ronnie Skillicorn, a bully generally dismissed as "thick," left school as soon as it was possible to enter the Merchant Navy. He retired a few years ago having spent the last ten years of his career at sea as the Captain of a cruise ship, an invitation to whose dining table was deemed an honor. And Brian McQueen, who was frequently absent from school and especially from Miss Green's Friday afternoon readings, is a widely published Shakespearian scholar at an American midwestern University. On the other hand the studious Billy Teare, authority on aborigines and boomerangs, who we were sure was destined to be a celebrated teacher, stayed in Ramsey to work in a hardware store which he now manages, a specialist in paint, nails and screws, hinges and knobs rather than more exotic anthropological arcana.

He's a patient man leading a quiet life.

CHAPTER NINE

WHILE OUR LIVES FOLLOWED SET PATTERNS THE WAR IMPINGED ON them in ways beyond those already described.

I may have made North Barrule my playground but that didn't stop aircraft from crashing into it, though on the mountain's other, steeper, and rockier side. The mountain was Janus-faced: one side a free and open natural playground, the other the site of death and destruction. I watched air force trucks drive past our house pulling long narrow trailers, wheeled coffins containing the battered fuselages and severed wings of dead aeroplanes.

Military ambulances picked their way slowly up the narrow valley track beneath that dangerous side of the mountain – right past the fearsome shepherd's house in fact – to collect the bodies and the pieces of bodies strewn about the scarps. I climbed up there not too long ago (the shepherd's place a roofless ruin now) and was surprised to find numerous shards and larger pieces of bent, jagged, weathered metal still embedded where they were violently flung over sixty years ago.

Aircraft got lost in fog and cloud and flew not only into Barrule but the higher Snaefell as well. Besides British pilots Poles (like my Spitfire pilot), Canadians, Australians, New Zealanders and American volunteers of the Eagle Squadron died in Manx valleys, on Manx mountainsides and in the waters just off shore. Seventeen aircraft were lost in this way in 1942, when I was ten, sixteen the year before and six the year after. Few crew members survived.

Then there was the night time bombing conspicuous, for us, largely by its absence but an ever-present threat nonetheless. When the air raid siren, set on the roof of a tall apartment building nearby, wailed in loud despair as fleets of German bombers approached we couldn't just turn over and go back to sleep. We had to take it seriously, get up and sit about in our night clothes "just in case" until the *all clear* sounded. The siren's lament heralded many nights of broken sleep as squadrons of German raiders flew over us headed for the shipyards of Belfast or Glasgow. It never occurred to me then that our lodgers were similarly disturbing the sleep of other families as they roared overhead in their bombers keeping Germans fearfully awake. Everyone had to have a bomb shelter to retreat to when an air raid was announced. Pop took one look at our front garden and decided that a steel-plated Anderson shelter was out of the question. It would have been just possible to build one in a fifteen foot square garden but at six feet six inches by four feet six inches it certainly wouldn't hold all the people living at *Rosetree Villa* and if one had been built there a direct hit would have sent our three-storey house down on top of it crushing us all. But no one really thought we would be the subject of the Luftwaffe's serious interest when there were more tempting targets in Belfast, Glasgow and the industrial north of England. The fighter aircraft stationed at Jurby and Andreas had been placed there to guard the approaches to the first two of these targets.

To satisfy official requirements for a shelter of some sort Pop decided to convert the pantry under the main staircase. A few shelves and their contents were removed. An electric light fixture was installed. Cushions, candles, bedding, some large containers of water and certain non-perishable foods were eased into what was a pretty confined space. Gas masks in their square boxes hung there. I asked what would happen to us if the house took a hit and collapsed while we were squeezed into this space.

"We'd be squashed like a snail on the road," said Pop cheerfully.

"Don't talk like that," said Ma, "you'll frighten the lad."

"Why are we going in there to get squashed?" I asked as broken, flattened snails oozed through my consciousness.

"We aren't," said Pop.

"Why are you getting it all ready then?"

"To satisfy the busy body nosy parkers who tell us we all have to have a shelter whether we want one or not."

"But it isn't a real shelter," I said, deeply troubled. "And what about our lodgers? Don't they have to have a shelter?"

"This place under the stairs will keep those busy body buggers happy and," said Pop, ignoring Ma who had interrupted to protest at his swearing, "our lodgers aren't worried that we don't have a shelter in the garden. Nobody around here's got one. Nobody wants one. Nobody needs one. Herman's not interested in us."

Ma went back to telling Pop off for swearing but he picked her up and whirled her in circles while she shrieked to be put down. Pop was only frisky when neighbors and lodgers weren't about.

I still had a worried look on my face so when Pop had finished whirling Ma around the room he said, "Don't fret about the shelter. We won't need it. The Germans aren't going to waste bombs on us. We're not that important here on the Island."

As things turned out he was right. A German aircraft off-course or pursued by a local fighter might release the odd bomb to lighten its load as it retreated – a few rush-fringed ponds in open country were originated in this way – but no one was killed by a bomb on the Island. When, after the war was long over, I visited the Manx Museum in Douglas I saw a minor exhibit, a small dead frog, a pauper relative of the one in the story with a manor house and a polished Rolls Royce car, the only Island victim of German bombing in the Second World War.

On the odd occasion the war could produce an airborne miracle. I remember a Christmas, probably in 1941, when Pop woke me up in the middle of the night because I had slept through the air–raid siren and he wanted to show me something remarkable. He took me out into the front garden. The whole night sky was brilliant with descending stars. There were thousands of bright silvery lights floating slowly down to earth like a throng of Herald Angels. They lit the landscape like a second daylight.

"What are they?" I asked Pop in wonder.

"Flares," he said. "Hermans in their aeroplanes have lost their way and they're sending these down to find out where they are."

I imagined eager German pilots straining to read the road signs by the light of their flares. I didn't hear the sound of engines, however, so I chose to think Pop must be mistaken. When I thought about what I had seen I fancied we had witnessed a heavenly host floating to earth to put an end to the war at the season of peace and good will. I was wrong of course, but one of the neighbors said it was a lovely thought when I told her about it.

We were not bombed and, unlike Cyril Bentley, we were not gassed though we had to carry gas masks with us everywhere we went. There were gas mask drills at school. A bell would ring, the teacher would declare that a gas attack was imminent, one or two credulous children would start to panic as the teacher ordered us all to put on our gas – masks which were stuffy and smelled strongly of rubber. It didn't take long for one's face to become hot, redden and perspire. The world turned green as we looked at it through our visors. We must have looked like little elephants with their trunks chopped off short. Our voices sounded like voices in a cavern. We were greatly relieved to tear the masks off when another bell indicated that the attack was over. No one thought to ask who would have time to actually ring the bell if a real attack occurred. The Germans were unlikely to phone Cyril Bentley to tell him they were on their way.

Of course our diet suffered because of the war in spite of Pop's Victory garden. We enjoyed its produce when it was in season but basic supplies such as tea, sugar, butter, meat and sweets were strictly rationed. We were allowed 12oz of sugar, 2oz of tea, 2oz. of butter per person per week but in an agricultural district barter could ease these restrictions.

Shopkeepers were suspected of favoritism, especially Joe Broom the butcher.

"He keeps the good cuts for his friends," said Bessie sniffing, lifting her head back a little, grimacing as if she had stepped on a dog turd – a habitual set of gestures when she uttered what she considered an unpalatable truth.

"Of course he doesn't – he can't," said Mrs. Corcoran, defending her husband's employer. "He's *regulated.*"

"Well, you *would* say that," countered Bessie. "I bet you don't go short. I bet you get more than your fair share. You're *well* regulated, I'd say. Must be nice for some people. Nice to be some!" (accompanied by a toss of the head).

"What a nasty thing to say!" protested Mrs. Corcoran her eyes filling with tears as they did whenever she felt herself ill-used. "Just because Fred works for a butcher doesn't mean he gets anything special put aside for him. That's against the law, that is. We're rationed same as you . . .same as everyone…"

Bessie begged to differ. She had convinced herself that the Corcorans sat down to vast cannibal-sized plates of meat every night and didn't hesitate to say so. She suspected that we might benefit from this bounty, which is one reason why she dropped in at mealtimes hoping to catch us wolfing illicit flesh.

"Think what them grocers is taking home," said Bessie longingly. "All that sugar and flour and salt and such. They're fat and well fed while we starve!"

I must say that I thought this excessive even when I was ten. I knew more than one cadaverous grocer. Ma said that Joe Broom the butcher had always been fat. Bessie demurred. She knew him when he was but an eagle's talon in the waist, it seemed. She declared that before the war he was a slice of his present self – "a shaving."

"He gets fatter every week of the war," she insisted. "And he's not the only one," she added with another vigorous nod.

Bessie confused always having to have the last word with being right though the longer she argued the more she convinced herself that she was uttering no more than the plain, unvarnished, truth.

If she had known what Pop got up to she would have turned apoplectic. He made deals. He used the fish he caught and the occasional rabbit he snared as media of exchange – for butter from a farming friend, for the odd bottle of sherry or brandy from people like Tony Wood's father and the housekeeper of the Sisters Quayle with access to a pre-war cellar. Bessie, of course, like most people, made her own arrangements offering her ration coupons for this commodity in exchange for coupons from others for things she wanted more than they did. She no doubt engaged in direct barter though she would have been the last to admit that she behaved like everyone else. She got by with less hardship than she claimed to be suffering.

She was certainly better off than Mrs. Dodd who lived in a flat in a four-storey building at the end of Ballacray Road where Ma visited her pretty regularly, often dragging me along. The place, unlike most in the neighborhood, was dingy and murky. The few windows off the main staircase were grimey. There was no light to turn on. The cobwebbed entrance hall with its grimy cold cracked tile floor was full of rusty flat-tired bicycles that had died there long ago. The stale marsh-gas smell of drains and boiled cabbage was thick on the air. I felt like throwing up whenever Ma hauled me there. The place needed new plumbing, fresh air and a squad of Aunty Doreens.

Mrs. Dodd's apartment was at the top of the building. When we labored up the stairs Ma usually brought something from her kitchen which she had me carry – a pie, a can or two of beans she could ill spare, some of Pop's fish, the odd rabbit he caught with snares in the hills. We always seemed to be delivering food. Of course I wanted to know why.

"Mrs. Dodd's poor," said Ma.

"Poorer than we are?"

"We are NOT poor!" Ma was indignant at the suggestion.

"We aren't rich. We're not like Mr. Woods. He's rich. He's got a great big house in its own grounds. He's got a huge greenhouse and a gardener. He grows grapes. He's got three cars and he sends Toby to a school that charges a lot of money. Toby can have anything he likes."

"We're not rich like Mr. Woods," Ma conceded, "but we're not poor either. We pay our way. So don't you go round telling people we're poor!"

I was surprised at Ma's vehemence in denying poverty but I hadn't experienced her fall from Middle Class grace. She had shown me a photograph once of the house she lived in when she was about my age. It was a mansion bigger than even Mr. Wood's. Like his house it stood in its own grounds, a long drive leading up to it from the road. It was an establishment that could not have been run without servants. It was a world away from *Rosetree Villa*, an engine driver's wage, endless labor on behalf of her family and a house full of billeted lodgers.

Mrs. Dodd always seemed glad to see us and was humbly grateful for Ma's gifts.

"I don't know what I'd do if I didn't have such kind friends," she would say, wiping the tears from her eyes with the end of the long, grubby apron she always wore over a shabby faded, flower-patterned dress. She plaited her hair in wheels like Mrs. Gelling.

"Hasn't she got a ration book like we have?" I asked Ma once after we had left the marsh-gas-and-cabbage house and I was gratefully gulping in the fresh, salty air. "Why can't she get food with it like we do?"

"You don't just need a ration book," Ma said. "You have to have money to buy what you're allowed and she hasn't got much. That's what being poor means."

"How does she pay the rent?"

"Once she has paid it she doesn't have much left for anything else. Her great lurricking son doesn't give her any. He's in prison."

"Like the enemy aliens?"

"No, not like the aliens. He's local. He's in the prison for people who break the law. He's a thief."

When I asked eagerly for an account of the wayward son's thievery Ma seemed to regret telling me that he was a criminal and wouldn't outline his nefarious career for me. She did, however, offer one intriguing detail: "He hits his mother when he's drunk."

I was appalled. The idea of someone hitting their mother seemed hardly credible to me at that age. I could understand why anyone might want to have a go at their father – there were times when I wished I was tall enough and strong enough to work Pop over – but to use their fists on their own mother – a mother who was poor – well, that to me was unimaginable. No wonder this son was in prison. That such conduct was not confined to Dodd Junior, however, I was made aware of one day when I witnessed a drunken brawl in the part of town Ma called a "slum." A fight between two brothers spilled out of a house on to the street. The combatants were bent on beating each other to a pulp and their mother tried to stop them. One of them turned on her, swore and punched her in the face, knocking her to the ground just as the police arrived. I watched long enough to witness the mother join her sons in hurling abuse at the local cops while her nose bled profusely.

Since Ma wouldn'ʒ say anything more about Mrs. Dodd's son I turned to Bessie who seemed to know everything about everyone.

"He's a ne'er-do-well like his good-for-nothing father."

"Where's his father?"

"In the army somewhere."

"Ma says Mrs. Dodd's poor. Why doesn't he help her?'

"They don't live together any more. He ran off with a tart, not before giving Edie Dodd a black eye or two. He was a nasty piece of work – still is I bet. His kind don't change."

I was confused about the tart. Bessie told me to ask Ma what they were. Ma said if I ever used the word "tart" again she'd have Pop rinse my mouth out with soap. Not relishing this prospect in future I always referred to Ma's pastry creations as "pies."

Fruits, except for local ones, were rare. Oranges appeared only at the occasional Christmas even after the war had ended. Food supplements and medications were being made from local blackberries and rose hips and we were given time off from school to gather them from fields, lanes, brooghs along the coast, the gorse-clad lower slopes of North Barrule.

The school was divided into groups – *houses* – each one identified by a color. Mine was Red House. A contest was established to see which house could gather the most blackberries and rose hips in late summer and early fall. Our efforts, we were assured, would be much appreciated by a grateful government.

It felt wonderful to be liberated from adult constraint in school time, especially with the blessing of our teachers. We even obtained the grumbling acquiescence of Mr. Jenkins the School Board Inspector, who wondered aloud and in public where it all would end. A conversation he had with Pop in a pub suggested his arm had been twisted.

"When I were a lad y'ad ter be i' school not gallivantin' ower field and 'ill and whatnot," he confided to Pop over a pint at the *Mannanin Arms.* "Did y'ever 'ear the like o' what's goin' on now? Rose 'ips and blackerberries, blackerberries and rose 'ips…I meantersay…there in't a thing I can do about it. Orders o' government. I mean, did y'ever 'ear the like o' that?"

"Strange times," Pop said he had replied and then added, "Still, nothing wrong with kids doing their bit for the war effort."

"That's all *you* know, said Jenkins the Lancashire Come-Over addressing Pop in the superior tone of an Arthurian knight confronting a Manx bumpkin. Pop took umbrage. Pop said there was almost a fight and added "silly oul bugger."

"Ernest!" Ma exclaimed. She ordered me to bed while she re-educated Pop on booze, swearing and violence.

As to the collection of berries and rose hips we would be judged by our results. I'm not sure that any of us went about the task of collecting them inspired by the idea of contributing significantly to the war effort. We couldn't see how our collected fruits would defeat Hitler. Rather, we were seized by the spirit of rivalry and competition. Each of us wanted our house to collect the most and thereby win the prize though I forget what the prize was. It might have been no more than a brief appreciative mention in the local newspaper which, for children, would have been fame indeed.

On our first expedition I had expected that Brian McQueen would simply take one of his days off and that Ronnie Skillicorn would put to sea with his fearless Dad but I was wrong. Like everyone else they were caught up in the excitement of the chase. Ronnie didn't even steal the blackberries and rose hips of weaker children, which I half expected when we set out. Everyone used their local knowledge to find the richest patches of brambles, the most productive clumps of wild rose, and then with full bags, jam jars, cans, sped back to school to empty their collections into the large tin containers waiting there.

We bore the scratches of brambles, the deeper cuts of wild rose thorns like badges of honor. As we stood before her at an assembly the day after our collecting was done Mrs. Gelling said we had exceeded our targets. Cyril Bentley coughed his way through his official congratulations. He didn't cane anyone for at least a week.

On that first occasion Yellow House won. Ronnie Skillicorn and Brian McQueen were both in Yellow House. I was moved to question that universal justice by which, the Vicar said, the world was informed. Ronnie and Brian soon lost interest, absenting themselves from future berry hunts. Red House even won, once.

CHAPTER TEN

WE DIDN'T GO OUT MUCH AS A FAMILY WHEN I WAS TEN. POP HAD to work long wartime hours. Ma had a house full of lodgers to feed and could barely spare the time or the energy to shop for groceries. Shopping entailed a walk of two or three miles, carrying steadily heavier bags and a return journey up a steep hill. Not everything was delivered to the door.

Bess envied Ma her access to the ration books of our wartime "guests."

"Must be nice to be some people," went her chorus when she was feeling more than usually peeved with the silent Willie and sought relief by stirring up trouble among her neighbors. "Must be nice t'ave all them coupons so's you can get whatever you want from the grocer, the butcher, the baker, the fishmonger…very nice it must be. Must be like owning a shop!"

On the rare occasion (usually, though not always, a Sunday) when Ma had had enough of Bessie's commentary and of her lodgers and Pop had one of his infrequent days off, they found time for an outing. Special arrangements had to be made. A jittery Mrs. Dodd was persuaded, with great difficulty and only out of her sense of obligation to Ma, to supervise the lodgers while Bessie took it upon herself to supervise Mrs. Dodd. If the day of the outing was a Sunday a note was sent to the Vicar to excuse me from Sunday School and choir for the occasion. A note invariably came back from the Vicar asking for proof that the original note was genuine.

Ma and Pop's idea of a relaxing day out was a six mile walk. Carlo could sink into his pushchair when he tired but I had to keep plodding even when overwhelmed by fatigue.

"You're a big lad now," Pop would say when I complained "so no, you can't share Carlo's pushchair. Your friends'd laugh if they saw you in it."

"Don't care, I'm tired."

I was told that if I forgot all about being tired the fatigue would vanish. That sort of mental trick might satisfy the credulous, the suggestible, the thick, but it didn't work with me.

There was one concession on such occasions. We paused to rest at a drab little shop run by an old woman with sparse black teeth who, I was sure, was a witch. She looked to me like the Lhiannin Shea – the fairy-woman responsible for all manner of mischief. She wore a faded tartan shawl over a long shabby black dress, she was bent over, cackled at Pop's quips and had a grim black cat that had never cracked a smile. She sold potions of her own manufacture. She even kept an old-fashioned broomstick in a corner, which Ma said was for sweeping out the shop.

Her drinks were cold ones made from dandelions, burdock, elderberries and simples, gathered from mountain, field, swamp, hedge, ditch and road-side. The liquids were deep black, ruby red and emerald green in color – refreshing in those pre-Pepsi days but I worried that we were swallowing pleasant-tasting poisons that would dismantle us later. When I confided this fear to Pop he said I had a wildfire in the brain. To my mortification he told my fears to the crone who kept the shop. She cackled loudly in what sounded to me like triumph. Pop said, "Ah take no notice… that's just the way of her" when I looked alarmed. None of us died from poisoning. None of us even had a stomach-ache after leaving the old woman's shop.

Very occasionally instead of their six-mile circuit Ma and Pop walked us out to a farm in Glen Auldyn. It must have been at least four miles each way but since we rested at the farm for a few hours before returning home the journey didn't seem as long as the more usual circuit.

The farm was owned and run by a couple Ma and Pop were friendly with, Talbot by name. Like most on the Isle-of-Man in those days the farm was mixed. There was a small dairy herd with a bull to keep it happy, some bullocks (carefully separated from the bull) fattening for market, a large flock of chickens and smaller ones of geese and ducks. The Talbot's fields were sown with hay, wheat, turnips, potatoes and cabbages. Since he had to put his tractor away owing to fuel shortages Tom Talbot relied on two very large, strong horses to pull his plough and a number of carts. There was plenty of work to do on the farm in all seasons especially since the Talbots daily delivered the milk from their dairy to their own customers and supplied the Mooragh Internment Camp with vegetables.

Up to the time I was ten I hadn't been to the farm that often but when we did visit I was told I could roam wherever I liked as long as I didn't leave gates open or throw stones at the animals. I was offended at the latter injunction. It was well known that I threw stones only at other boys. But I did have a weakness for swinging on five-barred gates.

To make sure that I behaved I was escorted everywhere I went on the farm by two firm but friendly border collies – *Rory* and *Tory* – who tended to jump up, put their paws on my shoulders and lick my face. When they did this to little Carlo their weight knocked him flat in the muck. He bellowed loudly. "Bad dog-hee-hee!" he wailed until rescued by Mr. Talbot. "Bad doggie hurtee meheehee!"

Mr. Talbot's hired man was wired oddly so that he had a unique way of pronouncing even simple words. He seemed to aspire to pronounce them as close to backwards as he could get. He was garbed in an antique mud-decorated sportscoat out at the elbows, worn over a pullover with many holes in it and a thick, faded blue flannel shirt. His trousers were ancient corduroy cast-offs tied at the knees with binder twine. He was shod in mud and dung-caked boots. His hair was hidden under a shapeless torn cloth cap pulled down over his forehead. He was tall, thin, boney, resembling a scarecrow, though scarecrows were, on the whole, better dressed.

"Them gods is doog gods," he said to set the record straight.

"What's a *doog god?*" I asked Mr. Talbot, never having heard of this deity at Sunday school.

"That's just Johnny's way of speaking," he told me. "He gets the words all round backwards. They come out arse-first the way Johnny did when he was born. What he was saying was that the dogs are good dogs. They are too…just a bit frisky. You don't mean anyone any harm do ya fellas?" He had to stop to embrace two wildly excited animals who came close to wagging themselves in half in gratitude for this character reference.

"Them gods," said Johnny pointing at the gyrating dogs and elucidating their function on the farm "is peesh gods. They hep drown up the peesh."

"The dogs help to round up the sheep," Mr. Talbot translated. "You talk funny don't you Johnny," he said, giving his farmhand a fatherly pat on the shoulder.

"I kort finely," said Johnny with dignity.

"Ay, that you do," said Mr. Talbot, who understood Johnnyspeak better than anyone except his mother.

Our visits to the Talbots, like those to our aunts and uncles, were of a social nature but where Pop refused to engage in the latter he relished our calls on the Talbots. He wasn't irked as he would have been by Emmeline's glass-filled rooms. He didn't fidget as he would have done in Agatha's book-lined Victorian interiors. He didn't sit in sullen silence as would have been the case in Aunty Doreen's house as she laid down the law on every subject remotely connected with housework and the paucity of cleaning products in war-time. The Talbot's farmhouse would have given Aunty Doreen a heart attack. It was rougher and readier even than our place and Pop felt very much at home in it. He and Mr. Talbot had a great deal to say to one another on matters such as farming, fishing, the conduct of the war, prices, the unavailability of whiskey and a myriad other issues. Pop frequently discussed his garden which he didn't do with anyone else. He often asked Mr. Talbot's advice on horticultural problems.

Ma got on equally well with Mrs. Talbot who fussed over us and gave us cream and home made jam and scones to eat – great treats in Spartan times.

"It's good to have kiddies in the house," Mrs. Talbot would say at intervals with a tear in her eye.

When I asked Ma why Carlo and I seemed to provoke this reaction she told me that the Talbots once had a son who, had he lived, would now be older than Ronald but he was killed in an accident on the farm when he was a year younger than me. He fell from the upper floor of the barn and broke his neck.

"I suppose you remind her of him," said Ma. "but she likes to have children around so don't worry about it."

I asked if Johnny had fallen from the second floor of the barn too, since he talked so oddly but Ma said he was born like that and then I remembered what Mr. Talbot had said about him coming into the world backwards.

The Talbots had given him work as a favor to his widowed mother when the local school despaired of teaching him anything. His employers had grown fond of him and he now lived with them, visiting his mother on weekends. The Talbots could usually understand what he said but when there was difficulty he drew them pictures – wonderful pictures. He could, apparently, draw accurately and beautifully. He felt safe on the farm, which he left only to visit his mother. At the village school he had been ruthlessly mocked and had responded with his fists, thus provoking beatings from gangs in the playground and elsewhere. Ronnie Skillicorn wasn't the only school bully in the area.

We generally had afternoon tea with the Talbots after which I paid a visit to the poultry, inspected the cattle and spent a bit more time with Johnny to see if I could begin to fathom what he was saying.

"Owes 'as to be klimmed," he observed leading me to the stone building that housed the dairy herd.

I was always amazed at how the cows filed into the farmyard from a nearby field at a call from Johnny after he had opened the gate to let them out. They walked in, slow and stately as titled ladies processing along an aisle, each one to her own stall in the cow byre, to dine leisurely on hay from a feeding rack while Johnny milked them in turn. These were the days before milking machines and Johnny was skillful at hand milking. When he gave me a turn the cow bellowed and kicked back nearly knocking me, the low, three-legged milking stool and the milk bucket, over. Johnny laughed at the stricken look on my face.

"Them 'owcs is awful dab if yer squidge 'dar," he said.

My owc was certainly awful dab. Its back hoofs just missed my head. Had they connected I might have spent the rest of my life talking like Johnny.

On one of our visits, this time on a Saturday after we had had tea and before Pop could decide it was time for us all to leave, I wandered in late afternoon to some rough land above the farm. The farm was situated below Sky Hill where Godred Crovan – "Orry the Dane" – founder of the Norse line of Manx kings, had defeated the native Celtic Manx. We could see the hill easily from our house four miles away. I remembered that when I was Carlo's age it was covered in fir trees. Now it was totally bald, not a fir in sight, and I wanted an explanation. I hoped to get it by climbing up to where the trees had once stood.

About halfway up I stopped climbing for a moment and turned to look down on the farm below and my eye traveled across the Talbot's fields. I was surprised to see a group of about six men working in one of them.

I thought the Talbots worked the farm themselves with only Johnny to help. On our more usual Sunday visits there was nobody around except Mr. and Mrs. Talbot and Johnny.

When I reached the top of the hill it was evident that the trees I remembered had all been chopped down. Their stumps remained but were already rotting away. I wanted to know who had cut down the trees and why, so I hastened down to the farm where Pop was stamping about the muddy farmyard looking for me. He had decided half an hour earlier that it was time to leave but couldn't find me. After he had promised me a "tanning" if I disappeared like that again, and thanked the Talbots for their hospitality, I asked about the trees.

"All cut down for the war effort," he said without further explanation. I asked about the men I had seen working in the field.

"Those'd be the aliens," said Tom Talbot. "They're allowed to leave the Camp and help us out when we're planting or harvesting…when we need the extra help. Makes a change for them f'las after being locked behind the barbed wire like our chickens."

"Why don't they just run off?"

"Well, there's a couple of soldiers there to guard them but where'd they run to?" Mr. Talbot asked. "Anyway they like working on the land…it gets'm out of the Camp, it gives 'm exercise, fresh air, something to do. They're not awkward customers."

This talk of prisoners led Ma and Pop to discuss them on the walk home. I wanted to know who they were and where they had come from and why they were cooped up behind the wire.

"They're Germans, Italians, and others from countries fighting against us now. Our government doesn't trust 'm so it locked 'm up over here to stop 'm helping the Nazis. They shipped off a lot to Australia and Canada too…spread 'm around a bit."

I asked why, if Mr. Talbot didn't think they were dangerous, the government did.

"Tom Talbot's doing well out of 'm. He sells meat, milk and vegetables to the Camp and he gets prisoners to help 'm work the farm. He doesn't have to pay them…they don't get wages like Johnny. Tom pays the people at the Camp for their work but it'd cost him a damn sight more if it was Manx f'las he had working for 'm. As far as Tom's concerned the prisoners are fine. They're not much of a danger now they're all locked up and guarded all the time but who knows what those f'las 'd get up to if they were out on the loose?"

"What *would* they do?" Those Friday afternoon stories at school led me to imagine lurid possibilities.

"Dunno," said Pop. "…spy for Hitler…blow up roads and bridges…send signals to German bombers and U-boats with lights at night…all sorts of things. Can't take chances in a war."

"Would they cut people's throats and steal their kids and rob their houses?"

"They might if they got the chance. But they're not going to get the chance because they're locked up in camps like the Mooragh and those ones in Douglas and Peel."

"Is that why people don't like them and say bad things about them?"

"There's a lot here don't like them because of what happened to the people with the hotels and boarding houses like them on the north promenade where the Camp is now. Those f'las was given five days to leave their homes…*five days*…as if those ones was causing the trouble. Government comes along and takes their houses…what can they do? Nothin'. Any trouble an' the police 'd have 'm locked up like thieves… an' its government's doing the stealing. Owners had to leave just about everything behind. They'd be paid for it all after the war…an' if ya believe that ya no better than Jimmy Simpson with only half a brain at 'm since he fell into the binder. So the owners had to leave everything behind except their clothes and what they could carry in suitcases. An' they had to find somewhere else to live in the five days. There's workmen out there in the street diggin' holes for the big barbed wire fences before people had time ta think. You could hear the racket at them road drills right up at our place."

"But it's not fair to blame the aliens," said Ma, who had been only half-listening to the conversation as she settled Carlo in his pushchair. "They don't want to be here. They don't want to be locked up" she went on.

"If the government didn't think them alien f'las was dangerous they wouldn't 've locked 'm up. And here they are livin' in boarding houses an' hotels belonging ta people who was kicked out…promised a prison cell if they didn't leave quickly…so don't go expecting people here to be sorry for the aliens."

I wasn't then in a position to appreciate the irony but there was Jakob Weiss thanking God for his escape from Germany in 1938 only to be seized by English authorities two years later and after a summary enquiry sent to the Isle-of-Man to live in a large barbed-wire-enclosed house in Ramsey, a house that had been as forcibly wrestled from its owner as he had been from his career. Neither had done anything to deserve their shoddy treatment. Both were victims of arbitrary authority but the house owners blamed the prisoners for their plight as if those prisoners had started the war that led to their dispossession, as if they wouldn't eagerly fight the Nazis themselves if given the chance.

Johnny had a more benevolent attitude toward the alien prisoners, at least to those who worked on the farm. He couldn't get his tongue round the word "alien." He called them "snails" but not as an insult.

"Them snails is doog. Them snails kwer doog."

And now it is time to introduce one of the "snails" who worked well, one who came to mean so much to me when I was ten. Jakob, who made Pop fearfully suspicious, was by far the most fascinating person I had met so far in my life.

CHAPTER ELEVEN

Perhaps I'd better explain how I met Jakob before I say any more about him. That will involve a brief explanation of the dairy side of the Talbot operation and how, with some difficulty, I became its humblest functionary.

The Talbots, as I've mentioned, delivered their own milk to their own customers. Liz Talbot didn't fancy driving a horse and cart like some of the local dairy farmers so with the help of the versatile Ramsey blacksmith ("Gone to lunch. Back in no time" read the note often fixed to his Smithy door) they converted their old, but sturdy, black Morris car into a milk van. The blacksmith carefully cut out the original back of the car, installed a door there, removed the back seat and modified the area it had occupied so that Tom could put in a raised wooden platform to support three milk churns with taps – a large one in the middle with a smaller one either side of it like a heifer with twin calves.

While Liz delivered the milk her husband worked on the farm alongside Johnny and the alien prisoners. They used the two Clydesdales, saving their petrol ration for the milk delivery and for an ancient truck, which they used sparingly to carry vegetables and farm supplies.

Ma bought most of her milk from the Talbots. Liz, like Willy Kneen, came to us at the end of her rounds but unlike Willy she came sober and with no evident desire to put the world to rights. She always had a cup of tea, a gossip and a helping of such baking as wartime restrictions allowed Ma to produce before she drove back to the farm. One day she arrived with a proposal. She asked if Ma would let me accompany her on her Saturday rounds. She needed a younger pair of legs to help her, she said. Ma understood what she hadn't said, which was that since I reminded her of Frank, having me around on a regular basis would be a bit like getting her dead son back.

Worrying that I would at once emulate Frank by falling on my head from the top floor of the barn or, alternatively, get myself mangled in farm machinery Ma raised practical objections. How could I be expected to walk to and from the farm four miles away along a busy road all on my own – an eight-mile round trip – on top of the work Liz would expect me to do? Would I be strong enough for the kind of work Mrs. Talbot had in mind? After all I was only ten years old, a soft town child unused to country labor.

Mrs. Talbot had it all thought out. "Tom'll pick him up early Saturday after he's delivered to the Camp and I'll leave him here when we bring your milk. I always come here last anyway. Don't worry, I'll look after him. All I want Erik to do is help me with the milk round. He'll have to carry nothing heavier than a full two-quart can. I'll give him a bit of pocket money for helping me. What do you say?"

"Well…I don't know…" said Ma dubiously as she imagined me hurtling from hayricks onto accidentally upturned pitchforks or trampled by one of the Clydesdales or gored by Gerald, the testy bull – which she admitted to me much later.

"He might not want to do it," Ma said hopefully.

"Well why don't we ask him?" Mrs. Talbot was a determined woman despite her mildness of manner.

"Let me discuss it with his father first," Ma countered hoping to persuade Pop of the incompatibility of farms and their second son.

"It'll do him good," said Pop when Ma tried to persuade him against the idea. "Helping Liz'll keep the lad outa mischief. A bit o' work never harmed anyone. It might toughen him up. Be the makin' of him."

"I don't want him *toughened up*," said Ma. "He's too young for farm work…he's only ten."

"Nobody coddled me the way you coddle him," said Pop, putting down his newspaper. "Before I was even a l'il f'la nine years old I was put out to work. I was made to cut wood, fetch coal, run errands, deliver groceries for the shop on the corner for a few pennies that I had to give to my oul man or else…and those were the easy jobs."

Ma groaned. Look at what she had done! She had as good as invited Pop to recite the epic tale of his childhood servitude – one she had heard with varying embellishments many times before – so much worse than anything she or either of his sisters or any of her sisters or his brother or her brother or his brothers-in-law or anyone else had ever had to endure since Viking times.

"While you and yours lived high and mighty and well-fed up that big fancy house in Douglas, with the grounds and the gardener at it and all the servants in the house fetching an' skivvying for you I was made to…"

"I'm not having Erik brought up like you!" Ma interrupted passionately. "I can't see why you would either if things were that bad."

"Oh," said Pop resorting to defensive sarcasm, "he's a gentleman is he? He's not to dirty his hands with a bit'v honest muck? Too dainty by half for that is he?"

"He's too young to be working on a farm."

"He's not going to be working on a farm. He'll be carrying cans o' milk for Lizzie Talbot not mucking out the cow byre or stookin' hay with the thistles in it or diggin' spuds out in the mud and rain with a coupla oul sacks to his back to keep from gettin' soaked but getting' soaked anyhow like I had to when we lived in the south down by…"

Appalled at her incaution in giving Pop another opening for bitter reminiscence Ma cut him short.

"All right!" she said," all right! Let him do it. But only for a week or two to see how he goes on. If he gets over-tired then he's not doing it any more."

"*Over-tired?!!* This f'la's the one that's off climbing Barrule…roaring round the woods up at Lhergy Frissel with that gang of kids…jumping all over the grave-stones at St. Mary's so the Vicar's always complaining! What's a few cans o' milk to all a that?"

"That's not the point," said Ma as she often did when faced with logic.

I had been listening to this exchange by way of a half-open door. Now I thought I had found out why Pop preferred to live away from his brother and sisters. His was a male Cinderella story. He resented being picked on as a child and made to labor while the other children were excused. I'd have resented it too…bitterly. Mind you, I had no way of knowing how strictly accurate Pop's tale of woe was.

I had to feign astonishment when Ma told me what Pop had decided and she had reluctantly, and only after a skirmish, gone along with. She did not, of course, mention that she had given in only because she had run out of ammunition and didn't want to hear any more of Pop's picturesque youthful slavery.

"You can help Mrs. Talbot…*but only if you want to,*" Ma emphasized, offering me a sly way out. "No one's forcing you," she went on in case I had missed the point, raising her eyebrows, tightening the muscles of her face, giving her head a slight negative shake by way of prompts that were lost on me.

"Yipppeee!!!" I yelled. "When can I start?"

Liz Talbot was glad to hear that I could help her but also slightly surprised. She had expected Ma to refuse when she had seemed so reluctant to let me go.

"It's against my better judgment," Ma told her, "but his father thinks it'll be good for him. Erik's only doing this for a couple of weeks, mind, just to see how things go on." Ma's tone suggested things wouldn't.

"It'll be all right," said Liz. "We'll take good care of him. Tom'll pick him up at seven next Saturday."

"Seven!!!" Ma only began to surface around that time. She was not going to get up any earlier to make sure I was awake and dressed in time. Her day was long enough without that. She rarely got to bed before midnight. "It'll have to be later than that," said Ma emphatically "or he's definitely *not* coming."

Negotiations began all over again. In the end it was Pop who said he'd have me awake and ready by seven. He had to rise around six to drive the first train of the day from Ramsey to Douglas after his fireman had seen to the tedious business of getting up steam. I would be given breakfast on the farm.

So began a new phase of my life. Instead of spending Saturdays invading abandoned farmhouses with the choir I was picked up while still half asleep and driven out to Glen Auldyn by Tom Talbot in his rickety truck – the one he had just used to carry vegetables to the Mooragh Camp for the alien prisoners to cook for themselves.

"I was up at four this morning," he would say as he saw me dozing off on the ride. "You town f'las have an easy life," and he'd laugh a superior rural laugh.

The Talbot's farm, as I have mentioned, lay on Sky Hill, not far above the foot of it. We had to cross the Glen Auldyn River to reach it. When we turned off the narrow road through the glen we drove over a small arched stone bridge. The first morning I drove out with "Uncle Tom," as Mr. Talbot suggested I call him, he stopped his truck on this bridge for a few minutes.

"See that big pile o' stones down there?" He was pointing at banks of rocks, some the size of a small car. "Well them f'las come down from the mountain in the flood o' '30. The whole road through the Glen was washed away. People by the river had water up to the second floor at them. Their cups and their saucers was floating up the stairs to meet them. We're a bit higher up so the water didn' reach us but ya shoulda seen all the mud and muck in all them houses along the river, rich and poor alike, didn't matter. That flood washed away our bridge and the one down the main road to Ramsey. It carried off all the bridges in the glen. They found garden seats, oul wheelbarrers, bitsa oul Mrs. Quilliam's outhouse down the beach miles an' miles away…out at Ballure on the shore near you. It took a long time to build back the road we've just been driving along. I had to pay for this new bridge we're parked on an' it didn' come cheap neither."

I'd had no idea that the Glen Auldyn River, nothing more than a shallow stream now, could have turned into a raging flood after prolonged torrential rains. I bet Ma didn't know the extent of it or she'd have used it to clinch her argument with Pop. *"But there could be one of those downpours… floods…Erik would be washed way out to sea…flung ashore in Cumberland…of course he can't go! Do you want your son to drown? Do you want him all soaked and dead on an English beach with his eyes pecked out by seagulls? Well then…"*

I decided not to tell Ma about this piece of local history.

What Uncle Tom had told me immediately made the farm a dramatic place to work. Suppose it rained again like Noah's flood and we were all isolated on the farm unable to cross the swollen river. People's tables, sofas and sideboards would float by, the new bridge would wash away and the farm would be like a desert island till the waters retreated to their banks. I'd be like a castaway! Whenever we drove across the bridge to the farm thereafter I checked the water level…just in case.

I asked Johnny if he remembered the flood.

"Terwa koot ridgeb," he replied shaking his head, amazed that the waters could exert such force that they carried away a structure he had believed to be fixed for all time like a feature of the landscape. "Terwa koot owcs" he added sadly. The sight of bellowing cows carried helplessly away from their riverside meadows had made him cry off and on for weeks said Mrs. Talbot (who said it was OK for me to call her "Aunty Liz").

I was introduced that first Saturday to the Talbots' idea of breakfast which featured thick pieces of home made bonnag plastered with butter they churned themselves and jam made from their own strawberries. "Door stops" the Talbots called these wedges of delight. Fresh bonnag, strong, salty, pure white Manx butter churned on the farm, jam from home-grown strawberries – a delicious combination at any time but in a war in a period of strict rationing the Talbot *doorstops* were luxury indeed. If Ma had eaten a Talbot breakfast she would have had fewer qualms about letting me help "Aunty Liz" on her rounds.

"These'll give ya muscle," said Uncle Tom as he buttered his third chunk of bonnag…these'll put hairs on ya chest."

"Dreb an' maj an' nagbon…hmmm!" Johnny said in appreciation. He then entered upon a lengthy discourse which I couldn't follow but which Uncle Tom said was an account of how his mother made the same sort of meal though in her case for afternoon tea rather than for breakfast. He was expressing the bliss he felt when he went to eat it on a Saturday afternoon. It was like having an extra breakfast.

Breakfast over, I went to the dairy with Aunty Liz. It was a stone building, very cold, very clean, the whitewashed walls spotless. It was close to the cow byre so the milk didn't have to travel far before it was pasteurized. There were milk churns, milk cans and pasteurizing equipment in the room, which had large stainless steel counter-tops all round it that shone from being well, and frequently, burnished. The place had a milky-buttery smell that made me feel relaxed and dreamy despite the cold. This was where that delightful butter I had just eaten was made and where milk was briefly stored before its delivery.

While Aunty Liz was explaining to me what everything in the dairy was called and what it was used for a truck drove into the farm street and stopped just outside. A small group of men jumped down from the back of it and Uncle Tom came from whatever he had been doing to greet them. As he began to explain to them all what the tasks of the day would be and where they would be carried out I realized that these must be the prisoners I had seen working in one of the Talbot's fields when I had climbed Sky Hill on that recent visit with Ma, Pop and Carlo.

I was a little fearful. This was the first time I had seen prisoners close-up like this without wire or soldiers between us. They didn't look very different from the townspeople even though they were called *aliens*.

One of them, a young middle-sized tough-looking man with a broad chest and very black hair, came into the dairy. Involuntarily I backed away so that Aunty Liz stood between us. She didn't seem the least bit perturbed. In fact she greeted the man affectionately before turning to me.

"Erik, this is Jaycob Wise. You needn't worry," she went on seeing me hanging back, "he won't bite."

"I may be wise…who knows?" said the young man, "but I am called W*eiss, Jakob Weiss*, pronounced *Yakob Vice,"* he said, "but Liz keeps trying to turn me into an Englishman by the way she says my name."

"A Manxman," Aunty Liz corrected him, "There's a difference."

"How do you do?" he said, offering me a hand roughened by hard work. I allowed my hand to lie limp in his much bigger one as he shook it. I was

100

now more embarrassed than anything else. I had never been required to shake anyone's hand before and felt foolish doing what only adults did – and rarely at that – where I came from. I could mentally hear the jeers of my gang of fern-stalk throwers or the other members of the church choir for that matter and felt deeply grateful they were all elsewhere.

"You'll get used to him, Erik," said Aunty Liz to reassure me. "He kisses my hand every time he leaves…imagine that!"

I turned bright red and whipped both my hands behind my back. Jakob laughed and went out to rejoin the others.

"He's very grand in his manners," said Aunty Liz. "He was an opera singer before the war," she added as if that explained his ways with hands. "I expect they get very emotional."

"What's opera?" I asked. She said I would have to ask Jakob. "It's like a play where everyone sings," was the best that she could venture.

And so on my first day at work after what I considered a luxurious breakfast I had met an "enemy alien" who sang in opera and came, as he later told me, from Mrs. Hochheimer's Austria.

From the war time routines of *Rosetree Villa* I had been transported not only to a farm where the way of life was quite different from the life of the town but also into the company of someone who proved to be very unlike anyone I had ever known and I bet even at that time unlike anyone Ma or Pop or Mrs. Dodd or Bessie or the Vicar or any of my teachers or relatives had ever known either. In fact I would have betted that even Mr. Wood, with his big mansion house and his acres of land and his greenhouse grapes hadn't met anyone like Jakob. I may have had to make do with Toby's hand-me-down car but I had met an Austrian opera singer and, for all his expensive education, he hadn't.

I couldn't wait to tell Ma and Pop about my meeting Jakob. My excitement was as great as in my tale of the crashing Spitfire. Their response was deeply discouraging. I was especially chagrined at Ma who had seemed so sympathetic to the aliens when she talked about them on that walk home from the Talbots' farm.

"You steer clear o' that f'la, said Pop. "Y' don't know what that f'la 'll get up to. Ya can't trust a Herman."

"I knew I shouldn't have let you go to the farm!" said Ma with feeling. "But your father knew best…the way he always does! Well I'm not having you mixing with dangerous foreigners! I'm going to tell Lizzie Talbot you're not going any more and that'll be that!"

CHAPTER TWELVE

I was glad for once that we didn't have a telephone. Ma would have called the Talbots right away to say that her son's experiment with milkmanship was over. There would have been no opportunity for sober second thought difficult enough in a place where, and at a time when, second thoughts were deemed a sign of weakness.

"The aliens could cut his throat in the barn," said Ma, "and neither Lizzie nor Tom would notice till it was too late. He'd be lying there bleeding into the hay…bleeding to death…and no one the wiser! He'd come home a white-faced corpse!! Then what would you say?"

Before Pop had time to respond to this lurid scenario Bessie, whose appetite for cheap thrillers was insatiable, declared "They'd garrote him with the baling wire. That's what foreigners do. Your foreigner sneaks up behind you quiet as a cat then…quick as greased lightning he's got the wire round your neck and the oul villain's pullin' it as tight as tight an' all you can do is choke to death an' make noises dreadful while your face is turnin' black as the tar on the road."

"F'las being choked to death all over the Island is it Bessie?" Pop resented her barging into every conversation while she was on one of her uninvited visits. "Farmers lockin' their kiddies away when the aliens come trampin' up the road in case a bit o' the baling wire goes missin?" Pop went on. "Guards from the Camp all asleep in the fields is it while the aliens rampage in the barns? Newspaper full o' these cases is it? Funny we haven't read about it. Police just report them to you do they...that it?"

"You won't be talkin' so sarky when they find Erik hangin' from a beam all cold and dead," said Bessie, miffed. "You'll wish you'd listened to me when he's swingin back and forth in the cold draught, the thick rope cuttin' his neck, not a bit o' the breath left in 'm."

The absurdity of the alternative fates Bessie was imagining for me helped to restore some balance to Ma and Pop's views. After Bessie had left I begged to be allowed to continue at the farm and sought to intrigue them by telling them about some of the customers whose milk I had just started to deliver and aspired to continue delivering.

I told them about the gaunt bearded professor from "across" with bad teeth who had retired to Glan Auldyn near the Talbot's farm and whose name was Kennet – Kenneth Kennet, like saying it twice. He reminded me of George Bernard Shaw, a photograph of whom I had once seen in Pop's newspaper and asked him who it was. I told Ma and Pop that Mr. Kennet said he lived on seaweed and dandelions, nettles, milk and snails and said that eating fish or animal meat was wrong and anyway very bad for us. Molluses, it seemed, were different.

"Look at me," he said that first day I brought his milk to his door, "have you ever seen a healthier specimen? I get my food from the seashore, my garden, even my driveway – all *natural*. I'll live to be a hundred!"

I was impressed but the cancer that claimed him a year later obviously was not.

"You're making him up," said Ma. "No one in their right mind eats snails."

"The French do," said Pop. "They taste pretty good when they're cooked right."

"Do you mean to tell me that you've eaten snails?" asked Ma, a look of distaste spreading over her face. There were, evidently, still aspects of Pop's early life Ma hadn't heard about.

"I'd've eaten cats and dogs after the rotten muck we had to eat in the trenches," Pop declared. "Compared to that snails tasted pretty good."

"Well this man's not in the trenches and I bet he doesn't eat snails. Don't you go spreading stories like that," Ma said to me, "or you'll get yourself into trouble. We could have the police at the door!"

"Don't be daft," said Pop.

"I'm not spreading stories," I said indignantly, "Ask Auntie Liz. She'll tell you."

"*Aunty Liz?*"

"Mrs. Talbot said I could call her "Aunty Liz." Mr. Talbot said it would be OK for me to call him "Uncle Tom.""

"The cheek of it! I'll have a word with Lizzie Talbot when I see her next!"

Ma felt that at the very least Mrs. Talbot ought to have asked her permission before appointing herself honorary aunty though she had allowed Bessie to do so with neither challenge nor comment.

To drag Ma's mind off what she felt to be a considerable liberty – "After all," she said, "there's got to be some standards even in a war" – I introduced the subject of old Mrs. Cannel who lived in a mossy, messy old stone cottage at the top of the glen (we delivered milk to customers in the glen first before heading for Ramsey).

"What's she got to recommend her?" asked Ma.

"She knows lots of Manx words. She told me the Manx for "butterfly" is *folican*. The Manx for spider is *doo-oalee*. She called me *millish* [dear]. She said I'd be the one to come first-footing on *Oeil Verrey* [New Year's Day] because I've got dark hair. She asked me if I wanted a *cuppa tay*."

"The woman sounds touched," said Ma.

"She empties her chamber pot on the grass in front of her door," I went on, hoping to impress Ma and Pop with my widening experience of the world and its varied customs, "and the grass there all turned white."

"She *is* touched," said Pop nodding to Ma.

"Filthy country habits! Don't you go anywhere near her again or you'll catch something and bring it home and give it to all of us." Ma was indignant.

I could see I had made a mistake here. Eccentric professors were one thing but insanitary rural nutters were another. I feared I was handing Ma facts she could use in evidence to end my new-found association with the Talbots so I hurried to describe my visit to the *Big House* (as it was locally called) at Milntown – a place Aunty Liz always spoke of in her capital letter voice.

Milntown is on the way to Ramsey from Glen Auldyn. We drove up to this square Georgian squire's house along a private road lined with tall ancient chestnut trees with rooks calling harshly from them as if warning the owner of our approach. Aunty Liz drove to the back of the house. She parked the converted Morris just outside two huge wide-open wooden gates painted in black. We walked between them with the day's milk into a cobbled courtyard where there were stables. Horses stood framed above the half doors taking a mild interest in us as we went up a few steps to a back door of the house, the one marked *Tradesmans Entrance.*

Aunty Liz introduced me to the woman who eventually answered the bell that tolled somewhere at a distance – a stout woman in a starched white uniform of some sort. She looked to me like an aging nurse in a hospital.

"Erik'll be bringing your milk now and then so I thought you should meet him on his first day with me. He'll be helping me with the round."

The starched woman seemed unimpressed by the news.

"Give us a look at yer 'ands," she said. Somewhat confused I showed them to her wondering if, like Jakob, she proposed to shake one of them. "Mmmm. They seem clean. Mind you keep 'em that way when yer delivering milk to this 'ouse," said the woman. "Mrs. Talbot'll be tellin' yer why," she added before informing Aunty Liz that she had brought a quart less than the household would need that day. Her tone was superior and obviously made Aunty Liz uncomfortable though she didn't say anything just then.

"You know about this house?" Aunty Liz asked as we walked back to the car for the extra quart of milk. I didn't of course, so she told me.

"In the Eighteenth Century it belonged to Fletcher Christian's family."

I was none the wiser so she sketched in for me the story of the mutiny on the naval ship *Bounty* – how Fletcher Christian, one of its officers and son of the squire who then owned this house, led the mutiny against Captain Bligh, who himself had been married on the Isle-of-Man – in the village of Onchan to a Customs officer's daughter. Wasn't that an odd coincidence?

Ma and Pop knew more about this story than I had expected. They were impressed in spite of themselves. Their son would be delivering the milk to the house in which Fletcher Christian grew up. Their son would be associated with History!

I didn't tell them what Aunty Liz privately called the cook – the uniformed person to whom she had introduced me.

"Skitterin' oul bitch," Liz called her in contrast to her deferential manner at the door. "I remember her growin' up…no schoolin' at her and now, because she works for the people at the Big House she won't put a sight on any of us. Acts like we're a smell under her nose the stupit oul bitch. But the moment the lady of the house is in sight you wouldn't recognize her. She behaves like one of our sheepdogs. Yer expect her to get down on the floor and crawl on her stomach and say *please walk all over me, woof*

woof. I could tell her a thing or two but if I say a word out of place she'll get the milk from someone else so I have to keep me mouth shut."

Aunty Liz normally spoke the King's English, unlike Uncle Tom, but when her temper was up she could be eloquent in vernacular insult. Ma was very concerned about the way we spoke and used to embarrass me by telling people "Erik has a real BBC voice." I didn't know what that was but I didn't like the looks I got, especially from the parents of other children, after Ma made the announcement. Had she known how Aunty Liz spoke when roused she'd never have let me go back to the farm on my own.

"He'll pick up the swear words and all sorts of bad speech habits from Liz and Tom," she would have said. She wouldn't have worried that I was in any linguistic danger from Johnny.

"You mean he'll talk like me?" Pop would have responded.

"If the cap fits…"

I encouraged Ma and Pop to tell me what they knew of the Christian family when they owned the Big House.

"Rebels mighty, that lot," said Pop. "That Iliam Dhone f'la was one o'them."

He was referring to William Christian, Governor of the Island under Cromwell, shot for it on Hango Hill when Charles II was restored. His family's farm at Ronaldsway (now the Island's Airport) was near the village where Pop was born and where, resentfully, he did his epic youthful laboring "in all weathers."

Now that Ma and Pop were impressed by my future association with the Big House, I thought I'd intrigue them further with a brief account of the Rand-Krueger establishment. Like the Trelawneys in their *Casa* the Rand-Kruegers were retirees from the old Indian Civil Service and had been attracted to the Island for the same reasons – the mildness of the climate and an income-tax rate lower than England's. Mr. Rand-Krueger, however, had been knighted on his retirement. He had been transformed into Sir Christopher Rand-Krueger. Mrs. Trelawney, who had met the Rand-Kruegers in India, felt quite bitter about Sir Christopher's elevation. Why had her husband not been allowed to retire as Sir Timothy? As far as she knew Timothy's career had followed much the same path as Sir Christopher's. Mrs. Trelawney became a lot more critical of her husband in his retirement than she had been during his colorful Imperial career. She was inclined to speak bitterly of his former Eurasian mistresses, sermonize upon the bribes he had taken, reminisce sadly about the houseful of deferential servants she had lost, the large garden their *Mali* had tended so well. That, at least, is what their housekeeper told anyone who cared to listen. When people asked what a *Mali* was the housekeeper looked at them pityingly and changed the subject. "Some days they're at it all day long, specially when they've been into the gin."

I got to know the Rand-Krueger establishment gradually, with passing time, but even after my first visit I was able to tell Ma and Pop that I was delivering milk to the house of a Knight who had come from India, was always complaining about the cold, and whose cook used all sorts of smelly ingredients in her work. Sir Christopher smoked a funny-looking pipe involving a long tube and a jar of water. When he pulled on the pipe the water bubbled. He said it was called a *hookah* and asked if I wanted to try it.

"Bugger's a dope-fiend!" Pop exclaimed in alarm.

"He sounds like a very cultured man to me," said Ma impressed by the title, the double-barreled name and the library I briefly mentioned. "He's got a room full of books," I had said in awe. The only other person I knew who had such a room was the Vicar whose heavy volumes on matters ecclesiastical were no doubt as dull as ditchwater.

"I bet he never reads any o'those books," said Pop. "Too busy knocking himself out with dope from that pipe."

"How would you know?" Ma spoke witheringly.

"Dope fiends are only interested in dope," said Pop.

"Like you with ale at the pub, you mean?"

"Mind you don't have a go at that pipe," Pop said to me, ignoring Ma. "It'll rot ya brain."

I was glad that Ma was impressed by Sir Christopher, but I have to say that I was disappointed in him. The knights I had read about were a lot younger, a lot slimmer, they wore armor, they rode steeds on which they charged to fight their enemies or to save damosels or to kill dragons – sometimes all at once. They didn't have deeply lined purple faces and pot-bellies; they didn't mope, shiver, whine about the climate and the servants and how they should have retired to the Bahamas. They didn't lounge about doing nothing in particular in hairy tweeds except drink gin and smoke hookahs. I wasn't interested in whether or not Sir Christopher used his library since the knights I had read about didn't have time for books. I hadn't yet met Don Quixote.

I wanted to make sure that on the whole Ma and Pop would find the Talbot clientele respectable, unthreatening, so in addition to the above I stressed that I would be taking milk to our Headmaster's house, to a town councillor, some shopkeepers, two doctors (one now too old to practice) and a few well-off old maids. There was also a retired General, so ancient that he might have fought the Russians in the Crimea. He was confined to bed and the milk was received by a tall woman dressed in black "with a face like a hatchet" as Pop would have put it had he met her. I never did ascertain her position in the General's household. Had she sported a bunch of keys I'd have said *gaoler.*

With the exception of Mrs. Cannel and her chamber pot I didn't mention other working-class recipients of the Talbot milk, of whom, in any case, there were relatively few. Most lived in Glen Auldyn itself. Ramsey's poorer people tended to go to one of the town dairies when they had money to pay for a jugfull.

"So can I help Aunty Liz?" I asked. "She says at Christmas I'll get Christmas boxes from the customers."

"We'll think about it," said Ma.

"What's to think about?" Pop wanted to know.

"Well, that dirty old woman in the glen for one thing. Do you want him to deliver milk to someone like that? He could catch something serious and bring it home. Then there's that daft professor telling him to eat snails and seaweed and other mucky stuff."

"They're harmless or Liz wouldn't 've let him near them."

"You've changed your tune. What was it you called Sir Christopher…a *dope fiend?* You wouldn't want him taking milk to someone like that would you?"

"As long as Liz keeps an eye liftin' he should be all right."

"And it's now all right for him to work alongside aliens who could kill him just to get their own back on us for locking them up?"

"They're not like that," I said.

"Know them all do you…know how they think and what they'll do after one day at the farm?" said Pop.

"No."

"Then you keep away from those f'las…don't you go anywhere near them or that's it. No more farm for you me-lad. You hear me?"

I nodded though I wondered why Pop was making this sort of fuss after his ridicule of Bessie.

"I'm going to tell Liz," said Ma "to make sure to keep you away from them and if I hear that you haven't then that's the end of it."

So on this condition I was allowed to continue to help Mrs. Talbot deliver the milk. But I was determined to get to know Jakob, somehow. He was an exotic. He intrigued me despite my initial fearfulness. I would just have to make sure that neither Ma nor Pop heard about any future meetings I might have with this operatic Austrian.

CHAPTER THIRTEEN

On the following Saturday when Uncle Tom arrived to pick me up Ma was ready and waiting for him. She had sacrificed sleep to be on hand to ambush him with a vocal list of conditions governing my future relationship with the farm, a list as comprehensive as she could make it. There were so many clauses and sub-sections of clauses that Tom was entirely bewildered. He had simply expected to install me in his truck as usual and drive off, but found himself instead unarmed in a combat zone.

I could continue to help Liz, Ma said, only if she did not send me to the doors of dirty old women like Mrs. Cannel, the probable source of many (unspecified) contagious diseases. I was to be protected from the obviously mad Professor whose notions of diet were crazy and would be highly dangerous to me if I should experiment with them which I probably would since children do, don't they? So there was damage done already, wasn't there? Above all I was to have no contact whatsoever – *what-so-ever* she repeated slowly, separating the syllables, enunciating each with care – with any alien prisoner who happened to be working on the farm in any capacity. *Was that understood?* There were many other conditions though, oddly, none involved the Rand-Krueger hookah.

"What's doin' on ya makin' all this fuss?" asked a bewildered Tom. Ma had never addressed him in this way before. "I'm takin" the chile off to a job not to his death! Yer'd think I was aimin ta chuck him off a cliff the way yer going' on!"

"I'll tell you what this is all about," said Ma grimly and launched into bitter complaints about my being allowed to shake hands with a prisoner, about my being exposed to germs, about Liz and he appointing themselves my aunty and uncle without asking her permission. In the middle of Ma's increasingly angry accusations a weary bomb-aimer and a pilot, both just back from raiding Germany squeezed past us in the hallway, apologizing to Ma for interrupting her flow which they hadn't because she carried on without appearing to notice either of them. They may have flown home on a wing and a prayer but what was that compared to the perils facing her son on the Talbot farm?

"Well, missus," said Tom when he could get a word in, "ya not short o'breath I'll give ya that but ya worryin' over nothin' at all, at all. I'll tell Liz what ya said but the lad's got to call us both somethin' so we thought *aunty* and *uncle* would be fer the best. Ya wouldn't want the lad to call us *Mr. Talbot* and *Mrs. Talbot* all the time as if we was the Mayor and the Lady Mayoress would ya? But if ya going' ter kick up a fuss almighty then…"

"You should have asked first," said Ma, "but what's done's done. You can't mend broken eggs so we'll say no more."

"What was that all about?" asked Uncle Tom as we drove down Ballacray Road.

I told him how I had met Jakob and made the mistake of telling Ma and Pop about it. I described Ma's Gothic fears concerning the primitive impulses of alien prisoners which had then attached themselves to some of the Talbot's customers.

"Nah, them prisoners is just like you and me," said Uncle Tom. "They wouldn't say *boo* to a goose. In fact your Ma could do a lot more damage than any a them when her temper's up and the wind's behind 'er. She gave me the willies I'm tellin' ya."

Tom told Liz about Ma's outburst and Liz said, more mildly than I had expected, "Well, we'd best not upset her then had we if that's how she feels."

I told them both that I thought Ma was being unreasonable and Uncle Tom said "y' can say that again" (an expression he had picked up, along with a cigar, from an American airman in a pub). I also told them both that in spite of what Ma had decreed I wanted to be able to talk to Jakob when I saw him around the farm and I asked them not to tell Ma and Pop about it.

"You're asking us to lie," said Aunty Liz dubiously.

"I'm asking you not to tell on me," I replied.

"Comes to the same thing, really. We'd be deceiving your Mum by not saying anything."

"Please!" I surprised myself by resorting to begging.

"What's doin' on Jaycob as ya want to talk to 'm that bad?" asked Uncle Tom. "Ya don't know that f'la."

"I dunno," I said unhelpfully, drawing an abstract diagram in the dust of the farm street with the toe of my boot. "He's different," I ventured unable to say exactly what it was about Jakob that had intrigued me during that one, very brief meeting in the dairy.

"Well if yer that desperate to talk to the f'la don't let Liz or me see ya do it. We can't tell yer Ma what we didn't see can we?"

With this piece of sophistry the issue of my talking to Jakob was put to rest – for now, at least. I looked for him in the farm buildings but he was out in the fields more often than not. When I did have a chance to talk to him and either Tom or Liz happened upon us they would go by with their eyes shut saying "can't see you, can't see you, you're not there." Jakob looked puzzled but said nothing. Perhaps he thought we were playing some childish game. I suppose we were.

❖

My initial conversations with Jakob were very brief and hesitant. I had to overcome the nervousness which his intense energy inspired in me – it was something literally foreign to the sedateness of my family. In any case I was always bashful with people I didn't really know but I had a child's urgent curiosity. I wanted to find out what Jakob the alien prisoner was like as a person instead of a label. I wanted to know about his opera–singing, about the Austria he shared with Mrs. Hochheimer and Hitler, about whether he had ever seen the latter in person, about why he had been imprisoned…about all sorts of things. I suppose I was what we might now call *star-struck*. And then Jakob had visited or lived in most of the places our lodgers went out to bomb every night as he told me one morning in the dairy when news of the war was being received by the wireless set Liz initially put there to distract her when it was her turn to do the milking.

After turning my questions aside with banter till he could figure out why I was asking them Jakob eventually became more confidential.

His work often took him to distant fields but sometimes he mucked out the cow byre or white-washed one of the stone farm buildings or did other work near the farmhouse while I was helping Aunty Liz to carry the milk out to fill the churns in the converted Morris. On these occasions or when he was dropped off at the farm earlier than usual I found opportunities to discover what I could about the real Jakob Weiss. What I initially learned was in consequence of brief exchanges over several weeks, sometimes interrupted by Johnny commenting on the weather – the force of the *dwin*, the frequency of *neray*, the appearance or absence of *uns*. Jakob was at least as baffled as I was.

I wanted to know how exactly Jakob found himself in a prison camp on the Isle-of-Man. What had he done to be thus shut away? Had he been caught spying? Had he refused to join the army, the air-force or the navy? Had he chalked anti-British messages on a wall somewhere? Had he threatened or hurt anyone? Had he been caught stealing (though I couldn't imagine him doing that)? What?

Of course at this distance in time I can't remember word for word what he told me but I recall the subjects we covered and the tenor of our, often brief, conversations. That's what I try to approximate here though of course from a child's point of view.

"I was interned because I am an Austrian Jew," said Jakob.

The only Jew of whom I had any personal knowledge, and that was slender, was Izzy McIsaac, the rag and bone man, the local recycler of his day. He may not literally have carried away any rags and bones we might want to dispose of but he took things like old bed-frames and springs, broken furniture, stacks of newspapers, what I would have thought were useless bits of metal, on his flat cart pulled by a decrepit old off-white horse that itself seemed to have been recycled. Besides Izzy I knew some-thing also of the Biblical Jews from my enforced Sunday school classes. They were the people chosen by God though I doubt that God would have chosen the rag and bone man. I was certainly glad I had not been chosen by God. Our Bible readings indicated that plague, floods, slavery in Egypt, being swallowed whole by a whale and over-close relations with a Jealous God who reminded me of my Aunty Doreen, and told you to kill your only son with a knife to demonstrate your obedience were just a few of the hazards of Divine Selection.

I asked Jakob if his being imprisoned had anything to do with such Old Testament events as those I had read about or listened to while Miss Kennaugh read aloud from an old leather-bound family bible, the cover of which was the color, and resembled the texture of, her skin.

"I'm here because I am not British," said Jakob. "I have a German name; German is my native language; I am a foreigner so the English Government thinks I am not to be trusted. The government is scared that people like me will work for the Nazis if we stay free so they have shut us away to make sure that we don't."

"Would you? Work for the Nazis?"

"The Nazis kill Jews. They round them up and put them on trains and send them to what are called concentration camps. I came to England to escape that. So did thousands of other Jews so or course I wouldn't work for them. I want to work *against* them any way I can. The Nazis treat Jews worse than they treat animals…they compare us to rats…to pests that have to be put down…how would you like to be compared to a rat?"

The Headmaster of our school sometimes compared us collectively to cockroaches but that didn't seem to be the same thing.

"How can you be locked up for just being who you are?" My limited experience of the world led me to ask naïve questions.

"Because the British Government doesn't like Jews either…everyone is frightened in a war, frightened of people who are different from the rest of the population, especially when they speak German as their first language. Or Italian. They lock up Italians too…and Hungarians, Bulgarians, Romanians, Czechs…lots of people the British Government doesn't trust."

From my initial conversations with Jakob it seemed to me there weren't many people the government in London did trust. There were camps like the one in Ramsey all over the Island, Jakob said…in Douglas, Peel, Castletown and Port Erin. Then I remembeed Pop saying that other people had been sent to camps in Australia and Canada though I didn't then know where these places were − we hadn't "done" them in Geography lessons yet. But they were a long, long way from Britain I had heard. What I hadn't heard about was that some of the ships transporting people deemed *alien* were sunk by U-boats and most of the prisoners they were carrying drowned.

Like other children I was interested in detail and not very diplomatic in getting at it. I probed Jakob's experience in a way that neither Ma nor Pop would ever have done had they surmounted their anti-prisoner prejudices to talk to him in the first place. I asked him how, exactly, he had ended up in the Mooragh camp, never thinking that re-living the sequence of events in talking about it might be painful for him. Once he began to tell me his story it was obvious that even now, two years after he had been sent to the Camp, he was still angry.

"I was singing in Birmingham," he said, "in a concert with a choir… an Oratorio…"

I hadn't a clue where Birmingham was, or what an Oratorio was, but I didn't interrupt to find out. I thought if I did that Jakob, in his angry state, would change his mind about telling me what had happened to him.

"The concert went well," Jakob continued, "everyone stood up and clapped for a long time when it was over. Afterwards the Conductor took the soloists…there were four of us…back to his hotel for a late supper and a drink. Singing is thirsty work."

I told him about my singing in the church choir so I knew what he meant though I have to confess that the kind of singing we did made us hungry rather than thirsty – hungry for freedom. I asked Jakob, superfluously, if he were hungry for freedom.

"Of course," he said. "Human beings in civilized societies are not supposed to lock each other up unless they have committed a crime. They are not supposed to say *"You came here from somewhere else. Your first language isn't English; you're not one of us so you belong behind barbed wire."*

"Is that what they said to you?"

"Not in those words but that's what the authorities believe. That is why they sent a policeman to my hotel room door at five o'clock in the morning the day after my concert. He told me I had a few minutes to get dressed and pack a toothbrush and my shaving kit. The clothes I wore and these things were all I was to be allowed to take with me. Of course I refused. I told him I had not committed any offence, that he must have made a mistake and confused me with a real criminal. He said if I did not change my mind quickly force would be used against me. There were soldiers nearby with loaded rifles, he said. So I did what he had told me to do and thought the mistake could be put right at a police station. When we went outside I was treated like a criminal...I was put in one of these police vans you call a *Black Maria*. I was pushed into it and driven to a nearby police station. No one would explain to me why this was happening. This is the sort of thing I would have expected in Germany but not in England."

"Were you locked up in a gaol?"

"I was put in a prison cell for a while. No one explained why. And then I was taken to a big red-brick building that looked like a school and I had to appear before what is called a *tribunal.*"

"What's that?"

"It's a sort of committee...a group of people who said their job was to judge whether I was a danger to the State in wartime or not."

"What does that mean?"

"They wanted to find out if I would do anything to help the Germans... become a spy, I suppose they meant. I told them I was an Austrian, not a German and the Chairman of this tribunal said 'What's the difference? Isn't Hitler an Austrian and isn't he the Dictator of Germany?' So I said 'How would you feel if I said there was no difference between an Englishman and a Scotsman? They both speak English and a few years ago a Scotsman was the Prime Minister.'"

"What did he say to that?"

"*I should say you were quite mad,* that's what he said. He treated me as if I had already been caught spying for the Germans and I was thinking all the time about how only the night before I was received as a distinguished artist – a whole audience had stood up to clap for me and the other soloists and now this fat little man in a pinstriped suit was telling me that I was a danger to the State and would be locked up. I protested of course. I told them I was an artist. I told them of my concert and the audience's appreciation. I said there was no proof that I was any kind of threat to England but it didn't make any difference. They said I belonged in Category A and like everyone else in that category I would be immediately interned. So overnight I became an Enemy of the State because of my German name. How would you feel if a stranger…someone who had never seen you before that day…called you an Enemy of the State and locked you up because you were living in England but had a Manx name?"

"I'd let Pop know and he'd come and get me."

"But suppose he and your mother and all your family were locked up too? That is what has been happening to people like me. If I had any family living in England they would have been arrested and interned as well. I don't have a British passport and that makes me a criminal in the eyes of the law. In ordinary times criminals have a right to a lawyer, a trial, they have a right to be thought innocent until proven guilty, but I was sentenced because of who I am and where I came from not for anything I had done."

"Why did they let you come to England if they didn't want you?"

"I came before the war. Once the war began everything changed. Before the war I was treated with respect, as an artist should be. It didn't matter then where you came from…people appreciated you for your skills and abilities. But soon after war was declared people became suspicious. They could, of course, tell I was of German origin by my accent. People I didn't even know told me to go home to Adolf when they heard me talking. They put filthy notes in my letterbox. They called me a Nazi. It became harder and harder to find work…I was lucky to get that concert in Birmingham. I don't have to worry about work now, though, do I? I have plenty to do here."

"Don't you like the farm?" I asked.

"I like the Talbots…they're good people…but no one should he locked up and used like a slave, especially when they have done nothing wrong. I spent many years studying and training to be an operatic soloist…now I sing only at the Camp to other prisoners and look at my hands! They are rough and dirty from digging in the soil, my nails are broken. I wasn't meant to be a farm laborer like poor Johnny. He likes what he is doing. He is free to do it. It suits him. But this is not my way of life. I have to work on this farm whether I want to or not. I can't leave and go home the way you can. You can go home to your family but I don't even know where mine is."

I asked him about that. His mother, father and two sisters had lived in a village about thirty miles from Vienna, he said, but he hadn't seen them since he left in 1937.

"They may have got out of the country before the Nazis came to their area to round up the Jews and send them to camps. I wanted them to come with me when I left but they didn't want to leave then. Maybe they made it to Switzerland or America. If they didn't and they are still in Austria then…"

He didn't finish the sentence but I could see where it was headed so I didn't press him with more questions.

Having told me this much Jakob seemed unwilling to confide in me further. I don't know whether he avoided me to evade my incessant questioning but I suspected so. Perhaps I made him think about things he'd prefer not to recall, especially family matters. It could just be that Uncle Tom had him doing jobs away from the farmhouse so that he was simply not around to be grilled by an eager ten-year-old. Whatever the reason it was a few weeks before I saw him again.

He would not have been surprised had he read among Home Office Guidelines the following confident ridiculous declaration: "In Britain you have to realize every German is an Agent. All of them have both the duty and the means to communicate information to Berlin."

Ma had got used to me working with Aunty Liz – she had even got used to me referring to Liz and Tom as "Aunty" and "Uncle." Since she had had no reports from them about any contact on my part with alien prisoners she assumed there had been none and no longer issued lurid warnings of violent death as each Saturday approached. Pop was happy to see me earning a few shillings.

"My oul f'la used to take what I earned and give me a few pennies back for sweeties but I'm not goin' ter take any o' your shillins to pay for yer keep," he said and waited for me to express my gratitude. When I didn't he was irritated.

"I could, yer know. I could take everythin' yer bring home. Some fathers would. Yer a lucky f'la."

"Don't be so daft," said Ma indignantly, "what do you think this is? The dark ages?"

"They were pretty dark when we were his age," Pop replied, "but in that big house on the hill I don't suppose you noticed. It'd be lighter up there."

"You keep your money," Ma said to me, ignoring Pop's remark. "Just don't spend it all, save some for Christmas. I'll find you a money box to keep it in."

I couldn't stay entirely silent at school about my very first wage-paying job or my new acquaintance but I tried to be circumspect so that disturbing details didn't circle back to Ma or Pop. I described the milk round and its more colorful customers with great particularity. My friends were especially taken by Sir Christopher Rand-Krueger and his hookah, which Ronnie Skillicorn declared he would have smoked if he'd been given the chance. No one doubted him. He also said that Mrs. Cannel was like his old grannie who lived somewhere in the country and smoked a clay pipe and emptied her chamber pot (which he called a *po*) in similar fashion. She had once thrown its contents all over the postman, his delivery of a rare letter fatally ill-timed.

I told the kids at school also about the prisoners who worked on the farm but didn't go into detail about Jakob. Not much went on in Ramsey without Ma eventually hearing some version of the news – even a school-yard conversation could be reported to parents – and what Ma might not find out Bessie certainly would. So when I was asked at school what the prisoners were like I stuck to generalities." They're like us, I said, "except they speak different languages as well as English."

"They're not like us," said Ronnie Skillicorn with his usual belligerence. "They're murderers and spies and Nazis…my Dad says."

I wondered how Ma would react if I told her that her attitude towards the alien prisoners resembled that of Ronnie Skillicorn's Dad whom she had declared "a drunken, ignorant boor" after he staggered out of *The Green Duck* on the harbor still wearing his thigh-high sea-boots almost knock-ing her over, yelling "gerouta me way yer stuck-up oul bitch."

CHAPTER FOURTEEN

WHEN I WAS GROWING UP OPERA WAS NOT A SUBJECT OF DISCUSSION on the Isle-of-Man among the people we knew. They had never heard of *Tosca, Norma* was merely a local girl's name, and if they had known about *Lohengrin, Tannheuser* and the Ring Cycle they would have declared them Nazi propaganda. So when eventually I began to have regular conversations with Jakob, I asked him about opera, what it was and how he became a singer and why. He told me a little about the opera form, which didn't register with me except that it seemed to deal – though musically – with the kind of melodramatic stories I found exciting on those Friday afternoons at school.

As far as his own career was concerned he said that when he was in his teens he realized that he had an unusually good singing voice which his teachers urged him to have trained. He enjoyed singing – he sang all the solo parts in the school choir – and when he realized he could make a living doing what he liked so much he went to music school. In fact he went to several so that he could benefit from the artistry and experience of a number of successful soloists. He told me about the schools he had attended; the teachers who had helped him develop his voice, the little gnome of a man who had taught him Italian, the elaborately gilded opera houses where he had begun his singing career, in small roles at first. Much as I relish opera now none of this information meant very much to me at that age and I can't recall any of the details but I was made to understand how seriously Jakob took his vocation and how bitterly he missed practicing it. He felt doubly cheated – by the Nazis initially and then by the British Government.

Just as he was beginning to be recognized in Austrian opera circles and parts were being offered to him in greater numbers than when he had started out and he had high hopes for his career, the murderous violence of the Nazis toward the Jews in Germany and the prospect of a German take-over in Austria had caused him to flee to England. He had begged his family to come with him but they stayed behind unwilling to uproot themselves. They chose to believe that the stories of atrocities, which they had been hearing were nothing more than exaggerated rumor or tales of isolated excess. When he began to talk to me of having to start his career all over again and build a reputation in England from the ground up and how difficult this was Jakob returned to that early morning in Birmingham when his hopes had been brutally crushed by a small fat man in a blue pinstriped suit.

This Chairman of the tribunal before which he had been brought, after grilling him about his reasons for coming to England and then for staying, all the while giving him to understand that he disbelieved Jakob's answers nonetheless wrote a summary of them adding notes of his own. He had then in a low voice conferred briefly with the other members of the committee who had also been taking notes before turning to Jakob and announcing in a solemn voice that the tribunal decreed he belonged in something called *Category A*. Before Jakob could ask what that meant he was ushered from the room by a policeman and handed over to a small group of soldiers who escorted him out of the building and into the back of an army truck. Membership in *Category A* despite its suggestive primacy was not, evidently, an asset.

He was not driven back to his hotel to retrieve his belongings but to a large echoing railway station to join a group of men like himself – disheveled, unshaven, bleary-eyed, roughly wakened before dawn, told to forget about having a wash but to dress rapidly in whatever clothes came to hand. Like Jakob they had been allowed only their toothbrush and shaving kit as luggage though they hadn't been given time to use either of them. Some of the men at the station spoke in anguish of their frantic English wives and children left weeping, bewildered, begging the police in vain for an explanation as their husbands and fathers were bundled off.

"There was an Italian," said Jakob, "a really angry man. He called one of the soldiers guarding us a *fascist pig just like that son of a pig Mussolini*. This Italian's English was very colorful. He used a lot of swear words on the soldiers…many I had never heard before. No (here Jakob held up a theatrical hand like a policeman stopping the flow of traffic), before you ask, I am not going to repeat them. Anyway, this man demanded to know why he had been dragged away from his wife and children for no reason. He had committed no crime. He was a loyal citizen of England, he said, even though it was true he had been born in Italy and his mother still lived in Napoli where her cooking was so good that the entire neighborhood said so even the fascists but…The soldier he had called a *fascist pig* told him to shut up and stop asking stupid questions. We were 'prisoners held at the pleasure of His Majesty's Government in time of war' and that's all we needed to know."

Jakob remembered the bleakness and cold of early morning in that cavernous, dirty, noisy railway station much bigger than any I would find on the Isle-of-Man. He told me it had a huge semi-circular glass roof but you couldn't see the sky because every inch of the roof was encrusted with soot and pigeon poop. Even the pigeons were sooty, he said. There was nowhere to sit down except for a few wooden benches along the platform to which he and the other prisoners had been taken. There was a chill early morning breeze that blew dust, discarded cigarette butts, scraps of dirty newspaper and stained wrappers of all sorts about. A few short hours ago he had been deeply asleep in a good hotel, in a comfortable warm bed, snug, well fed, satisfied with his Oratorio performance – as secure, he thought, as anyone could be in war time. Now he was literally out in the cold herded together with other men just as arbitrarily snatched from their private lives without benefit of soap, water or any normal legal proceedings and protection.

"Somebody asked to go to the lavatory," Jakob recalled. "He needed to pee. He was told to do what he had to off the station platform. When the poor man did so one of the soldiers called him *a filthy bloody foreigner with bloody filthy foreign habits.*"

Jakob and the others were kept on that platform for what seemed like hours…he had forgotten his watch in the haste with which he was forced from his hotel room so he had no idea of how much time had actually passed. The large ornamented clock suspended over their platform at the station had stopped and no one had seen fit to re-start it. None of the men standing around him had watches. Soldiers and the police brought more and more men to add to their number. Birmingham, it seemed, was ridding itself all at once of its foreign-born male residents and sending them into a timeless oblivion. It was while he waited for whatever was to come that Jakob first heard the term *alien* applied to himself and the other men on the platform.

He reflected bitterly as he stood there in the cold that overnight it had become a crime not to be British. The term *enemy,* was even being used by the soldiers to precede *alien.* No matter how long you had lived in Britain – and some of those around him had lived there previously unmolested for many more years than he had – no matter how well you spoke the language, no matter that you had (like the Italian) married an Englishwoman and your children had known no other country, no matter that you had an established business in England, a profession, a career, a reputation, a stake in the country – if you couldn't produce documents that proved your Britishness you were headed for internment and that was that. As Jakob discovered, this was what being classified as *Category A,* meant.

"That Italian man I mentioned…the one who swore at the soldiers… after we had been waiting on the platform for a long time he suddenly jumped off it on to the railway tracks and started to run away along the rails. The soldiers shouted at him to stop but he kept running. One of the soldiers aimed his rifle and shot him in the thigh. He fell across the tracks. The soldiers dragged him away and one of them told us that if anyone else tried that then next time they would aim for the head. We were all shocked by what we had seen. We had all gone quietly to bed and were wakened to this nightmare in a country we thought we could trust; in a place we thought we were safe, at least from each other."

I was eager to hear more of Jakob's story so I asked him what happened next as if it were written in a book that Miss Greene was reading to the class.

"We had to stand on that platform for hours," Jakob continued. "Some ladies from the Red Cross eventually appeared and were very kind to us. They brought us some hot tea to drink and some sandwiches. They insisted that the soldiers allow us to use the toilet facilities. One of the soldiers said 'these fucking foreigners can shit their pants for all I care,' but the women from the Red Cross shamed them for saying such things."

Jakob paused and looked awkward as if he regretted repeating the soldier's crude words. He said, "Please don't use that sort of language when your Mamma and Papa are listening or they will ask you where you heard it."

I was tickled to hear Ma and Pop referred to as *Mamma* and *Papa* but Jakob said that is what I would have called them had I been born in Europe. I added this to the many reasons I was glad I hadn't. As to the bad language, it was the common currency of the school playground.

When I steered Jakob back to the story of his detention he said: "After we had waited for what seemed like hours a train was backed up next to our platform. We were all ordered through a loudspeaker to get into the carriages of this train which were old and dirty and smelled of damp. Once we were all packed in the carriage doors were shut and locked so that we couldn't get out…the windows had been fixed so they wouldn't open… and the train set off. We had no idea where we were being taken. We went out beyond the city into the countryside passing hundreds of wet streets of dirty red-brick houses all of them looking the same. We traveled through other cities with similar kinds of streets all of them dismal in the rain. We went through some large railway stations without stopping and twice we were backed on to sidings out in the countryside while we waited for faster trains to pass. Hours after we had set out the train came to a small station near some ugly town…in Lancashire, we found out later."

Jakob paused, looked around him and then at me and said, "You know, living here on this Island with the sea in all its shades of blue and green, the mountains covered in yellow gorse and purple heather and all the green fields below them you have no idea what towns like the one that train brought us to are like. It was early evening when we arrived but this town was darkened even in the middle of the day by the thick black smoke from its tall factory chimneys. All the buildings were covered in soot and dirt worse than the railway station in Birmingham where we had started. It was raining so filth ran down brick walls into puddles like black ink on the road and on pavements."

He gazed at the hills above the farm, lost in memory. I was about to urge him to continue his story but he roused himself and went on unprompted.

"Soldiers unlocked the carriage doors and told us to get out of the train. They ordered us to hurry but we were cramped and slow after sitting for so long. In front of the station we had to form lines with four people to each line so that there was a long column of us. The soldiers then marched us in the rain toward the town. We were all soaked to the skin when at last we stopped at an old abandoned factory. We were going to have to stay here until the authorities decided what to do with us next. The soldiers called this run-down old building a *transit camp* but it was just a ruin, worse than a slum. Liz's cows have a better building to live in. They are warm and dry and properly fed, at least."

Ma frequently called the part of town where the fishermen lived a "slum" but it wasn't until I first visited an English industrial city that I properly understood what Jakob meant by the term. He was right. The Island had not prepared me for such a place.

"The factory roof leaked," he went on. "There were wads of old cotton and pools of oil on the worn wooden floors; bits of old rusting machinery were scattered about, the small window panes, too dirty to see through, were cracked and a lot were missing altogether so in places the rain blew in. There were very few lavatories and they were filthy and didn't work properly. There weren't many water taps and yet three hundred of us were crammed into this building. What water we could get out of the few taps was icy cold. In fact the whole place was wet and cold…there were dirty puddles of water on the floors below those places on the roof where slates had fallen off or been blown off by the wind. We had to sleep on damp boards with two thin blankets supposed to keep us warm in an unheated building. We were given stale bread and a lump of cheese to eat…that was our 'dinner' that first night, not that any of us had much of an appetite. Of course there were rats everywhere in a place like this squeaking round us in the night looking for any crumbs or bits of cheese we may have dropped. This factory was surrounded by barbed wire with armed soldiers on guard all the time in case anyone tried to escape. We had no idea how long we would have to stay in this foul place. So a day that began very badly for me turned into a nightmare. Also for all the others.

Some people complained to the guards that we were being treated worse than animals and the guards said things like, 'Did you expect to be put up at the Ritz? 'Sorry, all the hotels were full…we'll try again tomorrow.' 'Write to your Member of Parliament.' 'Why don't you emigrate?' They didn't want to be guarding us and blamed us for keeping them from more comfortable posts.

A few days went by and a lot more men were crowded into a space which was hardly big enough for us to start with. Every day brought more people like us snatched from their daily lives. They were artists, lawyers, doctors, dentists, architects, engineers, businessmen, rabbis (he explained who they were), scholars, shopkeepers, writers, painters…all of them the sort of people you'd think England could use to fight this war and all of us hating the Nazis if anything even more so than the English did. In a war countries behave like men with no brains. Prejudice and fear make everyone so stupid."

Getting more and more agitated as he talked Jakob said, "You'd think the lawyers among us at least would have found ways to avoid being arrested but they were taken by surprise like the rest of us and were hurried off before they could call on their friends for help. Most of them had been classed as *Category C,* which meant they were considered friendly to England but they were rounded up and imprisoned anyway. The police and soldiers made no distinction. The lawyers told us what we knew already…that what was being done to us was against the law…the law of the land when it isn't at war, they meant. In a war everything changes and governments can do as they please. It doesn't matter to the English what we did before the war. We are simply *aliens* and let me tell you that crammed in that old factory it didn't take us long to look the part. We were soon dirty, smelly and sick but the guards took no notice."

"What did you do all day?" I asked.

"Every morning we had to stand in a line and call out our names so that the guards could check them against their lists to make sure no one had escaped in the night."

"Did anyone escape?" I asked hoping to hear some exciting tale wherein a determined and outraged detainee – some Jewish Scarlet Pimpernel – had managed to get through the barbed wire fences and make his way stealthily back to his jubilant family without being caught – by stealing a ride on a train, perhaps.

"A few people tried to get out just for something to do…more because they were bored than for any other reason. I don't think any of them thought they could really get away with it. And, of course, they didn't. Two men managed to reach the railway station but they were caught trying to buy tickets. One man got all tangled up in the wire. He was taken away. Most people seem to feel like me…hopeless. They just sat around looking stunned. They couldn't believe that the country that had once welcomed them and allowed them to work without interference and seemed to appreciate what they did, could suddenly turn on them. I remember one man who owned a bookshop telling us that he was taken away before he could arrange for someone to look after it for him. All of us have property we don't expect to see again. Perhaps it is now considered patriotic to steal from the people the government has called *alien*.

Most of us became very depressed. I sang for them…they appreciated it and it cheered me a little to use my voice and be of some use in this terrible place. I gave a few little concerts…I sang some arias from operas I had performed in…some of the guards even came to listen. But most of the time we spent thinking about how wet and dirty we were, how hungry and cold, how badly treated we had been, how we had no one to speak for us or help us in any way. We had no idea how long we would be kept in this place nor what would happen to us when we were moved. Since the place was called a *transit camp* we did expect to be moved. There were rumors about where we were to go but nobody knew anything certain, not even the guards."

"What sort of rumors?"

"That we would be sent to Australia or Canada or somewhere else for as long as the war lasted. Some people said we would all be lined up against a wall and shot. Nobody really believed that the English Government would go so far but everyone was frightened just in case it was true. If the government could do what it had already done to us then what else might it make us suffer? Some of us had seen the soldier shoot that Italian in the leg so we worried."

"How did you spend the day after all your names had been called out like at our school?"

"Well, we weren't given anything to do so we talked to each other about how we had been arrested, about what we did before that. We found out a lot about each other. People showed each other photographs of their families if they had any in their wallets. We played cards. Fortunately some people had managed somehow to bring them. We of course tried to keep clean but found it almost impossible in that place. I sang from time to time. Others gave little talks on all sorts of subjects to anyone who wanted to listen. In some ways it was like being in school again. But we had to keep busy, we had to think about things that had nothing to do with the war or what had happened to us or we would have gone mad. It was hard as days went by and more and more of us got sick with colds, the 'flu, diarrhea…even pneumonia. The guards eventually became worried so they called in a local doctor who was so shocked by what he saw that he sent the worst cases at once to hospital. He protested to the authorities that we were being badly mistreated. We at least got better food after that."

Jakob had to go off to work in a field before he could finish telling me about the old factory in Lancashire with its rats and disease and its sick prisoners. I looked forward to hearing more about it the next time we met and also to find out how Jakob had got from there to the Isle-of-Man.

One of the military lodgers at our house at this time was a Lance Corporal Machin, a guard at the Mooragh Camp and thus one of Jakob's many gaolers. He cycled to work on an olive-green army-issue gear-less bone-shaker of a bicycle with his rifle slung across his back. On wet days he wore a voluminous cape the color of his bike to keep himself and his rifle dry. I used to wonder how he managed not to get it tangled in the wheels.

After I had listened to Jakob's account of his arrest and subsequent treatment I began to look on this soldier in a new light. He had seemed to me a pleasant sort of chap who missed his family and so treated Carlo and me in a kindly, playful manner like a sort of youthful uncle. But after hearing the details of Jakob's arrest I wondered if a man in his kind of war work would use his rifle the way the soldier at the railway station did to shoot the escaping Italian. The Lance Corporal didn't seem to me to be that sort of person but I had to ask.

"If a bloke scarpers and won't stop when ordered no matter 'ow loud y'are and 'ow often yer shout at 'im then yes, I'd 'ave ter shoot 'im," said the Lance Corporal in reply to my question. "I mean yer couldn't let 'im get away could yer? There's a war on. Yer can't 'ave prisoners runnin' off on yer and causin' all kinds o' trouble can yer? Not natural is it?"

"Have you ever shot anyone?" was my next question. He said he hadn't so I asked how he'd feel if he had to.

"I wouldn't want ter shoot a bloke if 'e were unarmed but if 'e were a prisoner, like, as was runnin' off and wouldn't stop as I told 'im to then I'd 'ave ter shoot 'im. Nuthin for it. Orders is orders. Yer can't go against 'em and yer can't get round 'em. If I didn't shoot an alien as was leggin' it I'd be in for it meself. I'd be up on a charge. They'd 'ave my guts fer garters."

"But how would you *feel?*" I pressed him for an answer since he appeared to be dodging the point of my question.

"Ow do I know since it 'asn't 'appened? I dare say I wouldn't be skippin' for joy if I 'ad ter do it but like I said there is a war on i'nt there? What can yer do? Y'ave ter do as yer told and make the best of it don't yer? Yer can't let them aliens escape neither…'oo knows what they'd get up to if they wasn't behind the wire? They could be doing all sorts to 'elp 'itler."

Ma appeared at that point and the Lance Corporal – whose first name was Wilfred but whose friends call him Wilf – said, "Your lad don't 'alf ask some funny questions Mrs. Cee…'e wants ter know if I'd shoot a alien as was getting' away."

"Erik has a vivid imagination," said Ma, "and he's always asking questions. Drives everybody mad with it. Don't let him bother you."

"'E in't bothrin' me Mrs. Cee," said Lance Corporal Wilf, "no more 'n that chap 'e was chattin' to…that Austrian prisoner chap on the farm 'as maybe put the idea in 'is 'ead."

Wilf seemed to think that the local imagination needed a bit of foreign stimulus.

"What Austrian prisoner was that?" asked Ma with a very sharp edge to her voice.

"E's a chap as works for the Talbots in Glen Auldyn…them friends of yours as Erik 'elps out at weekends. Well, I see Erik talkin' ter this prisoner bloke a lot. I 'ad ter go up there last week on account o' Reg Biggins bein' away, like. E's an odd beggar is old Reg. 'S wife's avin' a baby. 'E' took it into 'is 'ead the baby in't 'is. 'Is wife writes and says 'course it bloody is…'oo else's could it 'ave been?" 'I don't know,' says 'e ter me 'but I've an idea or two and I'm bloody well goin' ter find out.' There was quite a to-do before 'e got summat called *compassionate leave.*" Anyway 'e gets the leave and off 'e trots ter sort 'is wife out, like…though if y' ask me it's all in his 'ead. Anyway, I was up at the farm wi' the prisoners stead of 'im and I see Erik talkin' ter this alien bloke from the Camp. If I was a bettin' man…which I'm not…I'd say that…"

"Erik, come with me," said Ma towing me away by the collar of my open-necked shirt and into the presence of Pop while Wilf was left to address an empty room about his not being a betting man.

"I've just found out," she said to Pop, "that in spite of all we have said and in spite of all he has promised Erik has been talking to an alien prisoner on the farm. Liz Talbot gave me her word this wouldn't happen but it has. We can't trust either of them"

"This true?" Pop asked but the expression on his face was not a questioning one. I had been found guilty before I could open my mouth, before Pop had even asked who Ma's informant was.

"No," I lied desperately. "Wilf Machin's made a mistake. It was probably Johnny he saw talking to a prisoner."

Although Pop now knew who the informant had been he didn't question him. He said, simply, "Are you telling me that Johnny looks so much like you that Wilf couldn't tell you apart? That Johnny f'la's a walking scarecrow and a lot older and taller than you. And what prisoner could understand a word Johnny says? He speaks Double Dutch. He can't get his tongue round words. Words defeat him. But that's not your problem is it? You've got no trouble finding words. You find far too many of them. You never shut up. You've been caught stealing the jam, Sonny Boy, so no more stories…you may as well own up to it but be quick about it. I haven't got all day."

I didn't answer. I remained stubbornly mute while Pop promised me a "leathering" if I didn't reply. Ma persuaded him to postpone this vigorous exercise until she had had time to talk to Liz.

I had asked Lance Corporal Wilf an innocent question and it had led to this! I would never be able to see or talk to Jakob again! I felt the bitter injustice of Ma, Pop, Wilf, the world – more or less in that order.

CHAPTER FIFTEEN

I HAD HOPED THAT WHEN DOMESTIC PASSIONS COOLED I COULD PER-suade Ma and Pop that my talking to Jakob was not going to do me any harm. He wouldn't make me into a rebellious schoolchild intent on defying family and civic authority any more than I was naturally inclined to do already. On the contrary I was at pains to point out to Ma and Pop that I was learning a lot from him…about Austria, the opera, the situation of internees…all sorts of interesting things. But that, it seemed, was what Ma and Pop feared. They thought an alien prisoner would take the opportunity offered by my naivete to poison my mind against my parents and my country as a sort of revenge for being locked away in a camp. The fact that I manifested no signs of rebellion different in kind or intensity from those they had become used to didn't matter. I didn't utter any views savoring of Socialism, Communism or any other *ism* my parents might deem subversive, I didn't start to pepper my sentences with German words but they "knew," they said, that a man such as Jakob could only be a dangerous undermining influence on a naïve and unsuspecting lad with no experience of the world.

So Liz and Tom were summoned and, thinking the occasion a social one, innocently entered the house in jovial mood prepared for a drink and a chat and maybe something light to eat before they drove back to the farm. Their demeanor changed when Ma cleared her throat nervously and began to hold forth. She said that since neither they nor I could be trusted then my experiment with the dairy business was at an end. I had been allowed to talk to a possibly dangerous prisoner even after Ma and Pop had forbidden it. I had been put in peril. In peril! In vain did Liz argue, with some heat, that Jakob was not only harmless but a man of character and artistic worth who could teach a great deal of value to a small boy. It was a privilege few children would ever have. Ma and Pop ought to be grateful and thank them for my opportunity instead of blaming them for affording it. In peace time a friendship between a boy such as I and a man of Jakob's stature would never have occurred. We would have lived in different worlds.

Tom tried to sway parental opinion with his own blunt diplomacy saying, "What's doin' on yer both takin' on like this over a f'la as daycent as Jaycob? Yer both plain loony! He's as mild a f'la as yer'l see anywhere. He wouldn't say 'boo' to our geese no more than the other prisoners workin' on the farm. They're all daycent people. I'd has' thought yer both had more sense." Pop looked uncomfortable listening to this while Ma merely grimaced and glanced upward theatrically as though asking the gods for patience while she let a rural half-wit have his ranting say. She looked grimmer than before when he had finished.

"I don't care what you think or what you say," she responded, "Erik's not going back to the farm so you needn't come calling for him this Saturday or any other Saturday for that matter. I'm not having him talking to prisoners and that's that. There's more kinds of infection than the doctors deal with and I'm surprised you can't see it."

She folded her arms and looked like a grim Boadicea refusing the overtures of an uppity thoughtless but now repentant tribal subordinate.

Lis and Tom left *Rosetree Villa* in a mood quite the reverse of the one they manifested on entering it. Far from being repentant they were, naturally, angry that their integrity had been questioned, especially by people they regarded as friends. They were all the more angry because they felt guilty. They had knowingly gone against Ma and Pop's wishes by turning a blind eye to my meetings with Jakob. Ma had used some cutting language and that had added fuel to the fire as well, no doubt, had Pop's eloquent silence. The fact that I wept forlornly while the adults argued my future had no influence at all on the outcome of their exchanges. They had all forgotten me in the heat of mutual indignation.

"You can snivel and blubber and whine and carry on all you like," Ma said to me when she had calmed a little, "but you're not going to the farm again so make your mind up to it. A right mess you've got us all into."

Perhaps to forestall any rebellion against her edict Ma announced a visit to Douglas to see the relations. Adding insult to injury she said we'd be leaving the house just about the time on Saturday that in happier times (like last week) Tom would have arrived to pick me up.

I had never been so angry with my parents before in my young life than I was after Liz and Tom had made their flustered exit. I remained sullen and unresponsive for days.

"He'll come round," I heard Ma tell Pop, "Just give him time."

"He'd better," said Pop, "or it won't be time I'll be giving him…it'll be a leathering."

The "leathering" earlier promised had not been carried out, but remained a hazard dangling over me by a thread.

The train journey to Douglas that Saturday was the saddest I had ever taken. I could only think of Jakob on the farm and wonder what he was doing and if he would miss me now that I was prevented from seeing him. I missed him already and more than once Ma found me silently weeping. She tried some stilted words of comfort but, blaming her for everything, I refused to be consoled.

I stared out of the carriage window but saw nothing. When at last we stopped at St. John's to let passengers on and off and allow the thirsty steam engine to take on water a man in a thick tweed suit who had been sitting opposite me engrossed in a newspaper suddenly realized where we were, grabbed a bag from the rack over his head and left the carriage in haste. He slammed the heavy wooden door behind him and walked quickly down the platform. I had just stood up to see what was going on outside in the station and my thumb was in the space by the hinges created when the man opened the carriage door. When he slammed it shut my thumb was crushed. The pain was so immediately intense that I fainted while Ma, Carlo told me later, opened the carriage window and shouted frantically for help. The door was soon opened again and my thumb released but the damage was done.

I arrived in Douglas palely conscious but with a throbbing pain more severe than anything I had ever experienced or thought possible. Pain simply enveloped me. All I could do was moan feebly. I was immediately put to bed once we reached Aunty Doreen's house with much tutting and "eh, whatta ter doing" on her part. Clearly she was at a loss for words. My experience could not be dealt with by any of her ready-made verbal formulas. She insisted on closing the heavy bedroom curtains although it was only early afternoon for, she said, daylight was bad for pain. She thought her Cornish pasties might be good for it but the idea of food made me feel like throwing up which, when I said so, led to more tutting, "eh whatta ter doing" and "whatever nexts?" I was the only nephew to arrive at Aunty Doreen's house with a crushed thumb so my aunt who lived by precedent and protocol (often eccentric) was at a loss how to act.

That night I tossed and turned in an agony of pain unable to sleep amazed that such a small part of my body could create such turmoil in the rest of it. All I could do was moan the night away feeling that it would never end. Ma stayed up for most of it to look after me though there was little she could do to take the pain away. Aspirins only partly relieved it and not for long. The thumb turned an alarming shade of black. I feared this was a sign of rot and that eventually it would drop off.

Next day Aunty Doreen asked her doctor, an elderly Englishman called Fortescue, to come to the house and take a look at it. Doctors made house calls in those days as a matter of routine, even in a war. Dr. Fortescue was a tall Edwardian figure. His white shirt had an old-fashioned wing collar. He wore a black morning coat over it and had striped trousers and black highly polished shoes. He looked a bit like Neville Chamberlain and was the epitome of quiet authority. Aunty Doreen was unnaturally subservient in his presence. She stood at attention while he was examining me ready to procure anything the doctor should require. Had a bread knife or an axe been requested she would have produced either in an instant begging to know if they were sharp enough.

"Now let me see that thumb," said the doctor reaching out while I clenched my teeth, whimpered, and put my wounded hand as far away from him as I was able. I couldn't possibly bear the extra pain an examination would entail. The constant throbbing of my blackened thumb was torment enough.

"I can't help you with your thumb if you won't let me examine it," said the doctor.

He had a mild sympathetic voice. He hadn't tried to grab my hand, he seemed trustworthy so, wincing, I allowed him to take my hand in both of his. He gently turned it palm upward to scrutinize through a pair of pince-nez on a silver chain, which he took from the top pocket of his morning coat.

After looking at my thumb from a variety of angles he said, "It doesn't look good. The thumb is very badly bruised. Now," he went on, "I'll have to move it gently while I feel the joints. This will hurt but you'll be brave and I'll be quick."

I gritted my teeth and tried to be courageous while he manipulated my thumb. Though he did this carefully waves of pain and nausea swept over me and I whispered that I was going to be sick. The doctor finished his examination and softly laid my hand back on the eiderdown. The nausea faded without the arrival of any of the violent retching and wild vomiting that had signaled they were on their way.

"Well, there's nothing broken," said the doctor, "but the bruising is severe. I'll write a prescription for something to ease the pain. The medicine will make him drowsy," he said turning to Ma, "so he must stay in bed while he is taking it. Rest, in any case, will do him good. Extreme pain is very wearing."

He produced a bandage from his rather battered black leather bag and carefully bound my thumb with it. Afterwards wishing me a speedy recovery he left the bedroom and went off down the stairs Aunty Doreen at his heels kneading her hands together and offering obsequious thanks for his visit like a courtier fawning on a king. Ma went to the nearest chemist's shop for the prescribed painkiller while I lapsed into an uneasy doze. When Ma came back with a bottle of bright red liquid, which tasted vile, a single teaspoon of it sent me at once into a deep sleep. I was free of pain for the first time in nearly twenty-four hours. Evidently while I slept I rambled aloud about Jakob, about my grief at not being able to see him any more, at how unfairly both of us had been treated by capricious authority – all in the language of an aggrieved ten-year-old. Aunty Doreen told me about this and wanted to know who Jakob was. I told her the whole story while Ma remained silent. "Eh, whatta ter-do," said my aunt. "Who'd have thought?"

I was, of course, unable to pay the usual visits to the other relations. Ma started her rounds by taking Carlo off to see Aunty Emmeline, her crystal and her fruitcake. Next they proceeded to Aunty Agatha and her dusty books according to the time-worn ritual. They finished their rounds at Uncle Sidney and Aunty Avril's house late in the afternoon. Ma was offered a large sherry, which, as she later told Pop, she was glad to accept. I've no doubt she sipped her drink delicately with lady-like decorum and no doubt at all that Uncle Sidney downed several in the time it took Ma to sip one. This would act as preface to his early-evening whiskey and bed-time brandy. "One for the road," he would say drinking two or three of the latter before retiring to bed. He would certainly have appreciated the effects if not the taste of my medicine.

Sidney drove Ma and Carlo back to Aunty Doreen's house at his usual measured pace and with his usual uncertain sense of direction. He wouldn't have stood a chance with a modern traffic cop and a breathalyzer. Unusually for him he parked his car and came in with Ma. He normally avoided Aunty Doreen who despised men who couldn't hold their drink but on this occasion he said he wanted to see *the wounded soldier.* He sat down by my bed and told me how Ma had said I was being brave putting up with a lot of pain without whining about it. He said he had seen a lot of that in "the Great War." He'd seen many things a child should never hear about so he wouldn't tell me but he was glad to hear that I could "take" the pain.

"You'd be surprised. A lot of grown men can't, you know."

When I was older I recalled him saying this and began to understand how his drinking began and why Aunty Avril put up with it.

Uncle Sidney was being so kind and I was so weak from pain that I started to cry, a child after all and not the brave wounded soldier enduring his agony in stoic silence. I told him about my other source of pain when he asked me what was wrong. I told him about Jakob, about not being allowed to see him ever again, about Ma's injustice to me and to the Talbots, about how I wouldn't have had to endure the pain in my thumb if Ma hadn't first caused a pain in my heart by bringing us all to Douglas to prevent me from seeing Jakob. It was all Ma's fault!"

Sidney listened to me with patience and sympathy, patted me on the head, gave me a boiled sweet and smiled. He'd probably have offered me a drink if he'd had his flask with him. But he left my room without saying anything by way of comfort…he withheld the words I wanted to hear…the anti-Ma words, the poor mistreated Erik words.

After Sidney had left Ma came into the bedroom to say that Aunty Emmeline had sent me a big piece of fruitcake in lieu of a visit. She couldn't bear to enter sick rooms, they made her feel morbid and helpless. Aunty Agatha sent her best wishes for a quick recovery and, upon reflection, she had also dispatched Uncle Frank who arrived just as Ma was telling me about the fruitcake and Emmeline's aversion to the spectacle of illness. Uncle Frank said that that came from nursing her irascible elderly mother through her last long illness.

"I remember your Dad telling me about that," said Ma. "His mother would sit up there in that big brass bed, a queen on a throne ordering Emmeline around like a skivvy and never a word of thanks."

Ma hadn't got on with her mother-in-law. Pop said that was because they were too much alike.

Uncle Frank made sympathetic noises while Ma was telling him about my accident and how I had suffered. After Ma had left him to talk to me on his own I laid out for his inspection the entire Jakob situation as I saw it. I told him of course that had it not been for the quarrel over Jakob I wouldn't have been lying in the bed in front of him suffering the wracking pain I was enduring. I told him I would be glad of his opinion of the fairness of the case against Ma which I had just made. I told him that I respected his learning as an astronomer and trusted he would judge my case fairly.

"We'd best not go into all that if your mother's made her mind up," he said feebly.

I couldn't believe my ears! Was this the rational astronomer talking? Was he afraid to offer an independent view? My high opinion of his scholarly mind dropped like a stone down that long mineshaft in the cliffs near Maughold.

"But Ma's being so mean!" I protested.

"That's as may be," said Uncle Frank, now on his feet and edging his way toward the door, "but it's your Mum and Dad who have to bring you up so you should listen to them and do as they say. I hope you get well soon."

Having said that he disappeared in some haste. He was scuttling back to his telescope as fast as he left his own sitting room for that purpose when he felt he had done his social duty by callers to his house. He generally endured about five minutes of chit chat with a domestic visitor before leaving Aunty Agatha to entertain the intruder while he got back to his star-gazing. Agatha would rather have been reading a good book but she was gracious in enduring small talk. Had the word been current on the afternoon Uncle Frank left my room I would have called him "wimp." No, a "selfish wimp."

The result of my pointed conversations with two uncles in one after-noon was a boiled sweet and a lot of frustration. This and the pain in my thumb produced more tears. Ma found me sniveling when she brought me another dose of the medicine.

"Is it the pain?" she asked, a worried look on her face.

"I've got a crushed thumb because you brought us here so that I couldn't see Jakob on the farm. Uncle Sidney and Uncle Frank won't help me and Carlo's too little to understand. I'm all alone and everything hurts."

"I'm sure your thumb does hurt but everything else isn't as bad as all that. You'll get over it."

"No I won't," I said defiantly, determined not to 'get over' anything. "You're all against me and when we go home Pop's going to give me a leathering."

"He certainly is not," said Ma. "He's worried about what's happened to you. I got word to him about it through the Railway Company."

I was determined on self-pity so I continued to complain. "I don't care what you say. Nobody really cares about what's happened to me." I lay there, a solitary afflicted knight abandoned by his comrades to perish slowly and painfully of his injuries. Like King Arthur I knew the sting of betrayal by those closest to me.

"I care," said Ma. "Your uncles really do care. They've both been on at me about this Jakob at the farm." Ma surprised me by pronouncing his name properly.

I was astonishd at this news. I hadn't been abandoned in my wounded state after all. It seemed that Uncle Frank was neither such a wimp nor Uncle Sidney as ineffectual as he seemed.

"Well," I asked Ma, "what are you going to do?"

"If you take your medicine and promise to stop crying and feeling sorry for yourself I'll have a word with your father when we get home. We'll have to see if we can work something out."

Despite the inconclusiveness of this promise I took heart. I swallowed another large spoonful of the noxious medicine and drifted into a deep sleep. It would be illegal to prescribe it today. When I had to be treated with morphine after an operation four decades later its pleasant pain-killing effects and the sense of euphoria it produced seemed oddly familiar.

This visit to Douglas lasted longer than the intended weekend. After his employers relayed what had happened to me and how this would keep Ma in Douglas longer than expected Pop, with considerable difficulty, managed to persuade Mrs. Corcoran from next door to preside over the houehold for a few days. He didn't want Bessie anywhere near him. She was so indignant at not being asked that she dropped in on Pop only once to let him know that she would not be dropping in. Pop, of course, rejoiced. Ma told him not to worry unduly about me so he didn't.

After five days in bed and more of Dr. Fortescue's knock-out drops I was judged able to travel so we returned home. The very sight of a railway carriage door made me feel sore all over so I sat as far away from them as possible. Pop was a lot more sympathetic than I had expected. He looked at my still-black thumb and actually winced before giving me a careful hug.

"You've been in the wars, Sonny Jim," he said, "That thumb looks like it's been through a mangle. You'd best be wearing a leather glove till it gets better…that'll stop it from getting hurt again."

Ma and Pop conferred on the matter of Jakob. I was told that I could return to the farm if Liz would have me after all the trouble we had put them to. *We!* I thought but kept my indignation to myself till I had heard what else my guilty parents had to say. If Liz would have me back I could talk to Jakob but only if other people were nearby in case what Pop called "this Austrian Herman"was overcome by a Teutonic homicidal impulse, however remote I thought that possibility might be.

"You can't be too careful," said Pop wagging a soot-blackened finger as Ma filled his tin bath with hot water. "And never ever turn your back on that f'la."

"It's not funny business this isn't," Pop went on as I prepared to sneer at his melodramatic fears. "How'd ya think ya mother and I would feel if they brought ya home dead…run through with a pitch fork by this Jaycob ya so keen ta see…or all chopped up with an axe and sent to us in a parcel?"

"If you're that worried about him why don't you come to the farm with me and meet him? He's nice. He tells me a lot. He'd never hurt anyone. He'd never hurt me."

"We're not going to go that far," said Ma before Pop could reply.

"No. Germans is Hermans," said Pop as if that made any sense, "and you can't take the Herman out of the German whoever he is."

"What does that mean?" I asked.

"Never you mind," said Pop, "but it's true"

"Of course," Ma cautioned, "Liz and Tom might not want to take you back." She was no doubt remembering their angry departure after they had been accused and found guilty of duplicity. Ma no doubt also recalled some of the cutting language she had used on that occasion. "We'll ask anyway," she reassured me, "and I'll eat humble pie. I'll do my best to persuade them."

In the event Ma ran into Tom in the town, apologized in the most abject terms for her behavior, said there had been a terrible mistake though didn't explain what that might have been, offered to make a special journey to Glen Auldyn to beg Liz's forgiveness, said that Pop was of the same mind as she was and equally sorry and please could Erik return to their employment in the same job as before. She knew it was a cheek to ask but I had been so upset it made me ill so she felt she must. Tom, uncomfortably embarrassed by the spectacle of Ma penitent, sorrowful and apologetic said he would have to ask Liz.

Liz was willing to let bygones be bygones though she had been deeply hurt by some of the things Ma and said to her. An amnesty was declared and as soon as my thumb was more or less back to its normal size and color I resumed my dairying. Liz ended her rounds at our house once more. Ma apologized to her eloquently and they returned to their exchange of gossip as if nothing had happened to drive them apart.

The first thing I did on my first day back at the farm was to show one and all my healing thumb and describe in detail how it had been so violently squashed.

"Door made thumb sore," Johnny summed it up though he said it in Johnnyspeak: "Ord dame umth orse."

CHAPTER SIXTEEN

Jakob knew that it wasn't just my thumb that had kept me away from the farm. After that angry scene at our house Liz had told him of Pop and Ma's lurid fancies about what he might do to their unprotected child reassuring him at the same time that she and Tom had no such silly fears. They knew he was a normal decent man but my parents had been infected by local prejudice, she said – the product of social ignorance, she added. They just don't know you f'las an' we do," Uncle Tom said he had told Jakob the morning he picked me up after my absence.

"It will not be suitable for you to talk to me again," Jakob said as soon as I went to speak to him. "I'm a dangerous enemy alien you know. I can't be trusted. Liz tells me that this is what your Mamma and Papa think. Liz tells me that they are frightened for your safety even though they have never met me. They think I will eat you like a cannibal. I'm their bogey-man Liz says. They probably think I have horns on my head and play cards with the devil in the room I share with the three other prisoners."

"They don't know you," I replied simply.

"No, they don't. But do you? How do you know that in the next minute I won't pick up a shovel or an axe and smash your head in with it? How do you know I won't stab you with a rusty knife or cut your arm off with a sickle? Or push you off the top floor of the barn? How do you know I won't kill you to get my revenge for being made a prisoner when I have done nothing wrong…broken no laws? How do you know?"

"You're not like that," I said, perturbed by his excited manner and graphic questioning. I thought that perhaps opera singers resorted to this kind of exaggeration when they were angry the way most of the kids I played with did when they decided they had been insulted.

"But *how* do you know what I am like?" he insisted.

"I just do," I said, at a loss for proof. "If you wanted to hurt me you would have done by now," I added.

"So I would," he said, calming down. "So I would. Your Mamma and Papa are frightened like the government. I am a prisoner because the government is frightened. Putting us all behind barbed wire was like the government taking a pill to feel better when there was nothing wrong. You can see how silly that is. If a boy of ten can see this then why can't the government? Common sense is one of the first casualties in a war."

"Perhaps the government's like Bessie, our next-door neighbor. She says you'll strangle me in a barn."

"Such ignorance! Don't grow up to be like her please. Get a good education." He was silent for a while after he had said this. Then he said "It is sad but it is obvious you can't speak to me any more if I frighten your parents."

"But they've changed, they're different now!" I told him. "They say I can talk to you if Auntie Liz and Uncle Tom don't mind." I didn't mention the watchful eye the latter were supposed to cast upon us both. "You mind that Liz and Tom keep their eyes liftin' on that f'la" was what Pop had said to me.

"So," Jakob said, "you have to crush your thumb for this? This changes their minds? You must know Erik that we live in a crazy world. But we'll shrug our shoulders and speak when we can then. Your Papa and

151

Mamma will see that this does you no harm. You won't have to crush the thumb again."

"I didn't do it on purpose," I said unsure of what he meant by his last remark.

"A famous doctor in my country who died not long ago said there is no such thing as an accident. You put your thumb where it would be crushed so you could change things he would say, I think."

"Of course I didn't," I replied with some heat. "The pain was awful. I fainted. Dr. Fortescue knows I had an accident. He gave me medicine for the pain. He didn't say I crushed my thumb on purpose. Ma and Carlo don't think so and they were there. They saw. It hurt more than anything. I wouldn't do that on purpose."

"You wouldn't realize what you were actually doing nor why you were doing it," said Jakob, "but the mind has a way of playing tricks on us to get what it really wants. I was in an opera once with this very bad-tempered Hungarian soprano who nobody in the cast liked. One night when she was singing a very serious aria…telling me how much she loved me…I pulled this comic face. I didn't plan to. I just did. She was so surprised that she stopped singing for a moment and then had to sing very fast to catch up with the orchestra. She sang the rest of this love song with a very fierce look on her face. She was so angry with me that she had to turn away from the audience. After the curtain came down she yelled at me and insisted I should be dismissed for trying to ruin her performance. The theatre manager didn't want to lose her…she was very popular with audiences who didn't know how offensive she could be in private…so he did what she demanded. I lost that job but I didn't want to work with that woman so you see I must have deliberately angered her to get what I wanted. I had no other reason."

I wasn't convinced by this anecdote. I thought he'd invented it on the spur of the moment and considered Freud's theory of accidents the greatest nonsense when I was ten and had never heard of Freud. It stood to reason that no one would deliberately inflict upon themselves the pain I had suffered…would they? It was true that my accident led to a change. I could now talk to Jakob without worrying that Ma and Pop might find out. In fact occasionally Ma would ask what it was we talked about. Pop never did. He muttered about the immutability of Hermans of all brands…Austrian, German, Hungarian, whatever…and how they were never ever to be trusted.

"If ya talk to this f'la…an' I don't fer the life a me know why ya have to…mind somebody's not far away when ya do. Ya never know what a Herman'll do next. I know that much. I've seen 'm up close. I've seen 'm kill f'las with sharpened spades that split those f'la's heads wide open"

It was all Ma could do when Pop said things like this to shut him up and stop him whipping off his shirt to display the entry marks of the German bullets that had riddled his abdomen.

Soon after I was allowed to resume the delivery of milk to local doors Sir Christopher Rand-Krueger fell ill. Whether his hookah was responsible or his gin or some germs he had picked up locally or imported from India in a dormant but now active state wasn't immediately apparent though Malaria and Swamp Fever were widely spoken of. I mention this only because the day we found out Aunty Liz spent a longer time over her tea and cake with Ma than usual. They gossiped about the Rand-Kruegers wondering aloud whether Sir Christopher was about to set forth on his last safari unaware they were applying a Swahili word to an ex Indian civil servant. They examined the Rand-Krueger establishment from every angle their voices sinking to whispers when I wandered into earshot. At the end of their prolonged session Liz asked Ma if I could return with her to the farm. There was work I could help with. The Talbot's had been left short-handed because one of the prisoners had come down with the 'flu (eventually determined to be the prosaic cause of Sir Christopher's ailing state) and thus had to stay in the Camp.

"They do this on us, you know," said Liz referring to the Camp authorities. "They say they'll send the usual number of internees and no one bothers till the last minute to check to see if they're fit for work."

Ma was assured that the task awaiting me would not tire me out. I would be releasing a prisoner to do some of the harder work by taking his place at an easier job. Ma reluctantly agreed, softened up by the gossip session just ended, so I spent the afternoon with Jakob and two others picking the turnips that had already been turned up and trimmed. A lot of bending and stretching was involved getting the turnips off the ground and throwing them into a cart pulled by one of the spirited Clydesdales. Liz might consider this work light but I found it pretty tiring after the first half hour.

The best thing about this particular job on this particular day was that I got to talk to Jakob intermittently for a whole afternoon. The soldier guarding the prisoners didn't mind a bit. He sprawled against a hedge and dozed in the sunshine with a handkerchief over his face while Jakob, as we worked, told me the rest of the story of his journey to the Isle-of-Man and the Mooragh Camp in Ramsey.

"Remember me telling you that people fell sick in what they called a transit camp…that old Lancashire factory…and how some had to be taken to hospital?" be asked after I begged him to finish his story. "Well more and more people became ill because of the cold and wet and the dirt and the poor diet and the lack of sleep. I began to think we would all die in that place, one by one, day by day, until only the rats and the rain were left. I really began to think that this was the government's plan. Our bodies would be taken and buried secretly at night and no one would know what had happened to us after we were arrested. We'd have simply disappeared and our guards would be ordered to keep their mouths shut or face prison"

"But you didn't die," I said superfluously, "so how did you get out?"

Jakob didn't answer right away but stood looking at a kestrel falcon hovering against the wind searching out prey. The bird suddenly snapped its wings shut and dropped like a stone until it was near the ground when it opened its wings again to brake before seizing a small rodent with its razor sharp talons. It flew off with the hapless animal clamped fast.

"That's what Hitler did to Austria," said Jakob when he saw I had followed his gaze. Perhaps he was also admiring the bird's freedom to live its natural life, albeit a predatory one, while humans manacled one another.

"What was that you said?" he asked, coming out of his reverie.

"How did you get out of that old factory?"

"There was no adventure to it. One morning when we lined up as usual to call out our names to assure the authorities that we hadn't escaped in the night we were told we were to be moved to another camp for *aliens* as they were pleased to call us. We would be in this camp until the end of the war, we were told. When peace came the government would decide what to do with us. We were told we were taking a sea journey and that was all.

They didn't tell you where you were going?"

"No. They just said that we were being taken to a ship. We had heard of people being sent to Australia and to Canada and that some of the ships they sailed in had been attacked by German U-boats and torpedoed. We were frightened in case our ship, wherever it was going, should be torpedoed. The government wouldn't care. With all of us at the bottom of the sea the problem of what to do with us would be solved."

Perhaps bored with pulling a cart slowly across a field the Clydesdale suddenly decamped with the load of turnips. Jakob had to join the others in pursuit of the frisky horse. Clydesdales are very big, very powerful draft horses. When one of them turns frolicsome while attached to a cartload of turnips strength and guile are required for its recapture and the retrieval of the cart in one piece. The recapture of Nellie (as this huge horse was incongruously called) involved ropes, soft words, rather a lot of carrots and a fair amount of time. All the turnips in the cart had spilled out and Nellie had almost disengaged herself from the traces when the men caught up with her. They grabbed the trailing reins and held tight but that wasn't enough to hold the horse without additional ropes. When she was calmed down, had been bribed with her fill of carrots (supposed to have been given her in measured doses through the afternoon), was attached more firmly to the cart and all the turnips had been thrown back in we were able to proceed down the rows again at a measured pace but this time one of the prisoners held the horse's bridle and whispered endearments in her ear in Italian. At least Jakob said he was speaking in Italian. It was theorized that Nellie, feeling taken for granted, had bolted to assert herself.

"Like my wife," said the soldier guarding the prisoners who had been wakened from his nap by all the shouting and commotion in the field and had come to see what the fuss was about. "She was a bolter, my wife…bolted with Ernie my best friend…least, I thought he was my best friend…she said I was taking her for granted. I'll never understand women." When work resumed he walked slowly back to his place by the hedge and settled down to renew his nap.

Soon after order had been restored in the turnip field Liz arrived in the old black Morris, emptied now of its milk churns. She brought us jugs of tea and thick slices of bread smeared with Manx butter and homemade jam. This was "lunch" even though it was delivered in the middle of the afternoon. When I was a boy a meal in the middle of the day was "dinner." One at the end of it (usually lighter) was "tea." A snack before bedtime was "supper." On farms anything in between these established meals was "lunch" whatever the time on the clock might read. Liz was not informed of our communal romp with Nellie. There was no need to invite trouble.

Once "lunch" had been consumed – especially heartily by the military guard who had done nothing that afternoon except sleep – the Italian prisoner took Nellie and the cart-load of turnips back to the farm. Jakob and the other prisoner, with my feeble help, cut the stalks from the rest of the turnips lying on the ground and then piled them up ready for the returning cart. To take my mind off the fatigue that was settling on me I prompted Jakob to finish the much-interrupted story of his journey to the Isle-of-Man.

"There's not much more to it," he said. "The day we left that old factory we were lined up in twos and after a while we were marched out of the horrible place...it was like a ruined castle in a nightmare. Everyone cheered as we left, even the guards. Their officers weren't pleased by that but the soldiers didn't seem to be worried. We were marched back to the railway station we had arrived at and put on another train...as old and as dirty as the one that brought us...and we were taken to a place called Fleetwood. It's a port on the Lancashire coast. There was an old Belgian steamer in the harbor and we were ordered on to it. After we were all on board and the gang planks had been drawn in we were told where we were going.

'You're off to the Isle-of-Man,' an officer said. Most of us had never heard of the place and those who had thought it was just off the coast of France. 'It's in the Irish Sea," the officer said in reply to shouted questions. He added 'you'll all be out of the way there. You won't be getting into mischief helping Adolf in a place like that.' Boos followed this little speech."

"What was the sea trip like?" I wanted to know all the details as children do. "Did you see any German submarines? Did you see any seals?"

"No submarines, no seals...we didn't even see any fish...and it wasn't a *trip*. We were not coming here for a holiday the way I understand people did before the war. That little Belgian ship was packed tight...other prisoners from other so-called transit camps were on it too. There was nowhere to sit down. It wasn't long after we left the harbor when the sea became rough. Many people had never been on a ship before or had been on one so long ago they had forgotten what it can be like. People began to vomit as the sea got rougher and the boat was tossed about. The sailors cursed us and threw buckets of seawater across the decks to clean the mess away. We were soon out of sight of land and no one had any idea how long this voyage would take...no one on the ship had ever been to the Isle-of-Man before, not even the deck crew. The soldiers guarding us were as sick as we were and knew nothing of the island. We didn't know whether we would have to sail for hours or for days. After about two hours the winds calmed down a little and the sea was less rough and then we saw the smoke."

"Smoke?"

"We could see long columns of smoke rising up and hanging in the air. Later we found out that they came from gorse fires on the hills of the island. When we sailed closer we could see cliffs with mountains behind them rising up steeply from the sea. Everyone cheered up when they saw land. The sea-crossing had been shorter than many people feared it would be. But we didn't head straight for a harbor. We came in fairly close to the island so that we could see houses on top of the cliffs and roads with cars and buses and other vehicles on them. But instead of docking we headed north and sailed along the coast till we came to Ramsey Bay. There the ship moved in very slowly to your long pier. It took the sailors and the men on the pier quite a long time to tie the ship up so that we could get off it. There were soldiers waiting for us on the pier and they took over from the ones who had come with us from Fleetwood. The soldiers on the ship had been as sick as the rest of us so I'm sure they were glad that others took their place. They said things like 'if I wanted to go sailing I'd have joined the Navy.' They said such things with a lot of swear words which I won't repeat."

One of the annoying things about Jakob was that he'd be telling a story and say that people used these awful swear words but then he wouldn't say them. A contemporary Jakob would, of course, have no qualms about uttering them…would probably repeat them with glee. But this is now and that was then.

"We had to wait to get off the ship until we were given the order. Eventually everyone was lined up on the pier. Then we were marched along it by the new soldiers until we reached the promenade where we had to stop and be inspected by a senior officer. The look on his face was enough to tell us that he didn't like what he saw. I think there were looks on our faces that showed him we didn't much like what we saw either. Then we were marched along the promenade into the town with the soldiers guarding us, their rifles loaded we found out later. The surroundings were a lot prettier than in that dreadful place in Lancashire. The sun had come out and we cheered up even though many of us felt the lingering effects of seasickness. The road seemed to be going up and down like the ship as we went along so marching wasn't easy. I began to feel that our prison here might not be so bad after all. There was no thick smoke hanging over the town; no factories that we could see, there were mountains and seashore to look at instead of blackened rain-soaked brick and not much else. We dared to hope that our conditions would be better than they had been.

While we were trying to march down the promenade however we had to pass groups of people who had come out of their houses to stare at us. They weren't friendly. They yelled insults at us. Some threw stones. It was obvious that we weren't welcome. We found out later that people had been turned out of their houses when they formed our camp so that explained some of the bad behavior toward us though of course we didn't want to live in their houses. We wanted to go home to our own. It was all so stupid, so unnecessary."

I told Jakob that our house wasn't far from the pier but I had no idea that any such landing had taken place. Neither Ma nor Pop said anything about prisoners disembarking at the pier or marching down the prom.

"I suppose the authorities kept it all secret," said Jakob. "Some people obviously knew because they lined up to show us they didn't want us here. As if any of us wanted to be here…to go through everything I have told you about!"

I asked Jakob what he had been thinking about as he went down the promenade.

"The same things as everyone else I suppose. I was worrying what kind of prison we would be kept in. I hoped it would not be like a prison for criminals. We were not criminals but law-abiding people harmed by a government no longer guided by the laws of the land."

"What did you think when you saw the Mooragh Camp?"

"After we had marched along the harbor and were crossing the bridge I could see these tall hotels that were now surrounded by barbed wire and wooden sentry boxes. I was sure we were not going to be kept in luxury but I could see that there was no actual prison with high walls in front of us. We would be able to see the town and the harbor and the surrounding hills through the wire. We would not be shut away from the world completely the way criminals are. There was a beach nearby, the sea was on one side of us so whatever happened we had views to cheer us up. This was much better than the dirty wet brick walls of Lancashire so I felt relieved. I didn't know then that we would be allowed outside the Camp to work on farms or go for walks…with armed guards of course, but still we were not confined to the Camp every day and all day. We ought not to have been locked up at all but it was a relief to find that we were not going to be treated like dangerous criminals. Of course there are people who want us to be treated that way because they hate Jews."

"Why?" I asked in all simplicity.

"Why indeed," said Jakob. "To answer that question we would have to study over a thousand years of Western history."

I couldn't have known then that I would spend much of my adult life doing just that.

CHAPTER SEVENTEEN

ONE OF POP'S FAVORITE ASSESSMENTS OF ME WAS THAT "IF THERE'S
an easy way and a hard way to do a job you'll find the hard way." In this
perversity I am my father's heir. I have this clear mental image of him, in
the absence of a work bench which would have made the job so much
easier, kneeling on the cold stone floor of the back kitchen, very small
nails pressed tightly between his lips, about to hammer the newly-cut
soles of a pair of boots over the flimsy remnants of the old worn-out ones.
Before the hammering-on of soles another ritual had to be carried out.
When, somehow, Pop had acquired a piece of shoe-leather he set to work
– there were always shoes to mend. He made patterns for the new soles
by outlining the old ones with a pencil on pages from the local newspaper. Then he cut along the penciled line with a pair of scissors. He used
the paper patterns thus produced to mark out the new soles on the new
leather, again with a pencil. After that he followed the penciled line with a
razor-sharp, cobbler's knife. These operations were all carried out while he
knelt on that cold stone kitchen floor. Whenever I smell new leather (as
I've just done) I think of Pop on his knees bending over his cobbler's last.
I used to wonder what would happen if I slapped him suddenly on the
back and he swallowed all those nails.

"No point paying Billy the Cobbler to do what I can do just as well
meself," he would remark as he picked up a rough file to smooth the

edges of the new soles after he had nailed them over the old ones. I remember the look of suffering that used to cross Ma's face. She hadn't been brought up to this! When she had needed new shoes her father had given her the money to go to town to buy them with enough left over for lunch or afternoon tea. He didn't produce a sheet of leather, a cobbler's last, old newspapers, a pair of scissors and a knife and position a handful of little nails between his lips as he got down on his knees on the cold stone kitchen floor.

What anguish Ma must have felt at that point in the war when new leather for shoe and boot repair was unobtainable and Carlo and I had to wear wooden clogs for a while! It must have reminded her of that time in her Lancashire childhood when she was wakened by the dawn clatter of mill-workers tramping over cobblestones on their way to the looming factories. She must have shuddered that her children were forced to go to school in the footware of the very poor. What would the neighbors think she had been reduced to? What would the teachers assume?

I can't recall when I was given my first pair of shoes but I remember wearing boots as a matter of course all through the war years (except for the brief period of clogs) as did the other boys at school. A pair was kept apart all shined up for Sunday use – it was the weekly pair that was re-soled as often as the uppers would allow. When the weekly pair could be re-soled no longer the Sunday boots became the everyday boots and there was much anguished discussion about where the money for a new pair of Sunday boots was to come from.

"Tom Talbot should be buyin' your boots seein' 'as you wear 'm out worse than at school when you're working with Liz."

Ma reminded Pop that in effect this was what Tom was doing already since at Pop's insistence I had had to contribute some of my hoarded shillings to buy the leather for the latest pair of soles.

"I can't go bangin' new leather on oul uppers forever," said Pop defensively. "He's got to have new boots an' I can't afford 'm."

Boots provoked Ma and Pop to quarrel. Pop said Ma could easily afford to buy them for Carlo and me with the money she was being paid by the wartime lodgers. Ma replied that never in her wildest nightmares had she thought she would find herself married to a man who begrudged his children and his wife the very boots and shoes on their feet yet saw nothing wrong in spending money in a pub. He could do that without thinking twice. In fact he could do it without *thinking* at all. What sort of mind, Ma wanted to know (and wanted to know loudly) — what sort of mind would think that drink mattered more than the very shoes on his wife's feet…the boots on the feet of his children? What sort of mind…" Ma often managed a look of despair after having her repetitive say. Pop was left to splutter in self-defence but Ma always had the upper hand in that argument.

One day Lance Corporal Machin overheard one of these arguments and said he could steer some military boots Pop's way. Pop thanked him but refused. They wouldn't fit a child of my age and he didn't need any himself as, he said quite falsely, his work boots were provided by the railway company. Having introduced the notion of *steering things Pop's way*, however, the Lance Corporal generously offered other commodities from military stores to which he had access. He sounded like a pedlar in a market with a captive tourist as he eagerly listed possibilities. He seemed to have memorized a lengthy and tempting stock list.

"But that'd be stealin'," said Pop. "Oh no, I'm not getting' into the like o' that. There was this f'la up in Douglas got caught stealin' ration books at the Town Hall and that f'la was sent to gaol for years. He lost his job an' all. The f'la's job was to issue the ration books an' he thought he'd make a few bob on the side by sellin' some. Well he got caught. There was eyes out for the like o'him. He was hauled to court, he was sentenced to prison and he was called a *wretch* by the judge — a greedy traitor to his country. His wife left him an' took the kiddies…she couldn't stand all the gossip and the shame…so now this f'la's got nothin' but a gaol cell and no one to go home to when he gets out. Pinchin' things spells trouble so no thanks."

"Suit yourself," said Lance Corporal Wilf, "but yer fought in the mud in the last war and where did it get yer? Bullets was where it got yer. Was you ever given a 'thank you' for it as meant something? Yer got a few medals but yer can't live on medals. Yer didn't ask for anuvver war but yer gorrit just like the rest of us. We're all sufferin' from this war we didn't 'ave a say in startin' aren't we? We could all be done in by a bomb any night o' the week couldn't we? Bang! And we're gone. So I reckon we've earned a few comforts. They could be our last. Anyway, 'oose ter know? I'm not goin' ter tell. I'm not goin' ter kill the goose as lays the golden eggs. There's so much stuff in the stores they can't keep up with it. Goes out a lotta doors that does."

"Stuff? What sorta stuff?" asked Pop, intrigued despite his moral objections. He drew the Camp guard aside so I couldn't hear the rest of their larcenous conversation.

Soon after this discussion Pop produced a large bottle of whiskey from which, on special occasions, he measured sparing quantities. Ma gave some of it to Carlo and me on a teaspoon when we had high 'flu-like temperatures causing Pop to have minor explosions and issue lectures on waste. The whiskey tasted so vile on my ten-year-old tongue that I associated it with medicine and have had a life-long aversion to it.

Along with the whiskey a brand new pair of boots, smallest adult size, also appeared. With a bit of internal padding they were adapted to fit me. Since the boots had been illicitly acquired it was not thought morally proper for me to wear them on Sundays so they were put into everyday use at once. My feet slipped around inside them despite the padding. These boots were trouble. Pop should have listened harder to his conscience and then I wouldn't have ended up in gaol.

I occasionally mentioned our neighborhood Nazi when talking to other boys at school. They had asked questions. All I could tell them was that he had a wife and a daughter – when I was climbing some nearby cliffs

I had seen them walking together round the grounds of the estate the Government requisitioned for them. I mentioned that he wore a suit even on weekdays and that his wife and daughter always wore what Ma would call "nice clothes" – the kind she considered "Sunday best" to go to church in. I offered the opinion that he must be important to have a whole estate to live on with his family, to dress as if every day were a Sunday and to be guarded night and day by a platoon of soldiers.

"Let's go an' take a skeet at 'm, said Ronnie Skillicorn one day when I had been talking about them. "Let's," said Ronnie, "put the eye to 'm."

"You can't see anything," I told Ronnie. "The big gates are covered with sheets of metal so you can't see through the bars and there's a very high wall with sentry boxes all the way round. There's a soldier by each box all day and all night."

"You saw them from the cliffs?" Ronnie asked. I said yes and Ronnie said "Up them cliffs isn't near enough…not near close enough." He thought for a minute pressing his teeth down on his lower lip and then smiled the wicked smile that usually spelt trouble.

"Why don't we climb the wall and get a real good skeet at that Nazi f'la? Why don't we get in there and chuck stones at 'm all? Why don't we smash their windows with bricks? Why don't we friken the life out o' them?"

"How are you going to get in?" I asked scornfully. "The walls are so high we couldn't shin over them and, anyway, there's broken glass in concrete all the way along the top. I told you, there's guards all round too all day and all night. You'd get caught."

"Just you wait," said Ronnie, "I'll think of a way in. If you're too scared you can stay home."

"There's no way in except through the gate," I said but added something I regretted later, "but if you can think of one I'll come with you."

"So will I," said Brian McQueen, much to my surprise, since his general attitude to Ronnie was one of contempt. "Me too," said several others.

Ronnie couldn't bear to lose face so whatever his original intentions he couldn't back out now.

Nothing was said about the matter for some time but soon after I received my illicit boots, stuffed inside to make them fit me, Ronnie announced a plan. He had worked out how he could get us all over the wall. We just had to wait for the first moonless night. It helped that it was early winter and the sun set by tea-time. I ought to have backed out at this point but what boy would behave rationally when that meant being taunted at school as a coward? National governments behave as recklessly.

Inevitably the time for action arrived. A night was fixed upon for *Operation Well-Dressed Nazi*. Because it went dark early we would all still be up and not have to creep out of our beds at the risk of being caught before we could even leave the house.

I told Ma and Pop that Pierre Lamontagne had asked me to play at his house with his train set. He lived at the opposite end of Ballacray Road from us. Pop thought it would be educative for me to play with model trains. He smiled upon my new-found enthusiasm for railways and Ma hoped aloud that I would pick up more, and cleaner, French than Pop brought back from the Great War. Since Pierre's house was so close to ours I could go for an hour. I fled before either parent could change their mind, and quickly joined Pierre and the others who had decided to follow Ronnie's lead. They were assembled on that short promenade behind our house, the place from which I had seen the Spitfire crash when I was pedaling my toy car there.

Ronnie Skillicorn had brought some equipment with him: a small battery-powered detachable bicycle headlamp, a rope and a small but heavy anchor from his father's boat. He had tied the rope to the anchor. His supplies also included a tattered and dirty, but thick, woolen blanket that smelled rankly of dog. He was carrying it folded over one shoulder like a

Mexican serape. We all looked at these items dubiously wondering what use Ronnie proposed to put them to.

"Whose are them boots?" Ronnie asked just after I had arrived. "They look like yer Dad's." As the others stared at my footwear I told Ronnie to mind his own business. "I bet they *are* yer Dad's," said Ronnie and laughed.

He quicky got down to business and gave us our instructions. He would lead us to a place along the wall of the estate which sentries couldn't see from their boxes owing to the darkness of the night and a bend in the pathway down to the shore. He reckoned we would have about fifteen minutes after the last soldier marched from his sentry box along the wall down the path to the shore and back again until the next one did the same. To be safe we should all be over the wall in ten minutes. He told us how this would be accomplished but since no one had a watch the ten minutes would have to be estimated. We moved off on a roundabout route through bushes and undergrowth trying to make as little noise as possible until we were opposite that bend in the wall as it followed the path. When, from our hiding place in the bushes, we had seen a sentry march back up the path and round the corner to the sentry boxes we raced to the wall. It seemed a lot higher than ten feet to me now that I was standing up against it and had to get over it.

Ronnie was tall for his age and strong from hauling nets on his father's boat. He stood back a few feet from the wall and whirled the rope with the anchor fastened to it rather dangerously round his head like a cowboy with a lasso. When he had achieved the required momentum he let the anchor fly upward. It smashed through some of the broken glass set in concrete on top of the wall but lodged there, a make-shift grappling iron, with the rope trailing down. Whispering to us all to keep a careful lookout Ronnie tested the rope first by pulling on it and then shinned up it with the smelly dog blanket still over his shoulder. When he reached the top of the wall he threw the blanket over the broken glass meant to deter intruders and made the anchor a firmer fit. He urgently ordered us all to follow his lead. He shone his bicycle lamp on the wall but held it carefully downward so that it wouldn't be seen at a distance. Billy Teare climbed the rope like an avid pirate boarding a prize ship by walking his feet up the wall as he went up the rope hand over hand. Brian McQueen and Pierre Lamontagne followed but more slowly and with greater effort. As they dropped down into the estate via a convenient Traman Tree Ronnie urged the rest of us to hurry. A boy called Jimmy Gawne struggled up the rope and then it was Bobby Keruish's turn.

"Hurry up!" Ronnie whispered tensely from the top of the wall. "Gerra move on or they'll be at us!"

Once Bobby reached the top of the wall I started up it in my new boots. Since they were too big for me I found it hard to get my feet to walk up the wall as I climbed hand over hand in the manner of Billy Teare. I lost my grip and fell back to the ground when I was about halfway up the rope. Ronnie was hissing like Pop's engine by this time telling me fiercely that I would get them all caught. I started to climb the rope again, sore from my fall and finding it just as hard to manoeuvre my feet in the new boots, scraping them harshly against the rough stones and cement of the wall. I had labored back to about halfway up the rope with great effort when I was suddenly flooded with light. It was not the light of inner revelation that I experienced but the powerful beam of a small searchlight. I was blinded by it. The guards, no doubt alerted by the noise I was making trying to climb up Ronnie's rope, came down the rise and round the corner to see what was going on. Ronnie left me to my fate and dropped from the Traman Tree into the grounds of the estate to join the others. I was roughly hauled off the rope to which I was still clinging scraping my ungainly boots some more in the process.

"What you fink you're up to?" demanded a military voice after a military boot had landed on my backside.

"I just wanted to see what was over there," I whimpered, picking myself off the ground to which I had been sent sprawling by the military boot. The soldiers around me were angry. I thought they were going to beat me up.

"Pulley uvver one," said one of the soldiers, a sergeant I noted from his stripes. "Ow many of yer is 'ere, eh?"

"Just me," I said. I was going to be noble and protect the others. It was, after all, my fault that our enterprise had been discovered.

"D'yer want a clip owver yer ear? D'yer fink we're fuckin' blind?" asked the sergeant, a man Ma would certainly disapprove of for addressing a child the way he did.

"D'yer fink we couldn't see anuvver one o'yer on 'is wall wiv 'is light? 'Is light my be sma' but 'is light's parful enough ter pick out people onna coast o' Cumberland 'is light is so wha' yer fink a that 'en?"

If I understood his dense cockney speech correctly I doubted his claim but thought it prudent not to say so. I was very upset. I had caused our secret expedition to be discovered owing to my clumsy boots which any minute these soldiers might recognize as military issue and thus add stealing to my list of crimes. The last time I had been surrounded by a group of soldiers – during the Christmas tree foray – they had treated me with respect. This group seemed angry enough to commit violence. One had already kicked me. While I was feeling sorry for myself they found the dangling rope and the anchor on top of the wall to which it was attached. Next to the anchor of course they also saw the blanket draped over the broken glass. They returned to their interrogation.

"I'll arst you again," said the cockney sergeant, "nd I'll be noice and po-lite…ter start wiv. Now, ow many of yer is 'ere? A li'l bugger like you didn't get 'at anchor up 'ere all on yer own."

"There's just me," I insisted striving to be noble in the face of the evidence. "I was alone," I said, my voice suddenly low and hoarse, "honest I was."

"Izzat so?" said the sergeant mockingly. "'Ow d'yer expline 'iss lot 'en? Go on, 'ow d'yer expline 'em?"

He pointed back up the path where another small group of soldiers was coming from the direction of the nearest gate to the estate and with them trooped a downcast Ronnie Skillicorn and the others all looking as truculent as the young German soldiers who, later in the war, were sent to occupy the Island's prison camps.

"Yer was 'ere by yerself was yer?" said the sergeant in a mocking voice. "Funny 'is lot 'ad the same ardea as you did at the same time wannit? Great minds fink alike, tharrit? It's not full moon yet neiver."

"Pairhaps they were sent from Berlin to rarescue the Garman toff in thair," said a Scottish voice. "Pairhaps they came in a submarine that's oot thair in the bay. Pairhaps they're wee commandos who look like feckless laddies in short pants but are really grown as far as they'll go. Pairhaps they're a secret weapon – wee Gairman midgets trained to kill us all by the Gestapo – would that be it sergeant?"

More of these ironic pleasantries followed as other soldiers had a go at us. While they were uttered we were being marched back up the hill to a sentry box that had a phone. We heard the corporal call the local police. Had it not been so dark after the searchlight was switched off I'm sure I would have seen the color fade from the faces of my co-conspirators. I felt the blood drain from mine. I had a mental image of Pop in a frenzy when the police told him where I had been caught and what I had been doing while he thought I was playing with trains and Ma hoped I was picking up some respectable French.

We were driven, under guard, to the Police Station in Ramsey in the back of a small military truck, a soldier with a rifle guarding us, and I remembered Jakob's account of his journey in a similar vehicle to the Birmingham Railway Station on his way to that transit camp. I was beginning to know what it felt like to be a prisoner suddenly snatched from the relative safety of private life by a force that couldn't be resisted.

Ramsey Police Station occupies a building dating back to the Eighteenth Century but we weren't in any mood to appreciate its rational proportions, its tall elegant windows, its Georgian simplicity of line when the soldier in the truck handed us over to a police reception committee consisting of a sergeant and two constables. To my ten-year-old eyes the Station looked more like an ogre's castle. I feared we were going to be herded into the cells which I imagined were like dungeons or even the oubliettes of Peel Castle on the Island's west coast where in days of yore prisoners were left without food or water to be drowned, ultimately, by the salt incoming tide which flowed into those terrible places along channels built for the purpose. At best we would be held until a judge in a wig came to try us.

What happened in fact was that we were taken into an institutionally-painted room – the lower half of its walls a dull green and the upper half off-white with a narrow black band between. The room contained some wooden chairs and, at the front, a tall desk. It looked like a small classroom but without a blackboard. We were ordered to sit on the uncomfortable chairs while the sergeant stood behind the desk. The two constables placed themselves disturbingly close to us. The sergeant opened the proceedings by demanding an explanation of our wall-scaling. What had we intended to do once we had got over the wall? Didn't we know that we should have been nowhere near that place and especially at night? That it was off limits to the public? No one spoke. The sergeant began to shout at us and the constables loomed over us and began to shout too, ordering us to answer the sergeant's questions. Ronnie Skillicorn looked resolutely surly and said nothing. Most of us flinched and Jimmy Gawne started to howl like the Skillicorn dog whose favorite blanket we had used to cover the glass on top of the wall.

"Shut up!!!" yelled the sergeant. "Tell us what you were all doing up there or else…"

It wasn't the time to tell the sergeant that, logically, we couldn't do both.

Trying to summon a little dignity Brian McQueen said that we just wanted to get a closer look at the prisoners kept on the estate. That was all. We were just curious. He seemed to have forgotten that we were trespassing after dark.

"No we wasn't curious!" said Ronnie Skillicorn loudly. "We was going to chuck bricks at them Nazi buggers an' smash their windows an' friken them to death!"

"We didn't mean any harm," I found myself cravenly whining to try to undo the damage Ronnie's words must be causing.

"So…breaching military security with intent to inflict injury on the detainees and to damage property isn't harm is it? What would harm be? Blowing them up? Poisoning their food? Mowing them all down with a Bren gun? Why shouldn't I put all you lot in the cells and charge you with trespassing on military premises? Trespassing with intent to inflict grievous bodily harm? Why shouldn't I? Tell me why I shouldn't."

Wisely no one accepted this dangerous invitation. Jimmy Gawne geared down from howling to sniveling at the mention of the cells.

"I'll tell you what I'm going to do," said the sergeant after a theatrical pause. "I'm going to have all your fathers down here to collect you. I'm going to tell each male parent what you have done. I'm going to tell them that if they can't keep you all under control I'll bring *them* back to explain why in front of a magistrate. They won't like that. You've dropped them in it, see? When they get you home I dare say you won't like what they'll do. Now, I want all your names and addresses…give them to the constables here. Try any funny business like giving a false name or a false address and I'll have you in the cells so fast you won't know what hit you. You all got it?"

After making this announcement the sergeant had us all write out our addresses on slips of paper and went off to carry out his plan. The two constables remained to supervise us. Of course, in those days, none of the parents had a phone so the sergeant sent another policeman on a motorbike to spread the news. After a while the fathers straggled in, in varying degrees of rage. Growling feral threats they bore their fearful off-spring away. Ronnie Skillicorn's Dad was too drunk to appear so he was taken home and beaten by a violent lout of an elder brother. When he had sobered up his father beat him again for losing a valuable anchor, which the soldiers had forfeited. I received a "tanning" made all the more severe because Pop had to try to explain to the police how I came to be wearing a pair of what looked like military issue boots. I had obliged him to tell a string of lies involving my military brother Ronald. Ma kept out of the way until the tanning was over and then offered me a hot drink in a cup. In view of the rationing it could have been acorn tea.

I nurtured a sense of grievance for some time. When I told my tale at length to Jakob, expecting him to sympathize with me as a fellow sufferer from unfeeling and unjust authority, I was mortified when all he could do was laugh.

"What's so funny?" I demanded, angry and upset.

The answer was another fit of laughter. I began to think that imprisonment was making Jakob hard and unfeeling.

CHAPTER EIGHTEEN

It was the murder at the Mooragh Camp that made me change my mind about Jakob's state of sensitivity. But first I should explain Pop's rather sudden change of attitude about me working on the farm even in proximity to Jakob. It took a while for Pop to "simmer down" after "letting off steam" over the fracas with the military and the police. (Ma tended to describe Pop's emotional state in terms of the boiling water that drove his train). When he had regained his cool, so to speak, Pop said something that amazed me. He actually said he thought I was better off on the farm than getting "mixed up with the likes a that Skillicorn kid."

"They're ne'er do wells the lot of 'm. They live in a pig stye and it's always to the fists and the fight when they've had a drop. You keep away from that crew."

I could hardly believe what I had heard so I asked Pop if he meant what he had said – that I would be better off on the farm when I had time to spare.

"Well you wouldn't be getting up to much mischief there – not the mischief that brings the police to the door any rate. And you'd better not, neither. I hear you get into trouble there an' it's the last you'll see of the place."

For the sake of consistency with previous declarations of his he added, "That doesn't mean you don't have eyes at the back of your head for this Jaycob you're always on about in case that f'la tries somethin' funny. Herman's a f'la you've got to watch. If he thinks you're not looking he'll be at you like the hawk on the rabbit."

There was no point in arguing Jakob's case again when Pop's new attitude toward the farm meant in practice that I could spend more time there than I had before. The contraband boots that had caused Pop so much trouble with the police would be less in public view if I were at the farm instead of in town or even rambling through the glen or along the brooghs. Who knows who I might meet? Pop had heard enough bad jokes about "booty."

When I next arrived at the farm with Uncle Tom in his truck I told him I wanted to let Jakob know right away that I could be there more often.

"He's not…er, he isn't here," said Tom hesitantly.

"Why? Is he ill? Have the people at the Camp stopped him coming to the farm?"

I fearfully imagined all manner of occurrences that could keep Jakob away, all of them catastrophic though none of them involved murder.

"There's been trouble mighty at the Camp. It was all in the paper. Didn't ya put a sight on it?"

"I don't read the paper. I'm not old enough."

I was surprised that Tom thought otherwise. Only grownups read newspapers. I wouldn't be able to understand a lot of the words in them. Tom regarded me as something of a prodigy perhaps because of that "BBC voice" Ma was so proud of. Also he had been with Johnny so long that his standards of educational ability weren't high.

"Well if yer haven't read about it I'm not sure it's telling' yer I should be at."

"Why not? What's happened. Is he dead?"

My voice rose in panic as that thought struck me like a punch in the stomach. Before Tom could answer I went on hysterically, "Was he shot? Did a guard shoot him trying to escape? Was it Lance Corporal Machin? He said he'd shoot a prisoner if he tried to get away. He said orders is orders and he'd have to shoot. Was it the police? Why was Jakob trying to escape? He never said he was going to escape. Why did he try?"

My recent encounter with the law had given me a low opinion of it. The police shouted at children. They got their fathers to thrash them. They were pitiless. I wouldn't put it past them to shoot a prisoner trying to escape. As my fevered brain raced I thought it more likely that the police had shot Jakob than that a soldier had in spite of the fact that the prisoners were guarded by soldiers with rifles and the police didn't carry guns. Why had Jakob tried to escape? Why? Why? I started to cry.

"Hey, calm down! Calm down lad," said Tom amazed at my reaction. He had forgotten the emotional extremism of children.

"There's nothin' the like o' that doin' at all, at all. There's been trouble at the Camp. A man there been done in…killed…murdered."

"Why are they blaming Jakob?"

"Who said folk were blaming Jaycob?"

"You did…that's what you meant."

"Who says so?"

"I thought that's why you didn't want to tell me about it…about what it said in the newspaper."

"Well, you're wrong. No one's blaming Jaycob and he hasn't gone daft and run off. You've let yer imagination run away with yer at a gallop. The prisoners can't leave the Camp till them f'las runnin' the place 'ave sorted it all out. They've got to decide what ter do wi' the murderer is all I know of. It's made'm all worry so bad they've 'ad ter sit down and think what ter do fer the best before lettin' any o' the prisoners out again. Somethin' like this 'as never 'appened before."

"They'll blame it all on Jakob. I know they will."

"Who says so?"

"I just know," I replied as if I possessed occult knowledge. I began to weep again.

"Liz!" Tom shouted as she emerged from the dairy. "Will yer come 'ere and tell this lad nothin's goin' to 'appen to Jaycob. The lad says Jaycob's goin' ter be blamed for the trouble at Camp. Nothin' I say makes any difference."

"What did you have to go and tell him for?" Liz demanded. "You know kids imagine all sorts."

"Don't you worry," said Liz, as I got out of the truck. "Jaycob will be back when it's all calmed down, you'll see. So now your Dad says you can come here more often we'll have to find you extra work to do. How would you like to muck out the cows first?"

The look on my face made her laugh.

"I was joking," she said. "You can milk the cows instead…Johnny's busy."

I must say I found such levity at this time in very poor taste. Who knew what Jakob might be suffering? The Talbots were supposed to be his friends yet they didn't appear to be in the least bit worried. I'd worry enough for all of us. Perhaps that would help. Worrying was something I was good at.

❧

"Eh, look at this!" Pop held out the local paper for Ma to read the head-line. "Murder at the Mooragh," said Ma. Intrigued, she took the paper from Pop and quickly read the accompanying article.

"I know all about what's in there," I said dully, the triumphant tone with which I had announced the fall of the Spitfire notably absent.

"Aunty Liz says they're not but they are…they're blaming Jakob for it and it's not fair!" I was close to tears. "He didn't do it."

"See!" Pop exclaimed. "What did I tell you? Never let your guard down or a Herman'll have you quick as a wink! I've warned you about this f'la times out of number but you take not the slightest bit of notice. You've kept seeing him at the farm but that f'la's not safe. It was only a matter of time before he did somebody in. It could have been you! Now look what he's been and gone and done! You never listen!"

"Have you finished?" asked Ma with some heat.

"Well, I'm right aren't I?" Pop responded obviously bewildered by Ma's tone.

Before Ma could reply Bessie walked in without having either knocked on the door or rang the bell as was her habit. She was holding a copy of the local paper.

"Have you seen this?" she asked excitedly as she waved it about. Her eye fell on the paper in Ma's hand.

"Have you read what's in it?" Before Ma had time to reply she ploughed on: "It's what I've always said and said till I'm blue in the face…they're a murdering, thieving lot as 'd cut all our throats if they got past the wire. I bet this Jaycob yer think so much on 'as got 'is 'ands red in this. I'm warnin' yer," she said, looking at me with raised eyebrows and nodding head, "I'm warnin' yer if 'e gets away wi' this 'e'll 'ave 'is bony fingers round yer throat and 'e'll squeeze yer windpipe till its shut and yer eyes are out of yer 'ead on stalks like organ stops and yer as dead as a doornail!"

"For once Bessie's right," said Pop, startling her into temporary silence.

"Have either of you actually read what's in the paper? Have you got beyond the headline?" asked Ma.

"Why?" Pop asked, puzzled.

"Because if you had," Ma replied with some heat, "you wouldn't both be blathering away about Erik's friend. He isn't even mentioned in the paper. They've got someone for the murder. It says in the paper he's a Finn. It doesn't give his name but Erik's friend is from Austria. Austria's nowhere near Finland. At least it wasn't when I was at school."

Ma had been top of her class in Geography so she knew the whereabouts of Finns and Finland.

Both Pop and Bessie felt they had to save face.

"They don't put everything they know in the paper," said Bessie. "Not in a war they don't. It could be that Jaycob f'la's guilty as sin but they aren't saying. They'll 'ave their reasons."

She drew in her breath sharply to reinforce her declaration. The look on her face suggested Ma was hopelessly naïve to be so unaware of government strategy.

"Right," said Pop, backing Bessie for the second time in five minutes. "They've got their reason" he went on, actually quoting her. "I bet this f'la never turns up to fork a bale o'hay or pick a turnip again. They'll be runnin' him over to the mainland to hang him by the neck until he's dead. Hermans don't change. You can be damn thankful me lad," he continued turning to me, "thankful he didn't bump you off when he had the chance."

"So," said Ma theatrically, "the whole story in the paper's a pack of lies is it?" They've just made up a story about a Finn when the real murderer's an Austrian. And does it work the other way? Is Hitler really a Finn? Are the papers saying he's an Austrian just to fool us? What's the point?"

"To keep us in the dark," said Bessie.

"Why?" asked Ma.

"It wouldn't do for us to know too much in a war."

"Why not?"

"It's wartime," said Bessie unhelpfully.

"So you don't believe anything you read in the paper unless it suits you?"

"I never said that," Bessie replied sharply.

"Well how do you know what's true and what isn't?"

"I just do. It's a sixth sense…a gift."

"And I bet I know how it works," said Ma. "Anything in the paper that fits what you want to believe is the truth and everything that doesn't is lies or propaganda."

"It's time for Willie's dinner," said Bessie abruptly and left. Angry contradiction from Ma was something new to her.

"Why did you take after Bessie like that?" asked Pop.

"That's rich coming from you. You can hardly be civil to her most of the time. You're always calling her a crackpot. Then when she comes out with something really daft you tell her she's right. Here! Read the paper before you go throwing accusations about. They've got no reason to hide the truth about what happened in the Camp."

Pop scanned the newspaper report in a cursory manner then went out to fetch a bucket of coal from the coalhouse in the back yard. I had told Uncle Tom that I didn't read the newspaper but now I thought it was time to try. I picked the paper up from where Pop had dropped it and to my surprise found that I could understand at least the gist of what I read.

It seemed that there were these people from Finland in the Camp – sailors mainly, merchant seamen arrested in British ports after they had unwisely and publicly voiced support for Hitler because he was a potential ally of their country against the Russians. I didn't know anything about these people…Jakob had never mentioned them. I had thought everyone in the Camp was Jewish like himself. The newspaper story said that one of these Finnish sailors had thrown a bucket of dirty water over another of the same group. That had led to a fight between the two. The man who had had the water poured over him evidently pulled out a knife and stabbed the man who had poured it. The stabbing victim died right there on the spot "in a pool of blood" as the paper said theatrically. I remembered the line "a pool of clotted gore" that either I had read somewhere or that I had met in one of those Friday readings at school and I shivered.

The guards had seized the man with the knife and had eventually wheeled the body away on a small handcart. I had a vivid image of the victimizer-become-victim sprawled in death, his arms dangling loosely down either side of that small cart – perhaps like the narrow one the window cleaner, Syd Jennings, who always had a cigarette hanging out of the corner of his mouth, pushed round with his ladders on it. Mentally I saw the blood oozing through the dead man's shirt, his eyes still open but fixed, the brutal bullying face frozen in sudden horror. The man – a sort of adult Finnish version of Ronnie Skillicorn – had swaggered over with his bucket of filthy water to humiliate his fellow prisoner but that prisoner had had enough and the bully had gasped in agony and disbelief as the knife was shoved deep into him.

I retailed this story, with embellishments, to Pop later to make sure he understood the uncontroverted facts but he seemed reluctant to accept them.

"You wait…you'll see. That Jaycob f'la is behind this. It'll all come out at last. You just have to wait long enough."

Having just expanded my farm privileges Pop wanted now to revoke them once Jakob returned to work claiming to be protecting me from a murderer. Ma prevented him.

"This friend of Erik's had nothing to do with any of this," she said. "We don't know him…but fair's fair. He's done nothing to Erik except talk to him. Lizzie and Tom say he's the salt of the earth…a man who in peace time we'd be honored to know. The newspaper article is clear about who is guilty and the Editor has no reason to lie. Ask him yourself if you don't believe me. You drink with him often enough. I'm not getting into a silly quarrel with Tom and Liz all over again. Erik's been really upset at all this and I'm not having you making things worse by being too pig-headed to admit you're wrong."

Pop beat a strategic retreat behind the *Daily Expres,* the articles in which were less controversial. I remained anxious all week worried that Jakob might not have been allowed to return to the farm. As I said, I was good at worrying. Top of the class.

I wanted to know more about the murder than had been printed in the paper so I asked Lance Corporal Machin. He was no help at all.

"My lips are sealed," he said.

"What does that mean?"

"It means we've all been ordered not to blab about the murder, that is what it means so I can't say anything."

I was anxious until my next visit to the farm. "Guess who's here," said Aunty Liz as soon as she saw me getting out of the truck.

Jakob?" I shouted. "Where is he?"

"He's doing your job mucking out the cows."

I rushed to see him. I told him in a torrent all that I had feared when I heard the news about the murder. I omitted Pop and Bessie from the account but was careful to tell him that Ma had never believed him guilty of murder.

"Well, that's very nice," he replied "but no one ever accused me of murder except, of course, in one or two of the operas I have performed in. I did however, see the murder and it wasn't something you'd want to see again in real life."

"You saw the man with the knife stuck in him?"

"Unfortunately yes. The man who was killed was a bully and a brute. Nobody liked him. But isn't that sad – nobody liking you? Everyone needs friends – isn't that so? This Finnish sailor must have been an unhappy man to be always pushing other people around. The look on his face when this man he was bullying suddenly produced a knife and stabbed him – that look was horrible. He just couldn't believe what had happened. He tried to say something. He looked terrified – then he fell to the ground bleeding badly. The man who had done the stabbing was so shocked at what he had done so suddenly that he started to scream. He made such a noise that the guards came running. They took him away shouting and raving like a mad man."

Jakob shook his head. He had tears in his eyes. I was embarrassed. Grown men didn't cry – at least the ones I knew didn't, not in public anyway. But I realized that being locked away had not made Jakob hard as I had feared when he laughed at my story about my boots. He felt for this camp bully because of his friendlessness and the way he had met his death and he obviously felt for the man who had wielded the knife who hadn't meant to harm anyone but who had been provoked once too often.

Now I began to worry about Jakob's safety in the Camp – an issue that had never occurred to me before. I asked him if this kind of violence happened a lot.

"No, it doesn't. Most of the people there are like me…leading peaceful and productive lives until we were arrested and treated so roughly as I've told you. That hasn't made us violent but it has made a lot of us bitter. These sailors are different from the rest of us. They are not Jewish and unlike most of us they are uneducated. Some come from Finland and others from Holland. They were arrested because they support Hitler and said so in public. They are noisy and foolish. They often fight among themselves but the rest of us stay away from them just as we stayed away from the British fascists…the "black shirts" as they are called. They tried to make trouble when they came so they were taken away to another camp where they keep criminals – at least that is what people in the Camp are saying. This murder has shaken everyone…the guards as much as the rest of us."

I was most relieved to hear that murder was a terrible exception to camp routine.

"You laughed when I told you how I was caught and sent to the Police Station so I thought you didn't care about anything any more."

"I see," said Jakob, "and now?"

I didn't reply but stood looking foolish, scraping the toe of one boot about in the dried mud of the farm street.

Jakob looked down at me for a moment then knelt and gave me a warm hug. I didn't feel embarrassed as I would have done had an uncle broken the habit of a lifetime and embraced me. I felt happy that a serious misunderstanding had been sorted out and happier still that Jakob had been returned to the farm uninvolved in the murder except as a worried spectator.

"Opera singers kill people onstage with knives all the time," said Jakob, "but that is make-believe like those games in the woods you tell me about. The real thing is not something to sing about…"

I told Ma of Jakob's account of his horrifying experience as witness to the killing.

"He seems to be a sensitive person," she said, having evidently forgotten her previous nightmare imaginings.

Pop, who hadn't, rattled the newspaper he was reading but said nothing then. Later he came to warn me.

"This f'la could be pulling the wool over your eyes. This f'la could be planning to *escape.*"

If Pop couldn't reasonably convict Jakob of murder he was determined to convict him of something. Escape was the next best thing. He placed a heavy emphasis on the word.

"One o' these fine days, Sonny Jim, you'll see…you'll wake up and you'll find him gone. E'll 'ave flown the coop and be bobbin' about in the Irish Sea in a stolen boat, before anyone notices and that will be that. Maybe then you'll come to your senses."

CHAPTER NINETEEN

I WAS ON MY WAY TO SCHOOL NOT LONG AFTER THE MURDER AT THE Camp, early for once, when I met Shoveller Mylecraine. I once thought "Shoveller" was the name his parents had given him and speculated upon their sanity. Why would his mother and father saddle a child with a name like that? Why couldn't they have called him Jim or Bob or Dan or Billy or something else recognizable as a name for a child? "Shoveller" seemed to me like a pet name for a mole. When eventually I asked Pop about it he said it was a nickname. Shoveller had been a fireman on the railway. His job was to shovel coal into the firebox to heat the engine's boiler so his workmates began to call him "Shoveller" and the name stuck. His parents had actually christened him "Godred" but he preferred the nickname other railway workers had bestowed upon him. I asked Pop why, since he drove the engine, people at work didn't call him "Driver." "Because they call me "Smiler" he said.

Smiler? I must have looked amazed. Pop wasn't a dour domestic tyrant though he did assert himself upon such occasions as Ma permitted but he didn't go about the house conspicuously smiling either. He must really put himself out, I thought, when dealing with the public – like the toupeed manager of the *Plaza* movie house whom he despised.

Shoveller had to leave the railway before normal retirement age owing to a heart attack. He wasn't a resourceful man. He had never learned to read – he seemed to have managed not to go to school at all – and he didn't have a garden nor was he interested in renting a garden plot like Pop. Digging would be bad for his heart he said. Fishing was evidently not an attractive alternative; he had no hobbies so he didn't know what to do with all the time now at his disposal. He was to be found any day of the week from an early hour (his work had accustomed him to rising early) wandering aimlessly about the town in a dark blue pinstriped suit in which he looked entirely out of place. Mrs. Shoveller, having seen him for years wearing oily overalls, his face black with coal dust, insisted that he begin each new day with a thorough wash and that he pass each new day in what had once been his Sunday suit. He had long boring stories of his railway adventures to tell anyone he could trap into listening to them. The morning he approached me on my way to school I thought he wanted to launch into one of these tedious epics. I was prepared to tell him that I couldn't stop to talk since I would be late to school but for once he didn't want to recreate his past. For once the present was too much with him.

"Tell yer Dad," he said in obvious excitement, "that prisoners 'ave escaped from the Mooragh. They've swiped oul Skillicorn's boat in the night and buggered off with it."

"They stole Ronnie Skillicorn's Dad's boat?" I asked in awe.

"The very same," said Shoveller. "Tell yer Dad." He walked off quickly, a man with a sudden mission – to spread the news.

I spent the rest of the walk to school trying to digest what I'd been told. Whoever had made off with the Skillicorn boat obviously didn't know Skillicorn senior. He'd murder whoever had done it when he got hold of them. But then I thought how could Ronnie's violent father wreak vengeance when he was stranded on shore? But of course. He would borrow someone else's boat, using threats if persuasion failed, and set off in pursuit. By now he was probably already miles from land bearing down on the escaping prisoners. I wouldn't want to be one of them when Ronnie's Dad hove into view yelling in Manx and wielding a boat hook.

When I reached the school playground there was a mob of children standing round Ronnie Skillicorn who was recounting the night time theft of his father's boat. He described his father's epic Viking rage, his pungent vow to pursue the alien thieves and dispossess them of their private parts. His blood red promises of vengeance were uttered in the foulest language. Even Ronnie had been amazed at the depth of his father's feelings and the reach of his vocabulary. No one wanted to go into their classes when the bell rang. Everyone was seized by the excitement of the event, which Ronnie conveyed with unusual eloquence. The Head had to send out Harry Clegg to round us up.

Of course, I knew at once that when Pop heard of the theft he would declare that Jakob was behind it. He had, after all, not long ago predicted that I would wake up one morning to find that Jakob had fled. Having discounted such a notion at that time I worried now that Pop's prediction might have come true after all. I couldn't focus on the lessons in school that day. My mind wandered over white crests, circling gulls, jagged reefs and tall sinister cliffs. I skimmed the waves with the Stormy Petrel, I peered around the watery world like a myopic seal, I imagined Jakob bobbing about in the Irish Sea helpless as an Irish saint in a wattle coracle with the spray hanging over his stolen boat and the waves threatening to overwhelm it. I imagined him struggling to keep control of the rudder. What, after all, did a Jewish opera singer from land-locked Austria know about the management of a fishing boat in rough water? I wish I had told him about Skillicorn senior and his violent temper. Our exasperated teacher made me stand in a corner facing the wall as punishment for defiance when I failed to answer her repeated questions. I couldn't explain to her why my mind was, quite literally, at sea.

When, at last, the school day ended I raced home to see if there was any more news about the escape. I had hoped someone would have told Ma more than I knew but she wasn't in the house. Ruby, one of the Air Force wives who wore lipstick to match her name, told me that Ma had gone next door to Mrs. Corcoran's house. Too worked up to wait till she came home I rang Mrs. Corcoran's doorbell.

"Hello stranger," Mrs. Corcoran said when she answered it. "I seem to be popular today. Come in and join the party."

Puzzled by Mrs. Corcoran's unusually high spirits I followed her into her living room – so much tidier than ours, polished, better furnished, not a speck of dust in sight, all the china safely stowed in a china cabinet like money at the bank. There I found not only Ma but Bessie and Mrs. Corcoran's neighbor on the other side, a teacher at the grammar school called Mrs. White. She had unfortunately been christened Lillian but then her parents couldn't have foreseen she would marry a man called White and become locally known (though not in her presence) as *Lilywhite,* like a comic adjective. Mrs. Corcoran's brother Brian was there too. He pronounced his name *Bree-an* though no one else did. He was a coast guard and it was evident that my entrance had caused him to break off in the middle of a narrative.

"Come and sit here," said Ma making a place for me on the sofa where she was sitting. "Mr. Kissack was just telling us all about an escape from the Mooragh Camp."

Brian Kissack, it transpired later, had been told not to tell anyone anything but under the influence of his sister's hospitality and the flattering attention of a group of women eager for drama he had succumbed to temptation.

"As I was sayin', they stole oul Skillicorn's boat an..."

"I heard that this morning. Shoveller told me when I was going to school. He said to tell Pop. In the playground Ronnie Skillicorn said that..."

Bessie told me to shut up. If I wanted to hear the whole story I'd better keep quiet and not interrupt otherwise I could turn round and march right back out of the house.

"They stole Dickie Skillicorn's boat," Brian repeated raising his voice slightly and giving me an '*or else*' look. "Whover they were they were off in the dark of the night. Dicky comes down to the harbor at first light to get the boat ready for the fishin' and he stands there on the quay and he can't believe what his eyes are tellin' him. Somethin's not right. It takes a few minutes and then he realizes – there's no boat. It's gone! It's always there but now it's gone. Dickie starts to yell and curse mighty stannin' there on the quay an' shoutin' 'Where's me boat? Where's me bloody boat? Who's took me effing boat?'…ya know how ready he is with the language. Well he runs back home like he's got fireworks stuffed up his jersey and he sends his kids all over the harbor to look for the boat in case it's slipped rope and drifted up with the tide toward the river. But the kids can't find it. Not a sign! It's really gone. So Dickie's out there roarin' and yellin' like a chile whose toys have been swiped. Then he heads for Johnny Joughan the Harbor Master but Johnny's not down at work yet so he comes to us in the Coast Guard office all worked up and he says his boat's been took. He wants the Coast Guard to get it back. Well, we say, we'll do what we can and we phone the Mooragh Camp to see if they're missin' any f'las as might have took the boat and they say they aren't missin' any but 'ow they know without goin' ter look and see is a mystery ter me. We tell Dickie this but e's not 'avin' it. 'Who else,' says he, 'who else would want ter steal a boat? D'ye think a f'la's borrered it ter do a mornin's fishin?' He didn't exactly use those words…ya know his language…but that's what he meant in polite company."

I considered telling everyone what his actual words had been as quoted by his son in impolite company but decided not to. I wanted to hear the whole story as much as everyone else in the room.

"What happened then Mr. Kissack?" asked Lilywhite, caught up in the drama.

"We've got Dickie Skillicorn stampin' up and down the Coast Guard office on the second floor, turnin' the air blue with his swearin'. There's Fred Kermeeen tryin' to calm 'im down…Fred's always the one fer keepin' the peace. Fred asks Dickie if e's sure 'e tied the boat up and if so where exactly 'e tied it but Dickie's not 'avin' any o' this. 'E says…with a lot more of his bad language…'D'ye think I'm not knowin' where I tied up me own boat? Are ye hintin' I was so far gone in drink that I only imagined I'd tied it up? I tied it up where I always do o' course. It's not theer,' he says, 'an if yer don't believe me then get off yer fat arses and go and take a skeet for yerself and while yer at it,' says he, 'yer can all jump in the harbor.' Well this isn't the way Dickie's goin' ter get any 'elp from the Coast Guard but Dickie's stupit enough to go carryin' on like the blatherskite he is when the phone rings. I was the one who answered it. It's the Camp callin.' They say they've just 'ad a look and it seems there's three prisoners missin.' Three sailors, that is. So they think that might be where the boat's gone. We tells this to Dickie and 'e says 'Isn't that what I've been sayin' to you buggers since I walked up them stairs?' Sorry that just slipped out. It's hard not to swear when you're tellin' what Dicky said. We say to Dickie there's an officer from the Camp on his way over to talk to 'm. Dickie says 'Is he goin' ter get me boat back or not?' and we say 'We don't know…maybe…let's wait and see.'

Brian paused at this point in his lengthy narrative to sip some of his sister's pre-war sherry. I felt like telling him to get on with the story instead of making a meal of it but he was determined to take his time and the women in the audience – Bessie included – were prepared to wait. Having an appreciative group of women – one which included an educated teacher like Lilywhite – hang on his every word, including the bad ones, was a new and heady experience for Coast Guard *Bree-an* and he was obviously making the most of it.

"Well," says Brian resuming his story after putting his empty glass down on an occasional table, "this officer arrives in a bit of a rush." Brian stopped again when his sister began to refill his glass. "The officer 'ad worked up quite a head of steam (I thought of Pop) over the guards not even knowin' the aliens had got out and telling us no one was missing when three of 'm were. The officer asks 'oose boat's been stolen and Dicky o' course says 'mine' and then he's askin' what this Captain's goin' ter do to get it back. The Captain doesn't seem to like Dicky's tone of voice as Dicky seems to be blamin' im for losin' his boat. 'I'm sorry about your boat,' says the Captain in one of those English voices that seem to be tellin' yer an idiot for leavin' it lyin' about to get stole, 'but there are more serious matters to consider. Prisoners have escaped.'

"You know Dickie…e's not 'avin' some Englishman go all hoity-toity on 'im. 'Listen ter me yussir,' says he, poking this Captain f'la in the chest with a finger thick as a cable and black as in the inside of a drainpipe, 'I want me boat back. That's 'ow I mak' a livin' an' there's nothin' more important to the likes o'me an I'm tellin' yer that for nothin'. 'Well yes there is, actually,' says this Captain in his fancy English voice as he backed off from that finger o' Dickie's and him lookin' at Dickie as if he's just crawled out of the seaweed. 'There's a war on,' says the Captain. 'Prisoners have escaped. That's a serious safety issue here compared to which…' 'Compared to nothing,' says Dickie, getting' really mad now. 'I want me boat and I want ter know how ye's goin' ter gerrit back or ye's can pay me so's I can buy another one.' 'The Army,' says the Captain lookin' at Dickie now like he's right off his rocker, 'the Army doesn't compensate fishermen for boats lost.' 'What d'yer mean *lost?*' yells Dickie he's so wild, 'that boat wasn't *lost* – it was stole by foreigners ye's supposed ter keep locked up!!' 'That's not yet been proven,' says the Captain. Well, that was the last straw. Dickie really boiled over. Before any of us can stop him he punches the Captain on the nose with that big dirty nieve of his and knocks him flat on the carpet right there in the Coast Guard office. The blood's runnin' from the Captain's nose like a river in spate an' he doesn't seem to know where he is any more."

Brian was out of breath telling this part of his tale so he stopped to take a few more sips of sherry. His sister gave him a biscuit to go with them. While he took a little break Bessie entertained the company with her well-known views about alien prisoners. Lilywhite, who visited the Mooragh Camp regularly to help with the library there, firmly disagreed.

"They're just like you and I and all the people we know, Bessie," she said. "They're just ordinary people caught up in a war they had nothing to do with. But that's not quite true," she added on reflection, "some of them are much better than ordinary. Some of them are quite superior people."

Bessie in no way considered herself ordinary and was about to say so…I could tell from the way she held herself suddenly erect like a rooster about to crow…but Brian intimated he was now ready to begin the next phase of what was turning out to be a saga worthy of Shoveller at his most expansive.

"Turns out," Brian went on, "the Captain's not by himself. He's got a coupla military police with him…escapes are their trade. When they hear all the noise Dicky's making they come up the stairs to the second floor three at a time ter see what's what. They see the Captain bleedin' on the floor and Dickie rubbin' 'is fist and snortin' like the bull that just wrecked the china shop. Well these police f'las are across the room like a terrier after a rat…they're big strong f'las as made Dickie look small. They'ave him in handcuffs before yer can blink yer eye. So to end it all there's Dickie bein' hauled off ter the cop shop roarin' 'is 'ead off, there's the District Nurse called ter look after the Captain whose still on the floor babblin' about someone called Sylvia, and Dickie's boat, *The Cushag*, is still out at sea somewhere with three escaped aliens on it and no one yet the wiser where they are, where they're goin', or how they got out o' the Camp in the first place. And that's just 'ow the day began. We've spent the rest of it organizing a search for the boat."

"What's going to happen to Mr. Skillicorn?" asked Lilywhite in her formal way.

"'E's being charged with assault and disturbing the peace and 'e's being kept in a police cell till 'e calms down and sees sense and promises to behave himself."

A general discussion of Dickie ensued the majority declaring him a boor, a drunkard, a bully and a lout for whom prison was too good. Lilywhite demurred.

"Who knows?" she said, "he may have a kind heart. Who knows what he has had to endure in his life? And how would any of us behave if someone suddenly robbed us of our livelihood quite literally overnight? It's easy to blame and condemn but one should resist the temptation."

We all left Mrs. Corcoran's house subdued and sheepish after this admonition but the mood soon wore off.

"Who does she think she is preaching us all a sermon? Who gave her a pulpit for Christmas?" Bessie, who never resisted the temptation to blame others, demanded once Lilywhite had returned to her own house.

Of course, when Pop came home from work Ma told him the whole story and I added details I had heard at school.

"I've been hearin' about it all day," said Pop. "They're talkin' about it up in Douglas as well as down here. I hadn't heard about what Dickie got up to with the coast guards though. Serves him right they carted him off to the lock-up. He needs to be took to the loony bin that one. You don't go round punching Army officers when you need their help and they don't act just the way you want 'm to. What did Dickie think this Captain f'la was going' ter do? Pull out a big bag o'money and pay him for his boat right then and there? Dicky's got booze where his brains should be… always was like that. Musta been dropped on his head when he was a kid."

The subject of escape, which I thought would lead Pop to a lengthy indictment of Jakob, instead caused him to reminisce about Island escapes during the Great War.

"They had aliens locked up on the Island then as well as now," he said, preparing to reminisce for my benefit. "When I was away at the war there was this great big camp at Knockaloe, next door to Peel up on a hillside. They put all the aliens in this one camp instead of sharing 'm around the way they do now. There was close to thirty thousand of 'm in this one place. They turned this hillside into a sorta town for aliens. This camp was so big they built a railway into it. It was so big this place that prisoners were always getting' out of it. One a them got as far as Kirk Michael and held a knife to the throat o' the village bobby…that f'la was lucky the Army turned up just in time. Another f'la was found out at Kirk Bride by a fifteen-year-old lad who brought this alien f'la in to Ramsey. There was a f'la put in prison for spreading a rumor that thousands of aliens had escaped and was tearin' Douglas apart. Most of the ones who got out just wanted a bit of freedom for a while. They wanted to walk about wherever they liked and have a decent meal. There was a woman here in Ramsey sent to gaol for cooking dinner for some 'as had escaped…she did it for the money. We've had nothin' the like o' that this time. The powers that be learned from their mistakes."

I had never heard anyone discuss the aliens of the First World War – had never been aware that there were any – so I encouraged Pop to tell me more. He said there was an elaborate plot in 1917 for a mass breakout from Knockaloe. The leaders planned to steal one of the Island's ferries, pile all those imprisoned people on to it who wanted to go and sail it off to Germany. The U-boats would be given a description of the ship so they wouldn't sink it but would fight off any Navy ships sent after it. It was a daft plot and was found out and the leaders went to prison and that was that Pop concluded.

Pop had quite a few tales to tell of the Knockaloe Camp, "But in spite of all the escapes," he said, "no one got away. Even the few that managed to steal boats and leave the Island were caught and brought back and so will the f'las who stole Dicky Skillicorn's boat. In good time Dicky'll get 'is boat back but who knows what sort of a mess it'll be in?"

Pop was right. The Skillicorn vessel was recovered. The three sailors who had stolen it planned to sail it to the Irish Republic and seek help from the German Consul there in getting home. But a couple of hours after they sailed Dickie's boat out of the harbor in the pitch dark they ran into one of those storms coming in from the west that the Irish Sea is known for. The storm lasted for three days. It was only their skill as sailors that enabled the escapees to keep the boat afloat. They were eventually driven by the gale-force winds on to the Cumberland coast. When at last they put into a little bay exhausted by lack of food and sleep and by the constant physical effort they found themselves facing a welcoming committee hiding among the rocks. The boat had been spotted from the air. The Army knew exactly where to pick up the escaped aliens. Instead of returning to Europe via Eire they found themselves among the thieves and murderers of an English gaol and a lot worse off than they had been at the Mooragh Camp.

There was an inquiry into how the prisoners had escaped. Testimony indicated that they had first tried to break out by using a tall ladder but they still couldn't get over the wire so they resorted to cutting their way through it with tools they stole from a workshop in the Camp. Lance Corporal Machin also told us that some soldiers were sent to a military prison for being asleep when they should have been on guard. We also heard that the Captain, Ronnie Skillicorn's Dad knocked out, was demoted to Second Lieutenant. I wondered at the time what Sylvia would say to that – whoever she was.

The Skillicorn boat *The Cushag* had been knocked about quite a bit in the gale. Dickie was offered compensation by the government though he and his family protested it wasn't near enough, especially since the powers-that-be had added insult to injury by putting him in a prison cell for a few days merely for asserting his rights as a boat owner and loyal citizen. Dickie and Donald, his eldest son, had to go to England to pick the boat up and sail it home.

The night they tied up in Ramsey harbor Dickie and Donnie (as he was usually called) went straight to the pubs along the harbor to celebrate. They spent a lot of the compensation money on drink on that and subsequent nights. A week or so after they brought the boat home Dickie, blind drunk, fell into the harbor. Donnie just stood there watching while his father splashed about roaring for help. Donnie yelled "good riddance!" at him and made no move to pull Dickie out of the water. He'd have drowned if someone hadn't thought to call out the Air-Sea Rescue boat. Next day when everyone had sobered up Dickie tried to give Donnie a beating but Donnie had grown, he proved to be stronger than Dickie and sent his father to hospital after they had brawled out on the street for half-an-hour with a crowd watching. It was Donnie's turn to spend time in gaol. Dickie, meanwhile, had to have his jaws wired shut which didn't improve his disposition.

I felt I should draw Pop's attention to a moral lesson rising from Dickie's adventures.

"I thought you'd be blaming Jakob for stealing the Skillicorn boat. You said he'd try to escape but you see he had nothing to do with it…like the murder."

"You'll still wake up one morning and find him gone, son, so you'd best make your mind up to it."

Pop always liked to have the last word but I was troubled by the mixture of concern and conviction with which he had uttered these.

CHAPTER TWENTY

IT MAY SEEM AS IF I SPENT MY LIFE SIMPLY HANGING AROUND UNTIL I could visit the farm to see Jakob but all the daily routines I have earlier described were still in place. I went to school for five days each week, I sang in the choir on Sundays and went to choir practice on Wednesdays. I had argued – though in vain – that I was needed at the farm on Sundays, that the church, with so many supporters, could do without me but such arguments got nowhere either with Ma or Pop.

"Even Liz and Tom have a lie-in on a Sunday," said Ma," and if you're thinking of Jakob well the prisoners don't work on farms on a Sunday. I don't suppose they are allowed to lie in bed the way we do. I know they have to do housekeeping work on Sunday morning but then they're taken for walks round the town by the soldiers as long as they don't try to get away. That's what Liz tells me."

One Sunday the Vicar warned the choir not to leave the church in its usual mob-like rush after the service as he had an important announcement to make. What he eventually had to announce was as follows:

"The Bishop will be attending divine service here in this church next Sunday." He paused so that we could all exclaim with excited delight.

After a prolonged silence he continued, "It therefore goes without saying that I want you all to be present, dressed in your finest, on your very best behavior and in excellent singing voice. We want to make a good impression don't we?" Another lengthy silence. The Vicar hastened on with his message. "Yes, well there will be an extended choir practice on Wednesday. I have asked Mr. Beckett to go through the hymns that will be used next Sunday and the Order of Service which will be a little different from the usual form. The Bishop will be holding a Confirmation Service right after Matins and I want you all to be in good voice for those being confirmed as full church members. I want you to help make it a day they will all remember."

I had thought, naively, that since along with the rest of the choir I spent every Sunday and significant Feast Days in the church and every Wednesday night rehearsing, I was as full a member as you could get without actually being a vicar but evidently not. Confirmation conferred a privilege not enjoyed by the unconfirmed but when I heard that you had to take special classes with the Vicar every week for months in order to be confirmed, I was reconciled to my present infidel status.

The Anglican Bishop of the Isle-of-Man is known as the "Bishop of Sodor and Man." We called him the "bishop of soda and water", or "soda and bread" and other childish witticisms unaware of what the official title meant. "Sodor" is derived from the Norse "Sudreyjar" or "Southern isles" of which the Isle-of-Man, from a Norse perspective, was one. The term distinguished the Island and places like the Hebrides from the "Nordreyjar" or Northern islands – the Shetlands and Orkneys.

The Bishop of Sodor and Man officially lived on a six-hundred acre estate at Bishopscourt which, when I was a boy, had its own railway stop though I never saw the Bishop in his black gaiters with that large clunky crucifix hanging on a chain round his neck climbing into a railway carriage. He was ferried everywhere in a sleek black Rolls Royce. The ancient Bishop's

Palace is still there, gloomy, Gothic and dank under tall trees that shut out the light but are home to hundreds of loudly squawking rooks – a perfect setting for a Victorian murder. Modern bishops refuse to live in the Palace preferring smaller, drier, warmer and more practical houses with more generous amounts of daylight. One of the distinguished incumbents who endured the gloom and palace damps of yesteryear was the Bishop Wilson who Matthew Arnold loved to quote.

We were mightily impressed by the chauffeured black Episcopal Rolls Royce in which the Bishop would arrive – such a contrast to the Vicar's rusty old bike with its basket on the front and rattling rear mudguard. But we were not thrilled at the prospect of the Bishop's visit. I knew from a previous occasion that he would keenly observe us from his throne in the Chancel, set uncomfortably close to the choir stalls. It would be like taking an exam or being watched by a vigilant gaoler. We might enjoy treating the Vicar to our brand of high jinks but in those days when Authority counted for more than it does now Bishops were another matter. There would be a steep bill to pay if we tried to sabotage a Bishop though that prospect was unthinkable. We felt the same way about him as we did about the School Inspectors who frightened our teachers almost as much as they frightened us when they came calling. We thus sought to absent ourselves from the Confirmation Service.

The Vicar, a veteran of such occasions, had heard it all before. He had met our sick grandmothers in rural villages who simply had to be visited on the Sunday the Bishop came to town. He knew those neighborhood dogs that had to be walked and looked after while their owners attended Home Guard drill or ARP practice on a Sunday because it was war time and every moment counted. The Vicar was acquainted with harassed mothers and fathers who deserved a break from dreary routine. The bed-ridden aunties who required our help with household tasks – these and many other fictions the Vicar had encountered often and dismissed as he did now by saying, "before any of you offer me the usual not-very-creative reasons for missing church next Sunday and choir practice next week bear in mind that I used such excuses myself when I was your age and they didn't work then either. If any of you has a genuine reason for absence next week then bring me a note from your father."

The Vicar distrusted mothers. They were impressionable, gullible, too soft-hearted for their own good and thus easily fooled by an errant child.

"You ought to be honored the Bishop is coming," said the Vicar as we trooped despondently out of the vestry.

I tried to get Aunty Liz to persuade Ma that she really did need me on the farm the following Sunday but to no avail. I approached Uncle Tom who referred me back to Aunty Liz who asked me why I was so eager to avoid church and I told her that I was always eager to avoid church. Then I admitted that I had a special fear of bishops. Their strange black fancy dress costumes, their long white hair, their hooked hawk-like noses and eager, restless bright blue eyes under bushy eyebrows gave me the willies, I said. They were like sizeable birds of prey.

"And how many bishops have you known?" she asked. "They don't all look alike you know."

"I only know the soda one from Bishopscourt," I told her, "but he's got the evil eye."

"Well he might have at that," said Liz who, in private at least, was no respecter of authority, "but he's not going to use the eye on you in church is he? God won't let him"

"God lets the shepherd from the hills use it. Bessie says."

"Don't you take any notice of that one. She makes up the half of what she says and gets the rest all wrong. She tells anyone who'll listen that me and Tom are making a fortune from what we sell to the Camp. We're not. She's just a jealous oul bitch who says what comes to mind without thinking twice and then she spreads it as gospel truth. You tell her the

Bishop's coming and she'll cook up a feast of scandal about him. The evil eye'd be the least of it."

So I couldn't escape to the farm. I had to endure the Wednesday choir practice that seemed to go on all night. I was sure I'd forget the music we had practiced, all the details of the Confirmation Service – when to stand, when to sit, when to kneel. I didn't envy the servers – older boys in crimson cassocks and white surplices trimmed with lace who had to remember what to do with wafers on a flat gold-colored plate, the goblet with wine in it, when to hold up the big prayer book in front of the Vicar or the Bishop so they could read out loud what the book said, where to put things after they had been used, when to bow and when not to bow and to whom or what. I'd have bowed in all the wrong places in all the wrong directions, forgotten to hold up the big prayer book, produced the wine at the wrong time or, worse, dropped it on the marble floor of the chancel thus spilling Christ's blood all over again. I'd have made a real mess of things.

I was also thankful not to be one of those boys and girls who were to be confirmed since the Bishop would stand right in front of them, look them in the eye, put his hand on their heads, maybe even ask them some exam sort of question I couldn't answer. They were to be welcomed into full membership of the church by a man I tended to think of as a sort of baleful wizard in spite of his Rolls Royce. I even admitted to Pop that I'd be frightened.

"What of?" Pop asked. "People say he's a nice f'la with no la-di-dah to 'm."

"Of course he's a nice man," said Ma. "You just don't want to go to church…that's your problem. But you're going anyway," she declared, "so you can take that look off your face."

The day before the fateful occasion being a Saturday I was able to discuss the matter with Jakob.

"I know you'll understand," I said. "Ma and Pop say I have to whether I want to or not."

"But of course," said Jakob. "They want you to have a spiritual education."

I told Jakob I didn't know what that was but I had enough education the rest of the week so what was wrong with me spending Sunday playing or working on the farm?

"Your education goes on all the time, all your life," said Jakob, "wherever you are, whatever you are doing – not just when you are in school. So it goes on when you are in your church too."

This was news to me but my definition of what constituted *education* was narrower than Jakob's.

"Even this prison camp I am in,"said Jakob, "much though I hate it… it still teaches me and not only because my fellow prisoners…many of whom are excellent artists and scholars…offer classes for us all to take if we wish. No, the Camp also teaches me a lot about people…about human nature…about what makes people do the things they do, behave as they do, think as they think. We talk about such matters a lot. And here on the farm I learn about farming which is a subject I never thought I would concern myself with. We all learn from our friends, our parents, our aunts and uncles. Christians learn also from the church and its bishops and Jews from the rabbis…those scholars I have told you about."

I hadn't thought of most of these influences as "education," especially in connection with my aunts and uncles except for Uncle Frank. Though I didn't understand his little lectures on astronomy I was impressed by them. In general I thought of what happened outside of school simply as "life" – a set of customs and routines that everyone accepted. I didn't think of anything beyond the classroom as having educative force. Education to me was synonymous with school and textbooks and teachers and a fortress-like building barricaded with sharply spiked railings. To think of "life" also as "education" was thoroughly depressing to one who, like me, was bent on play. I told Jakob as much.

"But what makes you think that play is not teaching you? Opera teaches us about human nature as all the arts do. And the arts are a form of play. You make up whole dramas when you are playing those games in the woods you tell me about. All those books your teacher reads to you each Friday afternoon – they are a kind of play but they also teach you about people – how some are noble and brave and others just the opposite and why this is so."

I thought of Sir Christopher Rand-Krueger and how much he differed from Sir Walter Scott's knights and thought I saw something of what Jakob was talking about though as to why Sir Christopher was as he was I hadn't any idea, but then I hadn't met him in a book. Perhaps if he appeared in a novel I would understand him better.

"What has any of this got to do with the Bishop?" I asked.

"I have met your Bishop," said Jakob much to my surprise, "and he is a good man. He comes to the Camp to speak to us now and then. He tries to help us when we need things from the authorities. He argues our case. He tries to find out about our families. He doesn't have to do any of this but he does so even when he annoys the Camp Commander."

This was news to me but the Bishop didn't go about bragging of his feats of charity. The prisoners in the different camps on the island knew more about his work on their behalf than anyone else did except for the Bishop's wife and his Canons, some of whom followed his lead while others privately complained that he was helping the enemy.

I confessed that it was the Bishop's appearance as well as his high position that made me fearful.

"You must never judge people by their appearance," said Jakob. "Your Bishop actually has a very good sense of humor. He enjoys a joke as much as anybody. So you go to church. You could learn a lot from his example. He really does care for those who are in trouble and he does what he can to help. He's not like the people I told you about who came to the promenade to shout insults at us the day we arrived on the Island in that boat and the others who shout at us when we go for walks near the town with guards. He's not like that Bessie woman you often tell me about. He's a really good man and a good man is like a book…we can learn from him if we let ourselves see him the way he actually is. So don't be scared of him because of the way he looks or the way he is dressed."

I had expected Jakob to sympathise with me for having to go to church to be scrutinized by the Bishop and when he didn't I was not merely disappointed but felt hurt.

What Jakob had told me of the Bishop's charitable nature surprised me. It was difficult for me to associate a man to whom everyone in the church deferred, who was driven about in a posh car, whose very garb inspired such fearful emotions in me and other choirboys, with the acts of charity Jakob had described. Something else in Jakob's narrative surprised me. He had mentioned that the Camp offered classes in a variety of subjects. I hadn't thought that a man Jakob's age would still need to go to a school like me. I wanted to know more about that but when I began to question him Jakob said he was already late for work in the field by the Lezayre Road and would have to tell me about this side of Camp life another time.

So with Jakob's assurance that I had misjudged the Bishop, with Ma and Pop insisting that I attend church and sing in the choir as usual, with Liz and Tom refusing me sanctuary on the farm I reluctantly went to church where I found the other choirboys in a state of excitement, no longer as fearful or reluctant as they had said they were even at that Wednesday choir practice. In fact they were like actors – or opera singers – eager to go on stage to perform. The desire to show off had won out over their initial misgivings. They were making high-spirited jokes about the Bishop of Sodom and Gomorrah. I tried to act nonchalantly though it was a struggle to get into my purple gown and white surplice. I fought with an urge to flee. I was mortifed that Sammy Beckett felt he had to help me on with my robes and tell me not to worry, the Bishop wouldn't bite.

Suddenly the Verger appeared among us in his plain black gown and carrying his wand (or *verge)* of office to say that the organist was about to start playing the processional music. We lined up in the order we had rehearsed. We moved out of the robing room two by two and stopped in a corridor just outside so that the Vicar, a couple of Canons who had come with the Bishop as a sort of Palace Guard, the Bishop himself in his rich golden robes, wearing his tall mitre and the servers in their crimson cassocks could all take their places in front of us. The Verger inserted himself somewhere in their midst.

Once assembled we moved off at a dignified pace and entered the nave of the church through its main front doors under the bell tower. The organist played an inspiriting processional hymn, there was a wonderful smell of flowers in the air – the ladies who "did" the flowers had decorated the church beautifully despite wartime restrictions. The congregation was larger than usual and all eyes focused on the colorful procession led by one of the servers holding a tall ornamental cross and another carrying the Bishop's crozier. I began to feel more relaxed and actually started to enjoy myself as we sang the processional hymn. The perfume of the flowers, the music, the soaring organ, the sense that I was an actor in a ritual drama of interest to the entire congregation (many of its members in uniform) had an inspiriting effect. I began to feel excited at playing a part in this piece of ecclesiastical theatre.

We filed into the chancel. The Vicar and two Canons mounted two of the steps in front of the altar and turned to face the congregation. The servers arranged themselves a few paces behind and to one side of them. The Bishop stood in front of his Episcopal throne, brought from Bishopscourt for the occasion and a server placed his crozier in a stand beside him. As once before, his throne had been placed uncomfortably close to the choir stalls. The choir divided into those stalls on either side of the chancel and the Vicar then asked the congregation to be seated. Everyone sat down except the Vicar and the two Canons who would conduct the service. I glanced at the Bishop seated about twenty feet away and found his bright blue eyes moving over the choir. At once I felt nervous again as if the Bishop were biding his time to single me out for something I had done wrong and hold me up as an example of youthful wickedness to the entire congregation, an object lesson to those about to be confirmed.

The service proceeded as rehearsed. The ritual unfolded, the choir sang reasonably well even though its members glanced as much at the Bishop as at their hymnals. No one tried to pull any of the funny stunts to which we subjected the Vicar from time to time. All was going far better than my fears allowed me to expect. I relaxed and began to feel safe. I did wonder, though, why one of the servers left the altar steps for a brief word with Sammy Beckett. I looked down at my hymn book only to be startled by an urgent whispering in my ear. It was Sammy Beckett leaning over from the empty choir stall behind me. I was the last choirboy on the row and thus chosen to absent myself and run an errand as quietly as I could manage. I was to use the concealed door beside the organ behind me to go to the Vicar's robing room where on the desk I would find a prayer book bound in red leather. I was to bring it back without drawing attention to myself, step quickly into the chancel, bow toward the altar and hand the prayer book to the Bishop who had forgotten it. I was then to bow to the Bishop and resume my seat in the choir stalls. He needed it for the Confirmation Service that would follow immediately upon Matins. Sammy then vanished before I could tell him that Ma always said I was much better at losing things than finding them. Trembling nervously, all my new-found peace of mind gone, I stepped down from the raised pew and slipped through the concealed door beside the organ to retrieve the prayer book while cursing the Bishop's forgetfulness. Leaving a prayer book behind was the sort of thing I would do. Wasn't a Bishop supposed to be more careful?

It took me longer than I expected to find the book, which in fact was not on the Vicar's desk but on a small table buried under a pile of papers. Now I had to go out in full view of the congregation to hand it to the

Bishop. My mouth felt very dry. My hands began to shake. I felt that I was about to burst into tears and had to clamp that feeling down. I didn't want to be accused of cowardice nor to look like a fool so I picked up the prayer book and re-entered the chancel. I stood for a moment, invisible to the congregation like a nervous actor about to enter the stage from the wings, took a very deep breath and, with my heart thumping wildly, I walked out, remembered to turn and bow toward the altar, and then approached the Bishop. His piercing blue eyes focused on me as I walked toward him. That's the last thing I remember.

When I recovered consciousness I found Sammy Beckett, the Verger and the District Nurse (who happened to be in the congregation) staring down at me as I lay along an old pew stored in the choir's robing room. The nurse asked me how I was as she took my pulse.

"I'm alright," I said to everyone's disbelief. Had I been all right I wouldn't now be extended on that old pew.

"You fainted when you were handing the Bishop his prayer book." Said Sammy. "Did you have any breakfast this morning?" I said that I had.

"Surely you're not scared of the Bishop?" The Verger made this question sound like a statement of fact.

"Course not," I said feebly.

"Have you had any other fainting spells recently?" asked the nurse. I told her I hadn't. "Well," she persisted, "are you worried about something?"

I wasn't about to confess my episcophobia to any of these people so I told the nurse that I was sorry I had fainted but couldn't explain why. The Verger looked at me with narrowed eyes.

"I'll tell you for nothing what I think. I think that the Bishop scared you out of your wits." I remained silent.

"Well you certainly had him jumping to his feet," said Sammy Beckett. "He was the one who hauled you off the floor. I had to get one of the servers to help me carry you out here. The Vicar didn't look too pleased. I bet he thinks this was one of those tricks you boys are always getting up to. The service was interrupted while we carried you off. Are you well enough to come back? It's not over yet."

"Of course he isn't well enough," said the nurse before I could reply. "Look how pale he is. Don't you worry," she said addressing me, "I'll tell the Vicar that you had a bad turn and weren't playing a trick."

She told me to lie quietly where I was until I felt better. She went off to get me a glass of water. The Verger looked at me skeptically.

"I say the Bishop gave you a fright…I'd lay money on it." I scowled at him. "I ask you," he said, asking no one in particular, "how does a Bishop frighten anyone in this day and age?"

I lay on my pew feeling like an utter fool hoping that no one would tell Ma or Pop about what had happened. I shuddered to think of Bessie hearing the story. She would exaggerate it beyond recognition and make me look like a bigger idiot than I already felt. I wanted to get out of the church before the combined services ended to avoid the mockery of the other choirboys but the nurse insisted that I lie still. So I stayed put and actually fell asleep, to be wakened by the chattering of approaching choristers. Before they opened the door to the vestry I escaped into the street by another exit and hurried home feeling somewhat light-headed but otherwise all right. I told Ma I was tired. She suggested a nap and I was glad of the safety of my bedroom. I slept for most of the afternoon.

I hoped that would be the end of it but I ought to have known better. Nothing remains secret for long in a small island town and nothing remains undistorted. The other choirboys told their parents about me "falling in some kind of fit" at the feet of the Bishop and "lying twitching on the floor foaming at the mouth." The District Nurse called on Ma to see if I was all right.

"He's fine," said Ma. "Why wouldn't he be?" She was mystified by the nurse's interest in my health.

"He has told you, hasn't he?" said the nurse who, seeing the blank look on Ma's face then proceeded to tell her the whole story in dramatic detail including the "twitching on the floor" part as if she had witnessed that detail.

After the nurse had left, disregarding my protestations that I was fit and felt healthy, Ma took me to see Dr. Newsome, the doctor she had called in when Carlo hit me with his child-sized house brush. He was a dapper little man with consulting rooms on the promenade. His breath smelled of gin but Ma had an almost mystical faith in his abilities. He applied a stethoscope to my chest and abdomen, held down my tongue with a wooden depressor so that he could study my throat and then had me say "aaaah." He peered into my eyes with another instrument, asked me a lot of questions about my Sunday experience and then told Ma that in his medical opinion I had fainted from fright. But just in case there was something else amiss he prescribed a bottle of blue fluid that tasted as vile as medicine did in those days but did nothing for me except increase my loathing of this boozy Englishman. I much preferred Aunty Doreen's ascetic Dr. Fortescue whose medicine, though equally vile to the taste, had taken away my pain.

I faced derogatory laughter at school – the story was all round the playground when I arrived on Monday morning. Ronnie Skillicorn declared "That oul bugger wouldna scared me. I'd 've tol' 'm where to stick his funny hat. Y'ere real sissy."

I couldn't allow Ronnie to get away with that – concede an inch and Ronnie took a mile – so I punched him. After he recovered from the shock he punched me back and knocked me out. The District Nurse happened to be in the school and she was summoned.

"It's happened again," she said. "There's something wrong with you. You shouldn't be fainting like this. You'll have to see the school doctor."

I had to explain the series of events that had laid me low twice and beg the school doctor not to tell Ma and Pop what I had told him. He said he'd think about it. Then it was the Headmaster's turn. He summoned Ronnie and I to his office and informed us both in his gasping way that if he found either of us fighting in the playground again − whatever the cause − he'd cane both of us till neither of us could sit down comfortably for a week. Ronnie became quite friendly after that. He seemed to have concluded we were kindred spirits, both incurring official ire to the same degree of wheezing vehemence.

Bessie inevitably heard about the incident at the church.

"That Bishop f'la is one ye've got to watch. Who knows what he gets up to in the dark of the night in that there castle of his with the rooks all around. They say it's devil worship he's at. He put the eye on yer right enough − the evil eye. There's others could say the same if they were still alive. If yer near 'im again say a spell under yer breath and hold yer fingers up in a cross-shape − that'll cook his goose."

"Blathering on again Bessie?" Pop asked rhetorically on overhearing this advice. "It wouldn't be a day of shine fer you, would it, if yer couldn't make things up? What's wrong with the world the rest of us live in − no devils, no evil eye, no little people tryin' ter do yer in? Just a neighbor or two with time to spare and a nasty tongue to exercise."

"There's a lot you don't know," said Bessie looking at Pop with a mixture of pity and sorrow. "Yer know nowt about Unseen Powers."

"The ones I can see are more than enough for me," said Pop. "And there's plenty of 'm about in a war."

The lasting effect of my fainting before the Bishop was that Ma became permanently anxious about my health.

"The lad's right as rain" Pop would say. "You keep on about how he feels and you'lll turn him into a Mummy's boy."

"He's delicate," said Ma. "He's outgrowing his strength."

Determined to prove Ma wrong Pop gave me some heavy digging to do in his allotment. Fearful of the possible effect Ma told Pop that she would have to forbid me from working on the farm any more. This time it was Pop who told her not to be so daft. I had come close to losing my contact with Jakob because of the Bishop he liked so much. I seriously thought of becoming a Methodist – their chapel wasn't as colorful as our church but they didn't have Bishops.

CHAPTER TWENTY ONE

It is a cliché universally acknowledged that none of us can thoroughly, comprehensively, understand another person, not even those closest to us – parents, partners, children. If an adult finds it impossible ultimately to comprehend everything about those around him or her think what the world is like for children. Children have their likes and dislikes, their intuitions about the adults and other children in their lives – they fear or love or are indifferent to them without being able to explain why except in terms of instinct or in reaction to the way they have been treated by those others. They are not given to introspection or probing analysis but respond to what they experience with the very limited knowledge that Life has so far bestowed upon them. Or they push that aside entirely and bestow imagined identities on others to satisfy a personal need. At the age of ten I was, like other children, prone to magical thinking about the adults I knew or met as in the case of the Shepherd, the Bishop or of Jakob himself.

So there is difficulty in writing a memoir about one's childhood. Apart from the complex issue of memory and its wayward workings as a child one noted outward circumstances, appearances, and responded to them without much reflection so that it is impossible traveling back over the hilly roads that lead to the Past to depict, in the manner of a novelist (unless one resorts to fiction itself), a detailed account of the inner life and nature of those remembered. I might theorize now, as an adult with a long experience of life, about why Bessie required so much sensational drama in her otherwise dull life but I didn't give the matter a thought when I was a child. She either annoyed me or, occasionally, had me believe her fictions were factual truths. I knew even as a child that Pop's war had affected his temperament but I didn't try to determine how. Children don't. They can't. They live in the present. They have no detailed knowledge of past events and experience. This is why my account of Jakob lacks the analysis a novelist would afford it. I record what I remember – or think I remember – and have to guess at a great deal. I can't analyze him like a character in a fiction because I knew him in fact but only in the very limited way a child knows an adult. I couldn't get inside his head now without resorting to fiction because I couldn't, as a child, get inside his head when I met him on a weekly basis. Of course I can pretend to but in writing about Jakob I am all too aware that in many respects he is opaque to me. He was an adult with an adult's mind. His experience was of a world beyond my childhood comprehension – the Austria where he was born might as well have been the Wonderland of Alice. I tried to turn him into my imaginative property but in many ways he was indeed alien, though not in the government's hateful sense of that term.

It is obvious that he filled a need in my life. He became a sort of ideal elder brother in the absence of my actual elder brother. His tales of pre-war Europe, his artistry as an opera soloist, his status as a prisoner all worked on my imagination so that the Jakob I am writing about is probably a good deal more fictive than I'd like to think. I felt the injustice of his situation. I found what he told me of his former life and more recent adventures fascinating and had no doubt of their truth. I put him on a pedestal and resented my parents' periodic attempts to knock him off it. From time to time they tried to turn him into a scapegoat while I elevated him to the status of hero analogous to those I had read or heard about in Literature.

Jakob could do no wrong. But he wasn't my property, imaginatively or in any other way as I found when the Land Girl arrived.

I had experienced jealousy as a passing emotion when adults made more of Carlo than of me or when someone in my class at school was singled out for praise which I thought entirely unmerited. But I had no cause to feel jealous because of anything Jakob had done until Mary Kinvaig strode down the farm street one morning in her fawn-colored jodhpurs, her khaki shirt, her green V-necked pullover and brown greatcoat – her "walking out" uniform. She belonged to the Women's Land Army trained, ironically, at Knockaloe, the site of that huge prisoner-leaking, badly-drained internment camp of World War I that Pop had told me about. It had since been turned into an experimental farm. Members of the Land Army, formed in 1941, were paid by the government to help local farmers bring as much land into cultivation as possible. Some were billeted on the farms where they worked while others lived out nearby. I suppose I should have considered myself lucky that Mary lived out but I didn't see things that way. She had arrived for work on a Monday. By the time I came to work on Saturday it was obvious that she had cast some sort of spell over Jakob. He did everything he could to put himself in her way. He had no time for me.

When I encountered Mary for the first time she was wearing her working clothes, carrying a pitch fork over her shoulder on her way to clean up the cow byre – a job that Jakob felt he must help her with though he had never offered to help Liz when she did it. I hadn't felt jealous of Liz and Tom's relationship with Jakob but his response to Mary made it obvious to me that I had a rival. I was suddenly filled with an anger I didn't even try to understand. Murderous fantasies flooded my brain. How dare this interloper trespass on my territory – and do so while smiling at me in a friendly manner as if nothing was wrong when I came to see what she and Jakob were up to. I could have speared her with that pitchfork she had been carrying so nonchalantly. I stood surly before her while she told me who she was, said that Liz had explained who I was and then asked me if I had ever talked to Jakob (who by this time had left the byre). I stood silent but she went on to declare that he was so interesting! He had such exciting stories to tell! He had endured so much, poor man! She actually offered to introduce me to Jakob if I hadn't yet met him! I could have strangled her.

Here was an outsider patronizing me as if it was I who had just come to work on the farm. The fact that she could wring a chicken's neck with a quick twist of her hands without turning a hair or weed out turnips and potatoes without appearing to tire, milk a cow almost as well as Johnny (who thought she was a wonder of Nature), stook hay as fast as any man, muck out the byre while keeping up a cheerful conversation – none of these reported feats impressed me. She had already taken possession of Jakob. I couldn't see why he found her so appealing when he had me to tell his experiences to. I knew nothing then, of course, of sex or the sexual deprivation of camp life. I doubt that Mary had given this matter much thought either because of what happened later. She was a naïve nineteen-year old but to me she seemed an adult.

I accused Liz of introducing a dangerous inteloper into our midst. She was bound to cause trouble.

"Now why would that be?" asked Liz.

"Because she thinks she's '*it*'," I said, *it* representing any form of prideful self-regard one could think of.

"You're wrong there," Liz replied. "She's a nice young woman who already does a lot around the farm to help me. She's quick to learn and in spite of what you say she doesn't blow her own horn. She's strong, too. She's a lot stronger than she looks so you'd better watch out Sonny Boy."

"But why is she here? You've got the prisoners to help you, you've got Johnny and Uncle Tom, you've got me…so why her?"

"The government wants us to plant crops on as much land as we can and that includes land we've never used for crops before. They've sent Mary along to help us do that among other things. We weren't going to tell the government we didn't need help when they offered it to us because we do. We need all the help we can get. The prisoners aren't here all the time and neither are you. Mary will be here every day to do whatever needs doing including ploughing new rough land with the horses and that will take some of the load off Tom and me. We aren't growing any younger, you know. You wouldn't want to see us both drop dead from overwork like John Kennish's horse down the glen would you?"

I was being made to feel selfish so I blurted out a confession I hadn't intended to make.

"But she's working with Jakob and he doesn't want to talk to me any more. He's keen on her. She's put a spell on him. She's witchy."

"She's a pretty girl and Jakob doesn't see many of them…apart from me, of course," she said laughing. "There's no point hanging around looking grumpy and being mean to Mary. Tell Jakob how you feel. Tell him you feel pushed off the haystack."

"I'll tell her she's not wanted," I said. "I'll tell her she should be taken up Slieau Whallian and rolled down in a barrel of nails. I bet she'd be alive when she got to the bottom. That'd show how witchy she is."

"That's a bloodthirsty suggestion her mother won't take to. Her father won't neither…and neither will I. She's wanted here right enough," said Liz, "in fact she's *needed* so you'll have to make the best of her whether you like it or not. She's a nice friendly girl and if she's cast a spell on Jakob it's not because she's a witch. As you'll learn when you grow up."

Adults never tired of telling me what I'd learn about when I grew up, most often to put an end to some dispute. Having failed to make Liz see sense I went looking for Uncle Tom who I found about to take Rory and Tory up Sky Hill to look for some missing sheep. Both the dogs jumped up on me as they usually did and I played with them for a couple of minutes before proposing to Tom that he get rid of Mary forthwith since Aunty Liz was unwilling.

"Get rid of Mary?" Tom obviously found the suggestion bizarre. His tone of voice, the look on his face conveyed incredulity.

"And why would I be wantin" ta get rid o' Mary when them buggers in Douglas have just sent her here and me at them fer help fer months an' months and them doin' nothin' about it but send me orders ta grow more and more. When they've sent us some help at last why would I want ta get rid of it...of her, I mean?"

"Because she's put the eye on Jakob and he's not talking to me the way he used to."

"Oh, so it's the jealousy is it? Well you needn't worry. I'll keep an eye liftin' for them. They're here ta work not go courtin'. I'll see they work separate. Ya can still talk to Jakob when ya see him as long as ya don't keep Liz waitin'. Y'ere here ta deliver the milk don't forget. We've all got work ta do. There's a war on."

I had to be satisfied with that arrangement. Jakob would hardly have been pleased if he had found out that I had urged Liz and Tom to get rid of Mary or keep him apart from her. As it turned out Tom had far too much to do to track the movements of his farm workers so Jakob and Mary were free to talk to each other as often as they found opportunity and I was left out in the cold.

I was so angry that I had been put into this situation that I just had to tell someone about it. Adults didn't seem to understand so I confided in a boy at school called Lewis Corrin. I didn't tell him about Jakob but complained about this land girl who had arrived on the farm and was treating the place like her own, shoving herself in where she wasn't wanted. I told him that even the dogs had been fooled into thinking she was the bees' knees and jumped all over her. I explained about how Johnny too had been taken in but he was mental so that wasn't surprising. I asked Lewis what he thought I should do since my efforts at persuasion had all failed. He said he'd think about it. God knows what I expected him to suggest but certainly not the plan he offered the following day. He said I could borrow his father's hunting knife – the one he used to skin rabbits – and stick it in Mary's guts being careful to twist it round while I was shoving it in. That'd shut her up for good. Much as I would have liked to follow his suggestion its impracticality was obvious. I wasn't about to spend years in prison for murder however murderous my thoughts might be. No land girl was worth that kind of sacrifice.

Upon leaving school Lewis joined the Army and was later imprisoned in Germany for carving his initials on a naked girl's thigh with his razor-sharp bayonet. Army psychiatrists took a keen interest in him during his long imprisonment. His parents told everyone he'd emigrated. No one believed them.

School having failed to provide a solution to my problem I was led, reluctantly, to discuss the Mary issue at home in spite of my usual unwillingness to reveal any details of my relationship with Jakob to Ma and Pop. After I explained the situation Pop ran off with the ball I had thrown him in a direction of his own declaring his surprise that prisoners and land girls were ever allowed to work together. He put that down to Tom and Liz's laxity. He was sure there must be a rule against such fraternization. Then he went on: "I've said it before and I'll say it again a girl on a farm is a temptation to farm workers. Those f'las can't resist. This Mary's pretty I bet. What f'la can do his work when there's a pretty girl around ter tak his mind off it? I'm not sayin' it's the girl's fault. It's just Nature. That's the way of it. That's why I bet there's rules and Tom's not keepin' to 'm."

Ma generally manifested alarm when Pop began to pronounce upon the workings of Nature as distinct, say, from war or steam engines. It was all right as long as he kept to his garden but when his attention strayed or was drawn to livestock or farms with pretty girls working on them Ma didn't know what to expect. Rather than risk Pop touching on matters having to do with reproductive processes she sought to force the conversation into a less inflammatory direction. I was too young to have been told about the birds and the bees and Ma didn't want Pop to get round to the few scandals recounted in the local newspaper concerning farmers, farmhands and land girls with (allegedly) large appetites. If I had told Ma about what I had seen of the behavior of Gerald the bull she would not have allowed me to set foot on the farm again.

"Where does this girl Mary come from?" she asked as if I had been interested enough to find out.

"I dunno," I replied in a surly manner. "She's always talking to Jakob," I said, specifying my difficulty. "He doesn't want to talk to me any more. He likes her better. She's put a spell on him. She's like the Lhiannen Shea."

"She's put a spell on him right enough," said Pop who now seemed to find the matter amusing. "He's been at that camp without a girlfriend for so long that this girl Mary…"

Ma cut him off abruptly before he could suggest the sort of spell Mary Kinvaig might be using. She suggested it was time he went to his garden since he had digging to do and poultry to feed. Ma then sought to put my mind at rest so she explained that though Jakob liked this attractive girl he wasn't the sort of person to abandon me without a thought. What I had told her of him suggested as much. When I saw him next I should get him by himself and tell him how I felt. He seemed to be a sensitive person…after all he was an artist…so he'd understand.

"I've got all sorts of things to tell him but I can't with this Mary around."

"Well tell him that. He probably hasn't thought about how this girl makes you feel you're not wanted. And it's not her fault either. She doesn't know about your friendship with Jakob and how much it means to you. Folk can't guess about how other people feel…they have to be told."

Privately I considered that Jakob and I had known each other long enough for him to realize how ignoring me in favor of the new land girl would be hurtful. Weren't artists supposed to be sensitive? But if I didn't say anything Jakob might become so entranced with Mary that he would forget all about me so I decided to take Ma's advice. I'd remind Jakob that I had been his friend first before this Mary had come along. I had listened to his stories before he had told them to her. So he would have to let

Mary know this and send her away. He already had a friend so bye bye Mary. Ma, of course, would not have gone that far.

It was a while before I was able to catch Jakob by himself but one day when Mary had been sent to a distant field to weed potatoes with a small group of prisoners and a guard I found him with Johnny and the cows and told him I had to speak with him urgently.

"It won't keep," I told him after he said he was busy.

"Be quick, then," he said, "I've got to help Johnny.

My sense of grievance was only heightened by this brusqueness. I recited a catalogue of accusations against Mary for coming between us even though she had only just started to work on the farm and knew a lot less about him than I did. I told Jakob that since Mary had arrived he had been so wrapped up in her that he had no time for me even though I had a story to tell him about the Soda Bishop – the Bishop he had said was a good man who helped prisoners so it was a story he would find interesting but with Mary about there was no chance for me to let him know what I had gone through and what the doctor I was taken to had said while he breathed gin all over me. I said a great deal before pausing for breath. I let my resentment of Mary and my feeling of betrayal by him have their head. I finished by saying, "You'll have to get Auntie Liz and Uncle Tom to send her away so we can all be together the way we were before she came to ruin everything." I wept a bit for good measure.

Jakob didn't reply at once. He stood looking at me as I whimpered like a miserable puppy.

"I see," he said at last. "I hadn't realized. You know, Mary is a good girl. You mustn't dislike her because you are feeling neglected. She's a nice girl and she works hard. Tom and Liz need her so they aren't going to send her away. If I asked them to they'd think I had gone mad. They might have me sent to another farm and then we couldn't see each other at all. Is that what you want? We all have to get along together. I promise I'll tell

Mary how you feel…how we are old friends. When she knows about that you'll have another friend…aren't two friends better than one?"

I wanted to say "not if one of them is Mary Kinvaig" but I nodded faintly recognizing that if I remained openly hostile to her Jakob might not talk to me any more but devote himself entirely to the new Land Girl. I doubted that Jakob's friendship with me would be anything like his relationship with Mary. I might be ignorant of matters sexual but my limited churchyard experience of Elsie Smith had shown me that girls were a disturbing factor in relationships.

"I can't stay now," said Jakob, "but when there's time I would be very happy to hear about your adventures with the Bishop and the doctor. I hope you didn't slam another door on your thumb."

Jacob went back to helping Johnny and I stood mournfully looking out across the fields thinking of how things wouldn't be the same with Mary about. She'd be full of women's talk or I'd have to tell Jakob my stories with her there listening too. It wouldn't be the same. The intimacy would be gone. It would be as if Ma had produced a full-grown elder sister for me to cope with.

I was both angry and embarrassed when Mary stopped me the following week. "I didn't know you were Jakob's special friend," she said. "He's been telling me how you and he have had lots of talks about his adventures and yours. I didn't know. He says you're worried about me being here and speaking to him when you would prefer to have him all to yourself. He says you're his best friend on the farm. Now I feel like a fool for asking if you'd like me to introduce you to him. He's done so much and been to so many romantic places that I find him fascinating to listen to. Fancy having an opera singer from Austria working on a Manx farm! They didn't tell me about things like that when I was training. You could write stories about the like o' that."

I didn't know why Mary was talking to me like this. I had gone bright red with embarrassment – I felt my face burning. Now she knew of my jealousy. I didn't know what to say so stared hard at the toe-caps of my boots and drew diagrams in the dry soil with them. Mary stood there apparently waiting for me to respond to what she had said. I continued to stare at the diagram-drawing toe-caps feeling more foolish every second the silence lasted.

"It's not the same!" I finally exclaimed after the silence became unbearable.

"I just wanted to tell you that I won't get in your way," said Mary. "When you want to talk to Jakob about something just go ahead. If I'm there working with him I'll leave you two to talk. I don't want to cause trouble between you. I'm the new one here, after all, and I came to the farm to help not to put people out. So are we friends now?"

Mary held her hand out for me to shake. I felt very foolish and very guilty. I had been bitter, I had indulged lethal fantasies, I had resented this young woman who had been acting naturally, unaware that she had been stepping on delicate toes as she sought to make a good impression on her first posting. With this offer not to stand between Jakob and me she had shown herself to be remarkably generous and made me feel exceptionally mean. But children aren't good at suddenly becoming gracious when they have been in the wrong. I was surly. I didn't shake her hand but I did at last look up and mumble "'s'pose so" before shambling off to look for a place to hide.

"Mary tells me that you and she had a little talk about Jakob and cleared the air," said Liz when I climbed into the old Morris to start the day's milk round. "She says you didn't say much but she's sure you're both friends now. Is she right?"

"I suppose so," I said to Liz as I had to Mary. I couldn't admit to being wrong about Mary so I felt it was good policy to say as little as possible.

"That all you've got to say?" Liz persisted.

"She's okay," I elaborated.

"So you don't want her rolled down Slieau Whallian in a barrel of nails after all?"

"Only if she doesn't keep her promise."

"What promise would that be?"

"Not to push herself in when I want to talk to Jakob by himself."

"See, I told you she was a nice girl. She's from Sulby. Rides her bike to the farm every day in rain or shine and all the way back home again when she's finished work. We offered her a room but her mother's poorly so she wants to live at home. The neighbor keeps an eye on her mother when she's here working for us. She's got a brother but he's off to the war. Her dad's away too, working in an aircraft factory in England somewhere. So you be nice to her...she's got a lot to put up with for a girl of her age."

These details of course were designed to make me feel ashamed of myself and had that effect. I couldn't bring myself to apologize to Mary for my anger and jealousy. But since her life was a difficult one I decided to be civil to her when our paths crossed. I would try not to treat her like the enemy.

When I went home I told Ma where Mary came from now that I knew. Bessie wandered in while I was telling Ma the details and demanded to know who this Mary was. Ma explained.

"The like o' them land girls gets men all worked up so they can't get on wi' their jobs. They're like the mermaids from the sea as drag men down and drown 'em once they've got 'em where they want 'em. The government must be daft to let young girls loose in barns wi' working men who'll..."

"I don't think we want Erik to hear all that do we?" said Ma leading Bessie into the sitting room for a cup of tea.

CHAPTER TWENTY-TWO

WHEN MARY KINVAIG ARRIVED ON THE FARM AND I THOUGHT IT was as if Ma had produced an elder sister to put me in my place I was not to know how an unexpected birth would soon resonate in my experience.

Not long after I had confessed my jealousy to Jakob and he had reassured me that we were still the best of friends Carlo and I were wakened in the middle of the night by a commotion downstairs. Before we could discover its cause Pop, his hair uncombed, looking as if he had jumped out of bed and dressed in whatever came to hand, hurried into our room to say Ma wasn't well and had to go to the hospital. To forestall panic on my part and hysteria on Carlo's Pop explained that the hospital visit wouldn't be a long one and Ma would be home again soon. One of the Air Force wives wakened by the noise Pop had been making went to look after Ma who we had rushed in Pop's wake to see as he ran down the stairs again. We found her very white-faced lying in bed, her eyes closed. We stood watching helplessly as Pop went next door to borrow Mrs. Corcoran's phone to summon an ambulance. He subjected our neighbor, who had been deeply asleep, to what she called a 'fit of the flutterings.' "I thought me 'eart 'd stop," she said, "all that bangin' on the door in the middle of the night fit to raise the dead! I thought it were 'itler and 'is tanks comin' down the road!"

When the ambulance arrived (no sirens or flashing lights in war-time) I didn't believe that the hospital visit would be short as Pop had suggested. I feared the worst. Carlo, bewildered, started to wail while I subjected Pop to machine-gun questioning. Instead of answering me he had the Air Force wife take us into the front sitting-room to try to soothe us as Ma was being transferred from her bed to a stretcher and then out to the ambulance. Peering from the bay window of the sitting room we dimly saw Ma, her eyes still closed and looking especially pale in the moonlight, being carried along the garden path. Carlo and I began to bawl in fear. We relied on Ma and Pop to be with us and now Ma was being taken away and in the middle of the night. Hospitals, I thought, were places where you went to die. The idea that Ma was suddenly about to die was overwhelming in its enormity. Despite the fact that we were living through a war I hadn't thought our family was subject to mortality. I was quite sure that Ronald would return from battle unscathed to saunter through the town in his military kit. Although there were children at school who had lost a uniformed father, uncle, cousin, I was quite sure that such a calamity would never visit us. Yet we had been roughly wakened to face this very possibility at home where we least expected it. Pop came to reassure us that all would ultimately be well but we didn't believe him. We cried bitter tears while the pilot's wife tried in vain to soothe us.

When the ambulance doors had been shut after Pop climbed in to keep Ma company on the brief journey to the hospital and the vehicle had driven off at speed I felt that all in a moment I had been orphaned. All the petty worries and jealousies of the recent past became insignificant in the face of this sudden calamity. Ma was being taken to hospital to die and Carlo and I had been left with the lodgers as if we didn't matter. Had Jakob been living with us I could have trusted him for comfort but now, like him, I had become a plaything of Fate. All I could do was cry along with Carlo as the pilot's wife tried to persuade us both that Ma would be home again before long and we'd soon forget she had ever been away. Neither Carlo nor I believed her. I had seen ambulances at front doors

226

before. The white ambulance from the Isolation Hospital (diphtheria, scarlet fever) was a certain harbinger of death but the one from the small local hospital that collected Ma had borne off many on their last ride I had heard. I wondered if Ma was conscious, whether she knew what was happening to her, if she felt life ebbing from her like the tide going out as the ambulance raced along.

The last person I wanted to see on a night like this was Bessie who appeared in her nightie and dressing gown, her long gray hair hanging down in plaits over her shoulders instead of being sculpted on top of her head. Her eyes seemed to bulge more than usual behind her glasses. I expected her to launch herself into a tale of woe with prophecies of doom for Ma. I expected her to say that Ma's suffering was all my fault. I wanted to tell her to get back on to her broomstick and fly away to her favorite Buggane. But she didn't behave like the everyday Bessie who seemed to make a point of putting my back up. She was unbelievably tender. She squatted down beside us, drew us to her and gave us both a gentle hug. She told us not to worry. Ma was not sick in the way we thought. She was going to have a baby but the baby wanted to be born long before it was ready to face the world and the doctors were going to try to persuade it to change its mind and stay safely where it was for a while longer so that it could grow some more. The idea of reasoning with an unborn baby was arresting enough to cause me to stop crying and ask for details.

Why did Ma want a baby when she had Ronald and Carlo and I? Weren't we enough? Ma often called me a "handful" which suggested that she had plenty to cope with. Also she had a house full of people to look after in a war so why would she want to add to her responsibilities with a baby? I knew from observing other families that babies were hard work. They were always throwing up like Lilywhite's cat. They seemed to come in two states: asleep or wide awake, bawling, yelling, incessantly demanding. They often smelled worse than the cow byre. They were a constant nuisance and stayed that way for a very long time as I knew from having Carlo as my little brother. I had assumed that Ma had reached an age where babies were past history though I had no idea how old she was at the time. Ma, in fact, was about forty-one which of course seems young to me now that I have daughters of that age but when I was ten she seemed little different in years from the more elderly people we knew. Children don't make fine distinctions. To be told that Ma was going to have a baby was almost like being told that one of the elderly Misses Quayle was expecting.

"Doesn't Ma like us any more?" I asked Bessie.

"What a question! Of course she does. You're both her children and she loves you very much."

"Then why does she want a baby when she's got us and Ronald?"

"You'll understand these things when you grow up," Bessie said.

I had heard that before. It seemed to be a tactic adults used when either they ran out of answers or for some reason didn't want to answer the question. I allowed myself to be reassured when Bessie went on to say that the doctors would probably convince the baby to rest quietly where it was instead of struggling into the world before its time. Ma would then be able to come home. She would need to rest, though, so we'd have to promise to behave ourselves and not tire her out. We both vowed to do so. I was profoundly relieved that Bessie had dragged Ma back from the edge of the grave where my wild imagination had placed her.

It didn't occur to me to ask Bessie about the part Pop had played in this drama. I assumed at that age that there was a division of labor (so to speak) – babies were the work of the mothers who produced them and the father's job was to go out to work to earn the money it took to raise them. Thinking thus I wondered why Ma couldn't simply have told the baby to stay put when it showed signs of moving the way she told us what to do and how to do it. This baby, I thought, when it finally appeared was going to be spoilt and I decided that I would have to teach it a few necessary lessons.

With some difficulty Bessie persuaded Carlo and I to go back to bed and not to worry – it would all be sorted out by morning. She lit a candle, took us upstairs to our room, gave us both a goodnight kiss after tucking each of us up, told us to sleep tight or the bugs would bite and quietly closed the bedroom door. Carlo and I discussed this new baby for a while and resolved to make it toe the line even if Ma wouldn't and then we fell asleep. By the morning Pop had returned from the hospital but there was no sign of Ma despite Bessie's assurances. In fact Pop sat haggard, unshaven and grim staring into the fireplace where the fire had gone out. The pilot's wife of the night before gave us our breakfasts and looked after Carlo when, with a heart of lead, I left for school. Pop's silent gloomy abstraction did not bode well. I feared that when I came home I would find the drapes drawn shut on each window, the local sign in those days that there had been a death in the house, the drapes not to be opened again until after the funeral. It was a long day at school.

I raced home with my heart in my mouth convinced I would be met by shrouded windows and grave neighbors speaking quietly in little groups. The drapes however were still open. I felt the heavy sack of coal that was anxiety slip off my shoulders as I entered the house to find that Pop, still at home, had lost the haggard look of the morning but seemed sad nonetheless. He said he had something to tell me. My heart was no longer in my mouth – it had dropped into my boots. I knew with a terrible certainty that Ma had died. Pop, in shock, had simply forgotten to close the drapes. It wouldn't be long before the neighbors came to the door with condolences, conjectures, and casseroles.

Pop told me about the baby unaware that I knew already. He said the baby had been born before its time and had been born dead. It was a boy. Ma was all right but very tired, weak and upset. She was to be kept in hospital for a while. So, I thought, the little tyke had been wilful, hadn't listened to the warnings and the advice offered by the doctors but come wrestling and brawling his way prematurely into the world against all advice, run out of strength and died;. I simply thought "serve him right" but didn't say so as Pop was obviously in no mood to hear such a judgment.

"You and Carlo," Pop concluded, "will have to up ta Douglas ta stay with ya Aunty Doreen for a while. Mum will be in hospital for a week or two and then she'll be restin' at home. She won't be up ta lookin' after you kids and the house till she gets her strength back. Bessie's going ta take care of the house and the lodgers while I get ta work. Ya won't be away from home for long but there's nothin' else for it."

I objected at once. The prospect of living with manically tidy Aunty Doreen with her long lists of *don'ts* without Ma there to protect us was frightening. I had never been away from home without Ma and began to feel again something of the sense of abandonment I had experienced the night before until Bessie had explained matters. I promised that if we could stay at home Carlo and I would be paragons of virtue, no trouble to anyone. We would help with the housework and do whatever we were told without the slightest argument, without the least hint of a grumble. *Honest – we would – honest!*

"I'm sorry son," Pop replied, "but Bessie's not used ta lookin' after childer. "She'll have her hands full with the house and the cookin' for Willie and me and the lodgers. I can't be askin' her to look after you and Carlo as well…it wouldn't be fair."

Fair! What was fair in sending us to Douglas to Aunty Doreen who treated us as creators of dust, dirt and confusion? Anyway *why* couldn't Bessie look after us? She had shown us last night she could be tender and maternal. I told Pop about how she had comforted us, what she had done and said to reassure us.

"Ow aye," said Pop, "she's got a soft side to 'er right enough and she didn't 'ave t'offer ta take care o' the house and the lodgers till ya Ma gets back but I can't put on 'er. She'll 'ave 'er work cut out believe you me keeping the house going. Childer though need special lookin' after…that's work Bessie's not used to. She was nice enough last night but if she got 'er 'air off because she 'ad too much ta do then look out yussir! Ye'd be fer the high jump then I'm tellin' ya. Ye'd be beggin' me ta send ya both to Aunty Doreen's double quick."

I persisted in panicky disagreement until Pop clinched the argument by resorting to decree.

"Ya both goin' and that young fella-me-lad is that. It's off ya'll be termorrer, bright an' early – we'll all be up wi' the lark."

"Who's to take us?" I asked hoping that the unavailability of an adult would give me time to persuade Pop to let us stay safely at home.

"Ya comin' on my train. I'll see ya both into ya carriage an' the guard'll look out for ya to make sure ya both safe enough. Aunty Doreen's comin' ta meet the train in Douglas."

If I thought that Pop had spent the day mournfully gazing into the fire-place I was roughly disabused. He had obviously been out and about making these arrangements. It began to look as if there was nothing either Carlo or I could do to persuade him to change his mind. I told Carlo of the plan and he was instantly rebellious. He marched up to Pop and said threateningly "I eat my toat!"

"Will ya though," said Pop swinging him off the floor and tickling him till he shrieked with laughter. After a bit of horseplay he forgot all about the imminent exile to Douglas and I was left to imagine the horrors in store for us at Aunty Doreen's house. My only hope – a weak one – was that Uncle Bert would shrug off his inertia and be a protector if aunty got into one of her red-faced rages.

Pop dragged us firmly from the grip of sleep in the early morning. With the help this time of a tail-gunner's wife he got us ready for the journey. He had packed a suitcase for us the night before after listening to a comic show on the radio. He said we could each take a favorite toy. I took my battered bear, Bruno, but Carlo refused to be selective. He wanted to bring all his toys and had a tantrum when told either to pick one or leave the lot behind. Carlo found this condition unacceptable. Pop wasn't in the mood for irrational defiance so dusted Carlo's bottom with his heavy hand before we had even set out. For the first few hundred yards of our trek to the railway station Pop had to drag Carlo screaming in fury along Ballacray Road. Only the very loudly delivered promise of another bottom-dusting quieted him. That disconsolate walk to the station with our gasmasks in their boxes hanging by a string from our shoulders was the heaviest experience I had had for a long time. I thought as we trooped along that I now understood how refugees must feel driven by superior force along roads not of their choosing to a destination they didn't want to reach. I felt that I knew something of what must have been Jakob's state of mind when he was arbitrarily seized, labeled "alien" and sent on his roundabout journey to the Isle-of-Man, a place he had never heard of before.

We reached the station eventually. Pop put his bicycle away – he had been wheeling it holding our old scuffed leather suitcase flat across the seat. He took us to the station waiting room where there was a warming coal fire in the ancient cast-iron grate. He brewed us some tea in the kitchen next to the Station Master's office. After we had sipped it Pop left us in the care of Les Shimmin, the guard of the train, a man with an old-fashioned drooping walrus moustache that gave him a look of misery.

Unlike Pop in his oil-stained overalls and cloth cap that had seen better days, Les Shimmin wore a smart, clean, well-pressed uniform that made him look like an admiral of First World War vintage. He carried a silver whistle in his top pocket, which he used later, blowing it sharply as a signal for Pop to put the train in motion. I would have thought that wearing a spotless uniform and highly polished shoes and being in charge of a train which responded instantly to a blast from his whistle would have made Les Shimmin a cheerful man despite his moustache but he was as lugubrious as he looked. He certainly wasn't the person to brighten the day for two children en route to exile with a mother in hospital and an irascible aunt waiting at journey's end. Without saying a word, kind or otherwise, he installed us in a carriage once Pop had shunted his engine from the long wooden shed where his fireman had been getting up steam and hooked it on to the train. I had never seen Pop at work before and resolved to ask him to let me ride on the footplate one day soon.

This journey to Douglas was as painful in its way as that earlier one when my thumb was crushed. This time I was traveling against my will with a crushed spirit. Once the train had started Carlo forgot about our circumstances. He looked eagerly out of the window telling me about all the things he could see – cows, horses, sheep, sheepdogs, scarecrows with rooks perched on them in derision, houses, cars, barns, gates at level crossings – as I lay slumped against the back of my seat staring at the dusty carriage floor worrying about Ma and envisioning scenes of disaster at Aunty Doreen's house. There would be no one in it to protect us unless Uncle Bert discovered in himself more spirit than he usually showed when his wife became angrily dictatorial. Although Aunty Doreen worshipped the ground my cousin Herbert walked on she disliked children in general and made no effort to hide the fact.

But no one could say that she shirked her duty so when the train finally pulled into Douglas station there on the platform was the small squat figure of our maternal aunt dressed in her formal Sunday suit and looking business-like. She came to help us with our suitcase as we were getting out of our carriage. Les Shimmin had put it on the overhead rack so that Carlo and I had had to stand on the seat struggling to lift it down. Pop, looking sootier and more oil-smeared than he had in the early morning, came up just then to make sure we were all right. He gave Aunty Doreen a brief report on Ma's state of health ("poorly") and then drew her aside. I wondered what he had to say that he didn't want Carlo and I to overhear – not that Carlo was concerned. He was too caught up in watching various engines shunting back and forth shrieking in clouds of steam to attend to mundane matters like Ma's state of health. Children of Carlo's age, I had observed before with some disdain, were easily distracted. They seemed to live right in the moment looking neither ahead nor behind them unless forced to do so. While he watched the engines' comings and goings I feared that our life in Aunty Doreen's house would be like life in an ogre's castle – not altogether different from life in the police cell of my fancy after we had been caught climbing the wall that enclosed our neighborhood Nazi.

As was the case with our other arrivals Aunty Doreen's mind went first to food for which I was grateful since I was very hungry.

"When did y'ave yer breakfast?" was her first question. When I told her that we had only eaten toast at an early hour she exclaimed in alarm. "Nobbut toast? At six in 't mornin'? What was yer Dad thinkin' of? Folk need feedin' up specially when they're growin lads. Come wi' me."

Aunty Doreen handed our suitcase to a porter to carry on a little trolley and led the way, Carlo and I trotting in her wake, as she strode as rapidly as her short legs would allow toward the station café. When we reached it she paid the porter, parked us with our suitcase at a table and marched to the counter. Aunty Doreen marched everywhere as if on an urgent mission even when she headed to the corner grocery for some rationed item. She returned to our table with a tray on which there were buns and mugs of tea and presided while we gratefully and rapidly made our way through this unexpected snack. Maybe I had given in to my imagination. Perhaps my aunt wasn't the ogress I thought I remembered. I felt a lot better about being away from home when we left the station café to catch one of Douglas's yellow double-decker buses to aunty's house.

But aunty's house hadn't changed. Once its vestibule door had closed on us and we stood in the funereal quiet of its front hall inhaling the trapped musty air, the insistent smell of furniture polish, and listening to the only sound we could hear, namely the regular tick-tock of the grandfather clock, that old sense of foreboding crept back over me and my heart sank. I thought of Ma in hospital, I thought of the dead baby and I began to cry. Carlo was upset because I was upset so he cried too.

"Eh, whatta ter-do!" exclaimed Aunty Doreen. "What's got you pair? Look at them waterworks! 'Ave yer both got a pain or summat?"

I couldn't tell her that indeed I did have a pain – a pain in the heart. Boys had to be brave – Pop had said so – so they couldn't talk about pains in the heart. Anyway if I had done Aunty Doreen would think I was describing incipient thrombosis and, in a panic, hurried me to Dr. Fortescue. Instead I confessed to homesickness to which she responded "Yer what? Already?

Y' 'aven't been away five minutes." She went off to remove her suit and replace it with suitable work clothes and her omnipresent pinafore. When she came back she told us to go and play with Herbert's toys at the top of the house as we did on every visit.

"I can't be 'avin' you kids under me feet all 't time," she said, "ah've got too much ter do for the like o'that whether yer 'omesick, sea-sick or sick o' life."

So Carlo and I climbed the dark stairs of her dustless, sterile house to the third floor there to play listlessly with Herbert's train set and toy cars until summoned below. We had always enjoyed this kind of play in the past but then Ma was with us and there was the prospect of later visits to the shops along Strand Street and social calls on my other aunts and uncles. This time we felt as if we had been sent to a gaol. After our house, so full of the noise of communal life – doors opening and closing, many people talking, calling out, going about their daily lives – lodgers, neighbors, tradesmen, visitors of all sorts – this silent place was like a foretaste of the grave itself. Carlo must have felt its oppressiveness since he put down the toy car he was playing with to have a good cry

"What's the matter?" I asked.

"Want Mammy," he said, "Want to go home."

I told him that we couldn't go home until Ma was feeling better and back from the hospital. I told him that I wanted to go home too but that since we couldn't we'd have to be brave and not let Ma down. She wouldn't want us to be crybabies and, anyway, Aunty Doreen didn't like crybabies. I said we should try not to cause Aunty Doreen any trouble because she would only be angry if we caused trouble – "and you know what that means," I said slapping an invisible bottom with the flat of one hand. He quieted down especially after I let him have Bruno. We played sadly together until we were summoned to tea.

To give my aunt her due she always seemed to take satisfaction in our demolition of her cooking. Our empty plates were like a favorable review to a playwright, actor or singer. We relished the Cornish pasties, the salad and little cakes most of which she had made early that morning after Uncle Bert had been dusted off and launched and before she had come to meet us at the station. Uncle Bert returned in time for this meal – it was more than his life was worth to be late. He greeted us both warmly and said it would be nice to have children round the house to cheer the place up. Aunty Doreen sent him one of her best sour looks.

"Well, it would wouldn't it?" he said plaintively when he noticed the cloud settle on his wife's face.

"Children," Aunty Doreen replied, "is hard work…not that you or any other man would know about that since yer gone morning till night. Yer might not think 'em so cheery if ya 'ad ter look after 'em all the day long. They get inter everything. They turn t'house into a tip in no time but since yer don't 'ave ter clean up after 'em what do you care? What does any man care I'd like ter know?"

"There's more to life than keeping the house clean," said Uncle Bert, abnormally bold, drawing a little Dutch courage from our presence at the table.

"Is that why yer don't lift a finger about the place unless I make yer? If I didn't brush and polish t'ole day long besides mopping everywhere and cleaning the winders and the front steps yer'd soon 'ave summat ter say and it wouldn't be *there's more ter life than keeping t'house clean* neither."

I sat listening to this exchange feeling more and more worried. I didn't want Aunty Doreen to blame Carlo and me for her argument with Uncle Bert since it was his reference to us that had started it. I was also disturbed at the tone of dislike in Aunty Doreen's voice as she addressed her husband – a mild inoffensive man who would hurt nobody. Ma and Pop argued often enough but there was no undercurrent of resentment or hostility in Ma's voice while she argued, as there was with her sister. I wondered what sin or crime my uncle had committed to deserve to be spoken to in that way. I had never heard him so much as raise his voice to his wife.

"We'd best get out of the way," he said to us when the meal was over," else we'll be for it."

"That's right – go on," jeered my aunt, "shirk the washin' up the way yer shirk t'rest o't cleaning."

"I do offer," he said in his own defence, "but you won't let me."

"Yer'd make such a hash of it it's quicker to do it meself," said my aunt.

Feeling somehow responsible for Aunty Doreen's sniping at Uncle Bert I offered – much against my inclination – to dry the dishes.

"Yer'd be under me feet till I didn't know if I were comin' or goin'" said Aunty Doreen gracelessly.

When Uncle Bert asked Carlo and I if we'd like to go for a short walk we jumped at the chance. He took us to a local park where we could play on the swings and the roundabout while he sat on a bench nearby placidly watching us. At last he said, "Best be off now…we don't want your aunty riding her high horse over here to tell us all off for being late, do we?"

Once back at the house, even though it was still early in the evening, Aunty Doreen insisted we both went to bed.

"It's been a long day and I'm not 'avin' yer both sittin' about the place getting' in me way," she said as if she had momentous plans for the evening that involved the entire ground floor of the house – a ball, perhaps; a jeweled soiree, an important meeting of the Parish Council. So we were packed off to bed on the second floor of the house while it was still daylight.

The bedroom, not used for a long time, was musty, damp and very cold. Aunty Doreen wouldn't heat any of the rooms except the living room deeming such a step unnatural and unhealthy. We had not been offered the hot water bottles Ma would have provided. Neither of us felt particularly sleepy. Uncle Bert would have let us stay up longer and would have talked to us about our interests but Uncle Bert wasn't in charge here. His drill sergeant of a wife was. We were being got rid of. Both Carlo and I felt alone and forsaken. The terrible thought struck me that if Ma died despite the assurances given to us of her recovery then it would fall to Aunty Doreen to bring us up and we would be at her mercy until we were old enough to flee.

There was worse in store than simply being sent to bed early. Next morning at breakfast Aunty Doreen told me that I would have to go to school during our stay with her. Carlo was exempted only because the local school wouldn't accept a child so young. My aunt claimed that she was anxious for me to enjoy the benefit of an uninterrupted education but in reality she was eager to get me out of the house during the day. She could control Carlo more readily if I wasn't around. Together in the house we would "make a mess," distract her from the routines that comprised her life – who knew what mischief we would get up to? Anarchy stared her in the face.

"Yer mother spoils yer both rotten but yer'll get no spoilin' ere," she said to explain her actions. "Yer'll not run riotin' and rampagin' about this 'ouse like yer do at 'ome."

Her pugnacious look, her loudly combative tone of voice made Carlo whimper. I wondered how she knew what we did at home since she had never visited us there.

After breakfast on our first full day at aunty's house we were taken to the nearby school. It looked to me even more imposing and imprisoning than the one I attended at home and this one was full of strangers. My aunt took me to see the Headmaster who made it plain that my probably brief sojourn in his school would put people out. He would have to complete a multitude of forms, as if he didn't have enough to do already. I would have to be assigned to a class, the teacher of which would have to be given to understand that I would be leaving before long just as suddenly as I had arrived. He didn't say it in so many words but the Headmaster was declaring me a public nuisance. None of his staged petulance had the slightest effect on my aunt who was determined to leave me there. She sat impassively in the Headmaster's office letting him grumble away. When she felt she could do so she left, dragging Carlo with her screaming that he wanted to stay with me.

The Headmaster stared balefully at me for a while before taking me along strange corridors to a class full of strange children taught by a strange teacher. He left after briefly explaining my circumstances. In the event I only attended this school for two weeks but they were the longest two weeks of my life. None of the children there made any effort to befriend me. In the playground children gathered in groups that point-edly excluded me while making me the subject of their childish wit. The class teacher resented having an extra pupil thrust upon her and since I wasn't going to be at the school for long more or less ignored me. I spent hours in this school every day hating every minute of it, feeling painfully self-conscious, worrying about how things were at home and loathing my aunt for having me confined in this place.

When I returned to the house for lunch Carlo was nowhere to be seen. He was taking a nap I was told. In the evenings when we played together he seemed abstracted and flinched whenever my aunt approached. I asked him what was the matter but he simply said he wanted to go home. He cried a lot and that made me cry too. When Aunty Doreen happened upon us in this state she would say "Y'er a couple o' cry babbies and no mistake. Our 'erbert never cried the like o' that in all 'is born days."

Time went by. We weren't allowed to visit any of our other relatives in the town who would have provided us with some relief from joyless Aunty Doreen. Misery became our companion. I rivaled Les Shimmin in my dolor. Uncle Bert must have noticed but he didn't say anything though he did take Carlo and I out for walks from time to time, which we appreci-ated, especially since our walks usually led to swings and roundabouts. Whirling on a roundabout or urging a swing ever higher I could tempo-rarily forget the plight Carlo and I were in. Carlo was more like his old raucous self while caught up in playground activities but he became quiet and timorous as we went back to Aunty Doreen's house. I was puzzled. At home he was always boldly assertive even when his wilful conduct got him into trouble.

One Friday afternoon at the end of our second week in captivity I was let out of school very early in the afternoon along with the other kids after a gasmask drill. Glad of the escape and looking forward to walks with Uncle Bert at the weekend I entered my aunt's house quietly only to be instantly alarmed to hear Carlo screaming in a way I had never heard before. There was both pain and terror in his voice. I ran to the front sitting-room where these sounds appeared to be coming from and was roused to instant fury by what I saw. My aunt was holding Carlo down across the over-stuffed arm of a Victorian sofa while she lashed his bare bottom with a broad leather belt. His skin had turned purple where the lashes fell. I raced across the room and snatched the belt from my aunt's right hand. When she came to get it back, panting and wheezing in a fury, I struck her across the face with it with all the strength and loathing I could muster. Her glasses fell off. She yelled in pain. "Taste your own medicine!" I shouted as I grabbed Carlo and hurried him out of the room as fast as the pants round his ankles would allow. Aunty Doreen, beside herself with rage, bellowed for me to "come back 'ere!"

I kept her at bay for the rest of the afternoon by threatening her again with the belt. I told her what I thought of her cruelty and said that Uncle Bert would hear of it when he came home. I would certainly tell Pop what had happened. Aunty Doreen didn't try to take the strap from me by force probably realizing that in my state of fury I might cause her some painful damage. Carlo fell asleep, worn out by his encounter and trusting that I would protect him. By the time Uncle Bert came home my aunt had calmed herself by doing some violent baking. I was interested to see how savagely she thumped and kneaded her dough pretending I wasn't there holding the strap, watching.

Before I could tell my uncle of the afternoon's events Aunty Doreen took him aside. I don't know what tale she told him but he announced grimly that we were going home in the morning. I was so overwhelmed with relief that I didn't try to put him right about what had actually happened. He wouldn't have allowed himself to believe me anyway.

Pop put our early return home down to my aunt's impatience with children. I told him in detail what had happened but he chose to believe I was exaggerating. Life was less troublesome that way for one who sought quietude.

"Don't you go telling your Ma that story when she comes home on Monday. She's still weak and gets tired easily."

Not wanting to interfere with Ma's recovery I didn't tell her what had happened in Douglas. Neither did Carlo who was so glad to be home again that he seemed to forget about it. In the following years Ma took us to stay with Aunty Doreen from time to time as before but none of us spoke about the way she had treated Carlo. I buried my strong dislike of my aunt deep in my psyche for the sake of family harmony. Oddly, I became Aunty Doreen's favorite nephew when I had grown up, been to college, got a degree and become a teacher. She had obviously forgotten about this episode from my childhood. I thought I had too but in writing this memoir that scene of violence has come back to me in all its particularity and I have discovered a well of anger that surprises me. Aunty Doreen has long been dead but the anger is still there. I wonder if, for the rest of his life, Jakob too stayed angry at the way he had been so arbitrarily treated. If he did I understand why. Brutal injustice leaves its marks even if they can't be seen.

CHAPTER TWENTY-THREE

THE CONDITIONS IN CAMPS LIKE THE MOORAGH IN RAMSEY DID NOT, of course, resemble those in a German concentration camp. The Island's Camp Commanders were not sadists weeping in private over Beethoven's music or Goethe's prose while daily supervising time-tables for death trains, torture and mass killing. The guards were not physically brutal even if a few of the committed and more ignorant minority of Nazi inmates were inclined to be. The food was plain but prisoners were no worse fed than the rest of us. In fact at camps where professional chefs were interned the meals were probably a lot more appetizing than ours. What differentiated the camp occupants from the rest of us was that they were *prisoners*. They had been robbed of their freedom because significant people in government thought it likely that they would form a fifth column in the event of a German invasion of Britain, which, in 1940, seemed imminent. They had been imprisoned by a frightened country to which they had fled for protection from Nazi thugs, a country that had initially welcomed them. When Carlo and I were taken against our will to stay with Aunty Doreen from whom I felt we had a natural right to kindly treatment and when, in Ma's absence, she proved so arbitrary, so violent against Carlo, so cold in her general demeanor to both of us I really felt that I understood something of what Jakob must be enduring. I resented having to submit to authority; I felt as betrayed as the prisoners felt.

That is what I told Jakob once we had returned home and I had gone back to working on the farm. He evidently thought the comparison frivolous. He looked at me, smiled and shook his head. He said he was sorry we had been ill-treated but I could have no idea what being seized and locked away behind barbed wire was like, especially since he and most of the other prisoners hated the Nazis as much as any Englishman could.

Though Jakob had upset me by dismissing my notion that we had something in common owing to my experience of Ma-less and Pop-less exile I wanted to pursue the issue with him. I had a chance to do so the second week after Carlo and I had been sent back home. Saturday that week saw rain coming down hard. I had arranged to stay at the farm all day but by the time Liz and I had finished the milk round the rain made work in the fields impossible. I went to look for Jakob and found him in the hay barn but as I was broaching the matter of imprisonment Mary Kinvaig came in. She was obviously surprised to find me there. Though the daylight entered only dimly through the mud-specked windows of the barn I could see that she looked embarrassed.

"Erik was just describing life at his aunt's house," said Jakob smiling a curious smile at Mary who looked more embarrassed still. "He tells me his experience at his aunt's house and at a school he was sent to while he was away has made him understand better what it is to be locked up, to be thought of as foreign and dangerous."

"And how did that feel?" asked Mary trying to hide her embarrassment the cause of which was as opaque to me as some of the mud-spattered barn windows.

I didn't want to talk about this subject with Mary Kinvaig. Her tone suggested she wasn't really interested in any answer I might give. Nevertheless I explained myself, determined not to be silenced by her indifference. I said that living with my aunt was like being in a prison because I couldn't go out on my own except to a school I hated and which was another kind of prison; I wasn't allowed to visit my other relations; I was sent to bed far too early at night and confined to a bedroom while my aunt frantically cleaned everything in sight; she was frequently nasty to my Uncle Bert who didn't deserve it and was a sort of prisoner in his own house. Aunty Doreen rarely smiled and never laughed. Then I told her what my aunt did to Carlo and how I had saved him. I told her how Carlo and I were more miserable in my aunt's house than we had ever felt before – that it was just as if we were behind barbed wire with no more control over our lives than any prisoner.

"My granny's like your auntie," said Mary. "It's just the way some people are. They don't know they're like that. They're unhappy people who take it all out on those around them. But that's nothing like being in a camp on an island with armed guards and barbed wire shut away from your family for no good reason! Jakob has much worse to put up with (unlike most people she pronounced his name properly). He's been locked away for two years not two weeks! No one can get him out of the Camp unless the government lets him go. How would you like to live like that? Staying with your odd auntie wouldn't seem so bad if you had to choose between her and a camp. In fact if they put you in a camp you'd soon be begging to be let out to live with your auntie. You don't know when you're lucky! How would you like to be labeled an *alien* as if you didn't belong to the human race? You don't know you're born!"

I couldn't understand why Mary had suddenly become so heated on Jacob's behalf. Her initial embarrassment at finding me in the barn with Jakob had given way to anger which made her face redden. She seemed to think I had done Jakob an injustice by the comparison of my case with his. I was irate. I could think of many things I would like to have said in reply but while I was trying to fix on the most cutting Mary stalked out of the barn and disappeared into the rain.

"Why did she pick on me?" I asked Jakob. "What did I do to get her hair off?"

"Get her hair off? What is 'get her hair off'?"

I interpreted. Jakob glanced toward the door seemingly to make sure Mary wasn't about to come back into the barn before he explained.

During the two weeks I had been away, he said, he and Mary had worked together a lot. "She sees me, an artist shut up behind barbed wire, treated as if I had committed a crime, unable to do anything to help myself, forced to work in the mud as a farm laborer instead of singing before large audiences as I used to do and she thinks I am a sort of imprisoned hero like the ones you read about in books – or hear from in operas. You too see me like this I think. Mary has what Liz calls a "soft spot" for me. She defends me if she thinks I need a defense. She doesn't mean to be rude… her feelings carry her away so you mustn't be upset by what she said."

I was, to put it mildly, displeased by this news. I frowned.

"I see you are not happy about this. If you really knew what camp life was like you would understand better why I need all the friends I can get. Life behind the wire is much more unnatural than life in your aunt's house. It can crush the spirit. It can take away all your hope at the worst times. There is no one in the Camp I am really close to so if I find friends here on the farm you should be happy for me. You have your mother and father and brothers who love you. You are upset because your aunt doesn't…or doesn't seem to. Now think how you'd feel if you had to live in a camp full of strangers where no one knows you except as a fellow prisoner and where no one cares about you the way your family and friends do. Everyone in the Camp is troubled by this so we do our best to help each other but that isn't the same thing as the love of the people closest to you. People in the Camp begin to lose hope of ever being free again…of ever seeing their families. Two have killed themselves in despair. To drive away the bad feelings that make us unhappy we try to lift each other's spirits. We have artists in the Camp who paint and teach others how to do so. We have pianists who practice on old pianos the Camp Commandant has found for us and give lessons to any other prisoner who wants to learn how to play. They also give concerts as I do. I sing as often as I can. Everyone with a hunger to learn studies the way you do at school. I have mentioned this to you before. I have found some old books in our library that teach me about this Island of yours. I know things about it that you won't have been taught in school. I will tell you some time."

Jakob had indeed mentioned the subject of education at the Camp before and I had pictured him and other prisoners forced to sit cramped in rows of desks of the sort we sat in at school. I thought that the authorities must put them there as if they were in the medieval stocks – as a kind of punishment – since sitting on a hard wooden seat at a desk in a classroom had always seemed to me like a penalty for some offence. But the way Jakob talked about study as a way of staving off melancholy and his phrase *a hunger for learning* didn't sound as if he was referring to punishment. I asked him to tell me all about this aspect of camp life. The day being wet and Mary not returning he said he would indulge me by describing the mental pursuits of those fellow-prisoners who wanted to make the best use of time that would otherwise hang heavy on their hands. In language I could understand he let me into the intellectual life of an internment camp the artifacts of which can readily be seen today in the displays of the Manx Museum in Douglas.

Jacob was especially impressed by the painters – not the sort who worked on houses, he told me, but those who, in peace time, painted pictures that wealthy people would buy for large sums of money to hang on their walls. Owing to the absence in the Camp of the canvas they were used to, they painted on sheets of newspaper, pieces of wallpaper, stray bits of cardboard. These artists painted portraits of their fellow prisoners, they painted the Camp itself with its tall barbed wire fence and sentry boxes, they painted the sea and landscape beyond the wire – the coastline toward the village of Kirk Bride and beyond to Jurby Head, Ramsey Bay, the lower fir-clad hills with North Barrule rising behind them – my playground of an earlier chapter. The colors of these paintings are vivid still all these many years later even though the artists often had to find ways of making their own paints.

The camp also produced its own newspaper to inform the inmates of camp matters and some of the artists drew cartoons for it. The officers who ran the Camp and some of the more eccentric guards found themselves caricatured in it. Prisoners put on plays using the raised dais in the Camp canteen as a stage. As Jakob told me and as I knew from Lilywhite working as a volunteer in it the Camp had a library. At first it was small, consisting only of the books collected from the boarding houses of which the Camp was composed but over time it grew. Books were offered by sympathetic people in the town and were brought in from government sources. It was in this expanded library that Jakob had found the books on Manx history that he mentioned to me. The prisoners organized classes to teach other subjects in which they were expert – there were school–teachers and university lecturers in the Ramsey Camp eager to impart their knowledge not to mention professionals in other fields. They encouraged the authorities to continue to expand the library.

As Jakob described the cultural activities of the Camp I listened with growing amazement to his account of what seemed to be a parallel town with many of the features of the one I lived in but with an impromptu university besides. To listen to the diatribes of the likes of Bessie you would think that the so-called aliens were primitives who sat around doing as little as they could get away with while thinking up ways to cut through the wire and have their way with as many local girls as they could get their dirty hands on before stealing a boat to escape in. But Jakob's story was of a large group of serious-minded men using imprison-ment to improve their minds, increase their knowledge, raise their spirits, sustain a sense of purpose even though they had been arbitrarily seized and treated like criminals without benefit of trial for the offence of being born in Germany, Italy, Austria and other German-speaking places in the old Austro-Hungarian Empire.

"Don't you have time for play?" I asked.

"Remember what I said about play when you were telling me about the Bishop? To a painter creating a picture is play as well as work. It's the same for me when I sing and for musicians when they 'play' their instru-ments – we don't say that soloists 'work' the piano or the violin do we? Teachers feel as if they are at play when they give lectures…at least they do if they are interested in their subject. Of course we also do things that you would think of as play – we 'play' football in the Camp, we swim in the sea in the summer, we are taken to the cinema from time to time by the soldiers who guard us, we have games of all sorts to help us pass the time. If we didn't we'd all go mad feeling sorry for ourselves or angry at the authorities for locking us up. Of course for some people in the Camp none of this is enough. Being imprisoned troubles them so much that they become sick in the head. We all get angry from time to time...I certainly do as I have told you...but with my friends on the farm, my hours reading in the Camp library, the concerts I give and also go to I manage to pass the time without spending all my days yearning to escape and trying to find ways of doing so. Of course I want to be free more than anything...like all the others...but the things we do to occupy our minds and soothe our feelings help us to be patient...most of the time."

Uncle Tom came into the barn at this point and told Jakob it was time to go back to the Camp. The rain was going to last for the rest of the day. A small canvas-covered army truck driven by a soldier I hadn't seen before was parked on the farm street with its engine running. Four other prisoners and a guard who had been sheltering from the rain climbed into the back of the truck and Jakob followed suit. In my pre-occupation with Jakob I had never taken much notice before of the men who came with him from the camp. I now looked at them in their worn shabby clothes − torn pullovers, baggy mud-stained trousers, jackets out at the elbows, the leather of their boots cracked in a manner Pop would not approve − and wondered if any of them was a well-known painter before the war, or a university professor like Mrs. Hochheimer's son Friedrich (locally known as Freddy) − perhaps a lawyer in better days, a doctor or even a judge. Like most people in the town I had assumed that because the prisoners were shabbily dressed in what looked like hand-me-downs from some Charity most of them must be of the Skillicorn social level and with the same sort of habits. After my talk with Jakob I felt that I had to tell Ma and Pop that the people they called "alien" were more like Jakob than I had supposed − more like aristocracy fallen on hard times than social derelicts.

"That so?" sid Pop carefully taking a *Woodbine* out of his mouth so that he could pick stray bits of escaped tobacco from his lips in a manner that offended Ma who thought smoking a filthy habit and smoking the cheap loosely-packed *Woodbines* a social disgrace. "This Jakob fella tells ya that does he?"

"He told me that some of the prisoners are painters…not house painters but people who paint pictures. He said some are pianists and others were teachers or doctors or lawyers before they were brought here…they were important people."

"Well, Sonny Jim, if they were that important why are they behind barbed wire? Tell me that."

"Because they were born in Germany or places where they speak German and our government doesn't trust them."

"Right y'are and no wonder! They're *Hermans* up to no good. I've told ya before. When are ya going to learn? Never trust a Herman. They'll tell ya anything. And when the time comes they'll have ya before ya know it. Ya'll never learn if ya believe everything this Jaycob f'la tells ya."

"At it again?" asked Ma sarcastically. "As a matter of fact I was talking to Mrs. White about the prisoners and from what she said Erik is right. She says many of the men who use the Camp library were very distinguished in peacetime. They're the sort of people who used to write books on all kinds of subjects Mrs. White says. They'd still be doing it if it wasn't for the war."

"What does Lilywhite know about the way Hermans think? She wasn't in the trenches with me. And neither were you. I know what Hermans can do."

"I wish you'd use their right name," said Ma, "instead of that silly one. I'm sure that not all Germans think in the same way. Mrs. White says they don't and she should know since she works in the Camp library and meets prisoners all the time."

"You used to think this Jaycob f'la was going to have Erik for supper."

"That's because I listened to you before I knew better. We can all learn," said Ma looking at Pop dubiously. "At least some of us can," she amended shuddering as Pop made spitting noises as he removed more bits of escaped *Woodbine.*

Since Lilywhite seemed to be an authority on prisoners I decided to call on her to see what she could tell me about their educational pursuits in case Jakob had left anything out.

The Whites lived two doors up from us with Mrs. Corcoran in between. Their house was as big as ours but of no interest to the military since lodgers had lived there from before the war and there was no room to spare. Mr. White, who Pop called *Big Bill* owing to his height, girth and loud voice, was an auctioneer primarily of livestock though he prided himself on being able to sell anything that came his way.

"Bulls, heifers, horses, sheep, pigs, goats, ducks, chickens, sticks o'furniture, pots, pans, a load o'books, bikes, farm machinery...it's all the same to me. Someone wants to sell 'em and I can always get someone to buy 'em. Buyin' and sellin' makes the world go round, even in wartime. The wheels o' commerce is always on the turn," he would say, to the admiration of his fellow drinkers for he made statements like this in town pubs where he had had all manner of contacts and bought rounds to keep them happy. This is partly why Pop liked him and wished he'd visit his favorite local more often than he did.

"How a chap like him ever got hitched to the likes o'Lily I'll never understand," Pop said. "She's that posh and come-uppity and he's as rough as sandpaper. She's always tellin' folk what ta do in that la-de-dah voice like the Governor's wife and there's him goin' roarin' and swearin' round the town like a barefoot sailor on a herrin' boat with a hook in his foot."

"When we were married," said Ma "people said it was Beauty marrying the Beast so I wouldn't be so quick to talk about Lily and Bill if I were you."

"That daft li'll f'la in your dad's shop was the only one said that and he was gone on you."

"He wasn't daft and he wasn't little. You're not that tall yourself."

Tiring of this chat I asked why, since they seemed to have enough money, the Whites had filled their house with lodgers for years.

"To make more money," said Pop. "Some folks never have enough."

"Take no notice of your father," said Ma. "Mr. White has to be away from home a lot and Mrs. White feels safer with people living in the house. It's as big as ours and there's only the two of them otherwise."

"And the rent comes in handy," said Pop determined to have the last word.

After this discussion of the Whites I called on Lily to see if she could add to the information I had received from Jakob. She knew about Jakob since Ma, it seems, had had anxious conversations with her on the subject of prisoner reliability. She had reassured Ma from the beginning but it had taken her some time to accept the prisoners at Mrs. White's evaluation. They were, said Mrs. White, harmless people in terrible circumstances – many of them highly gifted people who could help Britain win the war if only the government would come to its senses and admit it had been wrong to persecute them in the first place.

"Pop calls them *Hermans* and thinks they're all dangerous," I said. "He's always warning me to watch out or they'll get me."

"Your father was in the Great War," said Mrs. White. "He saw men do terrible things to each other…so terrible that he can't talk about them. That happened to Bill…my husband…too. People think he's rough and

common because of the way he talks but that's his way of hiding his feelings. If he didn't behave rough and tough he'd go to pieces the way so
many who fought in that war did. Your father can't trust Germans because
of what he saw some Germans do and because of what the Nazis are
doing now. You have to make allowances. But that's no reason for you to
think in the same way…though of course I know from what your mother
has told me that you don't. You obviously like this Austrian singer, Jakob."

I told her all about him and how his account of the Camp's accomplished
people had interested me.

"There aren't any film stars there as far as I know," said Lily evidently
thinking my questions might be about such people.

"Jakob says there are famous painters, pianists, violin-players, people who
write books, teachers and doctors and people like that."

"That's true," said Lilywhite. "And wouldn't you think that the government could take these talented people…who all hate Hitler and what he
stands for…and give them jobs helping us to win the war? They want
to do that you know…except for the very few who think Hitler is right
about everything and all they want to do is go back to Germany. But
there's not many of them in the camps…most of that sort are ignorant
sailors. Prisoners like your friend Jakob are a lot more talented than the
small-minded people of this town. All those people can do is to complain
about the prisoners and think the worst of them. It's all prejudice. I'm
glad to see you're not like that. Never give in to prejudice," said Lilywhite
by this time quite worked up and out of breath.

To bring her attention back to the Camp and its cultural activities I told
her what Jakob had said about them and asked if he'd left anything out.

"I don't think so," Lily replied, "except the Debating Society. They have
a very active one and it is very popular. I haven't been to any of their
debates but I'm told that they're lively and that the level of discussion is
very high…very high indeed."

I must have been looking at her blankly since she didn't explain what a debating society was – how it worked, what it was for.

"It's a bit like the English Parliament or the Manx House of Keys," she said. "People get together and make speeches on important matters…they discuss problems and argue how they might be solved."

"So when Ma was ill with the baby and Pop said Carlo and I had to go to Aunty Doreen's in Douglas and if I had made a speech explaining why Carlo and I should stay at home instead…would that be like a debate?'

"I suppose it would," said Lilywhite looking awkward since no one in the neighborhood except Bessie and the lodgers had been told why Ma and been taken to hospital in the middle of the night.

"Pop would have sent us anyway so what's the use of a de-de…?"

"Debate," said Lilywhite retrieving the word for me. "In a debate," she explained, "both sides have to be willing to discuss things reasonably."

Pop, I told her, was never willing to discuss anything reasonably. He laid down the law telling us what to do and making sure we did it. "I wish we had proper debates at our house," I added.

Lilywhite said that I mustn't misunderstand her. The prisoners had to do what they were told every day too. "Their debates are about ideas, policies, philosophical issues but I don't expect you to understand any of this at your age. You will when you're older."

At this point Big Bill walked in.

"Caught ya red-handed seeing my wife behind my back did I?" he said. He frowned with mock severity and said "cheeky bugger. I'll tell ya Dad."

Lily explained why I had come to talk to her. He was immediately enthusiastic.

"There's some great brains in that camp," he said, "more than most people in this town realize. They should talk to Lily about it."

At home Bill spoke a different language than he used at the local mart, his place of work, or in the pubs where he made and entertained his many contacts. He was a highly intelligent man who, it turned out, took as keen an interest in books as my Uncle Frank and Aunty Agatha – or as his own wife. Unlike Lily but in common with many men of his generation raised in poverty he was entirely self-taught. When I was older and knew him better he would fire words at me whenever he saw me – words he thought I should know but had probably not met. It was from him that I learned words like "hegemony," "fallacious," "lubricity," "mordant." He loved the sound of such words as did I. When I was about twelve I once told Pop that he exercised an unfair hegemony over the family that might have been relieved by a mordant sense of humor if he'd had one – that his reasoning was often fallacious perhaps because Bessie was on hand to cast upon him an eye of lubricity.

"Ow aye," said Pop complacently, "swallered the dictionary again 'ave ya?"

He may not have known what the words meant but he was pleased that I evidently did. I suppose he thought they might come in useful when I was manager of a local bank.

When I saw Jakob next he told me that he had forgotten one very important group of men in the Camp. It was a small but distinguished group of scientists. They were not allowed to follow their interests since the authorities feared they might start making bombs out of everyday materials and other devices which could enable prisoners to break out of the wire and disappear. In fact they secretly put their knowledge and skills to work making whiskey from certain farm vegetables using sugar purloined from the stores.

"They don't allow us to drink in the Camp but we do so anyway and we have the scientists to thank for that bit of comfort."

Jakob told me that I was now possessed of one of the Camp's vital secrets and must never tell anyone about it – no one at home, no one at school, no one anywhere.

"This shows you how much I trust you," said Jakob. "I haven't told this to anyone else – not Tom, not Liz, not Mary – no one but you."

Of course I felt proud that Jakob had chosen me to tell this secret to. I didn't know why it was important to him or to anyone else to have whiskey to drink. As I mentioned earlier in the narrative when Pop illicitly obtained a bottle from army stores Ma occasionally gave me a teaspoon of it to bring down my temperature when I had a fever and I had never before tasted anything so awful. But grown-ups seemed to like it and if Pop could get hold of the stuff I didn't see why Jakob shouldn't be able to so I was glad for him that he knew scientists who could make it. It made camp life a little easier he said.

The problem with a secret like this is that it almost insists on being revealed. When Pop was being particularly difficult I felt like telling him that for all his laying down of the law I knew things he didn't. When a teacher at school accused me of colossal ignorance of some school subject I felt like saying "You think you know everything but I know something you don't. In the Mooragh Camp they…" When in the playground someone like Ronnie Skillicorn tried to make me the butt of his humor I would have loved to turn the tables by announcing the whiskey-drinking habits of the prisoners which only I on the outside knew anything about. The temptations to reveal Jakob's secret were strong but I never did tell anyone about the important scientific work of a number of imprisoned chemists at Ramsey's Mooragh Camp.

The authorities found out eventually when a drunken prisoner stripped naked and, pretending to be Mussolini, made a very public speech in loud Italian while standing on a chair in a camp dining hall. After that, Jakob told me, it took a long time to set up a new still.

CHAPTER TWENTY-FOUR

MA'S STRENGTH WAS FULLY RESTORED BY THE TIME OF THE GREAT Spring Cleaning in late May. Nowadays if people resort to Spring Cleaning at all they do so in the privacy of their homes and don't make a song and dance about it. They wouldn't refer to it in capital letters. In my childhood, even in the middle of a war, Spring Cleaning, at least on the street where we lived, was a public event, a communal ritual designed to rid us of mortal dust, cleanse us, renew us, burnish us brighter.

After the migrating birds had returned to build their nests, while sheep were lambing and cattle calving in barn, in field, on mountainside – when the sun rose higher in the sky and the air was warm, when bluebells and wild primroses scented the woods a spirit of renewal also affected Ramsey's householders. They started to behave like my Aunty Doreen but with saner minds and blither hearts. They went in search of dust and accumulated grime like missionaries stalking sin. They pulled wardrobes and cupboards away from walls to clean behind them; they moved gas stoves for the same purpose, they dismantled beds so that cobwebs were exposed, they cleaned the dark, less accessible corners of the house neglected all winter. They re-varnished and re-painted woodwork when they could contrive access to new paint and varnish or resurrect hoarded stock. They laundered all the household linen inspecting it for wear and tear. At a time of "make do and mend" worn fabric was converted to other uses or repaired depending on the degree of its divergence from minimal respectable standards. Those who were wealthy enough to employ household help (the Rand-Krueger class) expected their servants to carry out these seasonal tasks. The poor (the Dickie Skillicorn class) with little or no interest in domestic or personal hygiene whatever the time of year went about their daily lives unconcerned with cleaning – spring or any other kind. The Vicar's worn dictum that "cleanliness is next to Godliness" cut no ice in the lower town.

The cleaning of the house itself, of course, involved the family primarily though other residents and neighbors could be drafted to help with specific tasks where needed. Carlo and I, despite our protests, were handed dusters and told what surfaces to wipe. Ma busied herself with dry mop, wet mop, brushes and buckets of soapy water all over the house, her long hair tied up in a colorful headscarf, the rest of her covered by a faded smock. Occasional Air Force wives were handed other faded smocks and drafted to assist her. The ancient coal-gas-heated clothes boiler was in constant use and Carlo and I were obliged to turn the handle of the cast iron mangle the rollers of which squeezed the water out of the washed clothes and curtains. On dry days they were draped over clotheslines in the narrow back yard. On wet days they were hoisted up toward the ceiling of our living room on drying racks where they dripped on newspapers laid on the floor. Ma stayed up till late at night darning sheets or converting worn towels and threadbare ancient blankets into dishcloths and dusters. Such activities were domestic though the subject of Spring Cleaning was much discussed by the householders of the neighborhood.

The really public aspect of Spring Cleaning involved the carpets – all of them. In the days before more or less effective vacuum cleaners they were dust traps. In May the women of the neighborhood inefficiently aided by their children took their carpets down to an area near a concrete slipway at the beach and whacked them with beaters – the kind with long handles at one end, the bamboo from which they were made bent into a pattern of interlocking semi-circles at the other. The carpets were draped over low-lying tree branches or spread across blackberry bushes and beaten till their hoarded dust was given up to the air and blown out across the sands to the sea – an offshore breeze was essential for beating days. The practice had an incidental psychological benefit for the children who could imagine that the carpet being flogged was the Vicar, the Headmaster, Pop, Aunty Doreen, some annoying kid at school, anyone else one would love to thrash.

The beating of carpets was carried out near one of the entrances to the estate housing our neighborhood Nazi. The soldiers guarding him and his family took a dim view of all these people engaged in violent cleaning so close to the estate wall that I had tried to climb that painful night. When they had first arrived the guards attempted to put a stop to this rite of spring but faced with a restive, defiant mob of women armed with carpet beaters determined to knock hell out of their carpets in the usual place in the customary fashion the soldiers had backed down. They meekly decided that a week's prior notice would be a sufficient sign of neighborly co-operation. No one even thought of co-operating but having made their point the guards surrendered to local custom though refused all invitations to take turns with the bamboo beaters.

The carpets had to be deprived of dust on Saturday when the children were home from school and could lend a hand. Liz had to do without me on the farm for that one day. We wore our oldest clothes for the job while Ma, the other mothers and people like Bessie with no children but plenty of carpets wore a sort of floral smock over their clothes and covered their heads with colorful light wool scarves like peasant women. Bessie and the few other childless wives borrowed children for the day or part of the day from mothers who had them to spare. I thought it unjust that husbands and fathers with their superior muscular strength didn't do the job. When I suggested to Pop that he might lend a hand he replied "That there's women's work. I got a job to go to and plenty at me here at the house young fella-me-lad paintin' and stainin' and then there's all that diggin' in the garden. Carpets just aren't on the menu."

In later years when more efficient electric vacuum cleaners were a common possession Ma would affect not to remember the carpet-beating ritual of spring. It seemed to her by then a ceremony much too plebian for her to have been involved in. Lilywhite, Mrs. Corcoran, Mrs. Hochheimer, the sisters Quayle – none of them had ever beaten a carpet in public and Ma mentally joined their ranks denying she had done anything so undignified as lug carpets down to the shore like the household skivvies of her youth. It was only natural for more socially dubious women like Mrs. Dodd with her violent unfaithful husband, criminal son and smelly house to reminisce fondly about the occasion but Ma rewrote History absenting herself from a communal event she had once in fact enjoyed. Despite the hard work it had got her out of the house for a gossiping day in the sun. Along with the gossip came a picnic lunch that Ma always relished but denied in later years ever having eaten.

On carpet-beating days Ma listened and occasionally contributed to the common talk about certain young wives whose husbands "were away at the war." Those who were the subjects of gossip had, it seemed, formed illicit relationships with visiting young airmen, sailors, army personnel. These women…most barely out of girlhood…had been seen going into the local dance hall with uniformed young strangers. On other occasions young men had been observed entering the houses of these local wives at dusk after exchanging whispered greetings at the door. Such strangers had not re-emerged by the time the furtive, watching neighbors let their curtains drop and went to bed so dire conclusions had been drawn. Some of the more incautious young women in question had been seen passionately kissing men not their husbands in the town's dim, gaslit alleyways after the dances. At the annual carpet-beating the moral character of these young wives was condemned with as much vigor as the carpets were thrashed. If any of the children happened to overhear what their mothers were saying they were told that if they listened to conversations not meant to include them they would be struck with blindness, lunacy, diarrhea or some other affliction. In those comparatively innocent days such threats generally worked and chilren went back to the task of the day with occasional romps when they whacked each other's bottoms instead of the carpets.

From my surreptitious listening to Ma and Bessie and the others as they gossiped I learned that Dora Kewley, a shapely young woman who lived in a house half-way along Ballacray Road, was given to "going out" in general and had been seen with a variety of men. She had been married just before her husband was sent to fight in North Africa. Her alleged infidelities were deplored, especially by women who would have sold their grannies for the courage to act in the same way. Their voices formed a chorus of disapproval: "There's that poor 'usband of 'ers out there in the desert fighting the Nazis and the Eyeties and getting' sand in 'is tea and in 'is socks and 'is underpants and then there's the sunstroke at 'm too." "E'll he livin' in a tent full o' heat an' smells an' flies an' e'll be shot at an' bombed all the time an' what's 'is wife up to…'is lawful wife wed just a few weeks before 'e 'ad to leave? What, I ask you, is she up to? She's at it with anythin' in trousers!" "Out of'm more like!" [Boisterous laughter]. "There's words for women like 'er not fit for polite company and *hooer's* the least of 'm." [Murmurs of approval]. She doesn't want payin' but I bet she won't refuse if pay is offered." [Murmurs of agreement]. "Someone should write to 'er Wally and tell 'im what she's at!" "No, that could be 'is death! There's f'las have got themselves shot deliberate when they've 'ad news the like o'that!" "Silly buggers!" "If 'e ever got leave and came 'ome unexpected and caught 'er at it 'e'd throttle 'er." "Aye, e's got the temper at 'm…the whole family 'as. They must be blind with 'er carryin' on under their noses and the whole town knowin'." "She doesn't know what she's playin' with but *fire's* the name and someone should tell 'er before she gets 'erself burned…silly madam!"

"She's only a slip of a girl," Ma said in her defence. "She's not long out of school and never been off the Island. She works in a shop. She's pretty and now she has all these uniformed young men from faraway places she's never heard of after her and she's flattered. Her head's been turned. I bet she suddenly feels like a girl in a Hollywood picture. You can't really blame her…she's just young. Perhaps she's trying not to think of all the danger that young husband of hers is in by letting other men take her out and get her mind off the war."

"It's not 'er mind those f'las is interested in" said Bessie, "an I bet you wouldn't act like 'er if the shoe was on your foot."

"Of course I wouldn't," said Ma hurriedly, "but we're not all alike. Some folk can only cope with the war by doing their best to try and forget it. Dora's only nineteen. She wouldn't have been married at all if it hadn't been for Wally going off to fight and she wanting him to be happy."

"Are you tellin' me she got wed just to cheer Wally up?"

"I'm sure she loves him but I'm just saying that they wouldn't have got married so soon if he hadn't been going abroad to fight. His mother told me as much. She was against it but Dora persuaded her. Dora told her she couldn't bear it if she turned him down and then he went away all broken-hearted and got himself blown to bits. She didn't want that on her conscience. She has a kind heart that girl."

"Is she sleepin' with every f"la that come along to make them 'appy too in case they get killed? Is that 'ow 'er conscience and kind 'eart work? Next you'll be tellin' me this is 'er contribution to the war effort. With the numher of f'las she's slept with already she should get a medal when the war's over. A regular Florence Nightingale!"

"She's young," said Ma wistfully. "We were all young once. You remember what it was like to be courted and made to feel like the Queen of the May."

"Queen o' the May!" Bessie snorted. "Willy's idea o' courtship was ter tak me to a long line o' pubs with a fish and chip shop at the end of it. There were nowt ter do wi' the Queen o' the May wi' Willy. E's as romantic as a soggy chip and a wet cod."

"Well," said Ma, "I don't think Dora Kewley is as bad as everyone makes out. She's just very young. She might even be feeling that she did the wrong thing marrying Wally…she might be regretting it. Anyway it's to be hoped she doesn't do anything too wild. She'll only be hurting herself if she does."

"By getting 'erself pregnant you mean?" Bessie translated loudly. "It wouldn't surprise me in the least…*in the least*…if she in't in the family way already. There's that many f'las she's been out with it'd be a miracle if she in't in the club. An' how's she goin' to explain that to Wally? She can't tell 'im she found the baby under a gooseberry bush. Wally's not quick upstairs but 'e's not that daft."

"What's the club?" I asked forgetting that I wasn't supposed to be listening to this exchange.

"If you've been listening to what we've been talking about," said Ma, "then you'd best forget it or I'll tell your father."

I couldn't forget what I had heard because it seemed to me further evidence of the difficulty inherent in the relationships between men and women. I thought of Mary Kinvaig and Jakob. They weren't friends in the way he and I were. There was something between them that I didn't understand, something that for all the talk we had had on the subject nevertheless excluded me. I knew that if I asked most adults about this question I would be told to wait until I grew up and then I would understand. But I wanted to understand now. I decided that the next time I was at the farm I would risk telling Jakob about Dora Kewley and the things people were saying about her. I would ask him to explain why they said the sort of things they said. That would be simpler than asking him about his relationship with Mary which I was sure he wouldn't discuss. Perhaps after telling him about Dora I could work up to asking him why his friendship with Mary was different from his friendship with me. It had occurred to me that I could ask Pop for an explanation of such matters but I knew he would not find answering my questions conducive to a quiet life. He would tell me to go away and play or give me a job to do.

When Tom drove me to the farm the following weekend I resolved not to go boldly up to Jakob and ask for an explanation of the complications young women introduce into human relations. I thought that instead I would watch his reactions to Mary Kinvaig and her's to him so that I would know what questions eventually to ask. In effect I would make Mary and Jakob the subjects of study somewhat after the manner of modern scientists observing the conduct of chimpanzees. I would engage in some amateur behavioral research.

The first thing that struck me when I began to observe them more closely was that Mary always went up to Jakob as soon as he appeared, dropping whatever job she might have been doing at the time. He always seemed pleased to see her and more than willing to talk. He smiled a lot more than when he was talking to me and was altogether much more animated. He opened gates for her as if she couldn't open them for herself. He insisted on taking heavy objects from her even though I had seen her carrying sacks of potatoes and bales of hay over one shoulder without any sign of strain. I saw him hold Mary's hand from time to time when he thought no one was watching and once when they thought they were alone I saw her walk up to him at the edge of a field and kiss him bold as brass. It was obvious that they were more than just friends. It occurred to me that Mary was acting a bit like Dora Kewley as described in conversations between Ma and Bessie. I couldn't very well tell Jakob that given what Dora stood for in our neighborhood. I was also reminded of Elsie Smith who seemed to be headed in the direction our neighborhood attributed to Dora.

One Saturday, a week or two after I had begun my scientific study of Jakob and Mary, rain began to fall in the middle of the afternoon. It was heavy enough for everyone to seek shelter. I had been working in the dairy — washing out a milk churn with scalding hot water or some such task — and decided to have a brief lie-down out of the rain in the straw on the second floor of the barn. Here I would be able to have a nap undetected. After I had slept a while I was awakened by voices below me. The voices were soft as if the speakers wished to avoid detection. The second floor of the barn only extended about a third of the way across the building and was not walled off from the rest so I crawled to the edge and peered down through the gloom. I dimly made out Mary and Jakob on the floor below lying together in the straw behind a small wall of bales of the same that screened them from the main barn door. Jakob had his arms around Mary as if she were cold and he was trying to warm her and they were kissing in a way I had never seen adults kiss before. When Pop gave Ma a kiss their lips touched only briefly. Jakob and Mary seemed to have their faces locked together while they writhed about down there on the floor.

After a while Jakob rolled over on top of Mary at which point she seemed to emerge from a trance and struggled to get out from underneath him. "No!" she said, "no!" and pushed him aside. She quickly got to her feet brushing straw from her clothes. Her khaki shirt was entirely unbuttoned. She fastened it in a hurry and then ran from the barn leaving Jakob still lying in the straw and looking bewildered. It was obvious that whatever he had been doing had upset Mary yet until the point when she said "no!" so forcefully she seemed to have been enjoying her romp with Jakob as much as he had. I didn't want Jakob to know that I had been, albeit unwittingly, a peeping Tom so I drew back and lay silently in the straw until he got up muttering to himself and went off into the rain.

I thought about what I had just seen. I had heard adults talk about love and thought that probably this was what I had been looking at. Mary loved Jakob and he loved Mary so they had found time to come to the barn to kiss each other. But Mary had seemed suddenly frightened when Jakob rolled on to her and had hastily scrambled to her feet after pushing him away. He must have done something Mary hadn't expected. I would have to ask someone to explain to me what this all meant. I would be too embarrassed to ask Liz or Uncle Tom or Ma or Pop and even if I had found the courage to ask them to explain what I had seen they wouldn't tell me what I wanted to know. I'd just be getting Jakob into trouble for nothing. So I decided to take a risk and, without naming names, enqiuire at school about the meaning of what I had witnessed. Someone was bound to know – someone, perhaps, with an older brother or sister at home. My naivete about matters sexual will seem unblelievable to a generation with free access to the Internet.

Reluctantly I settled on Jimmy Gawne – the one who had made such a racket at the Police Station the night we were taken there after the wall-climbing incident. He had three older sisters and was the youngest member of his family, which might have explained his general timidity. I asked him what he thought might be going on between Jakob and Mary though I didn't mention any names – I pretended I was referring to a couple I had seen in the woods.

"I dunno," said Jimmy obviously embarrassed.

"But you've got three sisters," I said in exasperation, "you must know!"

"Me sisters don't go rollin' round wih big lads…me Dad'd leather 'm if they did."

"But why?" I asked in my naivete.

"Because the f'las'd be tryin' ta give 'm a baby a-course," said Jimmy seeking to put an end to the discussion.

So Jimmy did know after all. I was shocked to think that Jakob might have been trying to give Mary a baby in the barn that rainy afternoon. It was obvious that Mary hadn't wanted a baby. That must be why she said "no" so forcefully and pushed Jakob off her and ran out of the barn the way she had. I must say I found it unlike Jakob not to have asked first. He was normally very polite. Where the matter of having a baby was concerned surely the correct procedure would have been first to ask Mary if she'd like one not just assume she would and forge ahead. Another thought struck me when I recalled the gossip about Dora Kewley.

"Don't folk have to be married to have babies?"

"They supposed to," said Jimmy, "but there's them as aren't. Me Dad's always on at me sisters not to let any big lads near 'em. They'll take advantage he says."

"What would they do?"

"Well, the lads'd try to take their knickers off and…" Jimmy, not wanting anyone to overhear and make jeering remarks about his sisters, whispered a brief account of the process of fornication.

I was amazed. Ma and Pop must have engaged in this activity and not so long ago either since Ma had recently lost a baby. I couldn't picture my parents doing what Jimmy described and I certainly couldn't understand why Jakob would want to engage in this process with Mary especially since they weren't married. He could have made her the subject of the sort of conversations I had overheard at the carpet-beating. For the first time since we met I was disappointed in Jakob. He was like other people after all. I wondered if Liz and Tom knew how far matters had gone between Jakob and Mary. I didn't want to make trouble by telling them but I couldn't stay quiet about what I had seen in the barn even though Jakob hadn't got as far as Mary's underwear. She must have run away because he was about to reach that point. I remembered her open shirt which she had quickly buttoned up. I would just have to ask Jakob outright why he had tried to give Mary a baby when he hadn't asked her permission.

When I found the opportunity to tell Jakob what I had accidentally seen he went bright red in the face for the first time since we had met. Normally very much in dignified command of himself he seemed now not to know what to say. His first response was an angry one.

"You've been spying on us! You've never liked Mary! You're jealous of her! You're trying to make trouble! You're a Peeping Tom!"

I almost laughed at that slip of the tongue but his anger swelled and I quailed before it. A flood of recrimination followed, not all of it in English. The situation became truly operatic.

"Why didn't you ask her if she wanted a baby?" I asked, determined at least to have that question answered.

"You don't understand grown-up people," Jakob responded trying to control his anger. "When a man and a woman are attracted to each other in a certain way they like to hug and kiss each other…this has nothing to do with babies."

"Jimmy Gawne at school says it does and he ought to know…he's got three sisters older than him and their Dad tells them not to go round with big boys because they'd try to take their knickers off. You were going to take Mary's knickers off…I saw. That's why she ran away from you."

"That's not how it was," said Jakob.

"What would Aunty Liz and Uncle Tom say if they knew?"

"You mustn't tell them. They'd be angry and not let me work here on the farm. Don't you want to be friends with me any more? Are you so jealous because of how I feel about Mary that you'd have me sent back to the Camp?"

Right then with the way I was feeling I could easily have said "yes." But I didn't. Instead I changed tactics and asked him how Mary had felt about the experience in the barn. She had, after all, said *no!* pretty forcefully and run off into the rain. Would she tell Liz?

"What you will come to understand when you're older is that when a man and a woman feel attracted to each other sometimes their feelings just carry them away. Often they can't help it…those feelings are so strong as you'll discover. That's what happened in the barn. Mary and I came there at the same time to shelter from the rain. Things just happened. I have already told her how sorry I am to have frightened her and she said she felt silly at running away. She tells me she has never felt this way before."

I thought it was time to introduce Dora Kewley into the conversation. I told Jakob about the gossip circling around her and the conduct that was alleged to have given rise to it. I asked him whether he wanted Mary to be talked about like that. In view of my initial hostility to her it may seem odd that now I was speaking as Mary's moral champion but I had not suddenly become chivalrous even though I did think he hadn't behaved very well. I was still basically as selfish as children often are hoping that by revealing that I knew of Jakob's bad behavior I would cause him to distance himself from the land girl and talk to me more often the way he used to do.

"But Mary is not like this girl you are telling me about," Jakob protested. "If she had been would she have run away from me the day you saw us?"

"No," I replied "but if people found out about you and her they'd make things up like they do about Dora. They'd say that if Mary was kissing a prisoner from the Camp then she must be a traitor or something."

"So, in spite of our talks you do think of me as the enemy." Jakob shook his head sadly and stared at the ground.

"Of course not!" I replied flushing with guilt and embarrassment "but people might say that. Bessie next-door says things like that about people all the time."

"No one will ever know about Mary and I that day in the barn unless you tell them," said Jakob eyeing me sadly for my childish efforts at blackmail.

"I won't tell anyone," I promised feeling very much as if I had done something shameful.

"I wish I could believe you. But I'm not sure any more. You have been spying on me. That is not what friends do."

I tried to explain the difference between spying and curiosity. I just wanted to know what made his friendship with Mary different from his friendship with me. I wanted to know why he was closer to her than to me.

"Well," said Jakob, "that has to do with the differences between men and women. Your Papa loves your mother in a different way than he loves you. If you had an older sister she would love the person she wanted to marry differently than she would love you. That's the way it is. But that doesn't mean you and I can't stay friends. It's just different between us than between Mary and I."

"That's because of babies isn't it?"

"I suppose so…in a way, but it's more complicated than that."

It seemed to me that the longer I lived the more complications Life presented. I wondered if at some point it became simple again.

I tried to be nicer to Mary after this and as a sort of penance went out of my way to smile at Dora Kewley whenever I passed her in the street to make up for the gossip. She scowled whenever I did so.

"Listen kid," she said one day stopping as I was smiling at her, "what the hell are you smirking at? You're always smirking at me. If you've got something to say, spit it out!"

I stopped smiling at her after that and left her to her fate.

Wally came home on leave, heard all the gossip in the nearest pub, got into a fight and then went home and knocked his wife all round the house till she was covered in bruises. He then burst into tears and sat on the floor. After that they made up and she explained to anyone who would listen,"Wally's gone mental 'cause of the war but he'll get over it."

CHAPTER TWENTY-FIVE

As a rule Pop returned from his day's work more or less when he said he would unless some emergency arose whereupon Ma would be informed by the Station Master who sent someone to the house on a bike with a message. On a normal day after his last run to and from Douglas Pop would make sure that carriages and goods wagons were shunted to the proper sidings out of the way of later trains; he would put his engine to bed in the long red wooden engine house, sign various documents which he generally smudged with his oily right hand, receive instructions for the following day and then cycle home. He might be late at times by as much as half an hour when he had unexpected extra work to do – usually more shunting of carriages and wagons than usual – but he wasn't tardy because he had veered off the road home into a pub like some of the fathers of children I went to school with. Those children told dramatic tales of domestic strife. They described ambushes of reeling fathers carried out by furious sober umbrella-wielding mothers fearful for their grocery money and rent. They recounted fistful but fuddled retaliation on the part of men who, when sober, were the most inoffensive people you could meet – "wouldn't say *boo* to a *goose.*" "*The demon drink,*" said the Vicar, speaking with what some believed to be autobiographic passion, "*makes wild beasts of men.*" On the day Pop did not appear for tea at his usual time and after a couple of hours had dragged by I began to wonder if he had tired of his week-day temperance and was making a wild beast of himself alongside the more delinquent fathers of some of my school friends.

It was a Saturday – Pop often had to work at the weekend during the war. Perhaps he felt he had earned a drink. Driving a steam train was hot thirsty work. The pubs would be doing a brisk trade by late Saturday afternoon so maybe Pop decided to have a pint on his way home – and one pint had led to another and to several more until time didn't matter.

"Wait till he gets home…I'll murder him!" said Ma fiercely revealing the similarity of her thoughts to mine.

"Where's Pop?" I asked with affected innocence.

"How should I know?" Ma replied. "But what I do know is when he comes in through that front door I'll strangle him with my bare hands!"

Such an act might relieve Ma's feelings but it wouldn't help in the long run. Right then, though, Ma didn't give a damn about the long run. It was best not to argue with her when she had lost her temper. Her hands, hardened by work, were rough and heavy.

As time passed slowly and the sun set Ma's anger began to turn to fear. Even if Pop had stopped off at a pub on his way home he ought to be back by now. Ma had just decided that there was nothing for it but to fluster Mrs. Corcoran with a request to use her phone to call the Station to see if anyone there could tell her of Pop's wherabouts when in the dusk we saw a police car draw up to the house. We hurried outside to find Pop, very much the worse for wear, struggling to get out of the front passenger's seat with the help of the constable who had driven him home. Ma's worst fears were realized. Pop had been to a pub, got drunk, waded into a fight and been arrested.

"You're a disgrace!" Ma shouted as Pop clung to the police car evidently to avoid sagging on to the road. "Fighting like a ruffian at your age!" Ma continued. "How many bills won't be paid? How much have you poured down you?!!"

I couldn't see why the quantity of what Pop had drunk mattered. He was as we saw him however many pints it had taken to reduce him to this pitiful state.

"Whoa there missus," said the policeman, "ya goin' down the wrong road at a fine gallop. Ya don't unnerstan'. There's been an accident. Ya hubby's lucky to be alive with the breath in 'm."

"Accident? What accident? You should have put him in a cell overnight to sleep it off," said Ma unwilling to accept that Pop's condition was due to anything other than drink.

While Ma was offering the constable strong advice on how to do his job and the constable was trying to get a word in sideways I stared at Pop who seemed incapable of speech. His face was as white as the chalk at school. An elaborate bandage had been wound several times round his head. Blood had seeped through its layers. He seemed far from "all there." He stood clutching the police car with one hand, the constable with the other, as if they were the twin rocks that would save him from being swept away and drowned by some invisible flood. He didn't try to say anything. He seemed to have trouble focusing his eyes. He looked as if he had just wandered, shell-shocked, off one of those terrible battlefields of his youth. Something worse than a fight in a pub had reduced him to this.

"Why do you keep going on and on about an accident?" Ma asked Pop's new friend as she looked with growing horror at the battered version of my father swaying like the washing in a sea breeze.

"There was a bit of a riot on ya hubby's train," said the constable relieved at being allowed to explain at last. "It was the Air Force f'las. They'd all had a drop too many at them. Ya hubby's hearin' all this racket they're makin in the carriages, like, so he sticks his head out o' the engine to take a skeet an' bang! —he bashed it up against a piece o' the stone bridge the train was goin' under just then. If the fireman hadn't got a howl of 'm he'd have been off the footplate and down under the iron wheels. He was covered in blood an' didn' know where he was or what was at 'm. The fireman had to prop him up an' drive the train to the next station an' wait there for a new driver while they took ya hubby up at the hospital ta see the mighty man there…that f'la in the long white coat that does the operations. He stitched ya hubby up pretty good an' gave him some pills. Ya hubby needs a long rest that f'la says. He's got the shock that f'la says. That f'la says he's lucky he didn't smash the brains out of his head against that bridge."

"Why didn't you look where you were going?" Ma asked as if she were telling me off for crossing the street without checking the traffic. But her face was now full of anxiety while I contemplated an unwelcome mental picture of Pop's brains being smashed out of his head – oozing brains, which I imagined as a cross between writhing worms and rice pudding because of a picture I had seen in an encyclopedia.

"It was so fast, like," said the constable on Pop's behalf since the power of speech seemed to have deserted him, though in a healthier state he had many words for all occasions. "It all happened…bang! Fast as a dose o' salts" the policeman added.

"Typical of you to nearly kill yourself over a pack of drunks," Ma ventured before she started to sob. Perhaps she'd had a vision akin to mine of Pop's shattered skull. I had been watching the unfolding scene in wonder but when Ma started to cry with Pop standing there propped up by a policeman and staring at us all with a look of foolish astonishment on his face as if he had just parachuted down from the moon to find all these strange beings staring at him and speaking in tongues – then I started to cry too but more loudly. It was fortunate that Carlo was in bed asleep or the racket would have been doubled.

With the policeman supporting him on one side, Ma propping him up on the other and me trailing behind them Pop was helped into the house. I was aware that Mrs. Corcoran's window curtains had parted slightly and didn't doubt that other neighbors had furtively observed the scene despite the failing light. They would all draw the wrong conclusions, of course, the way Ma had at first. There would be no point in calling at all the houses in the block from which ours could be easily observed in order to interpret Pop's posture and bandages and explain the presence of a policeman.

"Ow, aye," the neighbors would say, "e'd best get some rest." Then they would tell others how Pop had been brought home by the police paralytic with drink and covered in blood.

That night Pop moaned in pain the way I had done when my thumb had been crushed. Ma gave him the tablets provided by the doctor at the hospital and, after protesting that it was the wrong thing to do, the medicine Pop preferred – namely liberal doses of his illegally obtained whiskey. This combination of remedies enabled him to sleep for a while but after a couple of hours he would be awake again moaning and so would require more of his medicines. The following day Ma looked as if she had been up all night. She told us of Pop's current state and warned Carlo and I not to make a noise while he was recovering.

Once the initial pain wore off Pop proved to be an *im*-patient. He wanted to go back to work right away. No one understood his engine the way he did. A replacement driver would reduce it to ruin in short order. It had to be handled delicately and only he knew exactly how to do that. Further, his wages were needed. A low-level guerilla war between Ma and Pop commenced over the issue of his return to work. Ma summoned reinforcement in the shape of the family doctor. She wanted him to impose a truce. The doctor, the trade-mark smell of gin on his breath, removed Pop's bandages, observed the wound through what looked like a magnifying glass, grimaced, applied new bandages, shone a small light into both Pop's eyes and told him he would have to heal properly before he could work again.

"I can't sit round here doing nothin'!" Pop said forcefully.

"He has to heal *in* his head, not just on it," the doctor said to Ma as if Pop wasn't there. "He's still showing signs of concussion. He's not fit to ride a bike let alone drive a train. He'd be a danger to himself and everyone on it. He could very well collapse especially with the heat he has to work in. He'd be playing with people's lives."

"You heard what he said," Ma told Pop as if he hadn't quite grasped the meaning of the doctor's words...*a danger to yourself and everyone else.* Make up your mind to it. You have to recover before you go anywhere near work." So Pop spent a querulous week fussing and fuming about his engine and how no one but he understood its temperament and how when he returned to work he would find it a wreck. By the end of the week Ma declared herself a wreck and begged the doctor to return Pop to his mechanical beloved.

"He's driving me mad," Ma told the doctor. "I've got too much to do already without fetching and carrying for him all day long and listening to him going on and on and on and on about that damned dirty oily engine as if it were his own flesh and blood!"

With misgivings the doctor let Pop go back to work early in the following week. "The blame will be on your head if anything happens," said the doctor with what, under the circumstances, I thought an undiplomatic choice of words.

Pop's accident really gave me a story to tell at the farm. Forgetting my recent difficulties with Jakob over Mary I told him and everyone else in the vicinity who would listen about Pop almost having his head knocked off by a bridge. I expected in-drawn breaths, "well I never's," eager questioning, a clamor for detail which I would be happy to provide – with suitable embellishments – but I was disappointed. Everyone looked grim and preoccupied.

"What's wrong?" I asked.

"Johnny's disappeared," said Aunty Liz. "He went home to have tea with his mother last Saturday the way he always does but he never came back. His mother doesn't know what happened...the last she saw was him going off for a walk before his tea. He loves working here on the farm. He wouldn't just not return. And he wouldn't leave his mother wondering and worrying. It's terrible! Something's happened to him! The police can't find him! They've searched the whole glen. They've even dragged the deep pools in the river."

Liz started to cry, the first time I had seen her do that since I came to work on the farm. Uncle Tom looked miserable and Jakob stared grimly at the earth. No wonder they weren't interested in Pop's misadventure. Even Mary when I met her later that morning had tears in her eyes which I assumed were for Johnny.

While I was delivering milk that Saturday it occurred to me that Johnny had disappeared the very day Pop had nearly been killed. Perhaps there was some connection there though I couldn't see what it might be. I didn't know if Johnny had ever been on a train in his life. The idea was far-fetched but I mentioned the coincidence of dates to Liz.

"That's all it is," she said, "just a coincidence. Johnny's had nothing to do with trains. Why would he have? He's only got his mother and us and we all live here in the glen. He hardly ever goes to town and when he does it's either with one of us or with his mum on the bus. People don't know what he's talking about. They think he's daft in the head and he knows it. He's been laughed at and got into fights in the past so he's not going to go alone into town and certainly not on the train. Anyway you said the trouble on your dad's train happened near Douglas. That's like a foreign country to our Johnny. If he won't go into Ramsey on his own he's not going to get himself into trouble on a train near Douglas. Where would he get the money for the fare? He gives his mum most of what he earns and we look after the rest for him. She would certainly have told us if Johnny had taken a train ride to Douglas and back. That'd be news in the glen worth the printing!"

Of course what Liz said made sense but I thought I'd refer the latter to Lance Corporal Machin, just in case. He might have learned something about the reason for the disturbance on Pop's train the consequence of which, for Pop, he heard from Ma as soon as he came back to the house from his guard duty. By then too, Pop had found the voice and clarity of mind to tell his side of the story to anyone who would listen.

The Lance Corporal was privy to general gossip among the military – at the prison camp, with the sailors and Air Force personnel he met in pubs or at local dances. He knew the private affairs of a surprising number of people. He knew that the Commander of the Andreas Air Station took his girlfriend for illicit rides on bombers which is how both of them ended up dead, along with the crew, when their plane clipped tree-tops when it was coming in to land. It was said the girlfriend was at the controls on the fatal day but that was probably a local embellishment.

"Oo's this Johnny then?" he said when I questioned him about the people on Pop's train and told him why I was asking.

I described Johnny as well as I could.

"Yer say 'is top floor's empty o'furniture?"

"No. I said he speaks words in a backwards sort of way. He can't help it. He was born like that. But he knows a lot. He can milk cows better than anyone. They'll come when he calls them the way the dogs do. He knows how to tie and undo really hard knots; he does lots of jobs on the farm and nobody has to show him how to do them. He can draw terrific pictures. Everybody likes Johnny. But he's vanished. No one has seen him since the day Pop nearly had his head knocked off."

The very recital of these deails gave me goose pimples the way mysterious disappearances in stories did except that in the stories I read you knew that those who had vanished would eventually be found whole and hale. Real life offered no such guarantees. Johnny could be lying dead or injured somewhere no one knowing where to even start looking for him.

"Where did folk last see 'im?" the Corporal asked.

"His mother said he went out for a walk in the glen while she was making his tea. There was a horse he wanted to see in a field nearby. He used to feed it bits of turnip. She says he never came back"

"What time was that?"

"I dunno…four in the afternoon maybe."

"I'll ask questions in the proper quarters," said Lance Corporal Wilf as if select doors invariably opened when he came knocking.

Wilf had some news the next day. Friends in the Military Police told him that the riotous behavior on Pop's train was the work of a group of very young officers who had just passed their flying training and had been to Douglas on a one-day pass to celebrate receiving their wings before being posted to various air stations round Britain. They had spent the day migrating from pub to pub and got back on to the train to Ramsey in such a state that it had seemed to them an amusing joke to unscrew all the fittings in their carriages and toss them out of the windows. After that they pretended to toss a few of their number out of the windows but contented themselves eventually with opening carriage doors and holding their victims upside down within a few feet of the rails as the train rocked along. The bellowed terror of those thus held was most amusing to the rest. They had all behaved disgracefully when the train had to stop because of Pop's accident. The Master of the station to which Pop's fireman had driven the train took two weeks off to recover from the shock of witnessing large-scale vandalism.

It seems that when the train — by now driven by a replacement driver — drew up at a small country halt near to Ramsey they had been presented with a civilian to torment. A man dressed like a scarecrow had been driven to this halt by a separate, smaller group of graduating airmen who had spent their day off having a liquid picnic in a park at the top of Glen Auldyn. They reached this place by means of an unattended jeep they had "borrowed" from the Jurby Airfield. On their way back down the glen in the late afternoon they had come across this shabbily-dressed chap, his cap pulled down over his forehead, his muddy boots fastened with string, and, for a joke, they had stopped and offered him a cramped lift. When the man ignored them and walked on they jumped out, grabbed him and hauled him into their jeep. He struggled to get away so they sat on him until the glen was behind them. When they heard the hooting of the approaching train they thought it would be hilarious to put their captive on to it like a goods item. They drove to a nearby halt – a single platform with no attendant buildings – and waved at the train to stop. When it did they heard the drunken racket being made by their friends. They presented their struggling prisoner to those on the train who made sure he didn't escape before the train moved off. His initial captors then drove away in their jeep roaring with laughter at the amazingly funny thing they had just done.

The drunken officers on the train suitably tormented the labourer who had been presented to them and hauled him on to the military bus sent to pick them up at the Ramsey railway station. When, however, they saw a reception committee of Military Police waiting for them at Jurby Airport they had pushed their hostage off the bus as it slowed down. The man had run away in the dark. No one knew who the captive man was nor had anyone seen him on or near the Base in the days that followed.

"But 'ere's the point," said the Lance Corporal as if he was underlining the moral of a fable, "when they was admittin' what they'd done to this chap as they'd been muckin' about with they said 'e wouldn't talk except the once when he went on about summat and they said 'e sounded as if 'e were off 'is rocker. No one could tell what he was sayin'. Now that sounds like your missin' chap dunnit? When them daft young buggers sobered up the next day and found theirselves all on a charge that's when they told the Military Police 'ow they'd spent their day off. None of 'em's much older than nineteen. The country's bein' defended by kids in Spitfires!"

It was obvious that the man kidnapped by the airmen was Johnny. All the details fit. The question was where had he gone to? It was no joke that he had been missing for a week and no one any the wiser as to his whereabouts. All manner of accidents could have befallen him. In the dark he could have strayed on to the airport runway at Jurby or at the nearby Andreas Fighter Station and been killed or injured by a plane either taking off or landing. He might have wandered over to Jurby beach where the tidal currents were strong and been swept out to sea in the dark. He could be hiding, terrified, somewhere in Jurby or next door in the Parish of Bride without food or water. My imagination ran riot with grim possibilities. Johnny was so child-like that I doubted he could take care of himself away from familiar surroundings. I had emphasized his abilities to the Lance Corporal but in the larger world outside the farm he would be like a rabbit at a fox's picnic.

Of course I had to tell Uncle Tom and Aunty Liz at once what I had found out. Such news couldn't wait till the next weekend when I was due at the farm again – I felt sure that Johnny's life depended on the speed with which he could be found and rescued from whatever predicament he was in. I told Ma the whole story and she took me round to Mrs. Corcoran's so that we could use that long-suffering woman's telephone. When she heard the facts in brief Mrs. Corcoran made local history by refusing the money Ma offered her for the call.

Tom and Liz of course rejoiced at what I had discovered. No time would be lost in finding Johnny they said. They would start a new search at once. I wished them good luck but went to bed that night with an odd sense of foreboding as though the morning would bring news of a body half-buried in seaweed and shingle or floating face down in a pond. I imagined Johnny stark and starved in a barn too frightened of strangers to make himself known to the farmer onto whose land he had strayed. I saw him spread-eagled on the runway of Jurby Airport with tire-marks across his back. Such imaginings made me edgy and I got into a fight with Carlo who was in one of his primitive cantankerous moods. We both received a "clip over the ear" from Pop as he responded to the noise we were making yelling insults at each other. He hadn't properly recovered from his accident and couldn't stand raised voices.

By the evening of the following day there had been no news except a phone call from Liz via Mrs. Corcoran to the effect that though they had criss-crossed the north of the Island right out to its northernmost extremity, the Point of Ayr itself, she and Uncle Tom had found no trace of Johnny. No one they spoke to – people walking the country roads, village shopkeepers, farmers driving carts, laborers in fields, a postman on his bike – no one had seen anybody matching Johnny's description. They had returned to their farm exhausted but were determined to try again the following day after the essential farm work had been done. Jakob and Mary, they said, were working twice as hard as usual to keep the farm running. I couldn't help feeling jealous when I heard that but I made no comment.

Liz and Tom didn't telephone after their second search – they drove to our house in Tom's old truck. They had traveled just about every road in the north of the Island; they had driven all over the parishes of Jurby, Bride and Andreas in vain. No one they had asked at the farms they had called at had seen anything of Johnny. No one cycling or walking along the roads they traveled had seen him. The local police had been persuaded to do a more comprehensive search than Liz and Tom could do on their own but drew a blank even after tramping for miles along beaches and cliffs. Johnny had evapaorated.

"Have you given a thought to the Curragh?" Pop asked eventually.

"My God! If he's in there he'll be a gonner!" Uncle Tom was appalled at a prospect that had evidently not occurred to him before.

"He won't have got that far away from the airfield, surely, said Aunty Liz, fear in her voice.

The Curragh is a large swampy region on the Island's northern plain between Ramsey and Ballaugh. It was said that anyone who lost their way in that morass would be sucked down by the volatile mud to join the bones of the Irish Elk, some of which had been found there. There were safe paths through this large swampy tract but you had to know where they were. What looked like a pathway might be a light covering of grass and other vegetation over deep sucking mud which, when it had you in its grip, would pull you down who knows how far? To hell itself some of the local ancients declared. If you blundered into this area in daytime you might stand a chance, however small, of pulling yourself free from the entreating mud but if you wandered there at night you were done for. You wouldn't be able to tell firm land from swamp. No matter how much you thrashed about and shrieked for help you'd sink and disappear while fiends laughed aloud – at least that was what was said in the school playground when the place was discussed. It was a place of which nightmares are made. The school playground was too at times.

"If that oul swamp gave up its dead," said the elderly, "howl armies'd march out."

The idea of Johnny lost and blundering about in such a region made me shudder. Pop had certainly not improved the mood of our visitors by introducing the Curragh into the conversation but before they went home that night Uncle Tom declared that the place would have to be searched. Johnny could have wandered over there from Jurby – the distance wasn't that great. Next day the police agreed to supply a few men for a one-day search but made it plain that they didn't expect success.

"Anyone in there who doesn't know their way'll be down under the mud," said the sergeant, a man not famous for tact.

In the event five constables, Uncle Tom, Aunty Liz and a local guide searched the marshes for a whole day shouting Johnny's name but getting no reply. All they found were an old pram, a rusted knife and spoon, a pair of faded blue knickers and the floating bloated corpse of a dog in one of the many ponds. There were also a number of spent cartridges left behind by hunters of pheasant and wild duck – one of whom had apparently shot the dog by mistake. There were various comic theories concerning the knickers. By the end of the day the policemen scratched by brambles, wet from blundering into pools, exhausted from their labours and from the fear of being grasped and pulled under by the predatory mud-gods had lost their sense of humour and were in a foul mood. Had their sergeant ordered them back to the search the next day they would have mutinied but were spared the necessity. The sergeant agreed with them that they had been on a wild goose chase. Having complied with Uncle Tom's request for help for a day the sergeant told him that his men had other more urgent matters to deal with. Tom said later that he felt empty and useless. He couldn't think of anywhere else to search unless it was the rest of the Island, inch by inch.

"Those f'las as collared Johnny and put him on that train should all be given the birch rod. He wouldn' hurt a fly if it was bitin' him and now he's gone and fallen over a cliff or been took in the Curragh. Those f'las are a disgrace – they don't deserve to be officers. I'd flog the buggers meself if I could lay a han' on them I'm tellin' ya."

Tom and Liz went sadly back to work grieving that they'd never see Johnny again, wondering anxiously day by day what had become of him. They refused to replace him on the farm since that would imply that they had lost all hope of his ever returning. Still, there was the farm work to be done and the extra load weighed heavily on those left to bear it.

Some weeks after Johnny vanished Tom heard a story going the rounds at the Mart in Ramsey where he had come to buy lambs. The shepherd of the hills – the man of giant stature who used to frighten me when he walked past our house with his dogs – had been there to sell some sheep he had paid a Ramsey carter to bring down from the mountain for him. He was not disposed to say much on such occasions and never joined other farmers when they went for a drink at the *Queen's Arms* across the road but he had had a brief conversation with Big Bill, Lilywhite's auctioneer husband. The shepherd told Big Bill that after all these years of working alone he now had a helper. The latter was someone who knew a lot about sheep and was willing to work for board and lodging. He had found this "young f'la" wandering lost on a lower slope of North Barrule one night. He was wet through and hadn't eaten in a long time except for turnips he had dug up in the lower fields. The shepherd had taken him to his home in a valley on the far side of the mountain, dried him out by the peat fire, fed him some lamb stew and had given him a bed. He had slept a whole day. The shepherd said this stranger couldn't speak properly so he assumed that callous relatives had abandoned him. Not a talkative type himself the shepherd appreciated the young man's companionship and especially his ability to draw wonderful pictures.

"That's how that f'la speaks," said the shepherd. "He wants ya to know somet 'n he draws ya a picture. He was use 'n bits o' coal till I give him the pencil."

As soon as Tom heard this he excitedly borrowed Big Bill's phone to call Liz. He told her he would look for the shepherd right away.

However, by the time Uncle Tom had heard this story the shepherd had left town for home. Tom didn't know where exactly the shepherd lived except that his place was somewhere in a valley under North Barrule. He set off in his truck along the coastal road to Douglas – the one that ran right past our house. There was no sign of the shepherd on the road. There weren't many people about of whom he could ask directions. Of the few people he encountered no one knew precisely where the shepherd lived. One said he thought the shepherd lived in a valley alongside the mountain but he wasn't sure. When Tom came across the entrance to this valley he turned up it and found himself on a very narrow track which wasn't paved but strewn with small stones embedded in mud.

The ride was a rough, bumpy one up a steep gradient. Tom had no assurance that he was on the right road to the shepherd's place but couldn't turn his truck round even if he had wanted to. After he had climbed for a while a level valley stretched before him apparently empty of human habitation. Apart from the track he was following the only other signs that anyone had been there since time began were dry stone walls built round what had once been fields but were now abandoned areas of gorse, heather and tough wild grasses. The only sounds when Tom stopped his truck to cool his overheated engine were the woeful cries of the curlews and the sighing of a light breeze blowing gently through the long dried grass stalks.

"That there's a spooky place I'm tellin' ya," Tom said when he later described his search for Johnny, "it give me the creeps. Ya wouldn' want to be caught up there with the night comin' on. It give me the willies in broad daylight. It was like everyone was dead and I was the only f'la left alive."

Once his engine had cooled Tom re-started his truck and drove along the track for another quarter of an hour until he saw smoke curling into the air as from a chimney. Ahead of him the track suddenly descended steeply down to a narrow stream flowing swiftly from the mountain. At the bottom of the hill was not the primitive tholtan he imagined the shepherd to be living in but a two-storeyed house built of stone with a slate roof that seemed incongruous out here in the middle of nowhere. Tom drove down the hill and stopped by the front door. He expected to be swarmed by barking sheep dogs but none appeared. He went round to the back of the house but there was no sign of the shepherd. The silence that pervaded the valley wrapped the house also. Tom knocked but no one answered. He tried the front and back doors but found them locked. He didn't know what to do. The shepherd may have taken Johnny up the mountainside. The two of them could be anywhere. Tom couldn't wait any longer since he had been away from the farm since early morning. If he didn't go home soon Liz would start to imagine all manner of accidents that might have befallen him.

Tom actually felt relief when he drove back up the track toward the valley and the main road after turning his truck in the shepherd's yard. He didn't really want to confront the shepherd by himself. There were all those stories about him suggesting that he had strange powers to do harm to people he didn't like. From what the shepherd had said to Big Bill he seemed to be fond of Johnny. Maybe he wouldn't let Johnny go and would put some sort of curse on him for coming to take Johnny back. Like most country people of my childhood Tom was highly superstitious.

When he got back to the farm he found Liz about to phone the police to tell them that her husband had disappeared. She was mollified by the tale Tom had to tell. They decided that there would be safety in numbers so they would both drive to the shepherd's place the next day to retrieve Johnny. His mother was told of the latest developments and rejoiced that her son was still alive.

Early next morning Tom and Liz drove back to the shepherd's lonely house. By this time it was pouring with rain and the climb up to the valley track was even more difficult than it had been the day before. The mud on the road under the pebbles had become soft and more than once the back wheels of Tom's truck began to spin. By the time they reached the shepherd's house the truck was covered in mud and so was Tom since he had had to get out at intervals to push it while Liz gunned the engine and steered to more solid ground.

Tom knocked at the shepherd's door but as on the previous day nobody answered. Tom was angry. He had had to drive up to this remote place twice, this time getting himself wet and filthy in the process. Yesterday he was willing to accept that Johnny and the shepherd were probably out on the mountain seeing to the sheep but today, in this weather, they must be at home. Johnny would have answered the door readily so he must have been prevented by his strange host. Tom started to bang on the door.

"What are you hammering on the door for?" asked Liz getting out of the truck to join him in the rain.

"Because that f'la's in there an' he's not lettin' our Johnny go. That f'la's after stealin' our Johnny!"

Liz moved her husband out of the way and knocked on the door more gently. "Hello!" she called out, "hell-o-hoh!"

There was still no response. The rain fell in buckets.

Together they walked round to the back of the house as Tom had done the day before and Liz knocked on the back door. "Hell-o-hoh!" No one appeared.

"That bugger's got Johnny in there and won't let him out!" shouted Tom now ready to knock down the door and confront the seven-foot tall shepherd.

"Can you hear dogs barking in the house?" Liz asked him.

"No, why?"

"There's nobody at home," said Liz. "Would Rory and Tory sit quiet if someone was hammering on our door with all the noise you've been making?"

Tom had to admit that any self-respecting dog would be barking its head off in the circumstances.

"What shall we do?" he asked. "We can't keep coming up here every day. The truck'll fall to bits on this oul track."

"We'll just have to tell the police," said Liz, "and let them sort it all out."

Tom had cooled off in every sense by now. He thought Liz's idea was worth trying. The shepherd wasn't likely to resort to violence if the police came for Johnny. They got back into the truck and drove off but Tom had to get out and push for much of the way up the steep hill.

The shepherd watched his progress as he and Johnny stood silently under a small stand of pine trees a short distance from the house, the sheepdogs at their feet.

It was three or four days later before Johnny returned in triumph to the farm. Uncle Tom picked me up in his truck so that I wouldn't have to wait for the week's end to greet Johnny on his homecoming – a grateful acknowledgment of such help as I had provided. Johnny came back in a police car. His mother was there with the rest of us to greet him. She was going to take him home for the night. When he saw us all standing on the farm street Johnny waved frantically but waited for his police driver to open the car door before getting out. He had rarely driven in cars.

There's no point in trying to record what Johnny said on his arrival since all he could manage were unintelligible sounds though it was obvious they indicated pleasure. He came back to the farm in the late afternoon and had to be prevented from going at once to the cow byre to do the milking. Tonight, Uncle Tom told him, he was to go home with his mother who had a grand tea waiting for him.

It had taken time to pry Johnny loose from the shepherd's grasp. The shepherd had become fond of him and valued the work he did which, of course, lessened the shepherd's load. The police had gone to the house and, like Uncle Tom, knocked on the door in vain. The house was invariably empty. So they sent a van containing a small party of policemen to the sheperd's district. The van was parked out of sight of the shepherd's house and the police fanned out into the heather where they lay concealed. When the shepherd and Johnny came back to the house the police quickly surrounded it. An officer knocked on the front door and when the shepherd fled with Johnny out of the back door he was arrested. They took the shepherd and Johnny to the police station, threatening to prosecute the shepherd for kidnapping. Eventually they reached a compromise. Johnny would be returned to Glen Auldyn and the farm but would be allowed to visit the shepherd when it was convenient. The shepherd then reluctantly agreed to let him go.

The story of how Johnny found himself on the mountain in the middle of the night at least ten miles from where he had been pushed off the military bus was pieced together from things he said over the next few months. When he found himself in the dark in a strange place he was frightened out of his wits and feared approaching anyone for help in case they treated him as badly as those youthful Air Force officers had done. He kept himself hidden wandering through fields and along lanes where there were few people or none at all even in the daytime. He preferred to move at night but had no idea how to get back to the glen and the farm, not even which direction to take. He wandered about as it turned out in an area parallel to the glen but a few miles off. He skirted the town of Ramsey and climbed up the lower slopes of North Barrule – my old playground. He walked up rough tracks that led him higher up the mountain until, miserable and wet through, he had been found by the shepherd.

The latter treated him kindly and said he could stay the night in his house while his clothes dried. Oddly enough though the shepherd frightened me he seemed to reassure Johnny. Fearful of wandering about on his own again Johnny remained with the shepherd and became quite fond of him. The shepherd appreciated his pictures and offered him a job.

Order was restored on the farm with Johnny's return to his proper place though he was allowed occasional visits with the shepherd. Pop recovered from his head wound. His fireman, locally known as "Squinty" Moore because of his "lazy eye," said that whenever they passed the bridge where Pop had hit his head he shuddered slightly but Pop vigorously denied this. His head had a slightly dented look I thought but I was told I was "seeing things."

CHAPTER TWENTY-SIX

I HAD SEEN THAT SPITFIRE CRASH INTO THE BAY AND I KNEW THAT its pilot had been killed. I had watched those long slender carriers of wrecked aircraft driving by our house with their shapeless loads of metal after they came down from the mountain and I had visualized in a general sort of way bodies flung artistically about the heather. I had gaped at many a funeral cortege and wondered with a shiver down my spine what the coffin's occupant looked like in death and whether that person was really dead or only unconscious to wake up again when he or she had been buried and no one was by to unscrew the lid of their narrow box. It was fortunate that I hadn't yet come across Edgar Allen Poe. I hadn't confronted Death in the raw, face to face. I hadn't seen the pilot's mangled body after his plane hit the water and I hadn't had to look at those other bodies or parts of bodies in shattered aircraft on the mountainside. I hadn't, like Jakob, witnessed one man bury his sharpened knife in another. I hadn't had to confront death domestically except when I feared Ma might die in hospital – Pop's father and mother and Ma's father had all considerately shuffled off before I was born. Thus, unlike quite a few other children of my age, I hadn't been taken to family deathbeds or had to stand by an open coffin for a final terrified leave-taking. Although we were living through a war and death on a vast scale was a daily occurrence the war was being fought elsewhere. Our neighborhoods weren't bombed into rubble. Battles were fought in the North African desert or in Europe. The newsreels at the children's matinees at the movie house omitted the fact of death and focused on alleged heroic achievement – our side's of course. Announcers with terribly posh voices insisted that "we" were winning as the screen showed allies allegedly advancing and "jerry" apparently in retreat.

But the spectacle of death would not be denied either on the battlefield or at home. The day came when it confronted me. I saw its terrible face, quite literally, and it frightened me so much that I shiver even now at the memory of what I saw despite the passing of decades.

In an earlier chapter I mentioned that I rambled along the cliffs above the estate where our neighborhood Nazi was kept imprisoned. For some reason, perhaps because if any rescue of him were to be attempted the authorities were convinced it would come from the shore, soldiers were posted at the foot but not on the top of the cliffs and thus were not around to ban me from cliff-walking in time of war.

After the affair of the wall-climbing had become an unpleasant memory a boy I knew at school but tried to avoid asked me one day to take him cliff-walking when next I decided to go. This boy was afraid of heights. In fact this boy was afraid of so many things that I was astonished when he asked to come with me. His name was Jimmy – Jimmy Curphey – only son of parents often mistaken for his grandmother and grandfather. They wrapped this unexpected child of their late middle age with great care as if he were a fragile ornament about to be mailed somewhere. He was coated, capped, booted, gloved and mufflered even on mild days. They impressed upon him the perils of the world – microbial, geological, mete-orological, animal, vegetable, human – so effectively that taking the sort of risks that excited the rest of us was unthinkable for him. No high jinks in churchyards or racing about the woods for Jimmy. He lived in terror of wet feet, bruises, conflict of any kind, closed spaces, wide open spaces, heights, depths, anything beyond a very narrowly conceived norm. I was thus astonished when he asked to come with me along the clifftop path.

"But you're scared of the cliffs? Aren't you frightened you'll fall over"

"I want to come so I won't *be* scared any more."

"It's dangerous to walk on the cliffs when you're scared. You could get dizzy, lose your balance and fall down on to the rocks."

I hoped that Jimmy would be discouraged by this piece of news. For good measure I described the entirely fictitious case of two people, a boy and a girl, who were frightened of heights but walked along the clifftops anyway to prove they could do it. They were drawn by some strange fascination to the very edge of the cliffs to look down. They held hands to feel safer. The boy felt woozy, lost his balance and, dragging the girl with him, fell, their screams mingling with the cries of the gulls. They were smashed like broken dolls on the pointed rocks. Their detached heads, guts, torsos and limbs had to be shoveled into blood-soaked sacks. Their brains were thickly smeared across the rocks. Their eyeballs popped into pools.

Jimmy shuddered but was persistent. He said he was fed up with feeling frightened of just about everything the way his Mum and Dad were. He wanted to turn a new page in his life by tackling the cliffs. He had decided that if he could bring himself to walk along the cliff path without being paralysed by fear then maybe he would no longer be afraid of all the other things that currently alarmed him – the neighbor's large dog, the cattle in the field behind his house, his senile auntie who always wanted to kiss him, the Headmaster, the prospect of a break-out by the internees…the list of his fears was a long and varied one.

I was intrigued by his evident dread of the internees and asked why he felt like that about them. I told him that I had got to know several from my work on the farm and had found they were just like everyone else – some in fact were a great deal better. I even told him about Jakob without going into detail about our friendship and I finished by saying that these people, apart from the fact that they were harmless anyway, were all locked behind barbed wire so what was there to worry about? His nerve-wracked parents, he said, often speculated tremulously about what would happen if the prisoners escaped, broke through the wire and came rampaging through the town bent on vengeance. They talked of being murdered as they slept, of the house being ransacked, their only son perhaps tortured. It was a tale worthy of Bessie at her most absurd. I told Jimmy about Bessie and how she was dismissed as a crackpot. But I felt sorry for a boy who was subject to such domestic influences so I agreed to let him come with me the next time I walked the cliffs.

Made reckless by the notion of doing something so adventurous, possibly even dangerous, Jimmy mentioned his intended expedition to others. When the day arrived – a Saturday when for once I wasn't needed on the farm – he turned up accompanied by Jimmy Gawne, the boy who had educated me about adult sex but who had gone to pieces when the police dealt with us after the wall-climbing incident. It was bad enough that Jimmy Gawne had invited himself to the cliff-walk but worse still, large as life and twice as nasty along came Ronnie Skillicorn. He was frightened of nothing but had come along to make fun of Jimmy Curphey, Fear's slave. Jimmy evidently thought that if he called off the event owing to the unwelcome company he had attracted he would have surrendered to Fear yet again so, in a shaky voice, he pretended not to mind the others coming with us.

I regarded the cliff-walk as my private preserve. I considered that I was doing Jimmy Curphey a great favor by allowing him to come with me so I was angry when he arrived at our house flanked by these two but especially the sneering hectoring Ronnie. We might be getting on better at school after the Headmaster had caned us both that day but I didn't want anything to do with him out of school. I was tempted to tell them all that I had changed my mind, I wasn't coming, they'd all have to go without me, but that would have given Ronnie an immediate excuse to jeer.

I ground my teeth together but said nothing. I had read about people in the Bible gnashing their teeth – there seem to be a lot of frustrated teeth-gnashers in the Holy Book – and I had wondered what this gnashing was and how it was done not realizing that I knew already. I gnashed silently at Ronnie.

I normally reached the path across the cliffs by way of the electric railway's bridge at the top of Ballacray Road. There was a locally agreed procedure for walking across this bridge that carried the rails over the glen lying a hundred feet or so below. First one put one's ear to the nearest of the hollow metal poles holding up the electric wires. If there was a hum then a tram was approaching and one waited for it to pass. If there was no hum one set off across the bridge. Sometimes I went under rather than over the bridge by way of the hollow girders below the bridge-deck. From that place the view of the glen with its silvered river sliding smoothly over rocks was spectacular but on this day of initiation for timid Jimmy Curphey there was no point in suggesting this potentially dangerous route. He would have been far too frightened to cross the glen on the unsteadfast footing of a hollow girder.

Strictly speaking it wasn't necessary to cross the bridge at all but the alternate route involved a lengthy detour and children are impatient of detours especially when roundabout routes are tame. The thrill of crossing the bridge, apart from the view it afforded, lay in the fact that it was illegal and potentially dangerous. Despite one's precautions an electric tram might appear to test one's mettle. It didn't take a tram to test Jimmy Gawne's metal. The son and heir of the Gawne family declared that he wasn't going to walk across the bridge. If a tram came along we could all be killed! Jimmy Curphey seemed relieved that it hadn't been left to him to point this out and proposed that we all take the detour "just to be safe." Ronnie marched off across the bridge shouting derisive comments about cowards and cowardice. I reluctantly trudged with the two Jimmies further up the main road and then down a long muddy lane, which brought us to the railway tracks just beyond the bridge. Once we had crossed the tracks we would pick up the path that led to the cliffs.

Ronnie was sitting on the five-barred gate separating that path from the railway tracks. He claimed to know the area we were headed into intimately since he and his brother often came up here at night to set snares for rabbits. I told him that I frequently walked this area in daylight and we wrangled about who knew the place better.

Jimmy Curphy nervously interrupted to ask where the clifftops were. We were by now standing on a path through vast high tangles of blackberry bushes and flowering gorse that blocked our view of more distant objects. We could not as yet hear the sea though the air had a salty flavor. Jimmy evidently didn't want to find himself suddenly on a cliff top, predatory waves licking the rocks below, without having prepared himself mentally for the experience.

"Wettin' ya pants already are ya?" asked Ronnie. "The sea's over theya!"

Ronnie pointed into the distance, scorn in his voice for the likes of the two Jimmies. He no doubt recalled Jimmy Gawne's terror of the police while Jimmy Curphey, as I have said, was timidity itself and thus a natural source of amusement. Ronnie had sacrificed an afternoon in order to relish the latter's reaction to danger. Ronnie wanted to work up a playground act based on Jimmy literally "shittin' the pants on 'm." I led the way along the path while Ronnie walked behind the two Jimmies so that neither of them could bolt. We tramped along in silence until we could hear the sea, no more than a susurration of waves at first but changing to loud crashing sounds as we neared the cliff edge.

I turned to see how Jimmy Curphey, walking right behind me, was faring. His face was the color of the worn ivory keys of our ancient piano, the color of jaundice. Any minute now he would have to stand near the edge of a cliff and look down from two hundred feet sheer above the water where seabirds swirled close to the tops of the waves. If he suddenly became dizzy he might fall "arse over tit" as Ronnie would put it and join those seabirds, his body shattering on the rocks like the imaginary dismembered couple I had told him about to frighten him off. From the look on his face I didn't doubt that similar thoughts were racing through his brain.

"It's all right, Jimmy," I said. "You don't have to do this. We can go back if you want to."

"An' I'll be tellin' them f'las at skyool how ya were that frikened ya wet yaself," said Ronnie. "That's a promise."

Jimmy Curphey didn't reply. Jimmy Gawne looked as nervous as the other Jimmy. To encourage them I walked slowly over to the edge of the cliff while they mentally decided what they could bring themselves to do. A long way below me seagulls and oyster-catchers were circling. I regretted that on this side of the Island we didn't have puffins, those colorful parrots of the sea. I also regretted that we didn't have white-bodied, yellow-headed gannets given to hovering then dive-bombing like stukas for fish snapping their wings shut before they plunged into the waves. To see them one would have to be standing on tamer cliffs made from clay and easily eroded sandy soil out toward the parish of Bride. The Jimmies might feel a lot bolder on those rockless cliffs. Round our rocky promontory the cries of thousands of gulls were as funereal in their way as those of the curlews on the mountainsides.

There were irregular lines of foam where the waves shattered themselves on projecting rocks. On the ledges in the cliff-face were seagulls' nests no doubt each containing three eggs none of which would be exactly the same colour. Like many Island children I collected seagull's eggs but followed Pop's advice to take only one from each nest so that the parent birds would not abandon it. I blew out the yokes through pinholes I made in the shell and kept the latter for my collection housed in shoeboxes lined with cotton wool. No two eggs were exactly alike. Their varied blues, greens and mottled browns fascinated me. I didn't go climbing down cliffs for them – I wasn't an entirely foolhardy child – but took them from nests I found on cliff tops.

Not so Ronnie Skillicorn. He bet us all he could reach a nest on the side of a cliff and bring an egg back from it unbroken. He showed how brave he was by shoving me aside and standing on the very edge of the cliff where, for good measure, he did his version of an Indian war dance. Jimmy Gawne responded by rushing back along the track by which we had reached this place. He told us later, at school, that he wasn't going to watch Ronnie fall and turn into red porridge on rocks as sharp as a wolf's teeth.

Ronnie yelled after him "Ya's a coward, Jimmy Gawne, and the Trammy Man'll getcha."

The "Trammy Man" was another of those mythic figures of our youth. There was actually a tall lean man who walked along the electric railway track knocking the rails with a metal rod to test for weaknesses. Because he chased us off the tracks when he found us walking along them roaring in fury as he did so we endowed him with supernatural powers and malice thus frightening ourselves unnecessarily. Tramping the tram rails with his long metal rod and uncertain temper he seemed to us an apt partner for any of the Manx witches. We said his wife had been rolled down Slieau Whallian in a barrel of nails and had survived the experience.

Jimmy Curphey stood as far away from the cliff edge as the gorse bushes would allow, his eyes bulging, more and more appalled by Ronnie's recklessness as he did his wild dance.

"You'll fall over, Ronnie," I said to him at last, "come away from the edge. You're only showing off."

"Am I then? That's all you know." He grabbed some long trailing vines that hung over the cliff – a form of ivy, old, thick and well-rooted. He turned his back to the sea, grinned at Jimmy Curphey now cowering against the gorse and looking terrified, tugged hard on the vines to test their firmness and reliability, then disappeared over the edge of the cliff. When I rushed to see what had happened to him I saw him rappelling his way down the cliff-side using the ivy vines as a rope. It was evident from his assurance that he had performed this dangerous feat before.

"Did he fall? Is he dead?" asked the remaining Jimmy on the verge of hysteria.

"Come and have a look," I said. "He's actually climbing down the cliff using those plants."

Curiosity proved stronger than terror, at least for the moment. Jimmy got down on his hands and knees and crawled to the edge of the cliff where he lay on his stomach and peeped timidly over. His fascination with Ronnie's reckless descent proved to be so strong that he temporarily forgot where he was. We both watched Ronnie make his way down the uneven cliff side, which sloped more gently after the vertical section toward the top. A third of the way down bushes growing from old eroded rock-falls provide extra hand and foot-holds. Abandoning the trailing ivy for these robust natural aids Ronnie was soon down close to those rocks against which the incoming tide hurled itself in white spray. He seemed to have forgotten about the gull's eggs. In spite of himself Jimmy was impressed by Ronnie's nerve, strength and skill.

"I couldn't do that," said Jimmy sadly, "not ever,"

"Why would you want to?" I asked worried that Ronnie might injure or kill himself when he tried to climb back up. "Anyway look what you've done. You've been looking over the edge of the cliff and you haven't been scared."

Once I had said this Jimmy, no longer distracted by watching Ronnie's mad escapade unfold, began to tremble. Here he was looking at the sea so far below and if the earth underneath him gave way he would plunge right down there to his death. They'd have to scrape him off the rocks! The jaundiced hue spread across his face again. He shoved himself rapidly backwards and then got shakily to his feet when he reached the gorse bushes. I stood looking down at Ronnie wondering what had diverted his attention from the ledges where the gulls were nesting. He was staring at the sea just below the rock on which he was standing. After a short time he turned to look up and seemed to be shouting something though I couldn't hear what. Then he began to wave his arms about and I became worried that he was in some sort of trouble and needed help. I waved and shouted back but he couldn't hear me any better than I could hear him.

"What's up?" Jimmy Curphey asked, his voice trembling.

"Dunno," I said. "Ronnie's shouting something but I can't hear him. I think he's in trouble down there."

"Oh, Lordy!" said Jimmy (an expression he had picked up from his perpetually surprised and distressed mother much given to instant panic over small things). "O Lordy, Lordy, Lordy! What can we do?"

I found Jimmy's use of that plural pronoun curious in view of his petrified state.

"I'll have to find a way down the cliffs to see what's wrong," I said with a lot more confidence than I felt.

"Don't leave me here on my own!" Jimmy begged.

"Why – do you want to come with me?" I was fast getting fed up with Jimmy whose voice had become a pleading whine. "Come or stay...suit yourself. I'm going to see what's up with Ronnie."

I wasn't going to repeat Ronnie's foolhardy trick with the vines so I walked further along the cliff-top path toward an area where I knew the cliffs were much less high above the sea. I was surprised to see Jimmy following me but he was more frightened at the prospect of being left on his own. I searched for a way down the cliffs for quite a distance beyond the point at which Ronnie had started his dubious descent. Eventually I came across a very narrow track zigzagging down cliffs much lower than those down which Ronnie had rappelled. If he had started at this spot he could have reached the sea and the gulls without his mountain-climbing act.

I started carefully down this track not much wider than one of my feet. I leaned against the rock face as I put one foot carefully in front of the other. Jimmy couldn't bring himself to follow any further. He said he'd wait for me and sat down in some tough grass while I made my way slowly twisting and turning with the narrow track down to the rocks just above the level of the incoming tide. A short headland separated me from where Ronnie was standing but I knew there was something like a cave at the end of it. I scrambled over the rocks to it, the waves breaking over them so that my feet got wet. I could hear Ma already telling me off when she saw the white marks left on my boots by the salt.

It was an easy climb of about seven feet to what I thought was the mouth of the cave in the headland but found it was a hollow. I could reach the area where Ronnie had been standing by getting through this hollow and climbing down to the rock-strewn beach beyond. Ronnie must have thought we'd abandoned him. When he saw me emerge from the hollow in the headland he waved his arms about and started yelling again though I still couldn't hear what he was saying.

I crossed the rocky beach as fast as I could and then finally I could hear what Ronnie was shouting about.

"There's a dead f'la down theya!" he shouted, "there's a dead f'la in a blue suit floatin' down theya with li'l fishes swimmin' round 'm!"

This sounded like one of Ronnie's practical jokes. It would have been just like him to have got me all the way down here for nothing. But his excitement seemed real enough so I hurried over the rocks to join him. What I saw was what looked like an inflated blue pin-stripe Sunday suit of the sort worn by Shoveller Mylecraine and a number of other local men of his age. It was turning in languid circles as the incoming tide sent more and more water through hollow passages in the rocks to the tidal pool where the body in the suit floated. Mecifully the corpse was floating face down so we couldn't tell if it was someone we knew. Perhaps it was a German spy who had been brought to the Island by U-boat but had drowned trying to reach the shore, no doubt in a dinghy which had been over-set by the waves. When I made this suggestion Ronnie agreed with me for once.

"Let's drag that f'la outa there," said Ronnie, "and see what's in his pockets."

"You go ahead…but I won't be staying to look at a dead body. They say people who've been in the sea look terrible."

"So ya just want ta leave this f'la bobbin' about like a cork and us doin' nothin'…is that the way of it? That f'la might have money on 'm."

"He might be a spy. We'e got to tell the police."

"Ya'll not be getting' me to them f'las…not after what they done when we was caught climbin' that wall beause ya couldn't get over it fast enough in them big daft boots ya Dad give ya."

"Well, you stay here so I know where to bring the police and I'll go and get them."

Without waiting for Ronnie to reply I set off back the way I had come deaf to Ronnie's protests against bringing in the natural enemies of generations of Skillicorns. I retraced my route across the flat rocks toward the hole in the headland, climbed up into it and down the other side and then began the climb back up the narrow track toward the top of the cliffs. The going was a lot tougher than on the downward journey and I arrived at the cliff top sweating liberally and panting for breath. Ronnie was right behind me. Jimmy Curphey, sitting where I had left him, had assumed Ronnie had been shouting to us because he was injured.

"What's wrong?" he asked in a puzzled voice since Ronnie looked no different than when he had last seen him launch himself over the cliff except that now he was wet, a lot dirtier and out of breath. Jimmy had evidently expected blood, wounds, fractured bones or why had Ronnie called us?

"What's wrong," Ronnie replied, "is that there's a dead f'la floatin' down there. He come in with the tide and got stuck in a rock pool an' he's goin' round' an' roun' in circles. And this f'la (pointing at me) wouldn't help me haul him out an' search the pockets on 'm."

At first Jimmy didn't believe him. He had been the butt of Ronnie's jokes on too many past occasions to accept anything he said at face value. I assured him that, for once, Ronnie was telling the truth.

"What are we going to do?" asked Jimmy who plainly would rather be a long way off, not called upon to do anything.

"We have to fetch the police," I told him.

"I'm not fetchin' them f'las" said Ronnie "and that f'la down there in the sea doesn't care what we do so I'm off home for me tay."

Matching his words with action Ronnie strode off along the cliff path in the direction of the railway bridge. Jimmy looked at me nervously as if I was going to insist that he come with me to the Police Station, a place of dread for him.

"Me Mum'll want me home for me tea," he said weakly.

"Please yourself," I said, "but I'm going for the police."

Jimmy didn't say anything further then and kept quiet for most of the way back to our house where he had left his bike. As soon as we reached *Rosetree Villa* he snatched his bike from the wall it was leaning against, said "S'long," and rode off. I didn't go into the house to tell Ma and Pop what had happened but took my *Raleigh* and raced to what we used to call "the cop shop" passing Jimmy on the way. That I would actually hurry to the building where I had been taken ignominiously as a prisoner not so long before only struck me as ironic long after these events had become distant memories. At the time I was so filled with excitement at having possibly found a dead German spy disguised as Shoveller Mylcraine that I couldn't get there fast enough.

When I reached the desk in the reception area just inside the Police Station I told my story incoherently and at top speed. The officer on duty managed to calm me down long enough for me to get the facts out in some order. He summoned the sergeant I had met on my last visit who told me that if I thought I was playing a funny joke the laugh would be on me since there were penalties for wasting police time. I was so overcome with frustration at not being taken seriously that I started to cry. The sergeant told me to repeat my story, slowly this time.

"Where did you say this body was?"

"It's up near the cliffs where we were walking. I can take you there but I can't explain exactly where the dead man was."

"Okay, you'll have to show us. But you'd better not be leading us on a wild goose chase."

Thus it was that in the late afternoon of a day in early summer I rode with two policemen and two auxiliaries in a small black van as far as the electric railway bridge across which we all walked to the place where Ronnie had gone over the cliffs hanging on to the trailing ivy. The policemen were carrying hip-waders, binoculars, powerful torches, lengths of rope and other gear that would have severely encumbered them had they descended to the rocks below. But the tide was now fully in and the water was so high that it was obvious we couldn't reach the body even by the route I had taken more than a couple of hours earlier. In any case a careful search of the area with the binoculars indicated that the body was no longer there.

"You promise you're not having us on" one policeman said once they had decided there was no body below us.

"He must have floated along the coast," I said.

The policemen considered whether they should call out the Lifeboat to cruise the shoreline looking for the body or perhaps the Air-Sea Rescue launch but first decided to search the coast in case the drowned man had been taken by the currents and deposited on rocks ahead of us. I went with them as they examined the rocks and sea through their binoculars. After we had walked for over ten minutes one of the police said he thought he saw something floating near the water's edge a few hundred yards ahead of us. Others focused on the spot and said it might be a body. They would go down the cliff to investigate. They looked around for a way down and found one much easier than the route I had taken by going a few hunded yards further along the path. There was a rough track down the cliff which here was nowhere near as high as the one over which Ronnie had launched himself so dramatically. I was told to stay where I was. Refusing to consider what I might actually have to look at and as excited by the drama of the events in which I was playing a part as on the night of the Christmas Tree Caper I followed the police down the track. I saw a blue heap in the sea moving back and forth with the waves a hundred yards or so from the shoreline.

"Ya shoulda stayed up there," said the sergeant "but since ya didn't ya'd better not watch this. If that f'la's been in the water a long time he'll scare the socks off ya."

The police found the body floating between two rocks lying close toether. They put on their hip-waders to go out to wind their ropes round the dead man and tow him in to the stony shore. In spite of the sergeant's warning I was still watching eagerly after they had hauled the body to the shoreline. The man in the water was rigidly stiff. When his legs jammed into a fissure in low-lying rock the efforts of the policemen hauling on the ropes reared the body upright. It swung slowly round until I was staring at the most terrible face I have ever seen – more terrible than anything I had experienced in a nightmare.

The face was white as marble and bloated to several times its normal size so that it looked like a huge grotesque devil-mask. There were broad, deep-red swollen rings round the dead man's open eyes. The expression on the face was hideous. I threw up as soon as I beheld this horror. One of the policemen took my arm and hurried me from this scene back up to the top of the cliffs. What made the apparition worse for me was that despite the effects of the sea and the ghastliness of that mask of a face I knew I was not looking at a German spy but at a diabolical caricature of Shoveller Mylcraine.

Why hadn't I gone home like Jimmy Curphey and Ronnie Skillicorn? Their departure had spared them the grotesque scene I had had to witness. Why hadn't I heeded the warnings of the policemen and stayed on the cliff path? Not only had I seen Death itself in all its terrible detail, but there were ramifications. The policeman who insisted on taking me home to explain the day's events to my parents told me that there would be an inquest and I would have to be a witness.

When Pop saw me coming up the garden path with a policeman he hurried to open the door to find out what mischief I had been up to this time. What imminent disgrace was I bringing upon the family?

"What's he been at?" Pop asked the constable. "Whatever it is ya can bank on it, I'll take the slipper to 'm."

"It's not like that," said my uniformed companion, "he's had a very frightening experience. He's had a real shock and maybe he should see a doctor. He found a body in the sea and showed us where it was. It wan't a pretty sight and the lad saw everything."

Pop groaned and said, "Why does it always have to be you?"

The Inquest was held a short time later and I was allowed a day off school to testify at it. News soon spread that Shoveller Mylecraine had ended his life in the sea – whether deliberately or not was left for the Inquest to decide. Public opinion had no doubts. The possibility that Shoveler had had another heart attack while out for a walk along the beach was summarily dismissed. Of course he had killed himself. To have died of natural causes or to have fallen into the sea by chance would be too ignominious. No. Shoveller could no longer face a life of aimless wandering round the town in his Sunday suit boring the pants off everyone he met with those tales of his working life. He saw other men going to work or war dirtying their hands or dying heroically and he felt useless even though he was an ARP Warden. So one day he went for a walk by the sea and ended it all with a final leap. Bessie, of course, loudly supported such a theory.

The children at school crowded round me in the playground asking for every detail of the story which, of course, enraged Ronnie Skillicorn, the actual finder of the body. He told everyone who would listen that my part in the business was a minor one, that if it hadn't been for him descending the cliffs with indomitable nerve the body would still be floating in the sea. If anyone had a day off school to go to an Inquest it ought to be him. But the story had got into the local newspaper and, on the best police authority, featured me as the finder of the corpse so no one believed Ronnie. He was accused of trying to cash in on my experience and this, of course, enraged him further. He kept challenging me to fights and got beaten up by Pierre Lamontagne who thought what I had done was heroic. Groups of friends accompanied me home in case Ronnie carried out any of his threatened ambushes.

"You wait! I'll getcha after skyool!" he kept saying.

Jimmy Curphey kept quiet about the whole affair. He didn't want his neurotic parents picturing their only child walking along a cliff path at a dangerous height marked for life by witnessing the consequences of a possible suicide in the company of someone like Ronnie Skillicorn. Jimmy Gawne was silent too. He didn't want it known that he had run away even before the corpse was found.

The Inquest itself was anti-climactic. I was questioned about the events of that fateful day but not about my companions. I was asked to describe factually what I saw but not obliged to dwell upon the horror of it all.

After about ten minutes at the witness stand I was dismissed with thanks. Shoveller, it emerged, died by drowning and not from a heart attack. Whether he had jumped into the sea or accidentally fallen into it could not be determined. Without evidence to show how Shoveller entered the water nothing could be decided except the fact that he had drowned, as an autopsy revealed. His wife was relieved that the infamy of suicide had been averted whatever the local gossips might continue to say.

I gave up walking along the cliff tops. I had no desire to find anyone else floating in on the afternoon tide. But I had learned what Death can look like and I have never forgotten.

CHAPTER TWENTY-SEVEN

IT WAS ALL VERY WELL FOR ME OR RONNIE SKILLICORN TO FEEL SUPE-
rior to the likes of the two Jimmies and the Curphy parents beause
of their timorousness but Fear was in plentiful supply in those days.
Whenever German bombers flew overhead and the siren's wailing woke
us up we did not adopt a nonchalant manner, say something wearily witty,
turn over in bed and ignore the sound like a minor nuisance. We got
up wide-awake, tense, squeezed ourselves into our converted pantry conscious that we lacked effective shelter, overwhelmingly relieved when the
all clear sounded.

In 1940 the whole country had been gripped by fear. Germany had con-
quered much of Europe with lightning speed. Mussolini joined Hitler's
Axis. America had not yet committed itself to war so after the fall of
France Britain stood alone. What was left of the British army in Europe
was stranded at Dunkirk apparently doomed to capture. Invasion seemed
imminent. It was the resulting panic that caused the government to round
up people like Jakob and send them to internment camps like the one
in my home town. A particular fear of invasion from the air by parachutists had the Island government ordering the removal of all road signs
including the historic ones dating back to the Eighteenth Century. What
confusion these removals would have caused any invaders equipped with
aircraft, up-to-date maps, compasses and recent aerial surveys of an island

thirty-three miles long and twelve miles wide no one seems to have paused to consider as they labored to remove the highway signs. They had to do something to allay their fear. They weren't going to "make it easy for Jerry."

Fear of invasion from the air caused farmers to block local roadways and scatter oil drums and old farm machinery across their larger fields to prevent airborne troop carriers from landing in them. These measures merely prevented the tilling of the land until tensions lessened and reason prevailed. For a long time the fear that the Germans would land on Britain's outer islands and use them as bases from which to invade the mainland kept numerous Dad's Army members keenly eyeing the sky and training binoculars on the sea.

One day Fear came to visit us on the farm in the guise of two men in dark hats and long dark overcoats attended by four soldiers with rifles. The men in long coats arrived in a khaki-colored military car driven by a soldier; the other soldiers came close behind in a small dark green army truck with a canvas-roofed back of the sort that had conveyed me and my wall-climbing friends to the local Police Station. The invaders got out of their vehicles looking curiously around them. Rory and Tory, taking an instant dislike to this odd platoon, began to bark and to circle it menacingly. The soldiers, who had taken their rifles out of their truck, pointed them at the dogs and threatened to shoot them unless Uncle Tom had them removed.

"What's doin' on ya?" Uncle Tom angrily demanded. "Put them guns away will ya. Yarn't in a war up 'ere. Y'ar trespassin' on my lan' the lot o' ya. Have ya gone foreign pointin' them guns at my dogs?"

"Call them off," said one of the men in long overcoats. "We're here on official business."

"What business?" Tom asked belligerently.

"None of your business," said the second long-coated man as if he'd just been witty. He glanced at the soldiers for a response but their eyes were on the dogs, which continued to circle them.

Tom whistled the dogs away. Reluctantly they stopped menacing the visitors and trotted over to him. They sat when Tom told them to – evidently against their better judgment since they panted indignantly and growled at the soldiers in intermittent protest.

"Well, what do you f'las want?" asked Tom. "I'm busy. I haven' got all day stan'in' here like a stook in a hayfield."

"You have a land girl working here, a Mary Kinvaig of Sulby?"

"What of it?" asked Tom. "What's she got to do with you? She's a good worker an's done nothing wrong as I know so why are you f'las all here with ya guns an' ya threats to shoot me dogs like them Nazi f'las. There's a war on an' farmers don't need you f'las getting in the way o' the work."

"Mary Kinvaig," said the long-coated man who had asked about her "has to come with us for questioning."

"Who *are* you f'las an' what's Mary after doin' but sweatin' hard here for the war effort?" asked Tom in exasperation. Tom had begun to worry – as he confided later – that some busy-body had seen Mary and Jakob together and told the authorities that a land girl was over-familiar with a prisoner. He should have been stricter with them both.

I wasn't present at this confrontation on the farm street. It took place on a Friday when I was at school. Had I been there I would have been terrified of arrest owing to my friendship with Jakob. I heard about what had happened the next day from Tom when he was driving me to the farm. Like most of the adults I knew when I was growing up Tom formed his more dramatic experiences into highly detailed narratives so I was told about what he was thinking while he confronted the military group, who was wearing what, who said what and to whom (verbatim) and in what tone of voice and the precise time of the whole encounter with a brief description of the prevailing weather. Everyone's conduct was described in detail. The threatening demeanor of the visitors was emphasized. Tom, of course, cast himself as a Manx David confronting an English Goliath (several, in fact) though in the event he had been powerless to prevent the invaders of his peace and property from taking Mary away in the military car without deigning to explain who they were or why they wanted her. *Force majeur* prevailed. By the time I reached the farm no one in an official position had telephoned the Talbots to explain why Mary had been arrested, where or if she was being held. Mary's mother didn't have a phone so Tom couldn't call her for information. It was all an ominous mystery. First Johnny had been lost and now Mary had been taken. Tom speculated uneasily about Fate. Had he somehow offended the Little People and were they now taking their revenge?

"P'raps we should call the police," said Liz. "I mean who were those f'las? For all we know they could have been German commandos…or spies."

"Listen at yerself!" Tom said testily. "And what would spies want with our Mary? Would they be puttin' the thumbscrews to her to find out how many spuds we dug up last week…or how many turnips? Would they be forcin' her to tell how many gallons o' milk a day the cows give? Would that f'la Hitler need ta know all this ta win the war?"

Tom, normally a mild-mannered man, was clearly provoked by the arrival of armed and arbitrary authority on his domain. The taking away of his land girl with neither explanation nor apology had him on the phone to other farmers to see if they had been similarly visited. Was a vast purge of land girls in progress for some reason? He was mortified to find himself in a minority of one. Everyone else's land girls were working away unhindered.

When we were alone I asked Jakob what he made of this event. He said Mary's arrest was his fault. Prisoners knew they were not supposed to be on close terms with anyone outside the Camp. A sympathizing friend on the outside – especially on a farm – could abet an escape all too easily. Like Uncle Tom Jakob assumed that someone must have seen him with Mary – holding her hand, perhaps, or, worse, kissing her – and that someone must have informed the authorities. While we were speculating on where they might have been seen together Uncle Tom shouted from the front door of the farmhouse that he wanted to talk to Jakob. His voice was uncharacteristically harsh.

"He's going to blame me," said Jakob, "as if I'm not as worried as he is about what's happened to her. People do such stupid things in wartime. I'm going to tell the Camp Commandant about us…I'll say it was my fault, not Mary's…I'll…"

"Jay-cob!!!!" bawled Uncle Tom from the farmhouse door, "gerrup 'ere when I'm callin' ya!!!"

As Jakob went off to tell Uncle Tom that he would shoulder the blame if indeed Mary had been removed for fraternizing with a prisoner Auntie Liz appeared. I asked her what reasons she could think of to explain Mary's arrest.

"Not a single one. I'm stumped like everyone else. Whoever took her must have made a mistake. It's these English come-overs! If the Manx police had driven up here they'd have given us an explanation. And they wouldn't have brought a lorry-load of soldiers with guns just to arrest poor Mary. What did they think we'd do when we saw them? Get the old blunderbuss down from the attic and blast away at them as if they were rooks in the corn?"

Johnny rushed up in a state of high excitement and interrupted her. "Arc income! Arc income!" He could hardly get his backwards message out. He had been really upset by Mary's arrest and more upset still when no one could explain to him why she was being taken away. The car whose approach he had just excitedly announced might contain someone who could offer an explanation.

The car in fact contained Liz's ideal expositor – a Manx policeman. It wasn't just any polieman, however, but the police sergeant with whom I had had dealings, a man I considered far from ideal.

Evidently the feeling was mutual. "You again!" he exclaimed as he got out of his car. "Where there's trouble there's Erik, eh?…runnin' at it like a ferret after a rabbit."

"What's the news about our poor Mary?" Liz asked ignoring the sergeant's characterization of me. Before the sergeant could reply Liz showered him with questions, pelted him with statements, offered heated opinions about the frightening way the poor girl had been dealt with so the sergeant found it hard to get a word in sideways.

"Two come-overs," she said, "looking like the Gestapo and a lorry-load of uniformed ruffians with rifles just to take away an innocent girl who had no idea what was going on! They treated her worse than an alien…and you know they're not treated right! They frightened her out of her wits! And here she is working dawn to dusk to help grow food for the war. She deserves a medal! But what does she get? She's dragged away by a pack of hooligans who'd run a mile if a real German soldier ever popped up to shoot at them. Does it bother them frightening a girl with their guns? Of course not. They love it! They'll be bragging about it at the pub. They even threatened to shoot our dogs! They're real heroes…I don't think. Why don't they pick on someone who'll fight back? I'll tell you why…"

Liz was quite prepared to continue with a minute pyschological analysis but the sergeant cut her short.

"Look, Missus, I'm sorry about all that but we're in a war. We can't take chances and we can't always be polite, not where people's safety's involved."

"My God! I never thought I'd hear a Manxman defending a gang of rough come-overs, especially not a policeman! And how, pray, is public safety threatened by our Mary Kinvaig who works her heart out here and then goes home to look after her sick mother and whose brother's in the army somewhere dangerous and whose Dad's working for the war effort on the Mainland in a factory after the army turned him down because he was too old or not fit enough or had flat feet…"

"Well, you got there at last Missus. It's the father, see…"

The sergeant drew Liz away from me at this point making it quite plain he didn't want me to hear any of what he had to say next. He talked to her at a distance for quite a long time and as he did so her resentment seemed to subside. When at last he got back into his car her demeanor was subdued. Of course I wanted to know at once what the sergeant had told her. She said that he had warned her not to mention what he had just revealed to anyone – except Uncle Tom, of course, but he had to keep the secret too.

"Anyway, why should you be worried about Mary?" Liz asked with some acerbity. "You never liked her and now they've taken her away you should be celebrating…you'll have Jakob all to yourself again…unless, of course, they come for him next."

I felt wretched…all mixed up in a manner I wasn't used to. I was hurt that Liz would accuse me of taking satisfaction at Mary's misfortune. I had been angry with Mary at first for coming between me and Jakob even if she didn't mean to cause trouble. I still preferred to talk to Jakob alone and didn't like sharing him with her but with time I had come to tolerate her, accept her as a member of the farm's society and was as troubled as everyone else by her sudden and forcible removal. Then I was terrified that they'd come for Jakob next whoever "they" were. That would end the most significant friendship of my childhood. The more I thought about all this the more upset I became until I began to cry. Here was I, a fearless stealer of apples and Christmas trees, hurler of bracken boomerangs, occasional taunter of the Trammy Man, provoker of the Vicar, discoverer of corpses, intrepid witness at Inquests at an age when I was beyond the tears that Carlo often resorted to, yet blubbering in front of Liz anyway, unable to stop once I had started.

"I'm sorry," said Liz, "I shouldn't have said that. I'm sure you're as worried as the rest of us really. It's just that what that copper told me about Mary has upset me."

Perhaps as a penance for alarming me Liz told me briefly what she had heard from the police sergeant but made me promise not to tell anyone else.

"You know what they're like in these parts for gossip," she said after I had sworn not to tell a soul. "The sergeant told me to tell only Tom so you have to keep it to yourself."

The gist of what she revealed was that at the factory in England where Mary's father worked, some plans for new aircraft parts had gone missing from the Manager's office. Mary's father, Charlie Kinvaig, it seems, wasn't patriotic enough for many of his co-workers. And he wasn't English. Indeed he had often been critical of the way the English government was directing the war. The Manx government, he said, would do it all differently and do it better if it had the authority. Then, ill-advisedly, he had told those he worked with that Hitler hadn't got everything wrong. He was, said Charlie, right to invade Russia to wipe out Communism. Such views didn't sit well with many of Charlie's fellow workers so when the plans disappeared one weekend a lot of people suspected him in the absence of other culprits. The Manager was informed and Charlie was conveyed to the nearest gaol as fast and as summarily as Jakob had been to his derelict "transit camp." Charlie's lodgings had been turned upside down but no plans were found so the police decided that he had somehow had them conveyed to his daughter on the Isle-of-Man. If they weren't with her then perhaps his wife had them or had hidden them somewhere on their property. So Mary had been removed from the farm to "help the police with their enquiries." Of course in the event she told the authorities she knew nothing of such plans and that her father would never ever be a traitor to his country but her protestations hadn't impressed the authorities. "Well, you would say that wouldn't you?" they had said. Mary had been told to stay at home after police and soldiers had examined every inch of the family house at Sulby and the entire extensive garden to no avail. To make sure she stayed put a guard had been left at her family's house. No one could enter or leave without permission. Mary's ailing mother's condition had not been improved by this arrangement nor at the news that her husband was being detained. Like Mary she vigorously denied he would have had anything to do with the theft, especially the sort of theft that amounted to treason.

"You can imagine what talk there'll be in the village now," said Liz. "The whole family will be found guilty by those Sulby busybodies."

I thought of a chorus of Bessies and shuddered.

I soon had further cause to shudder. The following Monday I came home from school still very much wrapped up in a scene from some adventure story we had been reading in class to find, as I neared our house, a military car parked outside. It matched Uncle Tom's description of the one that had driven up to the farm. I thought immediately that the men in long coats must have come for me. They had found out about my friendship with Jakob and had come to make me tell them about it. They would want to know all about Jakob and Mary so that they could punish him for making her his sweetheart. A month or two earlier I would have been glad of the chance to tell them all the bad things about her that I could think of but not now. The easiest way to avoid talking to these men would be not to go home so I turned back down Ballacray Road and went over to the churchyard to see if any of my athletic friends were leaping off graves.

There was no one about in the late afternoon of a school day. I loitered for a while hoping someone I knew would turn up but no one did, not even the Vicar. I spent the time trying to read the inscriptions on the weather-worn gravestones and was surprised at how old some of them were. Many were so old that their messages of wisdom, wit, or warning had been entirely erased by wind and rain. As I mentioned in an earlier chapter I normally took no interest in the graves except as impromptu pieces of gymnastic equipment to stand on or leap-frog over but on this afternoon the need to play for time and the absence of companions led me to pay closer attention.

When daylight began to fade I hurried away not wanting to be around when the ghosts of the buried dead left their narrow charnel houses to walk the neighborhood as it was locally said that they liked to do at nightfall, to catch a little fresh air. These ghosts might try to pay me back for heedlessly running about on their resting places.

I approached our house carefully even though the military car had gone. The relief to discover that the overcoated figures were not within pointing accusing fingers at Ma and Pop made me feel almost delirious. My good cheer was soon countered by Pop, not long home from work but long enough to have been given an account of the official visit by Ma.

"Where've you been an' what have you been up to now?" he asked.

"I've been playing. I haven't been up to anything."

"Is that why we've had visitors? Is that why police from across have been here asking after you?"

"What did they want?"

"Isn't that what your mother and me'd like to know? Isn't that why your mother's been in a state since those f'las rang the front doorbell and asked after you? What's goin' on? Not long since y'ad to go and find poor oul Shoveller waterlogged in the sea in 'is Sunday suit. What's it this time? Somethin' ta do with that Jaycob f'la I'll bet. What've ya been doin' at 'm? Tryin' to help him escape over the sea like Bonny Prince Charlie or what?"

Pop was angry enough to deal out a clip over the ear so I told him that Mary's father had been unjustly accused of something serious (I didn't specify what in deference to Liz) and the police were asking questions about him.

"What's all that got to do with you?" asked Pop.

"Search me," I said.

"Well somebody just might," said Pop, "because them f'las are comin' back after y've had ya tea so don't go missin'."

My loitering in the churchyard had accomplished nothing. I might as well have gone home in the first place and faced these men. They turned up again not long after we had finished the evening meal.

I had often been attracted to the most famous picture of W. F. Yeames, the Victorian artist. A copy of it hung on the wall of our upstairs sitting room. Its central figure is a small boy dressed in a suit of blue velvet of the sort worn by Cavalier children in Seventeenth Century England. The boy is confronted by a group of Cromwell's Roundheads. A man in a Roundhead helmet and metal breastplate has a hand on the shoulder of the boy's sister while behind this soldier is the mother, her face expressing anguish at what her young son might say as he stands on a decorative footstool that brings him to eye level with his Cromwellian questioner sitting across from him behind a long table. The caption reads "When did you last see your father?" It is obvious that Cromwell's men are sneakily trying to take advantage of the child's innocence to find out where the boy's Cavalier father is hiding and nab him. I felt like this boy when the tall men in long overcoats returned to question me about Mary. I felt that they were just waiting for me to say something incriminating about her or her father, something she might have given away in conversation. They were not of course aware that I already knew what they were after and that I wasn't an innocent like the Cavalier child. I decided to play dumb and give away nothing to these latter-day English Roundheads.

"You must have talked to this girl Mary when she wasn't working."

"S'pose so."

"Does that mean you did?"

"S'pose so."

"Look, we're not going to bite. Either you did talk to her or you didn't"

"Everyone spoke to her."

"Good. Did she ever tell you about her father?"

"No."

"Never? Not once? She never once mentioned her father when you were talking to her?"

"Nope." I'd taken to saying "nope" after hearing a character in a Western say it.

"I find that very hard to believe," said the man questioning me. "So do I" said the other man. They looked especially Cromwellian when they said this.

"It's true," I said and, of course, it was. My conversations with Mary concerned Jakob except for the time when Johnny was missing. I did not, of course, mention Jakob.

"Have you ever been to this Mary's house in Sulby?"

"Nope."

"You're absolutely sure she never mentioned her father? Not even once?"

"Nope."

Had Pop been in the room he would have told me to "quit foolin'" and "talk properly" but he wasn't and I didn't.

"What *did* she talk about?" asked the less talkative of the two Roundheads trying to be cunning."

"Things," I said determined to remain vague.

"What sort of things?"

"I dunno…the weather, the cows, the milk round, digging turnips, mucking out the cow byre…"

"Nothing about her family?"

"Nope…except about her mother being sick."

"That's strange don't you think? Most people talk about their families."

"Mary didn't."

After more of this the two men seemed to conclude that they were wasting their time with the town idiot. They had a few words with Pop on their way out and then went off into the black-out none the wiser for their visit. I felt rather pleased with myself at having given nothing away.

"D'ye know what them f'las said at the door?" asked Pop rhetorically. "They said that if y've been tellin' 'm lies and ya know more about this Mary than y've been lettin' on they'll be back for ya quick as a wink."

I didn't feel quite so pleased with myself after hearing this though unlike the boy in the Victorian painting I knew absolutely nothing about the father in question.

Nothing ever went unnoticed in Glen Auldyn. The following week many of the customers on the milk round wanted to know why government men and soldiers had driven up to the farm on a Friday with the police sergeant after them the next day. Liz was diplomatically evasive. I told the people I liked that the government men were police making routine enquiries on farming matters. They asked why a lorry-load of soldiers accompanied them. I said they would have to ask the police. I told the customers I didn't like – the eager purveyors of gossip – that there was a report that German parachutists had recently been observed from a distance landing near the farm at night and police had called to ask the Talbots if they had seen them. The story of the parachutists spread like a wild fire through bracken. Some claimed to have seen drifting white parachutes in the night sky. The local newspaper got hold of the story, a reporter was sent to the glen and an account appeared under a hysterical headline that wanted to know why the local government was denying the facts. The government reacted by sending soldiers to hunt for the invaders all over Sky Hill and the surrounding country. Road blocks were set up. House-to-house enquiries were made in the glen. Old sheds were searched, old wells peered into. Old Mrs. Cannel was accosted just as she was about to empty her chamber pot and was so startled that she dropped it and its contents on an officer's boots. Fortunately for me, in the general excitement generated by the tale and the flurried immediate response to it no one could recall who it was that had first mentioned the phantom parachutists. The gossips pointed at each other. Had anyone remembered me then the men in long coats would have been back at *Rosetree Villa* post haste.

I felt that I had to confess to Liz the part I had played in all this. She told me that I had been irresponsible, that I could get myself into real trouble by spreading such lies in wartime. But she couldn't help laughing at the thought that a group of local chattering busybodies had sent so many men fruitlessly combing the hills. We both hoped that the invaders of the farm were among them. I would have loved to tell my story to friends at school and watch Ronnie Skillicorn writhe in envy but, of course, I couldn't. War's restrictions were often burdensome.

When I next saw Jakob I asked him how Uncle Tom had taken his offer to confess his affection for Mary to the authorities. He told me that after Tom had stewed in anger over his confrontation with the men in long coats he had told Jakob to keep his mouth shut as Mary's troubles had nothing to do with him.

"He wouldn't tell me why she was taken away," said Jakob miserably. "I might never see her again," he added.

Knowing that I could trust his discretion I told him the actual reason for Mary's detention. I also told him the story of the fictional parachutists but made him promise not to share these confidences with anyone else. He smiled a bleak smile at the idea of the soldiers tiring themselves out all over the hills for nothing but about Mary he remained gloomy. He was convinced he would never set eyes on her again.

"I didn't know how much I would miss her until she was taken away," he said. "They're treating her the way they have treated me. She is an innocent person as I am. You see what stupid things war makes people do. In wartime there is no justice."

Bessie, who had learned of Mary's arrest from Ma, came round one night while we were in the middle of tea to say, "I knew she was a baddie as soon as I heard about her working on the farm. I told yer then that land girls is like mermaids draggin' men down. Now look! She's bin spyin' fer Jerry! She should be taken out one cold wet mornin' and shot!"

"Nice Christian thought that, Bessie," said Pop. "Any more y'd like t'ave done in while yer at it?"

"You, for a start," she said before departing to see what other shreds of gossip she could pick up in the neighborhood.

"That woman drinks poison for breakfast," said Pop. Carlo asked if he could have some on his porridge.

Just when the gossips in Glen Auldyn and in Sulby, Mary's village, had decided on the *there's no smoke without fire* principle that Mary must be guilty of spying since she had been arrested, and surmised that the Talbots must be accomplices, the military car returned Mary to the farm. The soldier driving it got out to open the door for her but Mary didn't wait. She opened it herself and rushed to give us all a warm hug. We had seen the car climbing up to the farm from the bridge and gathered to meet it. It was like Johnny's homecoming all over again.

There was of course a general clamour for information. What had persuaded the authorities to let her go? She told us what most of us knew already – the reason why she had been taken away in the first place – and said that just when she despaired that her father's innocence would ever be proven the English police, quite by accident, found the missing plans in the flat of a man they were investigating for stealing ration books. He was a petty thief who had broken into the factory, eluded the night shift, found the plans neglectfully left on the Manager's office desk and took them with a view to demanding money for their safe return once consternation over their disappearance had built up. Mary's father had been released from prison but no one apologized for his summary arrest.

"It's wartime," they said, "you know how it is."

"Yes, I know how it is," her father had replied, "and you can fight your war without me." He had returned to the Island by the earliest boat to look after his ailing wife and comfort his terrified daughter. The guard was removed from their house and a deputation of village busybodies who one day were agreeing that they'd never liked Charlie Kinvaig – "there was always something fey about him" – went to his house to welcome him home reassuring him that they hadn't believed a word of what was being said against him.

"You're all hypocrites and liars," Charlie told his turnccoat well wishers. "I've heard all the tales you've been telling while I've been across…and I'll not soon forget them"

"That Charlie Kinvaig!" the villagers said after Mary's father had slammed his front door on them, "he was always a hothead…always sure he was right and everybody else was wrong. It's his poor wife I pity and her not well at all. But she's made her bed so she must lie in it."

They shook their heads in sorrow at Mary's mother's perversity as they made their way to the village pub.

I asked Bessie if she still wanted to have Mary shot now it had been revealed that her father had been falsely accused.

"They've only let him go so they can follow him and see where he goes and who he meets so they can round up the whole nest o' them *sabotures*."

Bessie dwelt lovingly on that last word imperfectly picked up from radio news broadcasts.

Pop, who had heard these remarks, said "Y'know, Bessie, I've been drivin' a train through that village o' Charlie Kinvaig's for more than twenty year an' I'd no idea of it as a spy headquarters. Jus' shows ya how a f'la can go round with his eyes shut. An education is what yer are Bessie, an education. The government owes ya a job…ya wasted cookin' and cleanin'… wasted. A brain like yours should be used. Y'd find spies for the government under every bush on the Island…every bush. I'll put in a word for ya."

Pop went off laughing. Bessie tossed her head and told me never ever to forget that sarcasm was the lowest form of wit and won no friends.

The authorities eventually blamed the people in Glen Auldyn for imagining the parachutists and then getting a gullible newspaper reporter to print a story about them. It took only one rural halfwit to start the ball rolling, they said, as Lance Corporal Machin told us.

I expected things on the farm would return to normal but I was wrong. Not everything – or, rather, everyone – was as before. When I went to find Mary to see how she was feeling after her ordeal she began to cry. I asked her if she was having nightmares at being forced away from the farm at gun point but she surprised me by declaring "No, the nightmare is here."

"Where?" I asked turning sharply as if some apparition were standing behind me.

"Jakob won't speak to me. He says people will be watching us. If anyone sees us together Jakob says they'll phone the police and I'll be taken away again or he will. I told him that was silly talk…they've caught the thief who stole what my father was accused of taking but he wouldn't listen. Jakob says the police don't like being shown to be wrong so they'll look for any little thing, any excuse to arrest me again to get their revenge. I told him that the police here aren't like that but he just laughed and called me naïve. He said the local people think of him and all the others in the Camp as the enemy so if I have anything more to do with him I'd be accused of comforting the enemy and that's a serious offence. So he won't see me because he doesn't want to get me into trouble."

"He still likes you," I said, "he must do if he's trying to keep you out of trouble."

Leaving Mary with a dubious look on her face I went to find Jakob thinking ruefully about how oddly things turn out. Here was I about to try to bring him and Mary together yet I had done everything I could think of not so long ago to keep them apart. I met Liz as I was searching for Jakob and told her of my intentions.

"Well," she said with an ironic look on her face and tone in her voice, "times *have* changed. You tried to have me and Tom get shut of her not so long ago. If we had done p'raps you'd have liked her all the sooner."

When I found Jakob I did my best to persuade him that resuming their old relationship wouldn't cause difficulties for Mary either with the police or the army neither of which Force was interested in her conduct now that the case against her father had been dropped. Eventually Jakob allowed himself to be persuaded and Mary was so overcome when he apologized to her for keeping her at a distance that she flung her arms around his neck right out there in the farm street.

Uncle Tom was passing at the time and roared in fury "You silly buggers do that again an' I'll have Jakob sent back to the Camp for good! We've 'ad enough trouble up 'ere without beggin' fer more! Any oul gossip from the glen sees you two like that an' we'll have them buggers with guns back 'ere again. I've got a farm to run! Ya both 'ere ta work! Remember that. There's a bloody war on!"

"Don't you worry," said Liz after Tom had gone, "he'll come round in time. But you've got to be discreet, you two."

Liz was a romantic at heart and evidently saw some kind of future for Mary and Jakob no matter how unlikely that seemed given their backgrounds, circumstances and a war which by this time it was plain would not end soon. Perhaps she saw them as characters in an opera.

CHAPTER TWENTY-EIGHT

When Pop bartered with friends and neighbors for rationed commodities his currency, as I mentioned earlier in this narrative, was the fish he caught in Ramsey Bay. He and two other men – not only silent but invisible partners since their names were never mentioned in my hearing – had clubbed together to buy a rowing boat and took turns using it to go out to catch herring, mackerel, cod and any other edible fish that came their way. The enterprise almost foundered at the start over the choice of name for the boat. Pop favored "Ben-my-Chree" (Girl of My Heart) but his partners wanted to call it "Ben Varrey" which Pop thought was asking for trouble since it means "Mermaid." But there were two of them and only one of Pop so after a lengthy argument during which Pop's partners threatened to find another investor more attuned to mermaids he reluctantly gave in, the boat was bought and voyaging commenced not without misgiving on Pop's part. There had been no trouble with mermaids thus far so Pop began to feel easier about the name – he eventually denied he had once tried to veto it.

Pop told us heroic tales of his adventures at sea. There was the day he had to battle a sharp-toothed dog fish (a minor member of the shark family) to get it off his hook in order to throw it back into the sea (he called such rejects "sewer fish"). He claimed that this one barked like Milby the whole time he was disentangling it. He told us of the time an enormous floating jelly-fish stung his hand as he carelessly trailed it in the water. He claimed to have seen an undulating sea-serpent. He described little sea-horses. There were his stories of sudden squalls that came out of nowhere. They almost sank the boat. Pop made that kind of tale more dramatic by acting the part of a man about to be tipped into the famished waves. I thought how adventurous it would be to accompany Pop on one of his fishing expeditions. I had only seen his boat in the mildest of circum-stances: at anchor in the harbor when the tide was full or lying on its side on a mud bank when the tide was out.

The sea in its wildest moods terrified me. I remember standing one win-ter's day on the promenade in a gale with the rain and spray whipping like piano wire across the faces of those like me staring out toward the harbor's mouth. We stood behind a wooden barricade which the Town Council had ordered to be bolted into the road to prevent the waves that hurled themselves over the sea wall from flowing down adjacent streets entering houses, depositing sand, shells, seaweed, bits of driftwood. I was standing among women wearing black shawls who were crying, pointing, calling out in desperation since there, plain for all to see was the local fishing fleet trying to enter the harbor and looking as though at any minute it would either be swamped or shattered against the harbor walls. The sons and husbands of the watching women manned those threatened boats. It didn't look as if any of them stood a chance. The Lifeboat had been launched and was rearing up and down in mammoth waves as its crew kept a keen watch in case any of the fishermen were swept overboad. Several times it appeared to be in danger of capsizing but it was designed to right itself and it did so. I had never seen anything like this – the imminent destruction of the entire Ramsey fishing fleet on the watery threshold of the town with the Lifeboat gyrating in attendance. I haven't forgotten the terror we all felt at the wildness and manic force of Nature. By some miracle despite the gale-force winds all the boats managed to steer their way into harbor and shelter. There was much to celebrate that night in the little houses down by the quay.

When I thought of Pop's boat however, I did not imagine it in a scene like this. Pop's boat, despite some of his more dramatic stories, in my mind sailed a calm sunlit sea, gulls skimming the tops of mere wavelets, gannets diving way off in the blue distance, the odd Ginny-diver searching for fish and vanishing suddenly under the surface when it found them, the coasts of Cumberland and Ayrshire just visible in shadowy outline, the shore shimmering in summer haze – weather as far removed as possible from the black storm that nearly sank the fishing boats or the blinding autumn fogs that called forth the mournful music of the lighthouses and were just as dangerous.

One Sunday morning in summer I was startled when Pop asked me at breakfast if I would like to go out in the bay in the boat with him for a bit of fishing. The weather was much as I had imagined it in my sun-lit fancies. Pop had never asked me to go anywhere with him alone before except to help him dig his garden. Apart from that there had only been occasional family outings so this was something new. I said I'd love to go but Ma protested at once.

"You're never going to take the lad out in that old boat are you? He could fall in and drown! He can't swim! He could float about in the sea for days on end and be washed up at last on the rocks all black and bloated like poor Shoveler. Have you gone daft risking your son' life?"

"It's not an oul boat," Pop replied heatedly, "an' I go out in it when I can. I can't swim neither. You never tell *me* not to go out in case I come floatin back drowned and black in the face."

"I did when you first got it," said Ma, "I never stopped. I said time and again it wasn't worth the risk just for a few fish but did you listen? Of couse not. You knew best! It was like talking to the wind!"

"I haven't noticed you refusing the fish, though," Pop replied as if clinching a point.

"Since you risked your life to catch them and they're dead anyway I can hardly tell you to throw them back, can I? But," Ma went on her voice rising, "risking Erik's life is another thing altogether. Do you really want to drown your son with your stupidity?"

"Stupit is it?" Pop replied with a sharp edge to his voice,"what about all them fisher f'las that take their lads out on their boats all the time?"

"More fool them. Is it the gospel according to Dickie Skillicorn you're preaching now? You're in fine company there! And anyway his boat is a lot bigger than your little cockle-shell."

Pop appeared to drop the question in the face of Ma's opposition but close to lunchtime he asserted himself definitively. I was to go fishing with him in the rowing boat. He wasn't bringing up a sissy tied to his mother's apron strings, taught to be afraid of anything out of the ordinary. Men and boys had been rowing their way out of Ramsey harbor to fish in the bay since time began and the process wasn't going to stop with our family just because Ma said so. It was a fine day, the sea was as flat as a pancake… when was the last time Ma had heard of a local rowing boat sinking on a fine calm day in summer with the sea flat as a pancake? Anyway there would be plenty of other boats around on a day like this The RAF Air-Sea Rescue launch could be summoned in the remote event of an accident and so could the town Lifeboat. It wasn't as if we'd be sailing uncharted waters with no one by to help if help were needed. We were not, said Pop, risking our lives in some sparse region of Africa. Pop was an expert on Africa – when in a good humor he would tell Carlo and me elaborate bedtime stories set there about his adventures in head hunting country before he met Ma. He said Ma would make a good head hunter.

"Well, on your head be it," said Ma resignedly, recognizing that Pop was bent on taking me fishing whatever she might say about the danger. "When you're both washed up all bleached and blue and dead on the sand you'll wish you'd listened to me."

After losing an argument Ma could sound a lot like Bessie.

�֍

My Douglas uncles, had they been inclined to the sport, would have donned tweeds and pursued it with rods and artificial lures but men of Pop's economic standing couldn't afford such things. To Pop the possession of a rod (like the playing of golf, the wearing of tweeds and plus-fours and the drinking of gins and tonic) was a mark of Middle and Upper Class pretention. Pop used the fishing tackle of the working man – the handline wrapped around a small simple square wooden frame. Pop and men like him used as bait sand worms dug from those areas of the beach open to the public. While Ma had been quietly satisfied that she had prevented Pop from taking me to sea he had cycled to one of these areas and dug up enough worms for an afternoon of fishing. Ma thought the spade he had taken with him was headed for the garden.

Pop assembled our equipment in the back yard. He gave me a tin can full of writhing worms smelling strongly of the sea. He told me he'd show me how to put them on the hooks of the handline (each had several at different levels). He said I'd have to be very careful about putting worms on hooks since it was easy to get a hook in the hand if one wasn't paying attention.

"The idea," said Pop, "is to hook the fish and not yaself. The barbs of the hook are sharp and if ya get one a them in ya hand ya might have to go to the hospital so's they can dig it out. An' that, Sonny Boy, hurts. An' if the hook is rusty ya'd get blood poisoning and there's f'las have died o' that."

This trip wasn't going to be as easy as I had imagined. I could see myself, rusty hook embedded in my hand, telling Pop I could feel lockjaw coming on. Someone at school had told me that was what happened if you got jabbed by rusty metal. I was not to be a mere pssenger in Pop's boat or spectator of his fishing prowess. I stared at the writhing glutinous worms in the old tin Pop had handed to me. They looked slimy and disgusting as they wriggled and squirmed. The idea of picking them up and impaling them on hooks while they were still alive and writhing made me feel queasy. Pop said the worms didn't feel anything but how could he know?

He wasn't a worm. I suspected that an articulate worm would offer an entirely different point of view and a scathing assessment of Pop. I know I would if someone casually picked me up and stuck a hook through my head while remarking off-hand to someone else "he doesn't feel a thing."

When Pop told Ma we were about to leave she came to the back door, wiping the flour from her hands onto her apron. She gave Pop lengthy instructions concerning my welfare, repeated her opposition to the whole business and then gave me a weepy, floury hug while telling me not to do anything silly on the boat that would make me fall overboard.

"He's in your charge," Ma said solemnly to Pop, "so you take good care of him."

"When we're back with a bag full o'fish ya'll be glad we went out," said Pop.

We cycled off, our fishing bags holding our gear and a snack to eat while we were on the water hanging from the handlebars of our bikes. It was a unique experience to be cycling down the hill into town with Pop. I was excited about the adventure on which we were going to embark and looked forward to describing it in detail to Jakob and the others on the farm.

I couldn't have put it in these terms at that age but this trip with Pop was to be a sort of initiation into some of the practical skills of adult male life superior to the dull digging in the garden which anyone could do. I felt that by inviting me out in his boat at last Pop was beginning to take me seriously as a person instead of assigning me to the same bracket as Carlo – the one labeled *child*. When I looked at our afternoon out in this way I didn't mind that I was not simply along for the ride but expected to bait hooks, cast lines, pull in fish according to Pop's instructions. By the end of the afternoon I would be a fisherman and Pop would take me more seriously in consequence.

❦

The *Ben Varrey* was tied to a metal stanchion in that part of the harbor near the aliens' Mooragh Camp. In fact Pop had to produce a crumpled document to show the sentry at the entrance to the bridge that crossed the harbor and led straight to the gates of the Camp as well as to Pop's mooring place. The sentry, who obviously knew Pop, barely looked at the paper before motioning us on. We pushed our bikes across the bridge and then along a path close to the Camp's barbed wire fence until we reached Pop's boat floating now on a rising tide. We laid our bikes flat on the grass. As I looked around I thought that the authorities had made it easy for escapees to find a boat – Pop's wasn't the only one anchored there. Evidently those who ran the Camp relied on the tall wire fences, the armed sentries, the Coast Guard and other naval authorities and the grimmer moods of the Irish Sea as deterrents. A Camp guard came to see what we were doing. He too seemed to know Pop. They had a brief conversation before Pop turned to me and said, "When I pull the boat in jump in and sit at the back. Leave your bag – I'll put it in with mine."

Pop knelt on the grass, reached out and pulled on the boat's mooring rope. Slowly he hauled the heavy rowing boat alongside the bank of earth on which we were standing. While Pop held the boat in place I got into it. It rocked a bit especially when I stumbled my way over the seats to the stern. As soon as I sat down Pop dropped our fishing bags down by my feet and then stepped into the front of the boat. He untied the rope holding the boat in place and we began to drift out from the bank. The oars were kept lying along the bottom of the boat. Pop sat in the middle seat and lifted them placing each in turn into a rowlock (Pop called them "rollocks") which he had carried in his fishing bag.

"You okay?" Pop asked looking at me closely, "because now we're off."

As he pulled the boat away I told Pop I felt fine. Temporarily forgetting the business of baiting fishing lines I pretended I was a Pirate Captain being rowed out to his ship anchored in the bay and full of excitement at the prospect of adventure. Like Long John Silver I looked forward to the ships we would capture, the gold and silver, the jeweled treasures we would take wherever we found them. We would visit lush palm-treed islands with Birds of Paradise flying about. I even imagined that I had a green and blue talkative parrot that perched on my right shoulder. As we moved down the harbor over calm waters I could hardly believe I wasn't dreaming. I had never seen the harbor from this vantage point before. Normally I walked along the quayside looking wistfully at the ships anchored there but now I really was on the water and headed toward the harbor mouth with the bay beyond. Pop pulled on the oars while I invited my parrot to stand on my extended arm so that I could talk to it more easily.

"You alright?" asked Pop. "They lock up f'las who talk to themselves."

"I wasn't talking to myself. I was talking to my parrot. It's green and blue. It's called Bill."

"That so?" said Pop. "They lock up f'las who think they're talking to parrots called Bill."

"It's a pretend parrot, I said. "I'm a Pirate Captain and you're rowing me out to my ship."

"And here was me thinking we were goin' fishin'," said Pop. "Fishin' not exciting enough for ya?"

"Fishing's alright," I said, "But I want to be a Pirate Captain too."

"Well, there's a few o' them have passed this way in their time."

As we moved down the harbor Pop described the various craft – fishing boats, small coastal steamers, private yachts and launches – as we approached them. He knew who owned them all. A few people hailed Pop from the harbor-side and from the decks of ships and I waved to them feeling like an ancient chief receiving the homage of his subjects – a Viking Chief perhaps. They, too, had been rowed along this waterway in the distant past.

The harbor had been built where the Sulby River joins the sea and it follows the bends of the river. After these wide bends a straight concrete section of the harbor juts out into the bay. When we reached this point the effect of the incoming tide sweeping down the narrowed harbor channel made the boat rock and I began to feel rather nervous. Now there were no boats moored to one side of us to provide reassurance. Had I been able to see the bottom many fathoms down I would have been scared out of my wits. As it was the new motion of the boat quicky took my mind off Bill the blue and green parrot and off the pirate ship anchored in the bay. I was very much in the here and now and beginning not to like it. I clutched the woodwork of the boat as if mountainous waves were washing over us and any minute I'd be swept over the side eventually to be deposited somewhere disfigured and drowned.

"What's up?" asked Pop.

"Nothing." I said still clinging to the side of the boat nearest to me.

"If it's this swell that's worryin' ya then don't worry. When the tide's comin' in and the sea's bein' forced up the harbour then there's currents that rock the boat a bit. But after we're out in the bay ya won't feel that swell under the boat – it'll be calm out there an' we can get down ta some good fishin'."

I lied to Pop that I felt alright, that I was really enjoying the trip. I sat uneasily in the back of the boat trying to accustom myself to its new pronounced movements telling myself that we were not going to turn over. I would not be tipped into the water the way the sailors on the fishing fleet had almost been that wet stormy winter's day. I looked uneasily in the direction of the Lifeboat House as Pop rowed us toward the small twin lighthouses at the end of each of the projecting harbor walls.

Pop rowed in silent concentration while I tried to make my mind go blank. I found this very easy to do at school but impossible here. As we left the safety of the calm upper harbor further behind my thoughts slid full fathom five and stayed there.

Pop stopped rowing and looked at me speculatively. Without any forward momentum the boat rocked about in the most alarming way. It would have taken all of Pop's strength to pry my hands loose from the side of the boat about which they were clenched yet when he said "Ya frightened aen't ya?" I denied it. I said with a slight quavering I couldn't control, "No, I'm not…really I'm not. I want…to…go…fishing."

"Well…if you're sure…but if y'are frightened we can go back."

It was obvious to me that returning to the calm of the upper harbor was the last thing Pop wanted to do. He had come out to enjoy an afternoon's fishing on a lovely summer day. He couldn't enjoy such recreation often and to have it snatched from him by the fear of an inexperienced son would have been a bitter disappointment. So he allowed himself to be persuaded by my faint assurances that I felt fine and wanted to go fishing even though he must have seen me grasping the side of the boat with claw-like hands and known that this was hardly a sign of peace of mind.

"It'll be a lot calmer once we're out of the harbor," he said reassuringly and recommenced his rowing toward the twin lighthouses at the harbor's mouth.

When we neared it the waters calmed again. The boat didn't rock any more and I felt such relief that I let go of the side of the boat and sat back in my seat beginning to be more at ease with the world. But such a comfortable feeling was short-lived. As soon as we emerged from the harbor into the bay we were seized by powerful cross-currents and the boat swung violently to and fro and up and down while Pop fought to keep us moving straight ahead. I was absolutely terrified, sure we were going to be tipped over and having so far maintained a petrified silence I began to whine and snivel the way Jimmy Curphey or Jimmy Gawne would have done had they been with us. Pop didn't take any notice at first – he had his hands full getting the boat further out into the bay beyond the disturbing reach of the currents. As we entered less turbulent waters I stopped making a noise but I tensely gripped the side of the boat nearest to me again. I didn't dare to move an inch.

"Y're frightened aren't ya?" said Pop with an undercurrent of annoyance in his voice. "The worst's over," he went on. "That bit at the harbor mouth is always rough. Strong currents meet there but we're in calmer water out here. Do you want to go back?"

The idea of returning through the maelstrom we had just escaped was anything but appealing so of course I said, "No, I don't want to go back."

"Good," said Pop, "we'll soon be able to throw our lines out." And he rowed on.

Carefully I turned in my seat to look back at the shore only to find it had receded alarmingly. We were a long way from the nearest beach and headed out to sea. Before we set off I had thought that being free of the land would be exhilarating – would give me a feeling of release as if chains had been removed. That's how some local sailors described their experience of the sea. But now all I could think of was how far away the shore was and how terribly deep the waters below the boat. Only a few inches of wood separated Pop and I from those waters. Now I remembered Pop's tales of sudden squalls and wondered why I had found them funny. My mind went back to that winter scene and I imagined the terror those fishermen must have felt trying to reach safety in a high gale. I worried that the winds might suddenly awake from their summer sleep and sweep down from Barrule like roaring monsters stirring up the waves as I had seen them stirred in winter. Instead of taking comfort from the present calmness of the sea I dwelt on our vulnerability.

"Well," said Pop, "this isn't a bad spot. Let's try here first. Just throw me bag over."

He indicated his fishing bag, which was by my feet. I sat clutching at the side of the *Ben Varrey* paralysed with fear. I was convinced that even the slightest movement I might make would capsize the boat. Bill the parrot had long since flown off to find a safe tropical islet.

"What's up?" Pop asked. "Throw us the bag over."

"I can't," I said.

"What's the matter with ya all of a sudden?" asked Pop.

"If I move I'll rock the boat and I might fall into the sea."

"How d'ya make that out?" asked Pop genuinely puzzled. "This boat's a heavy one…ya should try rowin' 'er some time. She's not goin' ta turn over 'cause of a li'l titch like you."

"That's how it feels to me," I said.

"Well," said Pop, "try it. Do it slow. Jus' stan' up and get the bag an' ya'll see the boat won't even move.

"What would happen if the oars fell into the sea?" I asked. How would we get back?"

"I'll make damn sure they don't fall into the sea," said Pop looking slightly exasperated.

"You told Ma you couldn't swim," I said having just remembered this piece of salient information.

I never did learn," said Pop in a tone that suggested this omission was unimportant.

"So if the oars fell into the sea you couldn't swim after them to get them back. And if I fell into the sea you couldn't get me out either."

"Y' aren't goin' ta fall into the sea so don't worry about it."

"But what if I did?" I persisted.

"I'll get the bag meself," said Pop unwilling to play the *what if?* game.

But what if I did?" I persisted.

"So y'are frightened," said Pop. D'ya want ta go back?"

In viw of the fact tht Pop couldn't swim, that when he stood up to get his bag from near my feet the boat rocked dangerously, that he had no plan to retrieve the oars from the sea should they fall overboard, that the nearest other boats were mere specks miles away and remembering that if the tide went out before we could return to the harbor we would have to wait hours before it turned again I nodded. Yes, I did want to go back – desperately. I yearned for the safety of the harbor. Passage through those violent cross-currents would be worth it with the prospect of calm water and dry land on the other side of them.

"Why don't we just stop here and have a bit o'lunch?" Pop suggested temporizing in the hope that if I had something to eat and accustomed myself to the boat and its distance from the shore I would change my mind about going back. I told him that if I tried to eat anything I'd throw up. I really wanted to go back, I said, and added that I was sorry.

Pop must have been disgruntled at being robbed of his few hours of fishing but he didn't fancy having me white-faced, terrified, hanging on to the side of the boat for dear life. I couldn't have loosened my grip on it had I wanted to. I was in a most unpiratical state of terror. Long John Silver would have sworn at me and made me walk the plank. I envied the gulls and other seabirds their nonchalance as they bobbed about on the water. All I wanted to do was to get the hell off Pop's boat and never set foot on it again. I bitterly reflected on the wide gap between fancy and reality. The bold Buccaneer who sailed the seven seas in all their varied humours had become a whimpering, parrotless child. And that child was behaving as awkwardly as any mermaid Pop might have encountered sunning herself on a rock.

Looking at me with a mixture of annoyance, concern and bafflement Pop readied the oars and slowly turned the *Ben Varrey* round so that it was pointed toward the now-distant harbor mouth. We began the doleful journey back with me sitting there mortified at having displayed the sort of faint-heartedness I deplored in Jimmy Curphey. Pop rowed in grim silence leaving me in no doubt that I had not only ruined his day but also failed some sort of test. The boy about to be initiated into his father's world was in effect being taken home to mother. Pop never asked me to go anywhere with him on my own again – at least not until I was fourteen and we went to England for my elder brother's wedding and we both got blind drunk in the back garden of the new In Laws. So did the new In Laws.

The journey back to the harbor was a replica of the voyage out though much faster since the incoming tide bore us along with it. We still had to traverse the boiling waters where the currents collided but beyond was the harbor and safety, not the open sea.

"Catch much?" asked another boater as Pop was putting his oars back along the bottom of the boat after jumping out and tying it up.

"Never dropped a line." Said Pop. "It was a sight-seeing trip for the lad." I heard the edge in Pop's voice even if the other boater didn't.

As we cycled home in silence my thoughts were very different from those of the morning. I was a landlubber after all. I had proved myself to be a "sissy" afflicted with the sort of fears Ma had expressed before we set out. Ronnie Skillicorn would laugh his head off if he knew. When we got home I went off to my bedroom for a silent weep. I had let Pop down, spoiled his afternoon, and I had somehow betrayed myself. Living as I did much of the time in an imaginative world of myth and adventure I had cast myself as the heroic type. But when I was put to the test of experience I had behaved like a sniveling coward. I had whimpered to be taken home to safety. In the days that followed I wanted to ask Pop to take me out in his boat again so I could show him how brave I could be now that I knew what to expect but the nagging thought that I might well behave the same way and thus make things worse prevented me. Pop maybe compared me to my passive Douglas uncles. It turned out that I was more like the two Jimmies than I cared to admit. Ronnie Skillicorn, who I privately derided as "thick," had more raw courage than I had.

I lost my fear of the sea in my early teens. By then I had learned to swim and spent long hours in the bay well out of my depth, often under water, but this new skill never erased the sense that the first time my courage was really put to the test I failed miserably. And Pop was the concerned and deeply disappointed witness.

CHAPTER TWENTY-NINE

THE WEEKEND FOLLOWING MY INTRODUCTION TO HAND-LINE FISHING and small boat navigation I worried that those on the farm might have been given an account – by Ma or Pop or both – of my humiliating afternoon on the water. I was relieved that so far I hadn't been taunted about it at school, no neighbor had enquired or commented, but I worried that someone would be told who would then tell someone else until everybody knew. I hoped my parents had kept the matter to themselves as I had begged them to do but I couldn't be sure that they had. When Uncle Tom drove me to the farm he talked about the weather, an unexploded bomb found on the mountain, the sheep and the invasion of one of the hayfields by thistles. Auntie Liz said nothing about my adventure – not, at least, till we had delivered the milk to the house once owned by the family of the rebellious sailor, Fletcher Christian. Perhaps it waas the dubious association of the house with the Navy and the *Bounty* mutiny that caused Liz to remark, "Your Mum was telling me that you put to sea last Sunday."

"Oh?"

I didn't see how Ma could have passed on this news. As far as I knew she hadn't seen Liz since the previous weekend.

"Yes, I bumped into her in town in the week, shopping. She said it had all been a bit too much for you. Well…your Dad ought to know better.

You're not old enough to be taken out of the harbor. I know I wouldn't let your Dad row me out into the bay in that little boat of his…not for love nor money. I'd be yelling at him to put me ashore long before we got to the breakwater."

Liz no doubt intended her remarks to be a comfort but they only reinforced my sense of failure. It was all very well for women and girls to be frightened of the sea – they were expected to be. Nance Quiggin, who smoked a clay pipe and wore a sou'wester and oil-skins and was one of the crew on her husband's fishing boat was considered a freak by most people in the town. Boys and men, unlike women and girls, were supposed to take the sea in their stride. The sea was a medium as natural to them as to the fish they went out to catch. No one had actually told me this. It was just one of those assumptions I grew up with. Not wanting to describe my day on the water to Liz I changed the subject hoping that she hadn't mentioned whatever Ma had told her to anyone else on the farm. She didn't persist, to my relief.

It was one of those Saturdays when I went back to the farm after the milk round to help with the work. Mary found me cleaning up in the dairy, burnishing one of the metal counter tops. By this time she was happily re-established in her clandestine relationship with Jakob. I saw them together in various places on the farm furtively holding hands, occasionally hugging, when they thought they weren't being watched, often talking earnestly.

Liz, it turned out, had mentioned my sea-going adventure to her. She said, "You know, Erik, Liz is right. You're far too young for your Dad to take out to sea. I'd be frightened out of me life if I were out there rocking about in a small boat so don't you worry about it. When you're older it'll be you rowing your Dad to the fishing and then you'll think nothing of it."

If both Liz and Mary knew about my trip then probably everyone on the farm did. That being so I thought I would ask Jakob what I could do in future not to be found wanting when I was tested again. I hadn't done badly on the Christmas Tree Caper. I had got through poor Shoveller's discovery and Inquest creditably. I had tried hard to be brave when the soldiers hauled me off that wall and sent me to the Police Station along with my fellow climbers. I didn't blame myself for the wartime fears I shared with everyone else but there had been that disturbing incident with the Bishop when I fainted and now this trip out to sea saw me failing the test of courage again. I thought Jakob might help me to *steel my resolve* as the books I read might have put it. Jakob after all had seen a man shot and another one stabbed to death, he had been seized by police and then by soldiers and sent to a camp. He wasn't allowed to practice his profession properly but in spite of what he had suffered he had not let catastrophe overwhelm him. He had found a way to cope. I wanted to know what it was.

When I found him and had confessed my wretched spinelessness I asked him for his recipe for dealing with adversity.

"Being afraid of the sea at your age isn't something to worry about." He said, "It's natural to fear water. I was scared and so were a lot of other people when we were packed on that little Belgian ship to cross the Irish Sea. I told you how rough it was. That little ship went up and down so much we thought it might sink and that if it did the people who had put us on it wouldn't care. Even your Papa would have been afraid I think if he had been on the ship with us. You're not the only one to be frightened by the sea. There is, anyway, no magic to make us brave. Sometimes things will happen that frighten you even though you may have tried hard to be brave. This is true for everyone – even for the people we call heroes. There is nothing wrong with being afraid – this war makes everyone afraid. You will learn as you grow older how to live with fear so that it doesn't control you. But that takes time and it takes experience. You can't expect to have learned that lesson by your age. And it doesn't work every time. You can be brave in the face of one kind of danger and…do you say?…*scared stiff* when you meet another. Some things are so terrible they will always bring dread and make you feel helpless. Remember every-one…including your Papa…feels afraid and everyone from time to time surrenders to fear even when they have struggled hard against it. That's the way life is."

"But you haven't given in," I said. "You were brave in all the stories you've told me."

"I have told you only a little about what has happened to me. I haven't told you the most frightening things and how terrified I have felt sometimes. That's true of the other prisoners at the Camp. In fact a few have been so scared at being locked behind barbed wire not knowing what will be done to them that they couldn't stand it any longer and they have killed themselves. Most of us don't sleep well because we don't control our lives...other people decide what will happen to us. We have no idea where our families are...whether they are alive or dead...so we are fearful for them too. That's a nightmare that never goes away."

"But what you all do in the Camp isn't what frightened people do."

"Oh, but it is. If we didn't use our time to teach each other what we know, to put on concerts, to print our Camp newspaper, to paint pictures and so on we would think too much about being caged behind wire like animals in a zoo, we would imagine all sorts of terrible things the authorities might do to us...we would simply be crushed by our fears. Even that whiskey I told you about is a little medicine for fear."

"Would you be afraid if Gerald the bull got loose and ran round the farmyard?"

"Of course...and so would Tom and Liz even though they know this bull. And remember those soldiers with guns who came to take Mary away?... they made everyone afraid. No one knew why they had really come here or what they would do. And yet those soldiers for all their guns were scared of Rory and Tory and threatened to shoot them. Now you are not afraid of these dogs?"

"Of course not. That'd be silly."

"Well, there you are. The soldiers were alarmed by the dogs…we'd all be scared if the bull got loose…if your Papa were here when that happened he'd be shouting for help as loud as the rest of us…Mary was terrified by the soldiers…you see you are not alone in the panic department."

I began to feel better about myself after I had this talk. I thought that I should try to be as brave as possible in my daily life as a sort of moral gymnastics so that by practicing courage even in small ways I would, so to speak, develop a stronger courage-muscle. I forced myself not to flee at the sight of the approaching shepherd the way I used to do when he muttered his way past our house. I found that holding my ground was difficult though the shepherd in fact took no notice of me whatsoever. I deliberately picked a fight in the playground with Ronnie Skillicorn to prove to myself that I could be a tough guy too. Ronnie of course knocked me flat. Both of us were caned by the Headmaster for setting a bad example, and on that occasion I struggled especially hard not to cry despite the pain. Ronnie beat me up after school. His outraged sense of honor required it. I refused to tell Ma or Pop how I had come by a black eye and a very bloody nose. My new-found sense of honor required that.

"Ya start fightin' with other kids," said Pop," and ya'll answer ta me."

"You don't want me to be a cissy," I replied.

"I don't want ya turnin' into a bully neither."

I rather liked the idea of being thought a bully-in-the-making. It did a lot for my self–esteem. Perhaps I'd become a local version of my namesake, the Viking, Erik the Red, and lay about me.

Toward the beginning of this memoir I mentioned a Mrs. Kelly, elder relative of the Mr. Kelly at our school who was removed to the mental hospital by the police after threatening our Deputy Head. It seemed to me tht Mrs. Kelly, like a Victorian heroine, had taken to her bed as a form of protest against life or, perhaps, a prolonged rehearsal for death. Ma felt some sort of obligation to visit her now and then the way she felt she had to visit Mrs. Dodd in her smelly house. Ma had a social worker's instincts. I lacked such instincts but was dragged along anyway on both these occasions and hated them with equal revulsion. In Mrs. Dodd's house I sat bored stiff while she and Ma gossiped. I was thus at liberty to inhale the vile odours of the place and longed to escape the whole time we were there. When Mrs. Dodd offered me refreshment from her kitchen, more chaotic than ours, I invariably refused, stifling a shudder. Nothing edible or potable could possibly emanate from that dank hole with its ancient discolored, encrusted dripping taps and noisome slimy stone sink.

I was equally repelled by Mrs. Kelly's environs. She was invariably propped up by a bank of pillows in a large ornate bed that had been brought down from its proper place upstairs and now filled half of the ground-floor sitting room. There was always a sickly sweet smell in the air of that room, now and then varied by emanations from the porcelain chamber pot under her bed which Ma bravely offered to empty while we were there as if such a task were on a level with removing the tea things after a meal. I felt an urgent desire to be sick whenever Ma marched past me bearing this receptacle to a bathroom just down the corridor. I was annoyed on Ma's behalf that the occupant of the bed didn't seem to try to get herself to the bathroom. I wonder how she was looked after when we weren't there since she appeared to be the only occupant of the house, which Ma said she owned. Who did the cooking, the dusting and sweeping? Who did the shopping and made the meals and washed up afterwards? How did the dweller in the large bed take a bath? Maybe when there was nobody else about Mrs. Kelly suddenly became able-bodied, flung her covers aside and strode off to do these things for herself.

Apart from the smells of the improvised bedroom Mrs. Kelly's house didn't reek all over the way Mrs. Dodd's did but since our visits were confined to the invalid's front sitting room encampment that wasn't much comfort. I often sat there idly wondering what the rest of the house was like – whether it had any secret inhabitants, skeletons in closets or lying grinning in spare bedrooms. Mrs. Kelly with her ghastly white complexion and long pointed nose reminded me so much of a witch that I was ready to believe all manner of supernatural beings lurked about the house or in the chimneys. I wondered uneasily as I surveyed that converted sitting room if we were being observed through concealed spy-holes in the walls. I wondered what had befallen Mr. Kelly of whom no one ever spoke. Perhaps he lay mummified and decidedly dusty on a bed upstairs having expired years ago and been forgotten. Perhaps Mrs. Kelly had taken an axe to him while he slept, chopped him in pieces and disposed of him somehow – perhaps fed him gradually paper bag by paper bag (like chips) to seagulls who weren't fussy about what they ate. I had heard of a Sweeny Tod who baked his victims in meat pies. I resolved never to eat a meat pie if Mrs. Kelly offered me one.

I mention these details because not long after Pop had promised me trouble if I turned into a bully Ma suggested one Sunday morning that I take something or other to Mrs. Kelly – something Ma didn't have time to deliver. I don't remember what this something was, only the feeling that wild horses wouldn't drag me into Mrs. Kelly's house all on my own and unprotected. That lady's persistent smile had taken on a sinister character for me, like the knowing smile of a devil.

"I can't, Ma," I said, thankful that I had a legitimate reason for not going. "I've got to go to Sunday school."

"Since when did you *want* to go to Sunday school? You're always trying to avoid it and here I am offering you a chance to stay away – just this once."

"I have to go today," I lied vigorously. "It's my turn to read to the class from the Bible."

"I'm sure the teacher can find someone else to do that. You're not the only child in the class who can read are you? Why does it have to be you today?"

"Because it's my turn," I insisted doggedly.

"You'd normally jump at the chance to stay away from Sunday school, your turn or not. You're always complaining about having to go. I can't remember all the reasons you've given for staying away but I do know they'd fill a book. I've told your father so more than once. You wouldn't be trying to avoid seeing Mrs. Kelly would you?"

"Of course not!" I strove for moral indignation a bit too shrilly.

"So," said Ma, "you've no *real* objection to taking Mrs. Kelly this little parcel for me…it's just you feel…for once…that you must go to Sunday school…to read the Bible out loud?"

"Right."

"Well, then, don't you worry about it. I'll send a note to your Sunday school teacher to tell her that you wanted to be there but that you had to do your good deed for the day. Your teacher will be pleased. You'll be visiting the sick. Isn't that what they want you to do at Sunday school… things like that?"

"No, they don't. They want us to read the Bible and…"

"No *ands* or *buts*," said Ma. "Taking a little package to a bed-ridden woman is a good deed and you are going to do at least that good deed today whether you or your Sunday school teachers like it or not. Like it or lump it you're going to Mrs. Kelly's."

"And if you say *no* I'll clip your ear," said Pop who had come in on the latter part of the conversation in time to add this rhetorical flourish.

"I'll eat his toat," added Carlo who had come in with Pop.

"There's no need for threats," said Ma. "Erik doesn't really mind going to see Mrs. Kelly do you?"

"S'pose not," I mumbled knowing that any other arguments I knotted together would be effectively cut through with a further sharp threat from Pop.

After lunch while less burdened children were making their way to Sunday school I was dragging myself toward Mrs. Kelly's gloomy house close to where the main street of the town begins. I carried Ma's small parcel wishing I dared to drop it behind a bush in one of the gardens I was walking past and then tell Ma I had delivered it. This would not be a good deed but it would be good for me. I could amuse myself for a while and then return home to tell Ma the mission was accomplished. But on her next visit Ma would he sure to ask Mrs. Kelly how she had found the contents of her package and Mrs. Kelly would look bewildered and ask "what package?" and I would he plunged into a world of trouble. So I had no choice but to take the package to that baleful house and put up with the consequences.

I made very slow progress – like a perverse explorer trying to cross the arctic wastes without a dogsled. I drew out my reluctant journey by playing hopscotch at regular intervals on the flagstoned sidewalk. I paused to admire the gardens I was passing. I stopped to talk to an elderly neighbor couple by the name of Fayle – who were struck dumb with shock for a minute or two as I normally walked past them without much more than a curt nod and a grunt. I examined most carefully the window displays of the two shops on my route even though they hadn't been changed for years. The number of dead dessicated flies lying in those displays was surprising and I tried to count them all. I petted a couple of friendly dogs that had wagged their tails at me. It occurred to me to offer the contents of Ma's parcel to the dogs since I was pretty convinced they were edibles of some sort but Ma would never have believed me if I alleged I had been ambushed and robbed by dogs. So eventually despite all my foot-dragging I arrived at Mrs. Kelly's house. It was the last one in a row of dour slate-roofed, cement-faced two-storey houses the walls of which had turned a dirty gray with the passage of time.

I had asked Ma what to do when I reached this house. If Mrs. Kelly couldn't get out of bed who would answer the doorbell? Was someone else living there – someone I had not seen on previous visits – who would answer the door? I had privately thought it possible that after I rang the bell the door would open silently, impelled by some malign wraith.

"Just ring the bell and go in," Ma had told me. "Call her from the hallway, tell her who you are and why you're there and ask if it's alright to go into her room. Then when she says it is go in and give her the package…that's all I want you to do. She'll be pleased to see you. She doesn't get many visitors…even on Sundays."

So here I was despite all my delays standing on Mrs. Kelly's doorstep finding it hard to actually ring her doorbell. Once I had done that I would be committed to entering the house and confronting its occupant all by myself. Wouldn't it be simpler if I just left the parcel by the front door and went away? Another visitor would eventually find it there and take it in for me.

I had convinced myself that leaving the package on the front doorstep was the best policy when one of those nosey neighbors who inhabited the precincts of my childhood popped out of the house next door to see what I was up to. This one was a woman of middle age and bright ginger hair folding a very long red cardigan round herself as if trying to wrap herself up in it prior to mailing herself somewhere. She was wearing thick stockings with holes in them, had large dirty floppy pink slippers on her feet, paper curlers in her hair and a cigarette burning in the corner of her mouth that caused her to cough at regular intervals and screw her eyes up against the smoke.

"What yer after?" she asked in what Ma would call a "common" voice.

"I've brought a package for Mrs. Kelly," I said stifling an impulse to tell her that my concerns were none of hers.

"Oos it from then?" asked the slatternly woman, brazenly curious.

"My Mum," I answered politely though I felt a strong urge to tell her to mind her own business.

"What's in it?" the slattern asked again after a brief fit of coughing during which she contrived to hold the cigarette in her mouth.

This time she had gone too far. Despite my training in politeness I told her "That's none of your business." I wasn't willing to stand there bandying words with this woman so I rang Mrs. Kelly's bell at once and hastily pushed open her door and shut it on the red, pink and papered woman who had bounced out into the street at my last remark. I found myself in a hallway, a set of stairs in front of me disappearing up into the dark second storey of the house. Several doors along a corridor led to downstairs rooms. All were closed. I couldn't remember which one opened into the house-owner's daily quarters though the door nearest me was the logical choice since Mrs. Kelly occupied the front sitting room. The brief verbal duel with the neighbor, the dark of the hallway and my repugnance at being there at all robbed me of common sense. But I heard a faint voice calling "Hello…hello…who is it?" and I knew which door to open.

"It's Erik." I replied in a voice embarrassingly high-pitched and quavery. "I've brought something from me Mum."

It will seem odd to a contemporary reader that not only did ordinary people in the town I grew up in not lock their doors during the day but felt no impulse to do so even when they lived alone, even when they lived as solitary invalids. That anyone would enter the house from the street with felonious intent never occurred to them though it would to the Rand-Krueger class with advanced notions of private property fostered in Imperial outposts. Houses were occasionally robbed at night but so rarely that no one thought it would happen to them. Neighbors, friends, the men who read the gas and electric meters, tradesmen of all sorts rang the bell and then entered the house immediately announcing their presence by calling from the entrance hall as I had just done. So here I was about to confront the invalid, fearful of I know not what. I opened the door to that improvised bedroom very slowly. It creaked.

Mrs. Kelly was lying back on her many pillows clad in her usual voluminous faded peach-colored peignoir with a heavy shawl draped over it. She was very white-faced and looked weak. The persistent smile that I had found diabolic was missing. She struggled up in her bed to see me better. I explained why I had come and hoped I could then flee the house. She asked me to put the package from Ma on a sizeable bed-side table half of which was covered with labeled medicine bottles varying in the fullness and color of their liquid contents. Her table looked a bit like a bar counter. I was just going to say that I had to go – just had to get to Sunday school – when she asked me to stay a while and chat. She hadn't had visitors for a couple of days except for her household help who came in daily but only for a busy hour at a time and the District Nurse who visited on Mondays and Fridays but had no time for general conversation. She said she hadn't had a chance to talk to me by myself before so why didn't we remedy that now? I was about to mention the importance of my getting to Sunday school when I noticed something I hadn't seen on previous visits – a look of desperate pleading in her eyes – so reluctantly I agreed to stay though I was privately determined not to tarry long.

She asked me to tell her what I did at school, who I played with, how I got on with Carlo, what news there was of Ronald in the army. I was hesitant at first, wondering if these apparently innocuous questions had some sinister motive, but when she proved to be an enthusiastic listener I felt emboldened to launch upon a spirited account of my daily life. I even made her laugh a few times. I eventually told her about Jakob once I had begun to feel better about being there. I relaxed in my chair, observed the room more objectively than I had on prior visits when I had sat tense, silently begging Ma to stop talking and get me back into fresh air. The room now reminded me of several in Aunty Agatha's house. It had the same late-Victorian air – the same sort of thick, heavily embossed wall-paper faded over time, the same sort of prints on the walls in the same sort of gilded wooden frames, the same sort of brassware on the tops of drawers, the same dusty aspididstra lurking in the same kind of brass pot in a corner, the same kind of heavy lace curtains at the windows that seemed designed to keep out as much light as possible. The ponderous electrical fittings were like those in Aunty Agatha's house. Nothing in these surroundings was any more threatening than those of Aunty Agatha's much larger house now that I felt relaxed enough to notice properly.

Since I had a willing listener – a species not to be found at home where too many people competed for attention – I prattled on, beginning to enjoy the sound of my own voice. Mrs. Kelly seemed interested in every-thing I had to say.

Eventually she asked me if I would like some tea. I was a bit taken aback by a sudden vision of her leaping out of her bed to go and get it thus bringing into question the reasons for her living her life in bed in the first place. But she remained where she was explaining where the kitchen could be found and told me that the woman who came in to do the cleaning every day had left all the tea things ready (Ma, it seemed, had sent advanced notice of my visit) so that all I had to do was boil the water in the kettle and pour it into the waiting teapot which had the requisite amount of tea in it. So I set off to find the kitchen, which was at the end of the corridor.

It was a lot tidier than our kitchen ever was though of course ours had to serve the needs of an entire swollen war-time household and was never anything other than chaotic. There was a small wooden table in the middle of Mrs. Kelly's kitchen with matching chairs either side of it. The walls, in need of a coat of paint, were a faded brown in color. Framed photographs from the early years of the Century hung here and there. They featured old-fashioned-looking passenger ships, men in droopy mustaches, dark clothes and boaters, women in long white gowns and vast hats of the sort still favored by Mrs. Hochheimer, elderly tramcars on Douglas promenade – summer holiday scenes from before the first World War.

The kitchen was as dark as the rest of the downstairs since the projecting back of the house next door shut out a great deal of light. There was only a cement yard with a washing line suspended over it – not a blade of grass, not even a hint of a garden behind or beside the house.

I found the tea things ready on a tray on the kitchen table and a large kettle on the old gas stove half-filled with water. There was a box of matches on the table. I lit the largest burner on the stove-top and set the kettle on it to boil. This would probably take at least five minute so I wondered whether I ought to rejoin Mrs. Kelly while I waited but decided it might be safer to stay in the kitchen to prevent the water in the kettle from boiling over.

While the water heated up I stared out at the cement yard and then looked around the kitchen more closely but saw nothing that might explain anything of my hostess's background or current circumstances. I was relieved at what I did *not* find. The place did not contain any witch's paraphernalia such as a suspiciously large cooking pot in which to stew small succulent children nor a broomstick of the approved witch's type on which to fly about at night sowing trouble. There was no pointed hat, no black cloak, no ambiguous cat. The few cookbooks on a small improvised shelf did not appear to contain recipes for the cooking of small chubby children as far as I could discern from a very brief survey. Everything was respectable, shabby, normal. The last thing one would expect to find in such a place was a book of spells.

The kettle eventually boiled. I turned off the gas and made the tea. I walked back down the dark corridor slowly and carefully so as not to spill the tea nor cause any of the crockery to fall off the tray. I had left Mrs. Kelly's door ajar so all I had to do was push it open wider with my foot and enter.

"Here's the tea," I said unnecessarily, "I haven't spilled any."

When the occupant of the bed didn't reply I looked up from the tray to see that she had slipped sideways so that she was in danger of falling out onto the floor. Her eyes were closed, her mouth sagged open and she was breathing loudly and laboriously in a way that sounded far from healthy. I was so shocked by the contrast with how she was when I left her – weak, obviously, but upright and alert – that I dropped the tray and everything on it onto the floor. China teacups shattered, the teapot lid came off and scalding tea spread over the carpet mixing with milk from the broken milk jug. I stood there mid the wreckage gripped by terror. It looked to me as if Mrs. Kelly was dying right there in front of me. She was obviously unconscious. What could I do? My mind was in turmoil and my strongest impulse was to run away from that house as fast as possible and not stop until I reached home.

Instead of trying to haul Mrs. Kelly back upright in her bed – she was too heavy for that – I fled the room as if pursued by all the ghosts and goblins I once fancied occupied this house. Out in the street I gulped in the fresh air. I wanted Ma to cope with this crisis – she would know what to do but by the time I had run home to fetch her Mrs. Kelly might be dead. So I did the only thing I could think of. I dashed up the street to the house of a doctor I only knew by sight. Instead of politely ringing his doorbell I began frantically pounding on the door. The noise produced his pretty Irish housekeeper (and, said local gossip, the sharer of his bed) enraged by such an affront to good manners.

"What's all this racket yer makin' and on the Lard's day too?" she said, her Irish temper raised. "What for are ye bangin' away at the door ye leetle devil? Can't yer use the bell like any other Christian? If ye think that bangin' on the door's a funny joke I'll be makin' ye laugh outa the other side of yer face!"

I gasped out the reason for my frenzy but gabbled so fast she couldn't follow me. She could tell, however, that I wasn't playing tricks after all so she got me to take a breath and then repeat slowly what I had just said incoherently.

"Where did ye say this poor oul soul is?"

"Just down the street on the other side of the road."

"Come in and wait a minute," she said, "while I fetch the doctor."

So I stood impatiently in the entrance hall of the doctor's house, a place far larger than ours. It was all light polished wood, doors with ornamental glass panels, smart furniture (as far as I could see). There was a smell of furniture polish on the air. Its unobstructed tall windows let in light – it was the very opposite of the hapless Mrs. Kelly's shrouded domain.

The doctor appeared sooner than I had expected. He was carrying his black medical bag and told me to lead the way as fast as I could go. I needed no encourgement and was surprised at how fast the doctor could move in an emergency. We were soon back inside Mrs. Kelly's house. I showed the doctor into her room. By this time she had slid off the bed and was lying face down on the floor. Her breathing was even more labored and a lot more ragged than when I had entered with the tea tray. The doctor and I struggled to get her back into the bed where he laid her flat after pushing all the pillows aside. He took his stethoscocpe out of his bag, pulled her peignoir open (at which point I turned to stare at the wall) and listened to her chest. Then he fished a hypodermic needle from his black bag, filled it from a vial he had there and plunged it deep into her arm and pressed until it emptied. He swabbed the point of the needle's entry with something on a piece of cotton wool.

"Do you know the people in the house next door?" the doctor asked as he listened again to Mrs. Kelly's chest with his stethoscope.

I thought of the vulgar woman who had questioned me. "No," I said.

"Well, look, you run back to my house and tell Miss O"Neill to call an ambulance to this address. Say it's very urgent. Be quick now! This really is a matter of life or death."

Glad of an excuse to leave that front sitting room I again fled the house and again pounded on the doctor's door. When the housekeeper opened it she didn't waste time in lecturing me on proper social manners but listened to what I had to say and then rang at once for the ambulance, "And hurry!" she said, "the doctor says it's a life and death matter.

She suggested I return at once to Mrs. Kelly's house in case the doctor had other messages for me to carry. Not long after I had returned and made an effort to pick the tray and broken crockery off the wet carpet the ambulance arrived, its bell clanging. When it had come for Ma I was not allowed to see her being treated and then taken away. This time I was in the room with the doctor and the ambulance men so I saw everything. Not that there was very much to see. After a brief discussion with the doctor the two ambulance men carefully transferred Mrs. Kelly from her bed to a stretcher. They covered her with a thick blanket and got her to the waiting ambulance with some difficulty. Out in the street they carefully manoeuvred the stretcher into the ambulance, slammed the doors and drove off at high speed with the warning bell ringing. This operation didn't take long though long enough to draw the nosey neighbor out of her house again.

"Hey, kid," she said, "Wassup?" "Oos sick?"

I'd like to have replied "you are" but I only thought of that later. At the time I probably told her what she wanted to know.

"There's nothing more you can do here," the doctor said. "Go home and tell your mother what's happened."

Then, as one belonging to the small house-locking class, he added "and if she knows where the key is she should come and fasten the doors till we know more about the patient's condition. She might be in hospital a while. She might not come out alive."

I left the doctor to close the door of Mrs. Kelly's house firmly behind him. My journey home was a lot more direct and a lot faster than my halting progress the other way had been. In fact I ran almost bursting with my news which I gabbled out as incoherently as I had described Mrs. Kelly's condition to the doctor's housekeeper. Ma made me start from the beginning looking more and more alarmed as I described my afternoon's adventure in detail. She called Pop into the house from the backyard where he was mending a puncture in one of his bike's tires and had me repeat the story.

"I'll have to go up to the hospital at once to see how she is," aid Ma. Pop suggested that Ma disturb Mrs. Corcoran by telephoning first. Mrs. Kelly's condition sounded too serious, from what I had said, for her to be available to visitors.

"She has no family to speak of," said Ma. "She doesn't know many people at all. She could die up there in the hospital and there'd be few would know nor care. So I've got to go."

They discussed the situation back and forth. Eventually they turned to me.

"I'm proud of you," said Ma, "you were very brave this afternoon. You did just the right thing. A lot of kids would have run off scared stiff after seeing her taken suddenly like that but you didn't panic. If you had she might be dead now. She might be anyway for all we know but you did all you could."

Ma gave me a sudden hug and Pop added his word while she did.

"Aye, lotta lads would've run off in a sweat but ya didn't so good on ya." From Pop this was high praise.

When I had had time to think over the afternoon's event I realized that Ma and Pop were not praising me for physical courage of the kind you need to front rough seas or roaring bulls got loose or bishops in full ceremonial regalia. They were praising me for moral fiber, which was just as important. I had been tested again and this time, despite my fears, I had not been found wanting. I realized that I didn't need to become a bully to prove that I could be plucky. If I was faced with another crisis like the one this afternoon I would again have to ignore the rising panic and take action. It was a comfort to know that I could do just that.

Mrs. Kelly didn't die that day. But when she was brought home again in the ambulance she was much weaker than she had been before and had to have a full-time nurse. Even so she died alone one rainy afternoon a couple of months later. She had no memory of that frantic Sunday afternoon. She was irked that her daily help had broken some of her best crockery and refused to admit it.

CHAPTER THIRTY

WHILE MRS. KELLY WAS IN HOSPITAL I THOUGHT ABOUT HER A LOT more than I wanted to. I couldn't get out of my mind that terrible transition from the time I went to make the tea till I returned with the tray to find her limp, unconscious, slipping out of her bed. I may, at the time have been able to summon the fortitude to get help but the sight of her, as I had thought, dying, gave me nightmares when I recalled it – as I did, obsessively. It was the mysterious arrival of the man we knew as Mr. Smith that finally drove the images of Mrs. Kelly in her apparent death-slide out of my head.

Mr. Smith presented himself one night in dramatic fashion. I had been told to go to bed for the umpteenth time and had run out of excuses for staying up when the front doorbell rang. It was pitch dark ouside and the rain poured in a Manx monsoon.

Ma and Pop exchanged puzzled looks. "Who can that be at this time and on a night like this?" Ma directed her question at Pop as if he might have the answer. As it turned out Pop thought he did.

"It's them ARP f'las an' I'll be given 'm what for. There's no light comin' from *this* house. The black-out here's good…I've seen to that. But them f'las is always lookin' fa trouble. Give some f'las a badge an' a tin hat an' they're l'il Hitlers. That l'il titchy f'la Charlie Christian down the hill's a bugger for…"

Rather than explain what this diminutive Charlie Christian was a "bugger" for Pop was off to "have it out" with him for disturbing our domestic peace by falsely accusing him of aiding the enemy with illegal slits of light. Ma followed in his wake to calm him down and ensure he did not provoke tin-hatted authority. I trailed after Ma. Carlo would have done the same if he hadn't been firmly sent to bed more than two hours earlier. He had eventually fallen asleep after much bellowed incoherent protest at being forcibly removed from the family hearth.

Pop opened the outer front door causing enough light from the hallway's dulled wartime bulbs to leak outside and dimly reveal a man standing in the rain which by now was coming down as heavily as in a thunderstorm. He was not wearing an ARP uniform and had no interest in our black-out precautions. He wore an expensive raincoat and a sodden trilby hat. He carried a small leather suitcase with water running off it and he looked miserable. He told us later that he had walked all the way to our house from the center of town – a distance of more than a mile. "That f'la," said Pop a day or two later, "was all in an' looked just like a drownded rat."

The man in the rain introduced himself as Smith…Mr. Claude Smith. He had been sent to us by the Housing Authority as he needed somewhere to stay while he was in town on government business…English government business.

"We've only got the one small bedroom available at the moment," said Ma not knowing what the powers-that-be who assigned local billets had told this soaking stranger.

"If it's alright with you that will suit me nicely," said the stranger. "I was told you did meals and I've brought my ration book."

"Well, if you don't mind plain cooking and a pretty small bedroom then we can put you up," said Ma. "You come in out of the rain. You're all soaked."

Mr. Smith, well aware of this, stepped dripping into the front hall and took off his sopping hat to reveal a prematurely bald head. Ma helped him off with his raincoat while Pop stood by looking indecisive. But not for long. He eventually concluded that unlike the local ARP watchdogs Mr. Smith would pose no threat to his peace of mind so shook his hand and while Ma hung the stranger's wet things on the coat stand in the hall Pop led the way down the short flight of stairs from the hall to the kitchen. The coal fire we had been sitting by before the bell rang was still burning brightly. The stranger was invited to sit close to it to warm himself up.

This "kitchen" of ours was in fact a living room with the real kitchen beyond it through a door. It had been the housekeeper's room when in its grander days the house had held a single Victorian family with its servants. The wires that rang the bells to summon the domestics all ended in this room. They were activated by small inlaid porcelain handles set in the walls of the other significant rooms but by the time Ma and Pop rented the house they had either been disconnected or fallen into disrepair. I used to try to imagine the expression on Pop's face if any of our war time lodgers had had the temerity to summon either him or Ma with one of the bells.

The real kitchen beyond our living room we called "the back kitchen." This was a realm of chaos that only Ma could navigate without mishap. The daily meals were cooked there on a couple of ordinary gas stoves. Food was stored there. The laundry was done there in an ancient boiler with a mangle attached for squeezing the water out of washed garments. Utensils were scattered everywhere including the cold stone floors. Ancient shelves leaning toward those floors supported more than their fair share of plain crockery. The sink where the dishes were washed was made of stone and was as old as the house but did not smell like Mrs. Dodd's. The cloths with which dishes were washed had seen better days, as had the threadbare towels. In war we had to "make do" or, better still, "make do and mend."

The place we called "the kitchen" was a more orderly, cosy if shabby room heated by a coal fire in the center of an old-fashioned kitchen range built into one wall. When Pop had to resort to the tin bath to wash off his industrial grime it was placed on the worn carpet in front of this range and the doors to the room were carefully guarded so that Pop's cleansing didn't attract an audience. It would have been just like Bessie to have blundered in while Pop sat there naked in his foot or two of hot water. One of the resident Air Force wives might have meandered down from upstairs to borrow some sugar and been confronted by Pop in the nude stepping in or out of his tin tub so either Ma or I had to watch over him while he cleaned away the oil and soot and dried himself as well as he could on our threadbare towels. His ritual ablutions began at the back kitchen sink where he used a special kind of gooey substance to remove the worst of the oily dirt before he proceeded to the bath and soap.

But this is a long way from Mr. Smith. Ma asked him if he had had any dinner. It appeared that he hadn't eaten anything since breakfast and was ravenous. He had reached the Island by boat. The sea had been rough; he had felt so queasy that he hadn't even dared to think about food. But now, he said, he could eat a horse and would welcome anything Ma might have, including a horse. She produced some eggs and made some chips in the deep fryer. The potatoes for these, she pointed out, came from our own garden just as the eggs had been laid by our own hens. He'd get no war – time powdered egg here unless, of coure, the hens stopped laying.

"And I'm the f'la does all the work to keep 'm laying," Pop said giving credit where it was due but failing to mention that it was me who generally had to feed his aggressively peckish flock when I got home from school – a daily chore that I detested.

Mr. Smith was obviously as hungry as he had said he was since he attacked Ma's improvised meal with enthusiasm and HP Sauce. He had impressed her with his cultivated accent, his well-cut suit, his upper-class gentility of manner. Such incidentals generally caused Pop to behave like a truculent peasant with a "who does *he* think *he* is?" attitude but Mr. Smith was different. Pop evidently found in him the genuine article and urged more chips upon him. I was already fascinated by this man who had emerged so mysteriously from the dark and rain like an aristocrat (despite his name) seeking shelter from some nameless democratic peril. I wanted to ask him all manner of questions but I was sent to bed and had to leave it to Ma and Pop to find out who Mr. Smith was and why he had come to us at such an hour on such a day.

Next morning while Carlos and I were eating the thick gray porridge thinned with a little milk and sprinkled with a little sugar that formed our daily disgusting war-time breakfast we asked questions about the new lodger, questions that received no answer.

"He's a very nice gentleman, very well-mannered," said Ma, "but he didn't tell us where he came from or why he's here. Maybe he can't. There are all kinds of people doing secret work for the war and they're not allowed to tell anyone very much about themselves. They often can't tell their own families what they are doing."

"You mean he's a spy?" I asked.

"Now I didn't say that," Ma replied. "Spies are not gentlemen and it's obvious that Mr. Smith is."

I asked Ma how many spies she had known.

"None, of course. How could I?" said Ma with some feeling. "Anyway all that creeping about and poking into the secrets of people's lives is disgusting…there's plenty of gossips round here doing that and they're not the kind of people I care to know."

"Bessie's just like that and you don't mind her coming here to talk about other people. She's always telling you what she's found out about the neighbors."

"It's past time you went back to school," said Ma, "and don't forget your gasmask like you did yesterday. What would you do if there was a raid and you were caught without your gasmask? You'd go black in the face and choke to death, that's what you'd do, so don't you ever leave it behind again!"

Having vigorously diverted the conversation from the dangerous shoals of inconsistency Ma shooed me off to school none the wiser about Mr. Smith's occupation.

I thought that Mr. Smith's arrival was a subject I could safely open for discussion at school no one at home apparently caring very much either where he came from or why he had appeared unannounced late at night in the dark and rain. I confided first in the Polish boy, the refugee Jan Kosinski. I'm not sure why I chose him since we usually didn't have much to say to each other. I suppose it was because I was thinking about spying and felt that a refugee from Europe might have some special insight into this subject though Jan had never mentioned spies in the few conversations we had had. I recounted the circumstances of Mr. Smith's arrival and described his manner and appearance.

"So do you think he's a spy?" I asked.

"I don't know of the spies," Jan replied. "They are supposed to work in secret isn't it? This man knocking at your door at night…he isn't doing the secret thing. He has already begun you to think he's a spy. A clever spy isn't doing that thing. He wants you to think he is doing the other thing and not the spying."

Jan's English wasn't perfect but it was a lot better than my Polish. He had a point, I supposed, but then maybe Mr. Smith was clever enough to draw attention to himself by his mode of arrival so that people who thought like Jan would conclude that he was harmless. Or maybe he wasn't a very clever spy. There must be degrees of espionage ability.

I referred the matter next to Brian McQueen, another boy I spoke to only rarely. He did well in school examinations despite prolonged absences.

"What you say this f'la's name was?" he asked me.

"He said it was Smith."

"There you are then. Half the people on the mainland are called Smith and the other half are called Jones. If you want to hide who you really are these would make grand disguise names. If the f'la said he was called Fauntleroy Fitzherbert Smythe people'd sit up and take notice. They'd ask who the hell he was with a name like that. They'd be suspicious. But just *Mr. Smith* doesn't make anyone ask questions. You should try to find out the f'la's real name.

"How?"

"I don't know…get into his room when he's out. Look at his things. He probably thinks he's safe in your house so he'll relax and leave clues lying about."

"Would you search his room if you were me?"

"Of course, but make sure he's out first. You wouldn't want him nabbing you going through his things. If this f'la is a spy he might cut your throat and then go and do in your family while he's at it so there'd be no one left to tell the police about him."

You could never tell whether Brian was being serious or not. But I decided to watch Mr. Smith carefully, ply him with questions and, if I had to, examine his room while he was out of the house. That shouldn't be difficult since neither Ma nor Pop believed in locking doors so no one had a key to their own room.

"If we gave 'm all keys," said Pop, "that 'd be like telling 'm they couldn't trust us. And what if they took ill? How would we help 'm if they were locked in their rooms and couldn't walk to the door? Anyway we don't lock our doors so why should they lock theirs if they've got nothing to hide?"

The trouble with thinking of Mr. Smith as a covert agent was that he was unaffectedly pleasant to all of us. Instead of sitting with our other lodgers in the front dining room he took his early evening meal with us in the kitchen. He was out all day and joined us for "tea" (we had dinner in the middle of the day). He was never stuck for words, never moody or silent. He took pains to include Carlo and I in the conversation instead of ignoring us the way most adults did. He asked Ma and Pop lots of questions about the Island, its history and people. For some reason he was especially interested in the Island's native breed of mountain sheep – the Loaghtan – with its brown wool and two sets of curled horns. He told Pop he would like to see some of these. Pop told him that they were now rare but promised to ask along his daily route to find out whether any local farmers had any that Mr. Smith could inspect. Pop concluded from this interest that Mr. Smith might have something to do with the English Ministry of Agriculture.

Mr. Smith asked Pop about his favorite pub and sealed himself in Pop's good opinion by accompanying him there and buying him a couple of pints. If, on those occasions, anyone had said anything derogatory about Mr. Smith Pop would have defended him hotly and, if carried away, threaten to "knock" the offender's "block off." But no blocks required kocking off since Mr. Smith was as engaging to others as he was to all of us. He became popular at Pop's local where he played darts with the best the pub had to offer and lost just often enough to retain his popularity.

On occasion I found him on his own reading the daily paper or writing a letter at our kitchen table. The questions I asked him he answered willingly and with good humor not appearing to mind being interrupted. I found that he came from the South of England – somewhere south of London. I asked him about that region which, for me then, was a realm of the imagination where the King and Queen presided in a palace from which they issued at intervals in a large black car later getting out of it with worried looks to inspect bomb damage – whole streets reduced to rubble, docks smashed to pieces. The King wore a naval uniform and the Queen was better dressed in the day even than my Aunty Emmeline at Christmas. I had seen all this on news broadcasts at the cinema.

I asked Mr. Smith what the ordinary people in the South of England were like.

"A lot of them think anywhere north of London is where savages live. They think that up here you all go round in animal skins and live in tribes and fight each other and kill strangers. I'm sure some think you're all cannibals."

"Why?" I asked, taking him literally, appalled at such ignorance.

"Because they're snobs. They don't really believe what I've just said but they joke about such things anyway. It makes them feel very superior. I think a lot would be frightened if they had to live in the North."

"Why?" I asked again unable to see how the people I knew – with exceptions like the shepherd – could possibly frighten anybody.

"Because the North is where most of the industry is…the factories, the shipyards, the coal mines. You have to get yourself dirty when you work in places like that …the way your father does. Southerners don't like to get themselves dirty."

Mr. Smith's tone suggested a sympathy for the North so I asked him outright why he had come to the Island. I hadn't intended to ask this question but out it came.

"Well," he said, looking at me appraisingly," I can't tell you that. I work for the government and in a time of war people aren't allowed to talk about what they do. Gossip might get back to the enemy, you see, and cause ructions."

"How would the enemy find out?" I asked wondering at the same time what *ructions* were.

"Our enemy has all kinds of ways of finding things out," said Mr. Smith. "You'd be surprised. There could be spies in this very house. They could be pretending to be Airmen. I could be one. How do I know you're not one?"

"I'm not old enough," I replied taking him seriously.

I thought of Bessie next door and the sort of security nightmare she posed with all her gossip. I didn't mention her to Mr. Smith and thought it fortunate that she was temporarily away from the Island helping her niece, who in a fit of patriotism, had just had another baby.

Mr. Smith's evasiveness about his work, his favorable assessment of the North vis a vis the South made me wonder about him. He was so nice to everyone he met that he couldn't be genuine. Even the best people had their off-days. He cultivated Pop, he flattered Ma on her cooking, he behaved so much better than most of the adults I knew that I became convinced he must have something to hide. All his pleasantness and good humor made me decide to get into his room so that I could find evidence of his duplicity. I owed it to the war effort. A man as eager to please as Mr. Smith had to be a fake, a spy.

But sneaking into Mr. Smith's room in search of clues wasn't an easy matter. The first time I tried was at mid-day dinner time just before I had to go back to school. Mr. Smith, I knew, would be out of the house then. With Ma tied up in the kitchen washing dishes all I had to worry about were the other lodgers one of whom might catch me red-handed on their way to the bathroom. Mr. Smith's room was on the second floor of the house at the end of a short landing not far from the bathroom. I waited until all was quiet, darted up the stairs to the second floor, took a brief look round and finding the coast clear walked up to Mr. Smith's door and turned the handle. The door wouldn't open even when I pushed. It seemed to be locked. I retreated to the kitchen to direct at Ma what I hoped would be a diplomatic line of questioning.

"Do any of the visitors lock their doors?" I asked, trying to sound as if idle curiosity had prompted the question.

"Why do you want to know?" Ma radiated suspicion.

"I don't know. I just thought of it."

"Something must have made you think it."

"Well, I thought they didn't have keys but if they got a key and locked their door and there was a fire they might not get out of the house in time. They could be burned to death before they could get their door unlocked."

"Where *do* you get such fancies from? I don't know anyone else who would ask such a question."

Ma looked concerned as if she feared I had been afflicted with nightmares that had a lingering effect. Ma had a healthy respect for nightmares. She said they were always a sign that the person who experienced them was troubled so if we dreamed those sort of dreams we must tell her so that she could find out what was worrying us and put things right. Then the bad dreams would go away.

"I just think about things sometimes. I'm not having nightmares. What's wrong with asking questions?"

"Nothing," said Ma, "except that you never stop asking them. You're at it all day long, day in and day out. Why can't you just take things as they come without worrying why they are, how they came to be, what we can do about them and all the other questions you ask on and on and on. But you seem to lose your tongue at school. Your teachers say they never get a peep out of you there. When they tell me about how quiet you are they seem to be talking about a different boy than the one we know at home."

Now that the conversation had taken this turn – escalating from what I had hoped looked like an innocent question that would produce the answer to the conundrum of Mr. Smith's locked door to a critical account of my tendency to query the world around me – I felt it was time I left for school. The only consolation – a small one at that – I enjoyed at having to retreat without finding out anything about Mr. Smith's desire for secrecy was that I had left Ma puzzled.

When I came home from school I hadn't decided how again to raise the issue of Mr. Smith's locked door but Ma took that matter out of my hands.

"You know how you were asking me at dinner time about people locking their doors and maybe burning to death?"

"Can't remember," I lied. Ma reminded me.

"Well, she said, "Mr. Smith's the only one who really wants his door locked. He said he was sorry about it but it had to do with his work. His work is very hush-hush, he told me, and he has to keep important papers in his room. He's got nowhere else to put them. So your Dad gave him a key. He won't do it as a rule but he made an exception for Mr. Smith. Is your curiosity satisfied now?"

"Why can't all the others have keys to their rooms?" I asked though I already knew Pop's usual reply.

"Your Dad says if they're not up to mischief they don't need to lock their doors."

"What sort of mischief?"

"There you go again! I answer one question and you ask another. It's endless. I don't know what we're going to do about you...I really don't!" And off Ma went before I could say anything further.

Now that I knew the securing of Mr. Smith's room was a daily occurrence I hadn't a clue as to how to get into it unless he had a fit of most unlikely forgetfulness. People in storybooks opened doors with charms and magic keys, often golden. They said things like "open sesame" and doors flew open. I didn't have such useful means at my disposal nor did I know artful Dickensian boys skilled at picking locks. Mr. Smith's benign face and locked door continued to baffle me.

Then there were all those stories he told that made us laugh. I didn't associate spies with humor so I began to waver in my persuasion that Mr. Smith must be a secret agent hand in glove with the Germans. I still remember one tale he told us about a village in Yorkshire he had had to visit recently. The people there had peculiar views about how to fight the Germans should they actually invade the country. This place on the Yorkshire Moors, he said, feared it would be invaded by paratroopers. (I interrupted to tell my Glen Auldyn story about fictitious paratroopers in the moonlight but Pop told me to shut up). The local authorities decided that the first thing invading paratroopers would want to do after they had drifted down through cold air would be to pee. Being German and thus orderly they would all queue up for the available toilets in the village houses. So the villagers were to be shown how to fix bombs in their cisterns so that when the first paratrooper pulled the chain he would blow up himself and all the others standing in line. There would be a village of exploding toilets and dead Germans. And of course wrecked houses but no one had thought about that.

While the adults were laughing I asked, "But what if someone forgot about the bomb in their toilet and pulled the chain and blew themselves up?"

"Shut up," said Pop.'

Mr. Smith told us also about another place where the people were told to put dinner plates face-down all round the village if the Germans were advancing in tanks. The tanks would stop because the Germans would want to climb down to look at the plates thinking they could be mines and while they were looking the villagers would shoot them all from behind their stone walls. I asked Mr. Smith where he had heard this tale. He merely smiled and said "Ah, that'd be telling."

I took my difficulty to Brian McQueen. I asked him if he thought that spies would tell funny stories. The spies I had read about in tales were deadly serious and sneaky in their ways. They didn't buy boys' fathers drinks in pubs or share a laugh at the doings of villagers remote both from the world and from reality. They didn't offer to help boys' mothers do the washing up as Mr. Smith often did even though Ma generally refused. They stayed in the shadows. They never smiled. They dealt with as few people as possible and had code names for everything and everyone.

"Spies in books," said Brian after thinking the matter over, "may not be like real ones. Real spies wouldn't want people to notice them so they'd probably live like everyone else while they got on with their secret work. Where does this Smith f'la go in the day?"

"I don't know."

"Well he'll be doing his spying while you're here at school. At night he'll behave like other people...so he'll be going to the pub, telling jokes, getting everyone to like him so they won't ask too many questions about what he does. He'll...you know...live two lives."

I asked Ma when I got home if she thought spies lived two lives...one in the day when they were doing their spying and another at night when they were trying to make people think they were relaxing after a day at a regular job like everybody else.

"Why are you asking about spies all the time?" Ma asked. "What have you been reading? Who's been filling your head with such nonsense?"

"I talk to Mr. Smith about them," I said. "He says you never know who they might be. He said I could be one."

"What rubbish!" Ma exclaimed. "I'm sure he never said any such thing and if he did he was pulling your leg."

"He says people down by London are frightened of us and think we're cannibals."

"Now I know he was pulling your leg."

"Mr. Smith could be a spy," I ventured. "He could be a spy in the day and go to the pub at night and pretend he isn't one."

"So you're at that again. I told you before Mr. Smith is a gentleman and spies aren't. They are nasty snooping common people like that Willy Cregeen at the Post Office. It's well known he steams open people's letters and reads them before sealing them up again and sending them off but nobody does anything about that. They say he's paid by the government to do it! They say he crosses sentences out with a big blue pencil! He knows about everybody's private life. It's not right and his blue pencil isn't either."

Ma had never come to terms with wartime censorship. For Ma if there was a spy in Ramsey Willy Cregeen and his ilk fitted the bill.

"Mr. Smith would never stoop to read other people's private correspondence. It is not," said Ma with certainty, "in his nature."

"But what will you do if Mr. Smith is a spy?" I persisted.

"If Mr. Smith was a spy…which he isn't…then your Dad would have to tell the police.

"What would the police do?"

"They'd arrest him of course. But since Mr. Smith isn't any such thing… and don't you go round saying he is or you'll get yourself into very hot water…we'll have no need to bother the police."

Ma had provided me with another approach to the espionage problem though Willy Cregeen had mentioned it in passing. If I couldn't get evidence from Mr. Smith's bedroom I could always tell the police of my suspicions. But if I did that, I reflected, then I would have to explain why I thought our new lodger could be working for Hitler and all I would have to offer as proof would be my own unsupported feeling that he was up to no good in the security department. And because the common opinion was that he was an excellent chap I'd be blamed for telling lies and trying to waste police time. So I was back where I started.

It had occurred to me from the beginning to ask Jakob's advice. Normally when I came across anything perplexing he would be the first person I would ask for information. But after Mary was taken from the farm by soldiers and plain-clothes police and since the police had questioned me about Mary, I had a sense that it was all too easy to do or say the wrong thing and get people into trouble with the authorities. I felt that if I were to ask Jakob about spies somehow the powers-that-be would find out and punish him in some way so I didn't dare turn to him for help in my current dilemma. This was irrational but, of course, children often are irrational and rationality generally is one of the first casualties in a war. I would just have to lay hands, somehow, on those documents I was sure Mr. Smith must be keeping hidden in his locked room.

How would I know whether any document I found in Mr. Smith's possession was one he could have acquired legitimately? I decided that if I found any with SECRET stamped on them that would be enough to prove they had been stolen. Documents stamped thus, I thought, could never lawfully be kept in someone's private room. They would be locked away in filing cabinets in an office presided over by a man in a pin-striped suit and wire-rimmed glasses looking like our Headmaster but minus his terrible cough and ready cane.

I would never know what documents Mr. Smith had possibly stolen, however, unless I could get into his room so there was no use contemplating the issue of documentary legitimacy in the abstract. My opportunity came at last in the third week of Mr. Smith's stay with us. He had taken up Ma's offer to clean and dust his room for him while he was at work. Ma had to rush to make the mid-day meal after she had finished and had forgotten to lock Mr. Smith's door. In fact she had raced downstairs to see to a pan that was boiling over on the stove and had not only forgotten to lock the door but had left it wide open. I had come home from school while Ma was in the back kitchen so she served up the dinner and then didn't remember to return to shut and lock Mr. Smith's door. While Ma was washing up the dishes I went upstairs to the bathroom and saw the door still open. I walked right into Mr. Smith's room and closed the door behind me. After all my anguish it was as simple as that.

Once inside his room I was reluctant to touch Mr. Smith's belongings. I had never done this sort of thing before. I felt as guilty as if I had turned to thieving. I eventually picked up a small photograph on the table by the bed. A slender young woman and a small boy a little younger than Carlo looked back at me from the picture. Did spies have young wives and small children? I put the photo back on the small table, listened to make sure no one was coming and then nerved myself to start opening drawers. The drawers in a chest of drawers standing opposite the bed were old and stuck frequently and were almost impossible to pull open silently. In them were some spare shirts, underwear, socks, a pair of suspenders, a woolen pullover, a spare pair of glasses and, in one of the smaller drawers at the top, some letters. There were no other documents – nothing stamped SECRET. Still, I would see what the letters contained – perhaps instructions from the Germans about what to spy on, who to follow. That those instructions might be written in German or some sort of code never occurred to me.

I took the letters out of their envelopes one by one. The grown-up hand-writing was hard to read but I gathered that the letters were from the woman in the photograph. She told Mr. Smith how much she and "baby" missed him. She said she hoped he would come home soon. The only suspicious reference I could find concerned sheep. Surely Mr. Smith had not come all the way to the Island to spy on Manx Loaghtan sheep? I was bitterly disappointed. Private letters were no substitute for official documents. I felt embarrassed to be reading them. I recalled Ma's contempt for Wally Cregeen at the Post Office. I was just putting the letters back into their envelopes when the door opened and there was Mr. Smith, no longer looking pleased with the world and certainly not looking pleased with me.

"What are you doing in my room?" His tone was sharp, his voice raised.

"Ma left the door open," I said instantly fearful and trying to keep my voice under control. "I was just looking at the picture of your wife," I said.

"Is that why the drawer with my letters in it is open?"

"Ma must have left it open," I said. "She'd have been dusting the inside."

"When I came in your hand was in it."

"I was just shutting it," I lied.

"Do you make a habit of walking round the house going into people's rooms to look at their private things? If you do I think your father will be interested to know."

If Mr. Smith thought he could intimidate me with a statement like that he was absolutely right.

Before either of us could say anything else Ma appeared having just remembered that she hadn't re-locked Mr. Smith's door. She wanted to know why I wasn't on my way back to school.

"Because," said Mr. Smith, "he thought he'd just nip in here and go through my dawers to find my private letters and read them."

"Is this true?" asked Ma rhetorically. In an anguished voice she said "How could you do a thing like this? This isn't the way we've brought you up!"

I remained silent, staring at the carpet where one of my feet was tracing a pattern all by itself.

"Is this your stupid idea that Mr. Smith is a spy again?"

"Well, he could be," I said truculently.

No sooner were those words out of my mouth than fear grasped me tightly. If Mr. Smith was a spy now was the moment when he would whip out a pistol and shoot both of us dead so that we couldn't tell anyone else. But he did no such thing. He didn't just laugh briefly. He became possessed by laughter and, as they say in children's books, "roared his head off." I didn't get the joke and neither did Ma though she seemed relieved that Mr. Smith's mood had changed so radically.

"Did you really think I came here to spy?" he asked me when he could draw breath.

When I didn't reply but simply stood there feeling like a fool he said, "My job isn't as glamorous…or as dangerous…as that I'm afraid. If you want to know why I am here as desperately as you seem to think I can tell you that I work for the Ministry of Supply. It's not a secret that I'm here to take a look at different breeds of sheep on the Island. We want to improve the cloth from which some of our uniforms are made. That's why I was in Yorkshire before coming here. The details are secret but I can say that without getting myself or anyone else into hot water. My work is pretty much everyday stuff…nothing as exciting as what you have been imagining. You've been reading too many comics."

I must have looked pretty glum at this news because he said "Cheer up, you wouldn't have wanted a real spy here putting you all in danger. Can I assume this will be the end of the matter…that you'll leave my things alone from now on?"

I nodded, feeling myself to be an absolute fool. Ma apologized for my behaviour several times. Mr. Smith said something like "boys will be boys" and added "I came back to the house for this." He fished a large bulging envelope out from under the mattress of the bed. It was stamped SECRET.

"Can't leave things like this lying around," said Mr. Smith.

Mr. Smith left the Island the following week, his enquiry finished. When I told Brian McQueen what had happened and especially about the extra-large envelope marked "SECRET" he said, "So he was a spy and you let the f'la get away. You didn't believe what he said about sheep did you? What are you going to do about it now?"

"Nothing," I said feeling that I had done more than enough already. To be caught red-handed going through a guest's belongings in his room was a mortifying experience made more so by the rant from Pop when he came home from work and Ma told him what had happened.

"No son of mine's going to be a thief," he declared, "if I have to knock yer from here to Africa."

It wasn't easy but I trained myself to stop thinking about spies. Why should I worry about them if no one else around me did in spite of all the wall posters telling us that "loose lips sink ships." Spies could arrive on the Island by battalions to find out all our secrets for all I cared. I washed my hands of them.

CHAPTER THIRTY-ONE

When Uncle Tom picked me up on a Saturday morning he was always vigorously, annoyingly, wide-awake. He claimed to have done two hours work while I was still asleep, ready to joke about my decadent urban torpor. But one rainy Saturday he came to pick me up in a state far from alert. He was coughing, sneezing, shivering, his eyes streaming, his face flushed, his large never-very-clean handkerchief sodden. I asked him the obvious question: why hadn't he stayed in bed since he seemed to have the 'flu? I knew the symptoms because I had had it myself a month earlier and hadn't been able to summon the energy to get up. Ma had fed me some of Pop's vile whiskey on a teaspoon and I swallowed the noxious stuff because Ma said it would bring down my temperature. It had sent me back to sleep relieving my symptoms for a while but when I woke up again my temperature was as high as before. I asked Uncle Tom why Aunty Liz hadn't insisted that he stay in bed till he felt better.

"What f'las's goin' ta do the work if I put meself ta bed?" he asked as if the question were an irrefutable answer.

"Aunty Liz, Mary, Johnny, Jakob, the other prisoners," I said and then added a footnote: "me."

"Yas all got plenty at ya already," said Uncle Tom. "We're all flat out. Town f'las can lie in but country folk's got the work at'm as won't wait. There's cattle ta feed, cows ta milk reg'lar, fields ta plough, crops ta be brought in, sheep ta watch an' see to. It's all hands ta the pumps on a farm these days young f'la – there's a war on."

As to the war I didn't think its outcome would be materially altered if Uncle Tom had the few days in bed he clearly needed. The others could manage the farm work for that long but Uncle Tom, accustomed to generalship, seemed to feel that the whole operation would crumble into chaos if he wasn't there in person to direct each day's activities and issue plans of campaign to his motley troops.

When he drove into the farm street Aunty Liz was there to meet us. She didn't look pleased. In fact her face was flushed with anger.

"And what do you think you've been doing?" she asked Uncle Tom rhetorically. "I thought I told you to stay in bed. I thought I told you we could manage without you for a few days. I remember saying that I would take the vegetables to the Camp. That I would pick up Erik. So why have you been out and about spreading your germs in the town like dung on a field – even before I woke up? You've probably given Erik the 'flu all over again by now. What are you going to tell his Mum when she comes rampaging up here…as well she might? I told you last night how I would arrange everything. I've called the doctor. He's late, otherwise he'd have been up here only to find you missing…and what would I have told him then? Now you get up to the house and back into bed, take some aspirin and go to sleep. The farm won't fall apart if you have to have a few days off. If you don't watch out what you've got will turn into pneumonia and then what'll you say…if you're strong enough to speak at all? It'll be all your own fault. By that time you'll have spread germs all over the place… you'll be a German secret weapon…and we'll be quarantined and then nothing'll get done and all the milk will go to waste. Is that what you want? Is it?"

While uttering these words Liz was angrily driving Uncle Tom toward the farmhouse as though herding a flock of especially contrary geese.

When she came back again – minus Tom – she called all the farm workers together to issue new battle orders for the day. Four prisoners with an amiable guard, an ancient piece of machinery and a horse to pull it were sent to a distant field to make war on thistles and other weeds. Mary and Jakob were given jobs to do closer to the farm – Jakob to mend a dry stone wall (a skill he had learned from Uncle Tom) while Mary took Rory and Tory part-way up Sky Hill to check on sheep, a task Tom normally undertook. Johnny was to look after the cattle, as usual. Liz left Mary with a list of other jobs to do while she and I were away delivering the day's milk. Before we left on our round she went to make sure Uncle Tom had returned to bed as ordered. When she came back she said she had locked him in their bedroom.

"I know that f'la of old," she said, "and trust'm as far as I can lift and throw'm. As soon as we're out of sight he'll be down in the yard telling everyone what to do and rooting up all my plans for the day. He thinks no one can run the farm but him. He's a typical fella. Like that Hitler."

"Suppose he wants to go to the lavatory?" I said.

"He can use the open window or the pot under the bed," said Liz. "I'm not having him out and about rife with disease."

I imagined Uncle Tom relieving himself in unconventional disease-spreading ways.

"What about the doctor?"

"I only said that to make Tom go back to bed. I haven't called him yet but I will if that dafty gets any worse. What he needs more than anything is sleep."

After the milk round I returned with Liz to the farm instead of staying at home because I was eager to see what Tom had done to circumvent Liz's arrangements. I was sure he would have found some way to get out of his bedroom. I imagined him rappelling his way down the walls of the house using knotted bedsheets, one end tied to a bedpost. Liz was far from sure she'd find him where she had left him either.

"I wouldn't put it past him to have got out of the bedroom somehow and been working for hours for all I've told him not to. Men have no common sense. None whatever. Remember that when you grow up and get married."

When we drove into the farm Liz had to brake sharply to avoid hitting the ambulance – the very same that had taken Ma and Mrs. Kelly to the hospital. It was parked just round a corner out of Liz's sight. Liz was out of her improvised milk van in an instant. I imagined Tom climbing out of his bedroom window with his rope of sheets in hand but missing his footing and falling to the concrete pathway below. If he had come down head-first he could have replicated his son's fate in which case the ambulance was superfluous.

Mary began to talk before anyone could ask anguished questions. She had heard the milk van's engine as we climbed the hill to the farm and was explaining to Liz how Tom had taken a turn for the worse so she had sent for help.

"I got the key to the bedroom off the hook in the kitchen and went up an hour ago just to make sure he was comfortable and didn't want anything. I found him tossing about in the bed. There were rivers of sweat running off him. He was muttering, not making any sense. I ran downstairs and phoned the doctor. He said to phone the hospital so I did. Finally they sent the ambulance. They said there's a lot of this about and how important it is to control the patient's temperature."

Two ambulance attendants were carrying the semi-conscious Uncle Tom carefully down the steps from the house to the farm street. They put him in the ambulance and drove off after Liz had moved her home-made milk van. She followed the ambulance in it after telling Mary what to do next and asking me to help her. I stayed until the evening acquiring a new respect for Mary's abilities as I watched her work tirelessly at jobs that had to be done and finding it very hard to keep up with her. Liz returned to drive me home long after Jakob and the other prisoners had been taken back to the Camp in a military truck. A doctor at the hospital had managed to bring down Tom's temperature but it had taken most of the afternoon. He would have to rest in hospital for a few days so that the doctors could keep an eye on him and he would have to rest further once he came back home. Ma had been worried when I didn't return home by tea-time but listened with sympathy as Liz described her ordeal.

Bessie had by now returned from the mainland to darken our door. She marched into the house just as Liz left. After Ma had explained what had transpired at the farm and how I had been helping out Bessie said "Those germs were everywhere round us while I was away," as if to suggest we were rather backward on the Island to be getting them only now. "It was like the Black Death," she went on melodramatically. "People were dropping like flies in autumn. One minute they'd seem fit and the next they fell flat. The doctor did what he could and then the undertaker followed to measure people up. Bad dose, this. *An Island of health in a sea of disease…* that was what the doctor said about us over here. He couldn't say that today, could he? He had a real posh voice. He wore a pin-striped suit with a striped tie." Here Bessie sighed. "Lucky I got back home alive and well," she continued. "But it's followed me here."

Ma ignored all this and said "I'm sure Tom'll be alright once he's had a bit of a rest and his temperature's come down."

"But that's just it," said Bessie. "That's what people were saying over on the mainland but temperatures didn't come down…they kept going up and up till folk popped their clogs."

I had a surreal vision of exploding clogs. Ma steered Bessie out of the room.

"What does *popped their clogs* mean?" I asked after Bessie had left.

"I don't know," said Ma. "It's an expression Bessie picked up in Lancashire while she was across. They talk funny over there." Ma seemed to have forgotten that she had been born "over there" and had some of the speech habits of her birthplace still.

Tom recovered well enough to return to light work after a couple of weeks of rest. I came to regard his exit in the ambulane as the first of the departures. People came to the Island and went away again, of course, throughout the war but so far it had been the arrivals who had impressed me. New faces from places I had never heard of stimulated my imagination especially when recently-arrived people described the areas they had come from as the dubious Mr. Smith had done, or the girl-wife from Saskatchewan who had tried to give me some notion of the immensity and beauty of the prairies before melting into tears of homesickness.

Though I was glad to see Mr. Smith leave there were others whose leaving made me apprehensive. Mrs. Kelly's lonely death troubled me because she was part of my childhood world and if she could be removed from it by disease or age or both then so could Ma and Pop and others of their generation. I became newly apprehensive about my elder brother whose entry into the war had been delayed, much to Ma and Pop's elation, by his being sent to Sandhurst Military College to be trained as an officer. But after his training was complete he would be sent to a battle front to fight the way Pop had been in his day and unlike Pop, he might not come back. My childhood world became less stable when I began to dwell on loss, on departure actual or potential.

By late 1942 the Government had begun to consider that its "enemy aliens" might not be so inimical or so alien after all – might in fact become useful allies in the war against Hitler. Once the panic at the prospect of imminent invasion was over now that Hitler had turned his attention to Russia, with guilt mounting over the deaths of so-called "aliens" after ships taking them to internment in Australia or Canada had been torpedoed, with the belated recognition that those labeled "alien" had skills Britain could use in its war effort, prisoners on the Island were being released in batches and returned to England and their freedom. This was the subject of town gossip and I had also seen bus-loads of jubilant, newly-released prisoners passing our house on their way to Douglas where they would catch the boat to Liverpool. It would only be a matter of time before Jakob became one of them. I tried not to think of losing the most significant friend of my childhood but the thought would not be banished. I had to face the fact that one Saturday I would be driven to the farm to be told that Jakob was gone for good. Pop had warned me to expect this but the thought of never seeing Jakob again was hard to accept. It would be as if, like Mrs. Kelly, he had died. Ma found me looking gloomy and asked me what the matter was. When I told her she said, "People do come and go in your life and it isn't easy to face that. But you'll find new friends to replace the old."

"I won't find anyone like Jakob," I said sullenly, "ever."

"Maybe not," said Ma, "but you'll have other friends who will mean a lot to you even if not in the same way as Jakob. What has he said about going away, leaving the Island? Will he go back to singing in the opera? Will he have to do factory work? Will he have to join the Army or the Navy or the Air Force? What will he do?"

"He hasn't said anything," I told her wondering why he hadn't mentioned such a fateful development as leaving the Island. I would have to force the issue…ask him what his plans were after his release.

It was two weeks before I went back to the farm. The Saturday after Uncle Tom came down with the 'flu there was a choir outing which Liz grudgingly released me to attend. Sammy Beckett, with the aid of three younger Sunday School teachers, took us all by train to a glen on the West side of the Island for a picnic and a frolic in the glen and on the adjacent seashore. Pop was not the driver of the train we traveled on. Our walk to the beach took us through the glen which, though fairly remote, was still open to the public even if in wartime not many visited the place. Perhaps they were frightened by the signs emblazoned with skull and cross-bones warning of the possibility of mines floating ashore, of unexploded ordnance that might be lying around left behind by soldiers who trained in the area.

I remember that the day of our visit to the glen was fine and sunny. We forgot about war, about school, about whatever worries threatened and enjoyed an afternoon of sports on the sand while the tide was out and games of hide-and-seek in the glen after the tide came in. The following week the Government cut off public access to this glen. There was a rumor that a small boy had been shredded by a live grenade he had found there but the tale was eventually attributed to local invention as was the one about a stray mine blowing up a fishing boat just off the shore on which we had been playing.

When I returned to the farm I found Jakob still there, much to my relief. It was Mary who had gone.

"She's gone for good," said Liz sadly. "I'll miss her," she added. "She was getting to be like a daughter to me." Liz fumbled for a handkerchief and blew her nose vigorously. "I always wanted a girl," she said and then abruptly left the dairy.

I asked Uncle Tom what had happened to cause Mary to leave.

"Don't look at me…it's nothing' I've done" he said defensively. "That father of 'ers made up his mind that 'e can't stand them ones in Sulby… the ones that said he was workin' for the Germans when there was all that trouble at'm in England. They've moved down South. They've let the house to a f'la from across and gone down Castletown way. We said Mary could move 'ere. We've got the room. But the mother of 'er's a poorly woman and wants 'er with 'er so that put the top hat on it. She's applied to work at a farm down South an' she's gone."

"But what about Jakob?"

"Well, what about 'im?" Tom asked testily.

"How does he feel?"

"Ya'd best ask 'im," said Tom who whistled Rory and Tory to him and strode off with the dogs at his heels.

I was left with a whirlpool of conflicting feelings. Months earlier I would have rejoiced at Mary's departure. Then I saw her as an interloper coming between me and Jakob. But I had learned to tolerate her and eventually to like her the better I got to know her. I had been upset by the way the police treated her when her father was falsely accused of treason. I came to respect her abilities as I watched her work round the farm. I couldn't ultimately blame her for falling for Jakob though the relationship between them inevitably meant that I saw less of him than I wanted to. I wondered how she could bear to leave him behind preferring not to think that in all likelihood when he was released he would leave us all behind.

I found him standing by the wall surrounding the small field in which Gerald the bull was attempting, not very successfully, to take his pleasure with one of the cows. I wondered what was going through Jakob's mind. Since he was unlikely to tell I had to ask.

"I was thinking about Mary. I miss her. Everybody does. Johnny cried for two days after she left and Liz wasn't much better."

"She is very young," said Jakob, "even if to you she seemed grown up. We never talked of marriage…how could we? I am a prisoner here and have no rights, no freedoms. People in a camp cannot think of such things. We are not allowed to *fraternize*… that is the word they use…we are not allowed to have any kind of personal relationships the way you can when you are free. If they had found out at the Camp that Mary and I had feelings for each other I would have been taken away from here at once."

"But what are you going to do?" I asked my head full of tales in which the Prince overcomes apparently insurmountable odds to unite himself with the Princess of his choice.

"What can I do?" asked Jakob sadly. "Mary's family needs her. She has gone with them like a good daughter and I will never see her again. I'll always remember her. She has made my days lighter, she has made me feel like a valued human being again in ways that my other friends on the farm could not."

"Do you love her?" I asked. I felt that Jakob was dancing round the subject of Mary, not explaining how he really felt.

"What is love?" asked Jakob. "Do you know what it is you're asking me? Are you old enough to know? I don't think so. I have sung a lot about love on the stage but I have never been quite sure what it is. Is it what Gerald the bull is trying to do over there with that cow? I understand how Gerald feels but love is more than that. I wanted Mary to stay here but if we had known each other under different circumstances…if I had been free when I met her…maybe we would have found that we didn't have very much in common. I am a lot older than she is. I have seen a great deal more of the world. I am much better educated. Yet I feel her loss and I want her to come back. She won't, though, will she? She will fall in love with someone her own age. Maybe she'll remember me but maybe in time she won't. Who knows?"

It was obvious to me that Jakob was more affected by Mary's departure than he would fully admit."How could she go so quicky, without telling us?" I asked Liz.

"Actually, she told me weeks ago that she would have to leave," Liz confessed. "She made me promise not to tell anybody. She didn't want a fuss. She really didn't want to go at all but her mother needs her, especially now they are moving. She stayed longer than she meant to because of Tom being in the hospital."

I asked Ma if she thought Jakob was suffering in silence or whether he really wasn't as fond of Mary as I had believed he was.

"Bit o'slap an' tickle in the barn's one thing," said Bessie who had entered the kitchen while I posed my question, "but romance and wedding bells is another. There's a war on an' folk'll find comfort where they can which is why I've said till I'm blue in the face that having young women work with men on farms is askin' for trouble. The effort they're puttin' in isn't all fa the war effort you can be sure an…"

"Bessie!" said Ma sharply, "I don't think we want to discuss all that with Mr. Big Ears here taking it all in do we?" She steered Bessie into the cluttered back kitchen and closed the door between the rooms.

"Conference goin' on in there? Invasion plans bein' discussed?" asked Pop who had just come downstairs from the upper region where he had been trying to close a window one of the lodgers had said she couldn't shut.

"Ma doesn't want Bessie talking to me about land girls," I said and explained about Mary and Jakob. I asked Pop what he thought Jakob's feelings for Mary might be.

"I don't know, son, and I don't care. Aliens aren't supposed to have feelings for local girls. I blame Liz and Tom for letting them work together. Gives f'las ideas. Prisoners is prisoners and should be treated as such an' not like members of the family. They're out on the farms ta work an' not get girls into trouble…"

Pop was prevented from developing his views on this subject by Ma, who on opening the kitchen door to remind him of something was horrified to hear him uttering the prologue to a forbidden text. She imposed censorship at once and swiftly edited him out of the room. I was left to ask myself why Jakob wasn't planning to escape, to break out over the wire to be re-united with his Princess dragged from his arms by a wicked mother and a tyrannical father. I was frustrated that there was nothing I could do to change the course of events. I wanted to go to Mary to plead Jakob's case but at that point in my life I had never been to the South of the Island. It seemed then as remote as Timbuktu. I would be too scared even to try to reach Douglas on my own let alone somewhere further on. And then Liz hadn't mentioned exactly where Mary had gone to live. "Castletown way" was vague. That could mean Port Saint Mary, Port Erin, or one of the small villages like Colby, the one in which Pop was raised. When I asked Liz for details she had none to give. I had to comfort myself with the fact that now Mary was gone perhaps I could regain my old intimacy with Jakob and cheer him up.

Mary's replacement arrived after a couple of weeks. She wasn't at all like Mary. She was older…I suppose in her late twenties though she looked middle-aged to me. Where Mary was slender and pretty Elsie Cottier was plain, built on a robust peasant scale, bluff in manner, the sort of woman who could drink ten men under the table as she boasted to Uncle Tom prompting him to remark that she'd better not try it while she was working for him. He was still fragile after his serious bout of illness.

"It only taks a feather t'upset me so tak heed," he warned the new *girl* as they called this hefty interloper.

Jakob was a person no one could ignore. Elsie was clearly attracted by his good looks but she assumed that alien prisoners must have done something wrong for the Government to have locked them up. While she looked at Jakob appraisingly from a distance she asked me "What's 'e in the Camp for? What's 'e done? *What's 'e been at?*"

"He hasn't *done* anything" I replied hotly.

"E musta done summat or why's 'e in't Camp?"

"He's there because he's an Austrian," I said. "It's like you being locked up for being Manx."

"They're not lockin' us up," said Mary's unworthy replacement, "we didn't start the war."

"Neither did Jakob."

"Then why's 'e in the Camp?" And so we circled. I was pleased to see that Jakob treated her with a sort of polite contempt whenever she said anything to him.

"What's that f'la got to be so stuck up about?" she asked. Not waiting for an answer she would go on "an' him a prisoner with airs an' graces at'm like a pig in a party frock. It's that daft it maks ya want ta laff." She suited the action to the words but the laughter was strained.

"He was an opera singer before the war," I said thinking that information would wipe the stupid grin off this woman's face.

"An' what's that when it's at 'ome?" Elsie responded. After I had explained she said "Ya mean that f'la was paid money ta get up on stage an' wear fancy clothes an' warble about nowt in a foreign language? No wonder they locked 'im up."

Elsie at least would not distract Jakob from me in whatever time he had left on the Island.

With the prisoners gradually being released it didn't surpise me when Lance Corporal Machin announced his imminent departure. He was to have two weeks of leave with his family before being posted elsewhere. He hadn't been told where. He had got me into trouble over my friend-ship with Jakob but that was unintended. He had been useful to us in ways I have mentioned already. Pop especially was sad to see him go since his supply of whisky and other contraband goods would be cut off. We all genuinely liked the Lance Corporal and felt we knew his family who he talked about all the time. There was his wife Phoebe (*Feeb* as he called her), his mother Ruth (*Ruthie* to her three sons), his little boy Jimmy who had been sent to live on a farm to get away from the bombs but who pined for home so much that his mother had brought him back to their badly-damaged neighborhood. I had once asked Ma if she would mind if we called her by her first name the way the Lance Corporal referred to his mother and Ma said she *would* mind…she would mind very much… so we'd better not try it. It was all very well for the Lance Corporal to do it…perhaps that was the practice where he came from…but it would not be proper for the family of *Rosetree Villa*.

I told the departing soldier I would miss him. He said "Aye, we've 'ad some fun an' games an't we? I'll miss all o' yer. Still, mustn't dwell on that. Not the way ter win the war is it? I'll bet 'itler in't sitting around feeling sorry for 'is self is 'e? I get ter see me family before the next posting so I'm lookin' forward to that I can tell yer."

The day he left he struggled down the stairs with a very large cylindrical khaki bag stuffed full of what he called *kit* but which Pop declared was more likely to contain illicit goods from the military store to which he had access.

"That f'la'll be takin' a few presents that the Army knows nowt about home to the family. Look what he gave me," and here Pop held up a large bottle of whiskey for our inspection.

"Put that away before Bessie sees it!" said Ma in alarm. "If she catches sight of that we'll never hear the end of it."

We all stood outside to see the Lance Corporal off. A khaki-colored canvas-covered military truck stopped at our gate. Fellow soldiers in the back hauled him and his bag on board and the truck roared off up the hill on its way to Douglas and the ferry to the mainland, the soldiers all singing. The Lance Corporal was reduced to a waving hand and then the truck vanished round the corner at the top of the hill above our house.

"It'll feel strange without him," said Ma. "He's been with us a fair time."

I found it hard to remember a time when he hadn't been part of our household though I suppose he was with us not more than two years in all.

"Ma, why is everyone going away?" I asked. "Mary went, the Corporal's gone and Jakob's going to go...why?"

"They're all here because of the war," said Ma, "and in a war you have to do what you're told and go where you're sent. You don't have any say in the matter. No one asks you if you'd like go to one place or stay in another."

"It's not fair," I said.

"No, it's not. War's not fair. But we didn't start this one. The Germans did and we have to do everything we can to beat them or they'll be here telling us what to do."

Ma said this with vehemence. I suppose she was thinking of my brother shortly to become a Second Lieutenant, an officer the likes of whom Lance Corporal Machin would have had to salute but who would also have to lead soldiers into battle.

The more I thought about people leaving the more I wanted to ask Jakob what he would do when his time came. Would he leave joyfully like the Lance Corporal or with regret? I wanted him to promise to come back as soon as the war ended. I wanted him to seek out Mary and marry her and have children I could play with and settle on the Island and be my friend forever. I didn't then consider that one day I myself would want to leave the Island and would come back only for rare holidays.

CHAPTER THIRTY-TWO

As a baby Carlo was considered remarkably handsome if that is a proper term for an infant. This was a public verdict rendered in public. Infants in those days on the Island were entered into "baby shows" the way people now enter dogs, cats and horses in shows to have their "points" assessed by judges. Carlo had a surfeit of the right "points" as attested by an impressive list of cups, ornamental certificates and other prizes to his credit by the time he was three years old. Not that he cared much or even seemed to be aware of his growing local fame. Ma entered him into competitions in Ramsey and in the smaller towns and villages at the North end of the Island. Local mothers blanched when they saw Ma arrive with Carlo who smiled a lot in those days and eventually melted even the most competitive maternal heart. His temperament then was notably equable at home as well as in the shows to which he was taken. But during his third year there was a turning point. Some time in the course of that year Carlo tasted of the fateful Tree of Knowledge. His smile was replaced by a more or less daily scowl. He became prone to sudden acts of violence especially against me and was often as surly as before he had been charm itself. Ma wondered aloud if some night-tripping fairy had replaced her baby with a damaged copy, a tempestuous alter ego. She could display him in baby shows no more. At the last one he attended he spent his time screaming, roaring and kicking chairs. Formerly frustrated mothers smirked. Long hoped-for chickens had come home at last to roost.

Much of Carlo's new-found violence was directed at me. Whether, upon reviewing his babyhood, he resented being entered into public competitions like a pedigree cat and now despised the accumulated silver cups and certificates he had passively accumulated or missed being the center of attention at home as he grew older; whether he was undergoing some crucial hormonal change, was mixing with the wrong type of three-year-old or had begun to ingest the poisons of war I never discovered. Ma and Pop seemed to think that the Devil might have taken a hand in the creation of the new Carlo for one day they announced that he was to be purified by baptism. The Devil was to be cast out. I had been christened when I was a baby but I suppose the outbreak of war in the year of Carlo's birth had banished thoughts of church, font and holy water from parental minds.

Perhaps to make up for their baptismal tardiness Ma and Pop decided to associate Carlo with Island History and have him christened in Kirk Maughold (or Kirk Maughold Church as Islanders redundantly say). Unlike the bourgeois late-Victorian St. Paul's Church to which I was sent each Sunday as a matter of course, Kirk Maughold's origins lie in the mists of the Celtic past. The present church dates from the Eleventh – Twelvth Centuries but it was built on the site of a Seventh Century Celtic monastery and named for a Celtic saint variously called Machutus or Machaoi (though some authorities declare that in fact the church is dedicated to St. Magnus who wasn't a Celt at all). I rather like the no doubt apocryphal story of the Celtic saint sailing away from Ireland in a wicker boat – a coracle – letting God determine his course. God, via the currents of wind and water, determined that he would serve as a missionary Bishop on the Isle-of-Man – rather in contrast to his former careers as pirate, thief and Prince. In any event he seems to have been the sort of daredevil chap Carlo, as a now rampageous three-year-old, would have found congenial company.

This baptismal event served to emphasize the chronological extensiveness of our family. There was the absent Ronald, at nineteen almost an Army officer, me at ten constantly striving to be older than my years and Carlo only just getting round to a delayed baptism. I learned when I was older and thus regarded as mature enough for such confidences that Ma had had miscarriages between Ronald and me of the sort she had also suffered in 1942. Had this not been the case Carlo and I would either have been born into a larger, poorer family or perhaps never been born at all.

Carlo's christening involved expense since Maughold Church was several miles along the coast from where we lived which meant that Pop had to hire a couple of taxis for the family and a few guests. The taxis would wait at the Church and then ferry us all back to our house for a special baptismal tea. Carlo was to be treated like the silver cup winner he had lately been. The tea was made possible by extra ration coupons donated by some of the guests and a minor degree of grocer-bribery involving Pop-caught fish. Pop had originally suggested that the baptismal party travel to Maughold by means of the vintage electric tram but that would mean alighting at somewhere like the stop at Ballajora and walking from there to the Church, returning in the same manner. Ma had been horrified. How could a family hold up its head if the guests to the christening had to trudge sweatily in their Sunday best across hilly country to and from the Church just to save Pop a few pounds? And what if it rained? Everyone would be soaked. Did Pop think we were peasants? Did he want to scare the guests away? Had he gone mad?

Pop backed off and left Ma to organize the guest list while he arranged the transportation as duly instructed. He did it reluctantly making no secret of the fact that he intended to use his drinking fellowship with the owner of the taxi company to negotiate the lowest possible rate.

"Negotiate away," said Ma, "but just make sure those cars are here on the day and on time or else…"

Ma decided that Carlo's christening would be the social event of our year. Perhaps that is why Uncle Sidney and Aunty Avril turned up, amazing us all by driving all the way from Douglas without hitting anything. Pop was so shocked by the arrival of a brother he hadn't seen for years that all he could do was silently shake the hand he was offered. Ma hadn't told him that our relations in the Capital had been apprised of Carlo's formal entry into the Anglican Church and invited to participate in the event. Most were unimpressed by the news since Uncle Sidney and Auntie Avril were the only Douglas relatives to attend. Because they owned a functioning car and somehow found the fuel for it the other guests treated them with due deference.

As to those guests the Talbots, of course, were invited but had declined owing, they said, to the pressure of farm work. Bessie had readily accepted her invitation, much to Pop's disgust. Mrs. Dodd did so reluctantly and only after considerable persuasion. Unlike Bessie, she strove hard not to be noticed and thus was noticed all the more. To my horror the Miss Quirk who had embarrassed me so much with her theatrics in church had also been invited. A baptism would offer her wider scope than ever for dropping to her knees while fervently crossing herself and muttering incantations. Mrs. White the teacher thanked Ma for her invitation and came to the event readily enough though she made excuses for Big Bill who was conducting a cattle sale at the other end of the Island. Mrs. Corcoran whose telephone we commandeered so often brought her brother Brian Kissack, the Coast Guard, with her for reasons that were never explained. A Miss Geoghan, housekeeper to the sisters Quayle, also attended though neither Ma nor Pop could remember having invited her. Perhaps she felt entitled since from time to time she traded dusty bottles from the pre-war Quayle sherry collection for herring and mackerel Pop caught in the Bay. She brought one of those dusty bottles with her for the baptismal tea so of course no one queried her right to be there.

Our house was the rendezvous point for the drive to the church. The taxis available to us in those days on the very rare occasions when we afforded them were large square black cars mainly used in funerals but despite their size it was evident that there would be an intolerable squeeze if we all tried to climb into them. Had all those invited actually turned up we would have had to institute a shuttle system. Pop had obviously tried to keep down the costs by planning for as few people as possible.

At this point Uncle Sidney's arrival was reinterpreted as Providental. He volunteered to take passengers in his car. There was much milling about on the sidewalk in front of our house as people made the tricky decision about which car to ride in. Carlo was particularly difficult climbing into Uncle Sidney's car clutching our dog Milby and refusing to budge thus obliging Pop to haul both him and the yelping dog out again. While Carlo had a tantrum on the sidewalk the dog jumped back into the car. Pop's impulse was to "dust Carlo's rear end" there and then and "murder" the dog but he was deterred by Ma who explained to Carlo, as Pop was dragging the yapping indignant resisting dog up the garden path to the frontdoor of the house, that boys about to be christened arrived at the church by taxi with guests but without pets. A christening was a very special occasion to which dogs weren't admitted.

Once on the road, Carlo still clamoring for the dog, we proceeded at the leisurely pace of a funeral procession to which in fact the drivers were more accustomed. We drove up the hill to the junction with the coastal road and then down and up the steep hills whose contours that road followed until we approached Maughold Head, nearly four-hundred feet above the sea and bearing a lighthouse – one that when I was a teenager failed to keep a freighter off the sharp-toothed rocks and its cargo out of larcenous local hands.

Maughold Church is near the Head. It is a simple rectangular stone building without a tower entirely unlike the Norman or later Gothic churches of the mainland. It is an unostentatious chapel-like building in which John Wesley would have felt very much at home. There was a path from the road where the cars were parked to the church. Just off the path is the Island's most extensive outdoor collection of Runic crosses inherited from the Vikings. Beyond the churchyard inland at a distance of a few miles is the mountain range beginning with North Barrule and including Clagh Ouyre, Slieu Lhean and Slieu Roy. On this day the sun shone on those mountains, the sky was a clear blue and the sea, glimpsed in little bays as we came along, was a blue-green color. It was the perfect day for an outing.

Unfortunately Carlo, dressed in newish clothes with his hair properly combed for once and sporting a pair of new shoes, was as little impressed by weather and scenery as by the baptismal event itself. His behavior had been surly from the time he got up that morning and was not improved by his forced separation from the dog. When we reached the church in which he was to be transformed into a Child of God his impudence was such that Pop had to be physically restrained from "clipping him over the ear."

"Any more a' that an' I'll wallop ya one," said Pop.

"You'll do no such thing," said Ma. "Carlo is going to behave himself aren't you Carlo? He's not going to disgrace himself at his own christening in front of all these good people are you Carlo?"

"Wanna go home," wailed Carlo miserably.

"And so you shall after the service in the Church. Then we can all go home for a nice party all in your honor. You are the boy who is being christened today so stop scowling like that. If the Vicar sees that expression on your face he won't christen you at all! That look is enough to frighten strangers and turn milk sour." Not having realized the potency of his facial expression Carlo scowled all the more.

Pop took Carlo by an unwilling hand and towed him toward the Church. The guests all pretended they had seen and heard nothing untoward. They followed Pop up the path making loud remarks about the beauty of the day and what a good omen it was. They said they had heard that the Vicar was a nice man though his wife was a little dumpling of a woman, dowdy, retiring, though posh of speech. She was more like a housekeeper or a cook with social pretentions. She made excellent pastry, it was said, and her floors were so clean you could eat it off them.

The Vicar in question, a tall thin Englishman by the name of Elliot, met us wearing his full regalia at the foot of the few steps leading to the main door of the Church. He greeted Ma and Pop in one of those cultured English voices that so impressed Ma whenever she heard one but grated on Pop. Ma introduced him to all the guests and, pushing a reluctant Carlo forward, said "and this is our son Carlo who's come to be christened."

"What an unusual name for these parts," said the Vicar looking curiously at Pop who said nothing. The Vicar then turned to Carlo to ask, bending a little, "How are we today little fellow?"

The little fellow answered by kicking him swiftly in the shins and racing off down the path toward the gate and the waiting taxis entirely ignorant of the Church's history as a sanctuary for criminals. While Ma, appalled, apologized profusely to the Vicar, Pop set off in furious pursuit of the fleeing Carlo. Once he had caught up with him he held him with one hand while applying the other hand, hard, to Carlo's bottom. Carlo of course bawled his head off. As Ma arrived to lecture Pop for resorting so readily and so publicly to brute force Carlo lay face-down in the dust and screamed at the top of his capacious lungs making violent kicking motions with his legs, banging the toe of his new shoes against the hard but hallowed earth.

"I wonder oo 'e gets that temper from?" Besie asked the Church porch in which she and I were standing.

Ma, I learned later, ordered Pop to go back to the Church and apologise all over again to the Vicar while she tried to calm Carlo.

"It'll be the lad's nerves," said Aunty Avril trying to put the best face on his behavior. "He'll have the collywobbles with all of us around him and him the center of attention. He won't be used to it."

I contemplated reminding Aunty Avril of Carlo's cup-winning career but thought better of it.

Neither Carlo nor I had ever suffered adversely from being the center of attention but perhaps christenings were different. Eventually Carlo was persuaded to get up off the ground onto which he had thrown himself, submit to being dusted off, to having his hair combed all over again and his face wiped with one of Ma's handkerchiefs which she had dampened with spit. He accompanied her unwillingly back up the path to the Church – she had, in fact, to haul him along. When Ma ordered him to tell the Vicar he was sorry for misbehaving Carlo, his head down, muttered something graceless in a tone far from contrite. The Vicar, plainly angered by Carlo's attack and still in pain, forgave him in an unforgiving voice. I thought as I looked at the expression on the Vicar's face that he would have got more pleasure out of drowning Carlo in the font than baptizing him. The Rev. Clive Eliot entered the Church limping.

Once inside we stumbled about a bit in the gloom made more potent by contrast with the brilliant sunlight outside. Pop could be heard swearing loudly as he nearly fell over Miss Quirk who, upon crossing the threshold into the holy murkiness, had dropped to her knees in conditioned rapture to mumble one of her ready prayers. Brian Kissack, the authority of the Coast Guard upon him, suggested that everyone stand still for a moment until their eyes became accustomed to the darker interior.

Eventually we all stood around the ancient carved stone font. The Vicar briefly explained the form the service would take, told us where to find it in the prayer books with which we had been provided and was quickly seconded by Miss Quirk who told us where to find it all over again as if the Vicar had been speaking Swahili. Taking no chances the Vicar explained to Carlo that during the service he would have to pour holy water on his forehead but he said not to worry about this. No harm was intended to him. The water might be cold but since the day was warm he would find it refreshing.

The service began and as it proceeded Carlo sought to escape the restraining hands of both Ma and Pop. He seemed to be genuinely frightened and bewildered by the event. He couldn't understand why Ma and Pop had made him the central figure in this adult ritual when he could be at home playing with Milby. He was disturbed by the presence of all the guests, he was frightened of the Vicar and as soon as the Reverend Mr. Eliot began to explain about the holy water he started to whimper and beg to be taken home. It was rather as if we had all been assembled to witness Carlo's ritual slaughter Aztec fashion, than his christening. Ignoring Carlo's snivellings the Vicar, a veteran of such events, droned on with the service while Ma and Pop, with a series of loudly whispered promises and threats, tried to get their youngest child to shut up and behave himself.

I had been told about Godparents before the service and was shocked to discover that Aunty Doreen was one of mine the other being Uncle Herbert. Why had this information been kept from me like some dark family secret? Ma said Carlo's Godparents would be Bessie and her husband Willie but Willie hadn't come to the service and, indeed, never seemed to accompany Bessie anywhere. When I asked Ma why on earth she had chosen our bellicose and intrusive neighbor she said Bessie had offered and she didn't like to turn her down. The Vicar pointed out that both Godparents had to be present at the baptismal service upon which Brian Kissack offered to fill the gap much to his sister's amazement. As he stood next to Bessie at the font she smiled upon him warmly and he smiled warmly back and his sister seemed most put out. She made a sort of snorting noise and looked angrily at Ma as if she ought to have put a stop to this development.

When we reached the part of the service involving the water Ma and Pop handed Carlo over to Bessie who stepped forward with Brian Kissack to perform her Godmotherly part. Carlo looked more bewildered than ever. Why had his parents given him into the keeping of the next-door neighbor and this strange man he had never seen before? The Vicar told him to stand up on a stone step in front of the font. Bessie hoisted him off the floor and put him on it before he could make a move of his own. The Vicar put his hand into the water he had earlier blessed and saying "I baptize thee in the name of the Father, the Son and the Holy Ghost" let it trickle own over Carlo's forehead. Abandoned by his parents, having cold water poured onto him by a tall strange Englishman dressed like a wizard – one whose shin he had earlier kicked – Carlo had no idea what was going on. He bawled, he bellowed, he wept. He put both of his hands into the water in the font and splashed the Vicar liberally. He then jumped off his stone step, evaded adult hands that shot out to restrain him and raced vigorously for the door of the nave. He was out through it before anyone could respond and away as if the Holy Ghost was after him.

Pop again had to race after the fleeing Carlo and Ma raced after Pop in case, in his rage, he was tempted to maim his youngest. This time Carlo was more enterprising in escape. He climbed the hedge at the end of the churchyard and streaked across an adjacent field. Those of us who had followed Carlo, Ma and Pop out of the Church expected to witness an epic walloping when Pop caught up with his errant son. Instead Pop simply picked Carlo up, hoisted him on to his shoulders and carried him back at a leisurely pace to the churchyard. When he approached the hedge separating the churchyard from the field Ma and I, at least, were amazed to find that Pop was laughing and couldn't stop He explained later that the sight of Carlo splashing the Vicar with his own holy water was one of the funniest things he had seen in a long time.

"Serve the toffee-nosed bugger right," he said.

The Vicar, of course, didn't take the same view. Standing in injured innocence with his vestments all wet he had said that the child must be possessed by the devil. To baptize such a child would be a waste of time. But after Pop had persuaded Carlo that there wasn't much of the service left to endure and had made him promise to behave himself the Vicar relented and the rite proceeded. Carlo was finally declared a Christian and a member of the Anglican Church though the Vicar's tone of voice suggested considerable doubt about what he had just done.

Once people began to congratulate him Carlo cheered up. He didn't know why he was being congratulated but that didn't matter. Everyone seemed to like him again and that was enough. He not only behaved himself on the ride home but promised Ma, rashly, that he would never misbehave again. When she was told of this promise later in the afternoon Miss Quirk asked Ma if she didn't feel like shouting *hallelujah!* and offering a little prayer of thanks with her for this favor from the Almighty. "Not just now," said Ma backing away toward the kitchen.

Before we were allowed to eat and drink photographs had to be taken in the little garden in front of the house. Uncle Sidney produced a box Brownie to take a few snaps of an unusually docile Carlo standing alone in spirtual meditation next to a rose bush and then he was photographed in various groupings. Pop had found his elderly camera – bought at one of Big Bill's auctions but rarely used. He had put new film into it and he now took some pictures of his formerly recalcitrant son who had redeemed himself by giving the Vicar a bath. While Pop was in a picture-taking mood Bessie had propelled Carlo in front of a large hydrangea bush for further photos. She loomed over him like a protective goddess. As all this was going on Bessie's husband Willie who was supposed to have been Carlo's Godfather shuffled out of the house next door in a worn cardigan out at the elbows, shapeless trousers and a pair of dirty carpet slippers, a lit cigarette dangled from his lips. He wanted to know what all the fuss was about and I marveled at his skill in talking without removing the cigarette. In her sharpest tones Ma reminded him that he was supposed to have been at the Church acting as Carlo's Godfather.

"First I've heard of it," said Bessie's husband.

"Bessie must have told you! She's Carlo's Godmother and you were to have been his Godfather."

"First I've heard of it," Willie repeated.

Ma looked unconvinced but invited him to join the party anyway so he shambled over just as he was to mingle incongruously with the group dressed in its Sunday best. Ma took Bessie aside and asked her why she hadn't told Willie about the event.

"You know what he's like." Bessie replied. "I did tell him but he forgot. I didn't say owt when we set off beause I knew Brian'd be at the Church. He'll make a much better Godfather than our Willie. I mean, if he couldn't remember the christening after I'd told him all about it what good would he be as a Godfather?"

Ma didn't say anything more on the subject. I had overheard Bessie's excuse and didn't believe a word of it. Willie would do something to embarrass her at the christening…like lighting a cigarette while he was standing at the font…so she avoided embarrassment by not telling him about the event. When she left the house all dressed up Willie had assumed she was on her way to a meeting of the Mother's Union membership in which was not hindered by a state of childlessness.

After people tired of taking photographs we all trooped into the house. The front dining room had been cleared of lodgers for the afternoon. Chairs for the guests had been placed round the walls. Delicate sandwiches and cups of tea were served. Uncle Sidney furtively produced a silver flask from an inside pocket of his suit jacket and poured some of its contents into his tea. He offered the flask to Pop who accepted just to show that he could be sociable when occasion demanded even if he didn't make family visiting a priority. I noticed that Pop and Uncle Sidney touched their cups together before slowly sipping their contents. Willie looked wistfully in Pop's direction and took an extra-large drag on his cigarette screwing his eyes up in the smoke and coughing periodically without ever taking the cigarette out of his mouth except to swallow tea or take a savage bite out of a little sandwich.

Having people ranged around the wall of the room didn't make for relaxed conversation. Guests were able to talk to people either side of them but couldn't speak to others across the room without unseemly shouting so the little party had a stilted air once the guests were so awkwardly seated. For them all to stand up and move about the room to speak to others as the mood took them wouldn't have occurred to any of them in that more formal time.

"Haven't you forgotten something?" Ma asked Pop eventually with prompting nodding of her head.

"Have I?" said Pop. "And what would that be?"

There was a whiff of the combative in his tone which Ma reproved him for when all the guests had gone home. She said it was the brandy talking since she had seen Uncle Sidney put some in his teacup.

Since he refused to take the hint Ma had to go to the sideboard for the bottle of sherry that Pop had acquired for the occasion. She poured its contents into small sherry glasses, which she handed round to the guests. After the sherry had been delicately sipped the conversation became more animated. Eventually most of our Air Force lodgers drifted into the room to see what was going on and finding a sort of party in progress they stayed. They congratulated Carlo on his christening. Several of them went up to their rooms for bottles of their own and poured drinks both for themselves and for the original guests. The party became livelier. Milby raced about in a state of wild excitement which eventually caused him to pee on the floor. I was sent to find some old newspapers.

Pop moved to the old piano and began to play popular songs. The guests and the lodgers left their seats to gather round Pop and sing. Pop played by ear and, oddly, the more he had to drink the better he played. Eventually the staid christening party became something of a "knees up" with guests and lodgers dancing together and Pop played. I was amazed to see Miss Quirk being swept about by a young bomb-aimer enjoying a rare day off from wreaking havoc on Germany. Mrs. Dodd became quite talkative after a glass of sherry and another of something else provided by one of the lodgers.

By the time the guests left the house to stumble home in the blackout the boy whose day it had been had long since fallen asleep on the floor under a table that had held plates of sandwiches. Because he had to drive back to Douglas Uncle Sidney and Aunty Avril missed the jolliest part of the evening. I wonder what the Rev. Clive Eliot would have thought about this pagan enjoyment had he been present. I went to bed thinking that once the awkward parts of Carlo's Christening were over it had generated one of the best parties I had ever been to – not that I had been to many.

Of course I told Jakob all about the occasion when I saw him next and I said it was a pity he couldn't have been there. He could have sung for us all while Pop played the piano.

"That would have been pleasant," he said, "though I don't think your Mama and your Papa would have felt quite safe with a dangerous enemy alien in their house."

"They don't talk like that any more," I told him.

"Opinions do appear to be changing now that the Government seems to have realized we want to fight the Nazis as much as everyone else does." Then he added, "but if I had appeared at your little brother's baptism I don't think I would have been welcome. People are strange. They don't like it when they realize they have been wrong and have done harm to the innocent because of their prejudices. They blame the innocent for rousing their bigotry and that makes them hard when they should be asking forgiveness."

I didn't follow what he was saying so I said nothing.

It wasn't long after Carlo's christening that Ma told me that she and I were to go on a visit to my maternal grandmother, the legendary figure I mentioned early in this narrative. She was talked about so little and then only in the context of illness that I assumed we were going to her funeral. When I asked Ma if that was so she said, "Whatever gave you that idea?"

I explained. Ma then told me that far from being dead my grandmother lived with another of her daughters, a sister of Ma's called Aunty Phyllis whom I had never met. That would soon be remedied since we were to leave for Aunty Phyllis's house the following week. This news made me very excited – I had never left the Isle-of-Man before so I would now see a bit more of the world. Added bonuses would be a week off school and a brief holiday from the choir and from Sunday School. We would be taking the boat to Liverpool and then a train to Lancaster where my newly dis-covered aunt and my grandmother lived together. The prospect of such a journey was as exciting as one to any of those mythic places described in the storybooks I read. All of a sudden I was to have a Great Adventure.

When Carlo learned that I was to go and he was to stay with Pop he was overcome by fury despite the promise of good behavior he had made to Ma in the taxi. He was the newly baptized boy so it ought to be him who was going with Ma. The prospect of a week alone with Pop didn't fill him with joy either, especially since Bessie, his newly minted Godmother, had volunteered to look after them both.

"But you're still too little to come," said Ma.

"I not ickle! I big!" bellowed the new Christian who had to be dragged to bed kicking and screaming and threatening to stay awake all night eating everyone's coats.

CHAPTER THIRTY-THREE

My departure from the Island was not like those others, actual or expected, of people I knew and liked. When they went or when I feared they were about to go I brooded over how their absence would affect me. I felt not only left but left behind even before they had said their goodbyes. My own adventure, on the other hand, filled me with an excitement that drove out every other feeling. There was not only the anticipatory thrill of the unexpected to enjoy but also the prospect of being free of Carlo for a couple of weeks and I was pretty sure I wasn't going to miss Pop in his Old Testament moods. This time it wasn't me who was being abandoned and, in any case, unlike the Lance Corporal Machins of the world, I was coming back.

There were exciting preparations to make. Travel documents had to be obtained. Suitcases had to be searched for and when found, taken from their dirty hiding places and spruced up. There was much washing and ironing to be done. Ma gave me generalized accounts of the aunt and grandmother I had never met before and whom she herself hadn't seen for years. Carlo, feeling excluded already, misbehaved more than usual. He declared that he was coming with us. No amount of patient rational explanation by Ma did any good. No amount of assurance by Bessie as to the grand times they would have while we were away made any impression. None of Pop's guarantees that if he didn't behave himself he'd be "in for it" stopped the flow of rebellious protest from that small but ener-getic source. Carlo was coming too and that, in his own mind, was that. He began to make arrangements for the journey. Rummaging amongst his treasures he found an old wooden box into which he fitted his most precious toys. The night before we left he had a confidential talk with Milby. He told the dog that he was going to visit his "gammar" but Milby mustn't worry as he would be back after a while and would bring him a bone as a present – an English bone.

The dog licked his face in gratitude.

It came as a terrible shock the next morning when Carlo had to watch Ma and I, dressed in our Sunday best, prepare to leave the house while he was prevented by Pop from accompanying us. Only then did it sink in that he was indeed being left at home. In vain had his little wooden box been filled with portable toys; unnecessary had been his discourse with the dog; futile had been his promise of an English bone.

Carlo cried loudly and bitterly. He wailed. Pop picked him up but he kicked the air violently refusing to be mollified. Pathetically he held both his arms out to Ma but Ma, who until recently had so proudly exhib-ited him at baby shows, had to refuse what that gesture begged for. I began to feel guilty at relishing my temporary freedom from my little brother's company.

The ferry to Liverpool from Douglas left around nine o'clock in the morning so we had to get up earlier than usual to catch the bus for the sixteen mile journey. With many bends to negotiate, many steep hills to climb and descend, many stops to make along the road the bus took over an hour to reach Douglas. Pop brought Carlo out into our little garden to wave goodbye but he refused to look at us. He had tantrums all day we heard when we returned home. Whatever his christening had accom-plished it evidently hadn't driven out the Evil One. "He was a little divil all that day…and the next," Bessie reported when we returned home.

The bus ride to Douglas in the early morning would soon have made me forget Carlo and his hurt feelings had Ma not worried aloud about him at intervals.

"I hope he's going to be alright," she said from time to time. "Poor Carlo…I hope your father can cope with him without losing his temper…"

"He'll be all right," I said brusquely, wishing she'd drop the subject, not caring much whether Pop kept his temper or lost it so long as I wasn't involved.

We had always traveled to Douglas by train so this bus journey close to the East coast of the Island – at one point the road had been cut into the cliffs – lay through territory unfamiliar to me. When I wasn't listening to Ma on the subject of the bereft Carlo I eagerly observed the passing countryside. I took note of villages I had never seen before and saw such an exciting phenomenon as the huge Laxey Wheel, not far from the Laxey bus station. It was the largest waterwheel in Europe and maybe in the whole world Ma said. It had been used to pump water out of the now defunct lead mines. I was actually sorry when we reached the outskirts of Douglas though my interest was piqued again as we drove along the wide promenade. All the sea-front hotels, like those boarding houses in Ramsey, were surrounded by high barbed wire fences and for the same reason. Douglas had several camps for "aliens" and they were larger than the one in Ramsey. There were many soldiers on guard. My relatives lived at a distance from the sea-front so I had only heard of the Douglas camps which now I was seeing for the first time. It became evident that the government had locked away many more people than I had supposed. Had I seen the camp at Onchan, next door to Douglas, or the one at Peel on the West coast of the Island or the women (some of whom committed suicide by jumping off the cliffs) confined in Port Erin, Port St. Mary and Castletown in the South I would have been more surprised still. The whole island was one vast internment camp from which I was, if only temporarily, escaping.

My thoughts were diverted from prisoners to the prospects of a sea voyage when the bus turned a corner and I could see the harbor and its ships. I was as excited at the idea of sailing to England as I would have been if we were sailing to America. Anywhere across the Irish Sea promised adventure to a child who had led my sheltered life. My enthusiasm for what lay ahead abated somewhat, though, when I remembered Jakob's account of his journey to Ramsey in a rough sea with everyone on board throwing up and also when I recalled my own experience in Pop's little boat. I began to wonder if, when the ferry left the dock and headed out of the harbor into the swell I might, despite the reassuring size of the ship, be overcome by the fear I had felt that day and thus find the journey not an exciting adventure after all but a torment to be endured. Terror and seasickness were not the traveling companions I had anticipated.

After we got off the bus Ma and I found ourselves in a crowd of people who all seemed to be leaving the Island that day on the same ferry. We lugged our heavy suitcases after Ma, to my disappointment, refused to hire a porter to carry them for us.

"Porters charge far too much," said Ma. "They tell you not to worry about your cases but I know people who gave their luggage to porters to carry and never saw any of it again. I don't trust them." So we struggled, burdened, along the harbor stopping every now and then to put the cases down and rest.

A long way ahead of us we could see gangways stretching out from the harbor like arms beseeching the ferry to stay. We could also see that there were literally hundreds of people between us and those beseeching arms. We eventually were forced to shuffle toward the boat a few feet at a time with more and more people queuing up behind us. A lot of those prospective passengers, male and female, wore Army, Air Force and Naval uniforms and carried kit-bags like Lance Corporal Machin's. They seemed to be in a cheerful mood despite the earliness of the hour. I realize now that they were mostly in their late teens but they seemed very grown up to me then – as grown up as my elder brother.

After shuffling forward with the slowly-moving crowd, our gas masks in their cardboard boxes hanging over our shoulders by their strings and threatening to fall to the ground every time we bent to lift a case, we eventually reached the gangways. A ship's officer clipped our cardboard tickets after inspecting our Identity Cards. Two strong sailors helped us across to the ship by carrying our luggage ahead of us along the gangway. Once we were on the ship Ma led me to a place manned by a sailor where we could leave our cases, which were then locked up in one of the luggage respositories provided. Once our cases had been taken care of we could move about the ship freely – or as freely as the press of other people would permit.

Ma said she absolutely had to sit down or she'd faint so she led me hurriedly along the deck we were on to the large public third-class cabin which, when we reached it, seemed full already. Ma diligently searched the rows until she found a seat still unclaimed. She said that if I felt tired I could sit on her knee but I was far too excited to do anything like that so she said I could go out onto the deck as long as I didn't do anything silly, like trying to climb the outside rails to get a better view. Some foolhardy people had fallen off and drowned doing that, she said. Cases had been reported in the local paper but that was before the war when Lancashire mill-workers coming to the Island for their two-week holiday in their noisy exuberant thousands drank too much beer at the ship's bar.

I was puzzled even then by Ma's allowing me to walk round the ship on my own though I suppose she thought I couldn't really come to harm with so many people about – a circumstance which today might raise alarm rather than quell it. I had to promise to return to the public cabin before we reached Liverpool. It was stuffy in that cabin and I had started to worry again that I might be seasick when the ship began to move up and down with the waves so I was relieved to be allowed to wander about in the open air. I had not been reassured by the sailor who came to tell the passengers in the cabin where to find the sick bags if they needed them.

Leaving my gas mask with Ma I went out and climbed the stairs to the top deck where I found uniformed young men and women crowding the rails to watch the ship leave the harbor. Two good-natured airmen, noticing me hovering near in the hope of seeing what was going on down below on the dock, made a space for me by the rail so that I could survey the quayside from what seemed to me a very great height. People were still boarding the ship and there were still long lines stretching down the quay.

The Airmen asked me where I was going so I told them of the visit to my grandmother.

"What's she like?" one of them asked me. "Mine's a bad-tempered old biddy I wouldn't walk a hundred yards to see…always complaining. If it isn't one thing it's another. Never been happy in her life me Mum says and doesn't want anybody else to be neither. Wants everyone to be as sour and miserable as she is. And that's as miserable as sin. She drove me grand-dad into an early grave me Mum says. Mind you, what with the drink and the cigarettes and the women he found in pubs he'd have driven there fast enough without a chauffeur anyway."

"I don't know what my grandmother's like," I replied. "I've never met her."

"How's that, then? Never met your own granny?"

"She lives in England and we live on the Isle-of-Man," I said, thinking that the airmen ought to be able to work out what that implied.

"My gran's alright," said the other airman, "but she can be a bit daft in the head. Like she asks you things she's asked about already. Some days she can't remember who I am and then she'll get me and me brother all mixed up in her mind. She talks to me Mum sometimes as if she's still a little girl at school. Other days she is as normal as anyone else and you wouldn't think there was anything wrong with her. Sharp as a butcher's knife on those days. Odd, that. You never know what to expect with my gran."

Neither of these versions of Grannyhood inspired me with confidence. Were we traveling all this way to spend time with a bitter complaining old woman who never cracked a smile or with one who had gone off her rocker and perhaps would mistake me for my brother Ronald, the only one of Ma's children she had met so far? In either case Carlo would be better off at home and the joke would be on me. I decided to question Ma more closely about her mother than I had done so far.

At last all the passengers had crossed the gangways which were then raised by some mechanical means and the entreating arms were hauled back onto the quay. I jumped when the ship announced its departure with a tremendous blast from its steam horn. It slowly began to move sideways away from the dock out into the middle of the harbor.

"You've gone all white-faced," said one of the airmen. "You're not going to be sick are you? What'll you do when we're out at sea?"

I explained about the horn catching me unaware not wanting to hear any more talk of seasickness. Then the airmen drifted off after wishing me a good journey and a pleasant visit with my grandmother.

"Maybe she's the cheerful type with all her marbles," said the one who had just commented on my suddenly white face." I wasn't sure what he meant. "You'll like Lancaster anyway," he added, "it's a lot bigger than any town on your little Island."

Now that I was on my own, at liberty to study the ship's movements, I was keenly interested in every detail. I noticed that the bow of the ship was pointed toward the top end of the harbor and wondered how the Captain would be able to turn the boat round since the harbor didn't seem wide enough for the purpose. The Captain had another plan in mind. With increasing speed the ship left the harbor backwards. Then I worried that it would run into the small lighthouse on the end of a projecting arm of the harbour or up on the rocks. I needn't have worried. The ship left the harbor smoothly in a wide semi-circle. Once clear of the harbor, when the ship's stern was close to the Gothic Victorian Tower of Refuge on its rock in Douglas Bay, the Captain pointed the bow to the open sea, the propellers churned the water white and foamy, the deck and the side rails shuddered and we began to move forward faster and faster until we reached our traveling speed and then we sailed along smoothly leaving the troubled wake behind us. The ship did move up and down and from side to side but with a gentle motion so that I no longer thought about seasickness though of course the thought would have recurred in a flash had we encountered an unexpected wind whipping up the waves.

I was about to leave my post by the rails to explore the ship when I saw that we had company. A low-lying, long, sleek and slender gray naval vessel – a corvette, I imagine it must have been – had detached itself from a small fleet anchored in Douglas Bay. It came toward us very fast taking up a position parallel to the ferry, just a few hundred yards away, and pre-pared to escort us across the Irish Sea. I hadn't thought of our journey as a dangerous one. Ma had said nothing of menace or threat from U-boats that might find a ferry crowded with military personnel a tempting target. I was used to the danger posed by bombers passing over us in the night but I hadn't thought much about the wartime perils to be found at sea. I was more interested in and excited by the ship escorting us than I was inclined to think about the potential dangers its presence indicated.

It steamed along beside us a few hundred yards away seemingly operating automatically. Only a very occasional sailor appeared on its deck during the journey and then only to do something mundane like throwing dirty water from a bucket over the side. None of these occasional sailors waved back when I waved to them. What was an exciting novelty for me was all in a day's work for the crew of the corvette.

Having stood by the rail watching our escort for a long time I looked up and behind our ship to find that the Island had become a distant shadowy pale blue outline. I went to find Ma to tell her about my adventures so far. She was knitting and talking to someone in the next seat. She suggested I have something to eat since we had a long day ahead of us. I had some of the sandwiches she had made and some of the tea she had bought from a small kiosk on deck. After that I returned to exploring the ship, not an easy task since the decks were crowded with passengers many of whom were sitting on their kit bags and suitcases. There were very few children on the ship, I noted, and none seemed disposed to talk to me. So I went exploring on my own going from stem to stern on all the deck levels before I returned to the top deck where the view was the clearest. I had found the engine room, down into which one could peer from an upper porthole, the most dramatic part of the ship. I wondered how those who worked in the engine room could stand either the heat or the constant deafening noise.

As we neared Liverpool the waters became muddy, the number of seagulls following the ship increased considerably as did the number of ships in the waterway. There were gray warships far larger than our guardian corvette. There were merchant ships of all sizes. There were dirty-looking dredgers keeping the mouth of the Mersey river navigable by battling the ever-encroaching silt. There were tugs pulling garbage scows and low-lying barges. There were ocean liners turned into troop carriers and painted in dull war-time colors. The Mersey estuary and river became an increasingly crowded waterway. The loud steam horn of our ship sounded frequently in all that nautical traffic. And now the shores could be seen on both sides of the ship. They seemed to be depressing mud-flats not at all like the Island's bright sandy beaches. We passed light-ships and buoys the bells of which clanged mournfully as they rocked in our wake. I was so absorbed by all these new sights that I entirely forgot Ma's injunction to join her in the cabin before we reached port. I didn't notice our corvette leave us, changing course to accompany another ferry sailing back from Liverpool to Douglas.

As our ship slowed right down after a series of bells had clanged I stood looking at the New Brighton shore on our starboard side but eventually I became fascinated by the tall buildings of Liverpool across the river, which appeared as our ship slowed further and turned toward them. One especially stood out. It was bigger than any building I had seen on the

Island. It was a building (the Liver Building) surmounted by two gigantic golden bronze statues of the eponymous mythic Liver birds. I was also taken by the miles of docks that were now visible as our ship neared the Liverpool shore going very slowly now as it moved toward the dock used by the Isle-of-Man Steam Packet ships. Only then did I remember that I was supposed to have rejoined Ma in the public cabin some time ago. Now, when I tried to get back to that cabin, I was hindered by the passengers on the decks who had begun to mass in preparation for landing. I had to try to force my way through a virtual wall of people. No doubt individuals who formed that wall would have let me through if they could but the press of numbers prevented them and I felt myself being pushed much against my will toward the stairs descending to the lower decks. I began to feel panic rising.

Luckily for me a sailor appeared and asked me where I was trying to go. After I had explained he took me off to one side and guided me to the public cabin through areas of the ship off-limits to passengers. I found Ma close to tears as she tried to explain to another sailor that she had lost her son who must be found at once. When Ma saw me with my rescuer she first slapped my face and then gave me a long weepy hug followed by a lecture on never doing anything so foolhardy again. She said I had succeeded in shattering her nerves already yet the day and our journey were far from over. She didn't know how she was going to recover from the shock of nearly losing me. She could, she said, have left me at home but out of the goodness of her heart had thought to give me a treat by letting me travel with her – and this is how I repaid her!

It took a long time to disembark. I felt guilty at every step. It was not until we had descended the steep gangway onto the dock burdened again with gasmasks and luggage that Ma recovered from her shock and her anger dissipated. I found myself doing what Carlo had done on the way home from his adventurous christening, promising Ma that I wouldn't misbehave again for the rest of our trip.

"Don't make promises you can't keep," said Ma curtly.

We now had to join the hundreds of other passengers waiting for the buses to take us across Liverpool to Lime Street Station. There was a fleet of double-deckers for the purpose but the wait was a long one nonetheless. To pass the time I engaged Ma in the sort of conversation I hoped would make her forget my disappearance on the ferry. I asked her about the gigantic golden birds I had seen on the roof of that tall building near the docks. She told me they were called "Liver Birds" (pronounced "lie-ver") but she didn't know why…something to do with the first half of the name "Liver-pool" perhaps or maybe it was the other way round. I asked her about the grandmother we were visiting, telling her about my conversation with the two airmen before the boat had left Douglas. I asked apprehensively if my grandmother had anything in common with theirs.

"I should hope not!" said Ma. "Your grandmother isn't loopy and she certainly hasn't lost her memory. I don't know how old you think she is but she's not so old that she's gone gaga. She has been ill but she's getting better now. Normally she's as fit as a fiddle but she had a nasty bout of pneumonia and that takes a lot of getting over at her age especially. She wrote to say she'd like me to visit her so as she hasn't seen you since you were a baby a few weeks old I thought she'd want to see you too. You'd better not try any of your stunts with her, though…she hasn't got my patience."

I was relieved to hear that my grandmother was both mentally sound and basically healthy and also surprised by the news that she had indeed met me before, not long, it transpired, after Ma had brought me home from the hospital in Douglas where I was born. We shuffled forward in our long queue a few feet at a time as the green Liverpool double-deckers came and went grateful for the glass roof over our heads when we heard heavy rain begin to pound on it. We had left the Island in sunshine but the sky had become dull an hour or so before we docked. Now the formidable Lancashire rain drummed on the roof.

"Good job I brought an umbrella," Ma remarked after looking up at the grimy glass high above our heads. I suddenly thought of Jakob's account of the dirty railway station in Birmingham the day he had been arbitrarily seized and declared an "alien." And I remembered that he had said the disused factory in which he was first imprisoned had been somewhere in Lancashire − somewhere perhaps not very far from where we were now standing. Remembering these things I felt guilty that I had left the Island without telling Jakob how much I would miss him while I was away though, truth to tell, the novelty of this trip drove him, like Carlo and Pop, out of my head much of the time.

After we had stood in line for close to an hour we were finally able to get on a bus but had trouble managing our luggage since the small compartment under the stairs of the double-decker was filled with the suitcases and kitbags of those who had boarded before us. We had to sit with our cases flat across our knees with the inevitable gasmasks in their boxes on top of them. But as we drove away from the docks and into the city traffic I was far more interested in what I could see on the streets than concerned about discomfort.

There were so many streets going off in so many directions; so many buildings of all ages and, among them, buildings taller than any I had ever seen except in pictures. They all seemed to be built of some kind of black brick or stone. I was amazed many years later, when coal was no longer the common fuel and the city got round to cleaning itself up, to find that the black color had been imparted by soot and other industrial grime over many decades lending a grim uniformity to facades that were in fact varied and colorful.

I had never seen so many vehicles before − cars, buses, military trucks, other kinds of trucks, motorcycles − an endless and noisy parade. There were people everywhere and they all seemed to be in a hurry. A lot of them were in uniform and those who weren't looked drab and down-at-heel for the most part. I had never seen so many people before yet I had thought our town a large one when I compared it to the Island's rural villages. Some of the effects of recent bombing stood out − there were buildings that had collapsed into piles of rubble that was still being cleared away. Some had a wall or two still standing amid the general destruction. People here had obviously got more reason than we had to fear German bombing raids so it was no wonder that many of the faces I could see when the bus stopped at traffic lights had care and fatigue stamped upon them. I had seen barrage balloons before, in ones and twos, but here there were many flying above significant buildings especially in the dock area. On this relatively brief bus ride I was looking at last at the urban England I had only heard about before from programs on the radio and from the people who stayed with us during their Island exile who told us how lucky we were to grow up in such a lovely unbombed place.

The bus we were traveling on was a special one from the boat to Lime Street Railway Station so it only stopped for traffic lights. When we had struggled off it at the entrance to the station I was amazed at the hordes of people streaming in looking for their trains.

The station had a vast number of platforms at many of which the large steam trains of the time were waiting to leave for destinations near and far. The place was incredibly dirty, fouled by soot from many years of steam engines and by the carelessness of thousands of passengers daily tossing their candy-wrappers, cigarette butts and packages, matchsticks, used tickets and other personal debris on to the ground without a thought. The railway station at Douglas the size of which always impressed me could be fitted inside this station many times over but it was a lot cleaner. I was so amazed at the size of everything that Ma had to tell me to stop standing with my mouth open like some country bumpkin just come to town and hurry along with her. We had tickets to obtain, a train to catch. We had to rush like everyone else.

Of course obtaining the tickets meant joining the inevitable queue once Ma had found the relevant ticket offices. Ma had some sort of pass from the Isle-of-Man Railway that would enable her to obtain our English tickets cheaply or for free but she had to present the pass to a ticket-seller so we had to line up. We shuffled forward at the same snail's pace as at the dock and as we did so the ground seemed to move under me as the ship's deck had done on our brief voyage. I told Ma I felt sick. Ma said to breathe deeply and regularly and try to forget about the ground moving and I'd soon feel better. The unpleasant sensation faded as the afternoon wore on but I thought it very strange and most unfair that I should feel seasick in a railway station when I hadn't felt that way on the boat.

After standing in a long line of would-be ticket buyers for what seemed an age Ma managed to get our tickets though only after a suspicious clerk had consulted a supervisor about our pass from the Isle-of-Man Railway which the clerk had obviously not seen before. Putting the cardboard tickets in her purse Ma then led the way to a café. She was, she said, "dying" for a cup of tea. Since we had at least an hour to wait for our train having a cup of tea and a scone would pass the time nicely. The tea reminded me of dishwater and the scone was as hard as a rock.

Eventually we were able to board the train that would take us to Lancaster. It was as dirty as the railway station. There was thick dust and waste paper on the floor of the compartment and sooty grime on the windows. What might have been ground into the seats didn't bear thinking about. Every train seemed to have a horde of people waiting for it so we were lucky to find seats however dirty they may have been, and seats by a window at that. But as the carriage filled up Ma made me stand next to her so that a woman could sit down. I felt really tired and still a bit seasick and I desperately wanted to sit after all my standing but having promised Ma better behaviour I had to get up. It would be Ma's fault if I fell down in a swoon like some over-used knight in the stories I liked to read. I remembered Jakob's account of his awful train journey to that dis-used factory and prayed that this one wouldn't last as long as his had done. I had no idea how far from Liverpool Lancaster was.

The train started just when I was thinking it was going to remain at the platform for the rest of the afternoon. It announced its departure with a piercing whistle supplied by the guard and a series of jolts as the engine wheels found purchase on the tracks. The jolts almost threw me into the lap of the woman who had taken my seat. She hadn't said "thank you" when I had reluctantly ceded it to her and now she glared at me as if

I was lurching toward her with hostile intent. If Ma hadn't put out a restraining arm I would have been pitched on to the scowling woman. Restored to balance I turned to look out of the window as the speed of the train increased. At first there wasn't much to see except for the grimy girdered structure of the station itself and then the high sooty walls of embankments. But once we were away from the City Center soot-encrusted embankments gave way to vast rows of streets. The city which I had thought huge when viewed from the bus now seemed to be unending as street after identical street flashed by now that the train was traveling at high speed – much faster than any train Pop had driven. The whole of Lancashire seemed to be filled with seedy streets of small dirty red-brick houses near to long buildings several storeys high with very tall chimneys emitting columns of black smoke which Ma said were called factories. I felt glad I lived in *Rosetree Villa* instead of in a house next door to one of these smoking factories. I began to worry that my grandmother might live in a street like one of those past which we now were rushing in noisy commotion.

I asked Ma if I could open the window to get a better view but she said that all I would get would be soot in my eyes from the engine and I would make the whole carriage cold so I would have to put up with things as they were. The woman who had taken my seat nodded in approval.

"Children need restraint," she said to Ma, "don't they?"

"Sometimes," Ma conceded, unwilling to commit herself to the notion of wholesale confinement. I stared at this joyless woman wondering what she would have said had she known that I had spent the morning wandering round a ferryboat unsupervised not to mention my unfettered play on the mountainside and in the woods at home.

"In my opinion children need restraining most of the time," said the woman giving Ma a dubious stare. "If that monster Hitler had been disciplined as a child he wouldn't now be having his tantrums rampaging about trying to conquer the world and causing havoc like some great spoiled lad. Look at what his fits of temper are doing to all of us! A good spanking would have saved us!"

No doubt Ma thought the woman had strayed pretty far and pretty fast from the instance that provoked these remarks since she didn't reply. The train charged noisily on, streets at last giving place to fields. Towns much smaller than Liverpool appeared. Some we stopped at, some we didn't. The obnoxious woman got off the train and at last I was able to sit down aching all over from having been so long on my feet. When the train slowed down again Ma said we were coming into Lancaster station. We got the suitcases down from the overhead racks and I began to worry about what I would find on the platform. So far, on the whole, I had enjoyed the adventure of the journey but I was about to meet an aunt and a grandmother I didn't know. I hoped that neither of them would bear any resemblance to the woman who had taken my seat. Then I had another thought. We were to spend two weeks in Lancaster – an age if I should find my relatives as unpleasant as my Aunty Doreen. My Aunty Phyllis, after all, was Doreen's sister as well as Ma's and my grandmother had given birth to Aunty Doreen. I don't know why the possible implications of these facts hadn't occurred to me before.

We struggled out of our compartment with our luggage while a porter sprawled on a small luggage wagon on the platform chewing on a matchstick and watching us without offering to help. The English, I thought, were a careless rude lot but then I remembered the helpful airmen on the boat and the many pleasant people who had stayed at *Rosetree Villa*.

There were a lot of people on the station platform but as we walked towards the exit a woman about my mother's height (Ma was short, not much above five feet tall) but thin where Ma was "well upholstered" as Pop put it – this woman detached herself from the crowd and uttering a cry of welcome flung her arms around Ma. Then, though I had never seen her before, she bent and gave me a welcoming hug and a kiss. I noted with relief that here we did not have a replica of Aunty Doreen but quite the opposite as subsequent experience affirmed. Aunty Phillis was Ma's eldest sister who although she had lost her only son a year before somehow managed to stay cheerful making our visit to Lancaster an easy and memorable one. I took to her at once. As to her son, by a bitter irony my eldest cousin had joined the Air Force and gone off to war only to drown at the seaside while on a day's leave from his squadron.

Having met my aunt at the station I dared to hope that I would find my grandmother to be like her and like Ma – essentially kind and cheerful unlike my doleful Aunty Doreen who it was said, resembled my long-deceased irascible maternal grandfather. Meanwhile I enjoyed the ride on the top deck of a Lancaster City bus enthralled by another large urban area – one nowhere near as large as Liverpool but much larger than any town on the Isle-of-Man. It occurred to me that in the course of his life Jakob must have seen many such places. I now wished I had asked him more about them.

After the bus ride we had to walk a short distance up a busy street that followed a gentle hill slope. Along this street were much larger and cleaner-looking houses than I had seen from the train. There was no dirty red brick here. These houses were faced with an attractive light gray stone. Each had a flight of steps rising to a front door which in most cases was painted black and sported a shiny brass door-knocker and equally shiny brass street numbers. It was toward one of these houses near the top of the street beyond a row of shops that we headed.

Aunty Phyllis led the way up the steps of this house, opened the door with a key and ushered us into a long hallway the very opposite of the one in Mrs. Dodd's smelly house. Here there was light instead of gloom; here there were no dead or dying bicycles in a jumbled heap but well-polished oak furniture and thick expensive-looking carpets. As soon as we entered the house a feeling of comfort enveloped me and I knew that we were going to enjoy our stay here. *Rosetree Villa,* whatever our pretentions about it, was threadbare by comparison and a lot noisier for here there were no occupants but my aunt, my uncle (who hadn't yet come home from work) and my grandmother. Had Carlo come with us he would have altered all that in seconds but he was at home making life difficult for Pop and for Bessie. I no longer felt any of the anxiety provoked by the airmen on the ship so when Aunty Phyllis opened a door off the hallway and said "Erik, come and meet your Granny" I followed her into the sitting room of the house with alacrity.

CHAPTER THIRTY-FOUR

THE FRONT SITTING ROOM OF MY AUNTY PHYLLIS'S HOUSE WAS NOT unlike Mrs. Kelly's in size, shape, and the sort of framed prints on the walls but where Mrs. Kelly's room had been dark, swathed in heavy curtains and smelling of medicine, mothballs and its bed-ridden occupant my aunt's front room was bright, the long dark green velvet curtains pulled aside and fastened with gold-colored cords, daylight entering freely, the room smelling faintly of furniture polish and more prominently of the flowers in a cut-glass vase set on an occasional table by the window. Dressed somewhat after the Edwardian manner of Mrs. Hochheimer though not as flamboyantly and with a light shawl draped around her shoulders my bespectacled Grandmother was sitting in a comfortable armchair beside an ornate dark-green tiled fireplace in which a coal fire was keeping the room warm. She had been reading but put her book and her wire-rimmed glasses down and stood up as I came in ready to give me a welcoming hug to which I ruefully submitted. She proved to be as affectionate as my Aunty Phyllis.

"Well, you've grown a streak since I saw you last," my Grandmother said and added "but that's not surprising...you were just home from the hospital, about three weeks old. You were a noisy handful then...are you still like that?"

I was surprised by my Grandmother's voice. I had expected her to speak with a Lancashire accent like Aunty Phyllis and Aunty Doreen…and Ma, too, now and then when she was distracted and irritated. My Grandmother didn't express herself in what we used to call "BBC English," which was highly mannered when I was a child, but in a voice free of regional vocal coloring if not of regional turns of phrase.

"She went to elocution lessons when she was a girl," Ma told me later when I commented on the way Grandma, as I took to calling her, spoke.

"Electrocution lessons, more like," said Pop when I later gave him a minute account of our trip. "She's got a keen tongue your Grandmother has," he added, "when she decides to use it."

In answer to Grandma's question as to whether I was still a handful Ma described our day's travel – me vanishing on the boat with near-disastrous consequences. She told her mother how frantic she had been and said, "It's taken me all day to recover."

"We shall have to keep an eye on you," said my Grandmother. "You're a wanderer…like your Grandfather."

Ma dived into the conversation to change the subject leaving me to speculate on where or how my Grandfather wandered.

My Grandmother wanted to know all about my life at home. I was only rarely invited to hold forth to adults so I launched into a lengthy account of our military lodgers, school, my friends there, Sunday school and the choir, my difficulties with Carlo, my adventure with the police and the floating corpse, my suspicions of Mr. Smith and my experience of the day Mrs. Kelly began the last phase of her slow demise. Last but not least I described my work on the farm and my friendship with Jakob. Aunty Phyllis's arrival with a tray containing tea and Eccles cakes interrupted my headlong narrative.

"Th' afternoon's drawin' I know," said Aunty Phyllis, "but we weren't sure what time y'd be 'ere, ye see, as trains don't always run to time these days and sometimes they don't run at all so we'll be 'avin dinner a bit later than usual. 'Ere's a bite to put yer on."

The "bite" in question consisted of the Eccles cakes which I had never seen before but, once tasted, captured my whole attention. The sweet light raisin-filled puff pastry was a delight. These cakes were as good in their way as Aunty Emmeline's fruitcakes and, like them, to be savored in silence. I thought of Jakob's remark that there were other benefits to travel besides a change of scenery.

"Well, you certainly lead a busy life," my Grandmother said when the tea had been drunk and the Eccles cakes disposed of. "You've got a healthy appetite too I see." Abruptly changing the subject she asked "And who's this foreigner you were mentioning…this chap Jay Kob?"

Before I could reply Ma said "He's an alien at the Mooragh Camp. He works on Tom Talbot's farm…you remember him and Lizzie Talbot? You met them both years ago when you came over to see Erik just after he was born. They've got a farm in Glen Auldyn. Erik works there helping-out at weekends. He goes with Lizzie to deliver the milk. Aliens from the Mooragh Camp work there on the farm too. This Jakob's one of them. Erik's very fond of him"

"Fond? Of an alien? Well…I don't know about that," said my Grandmother looking at me dubiously for the first time since we entered the room. It was obvious that friendship with anyone the government labeled "alien" was a state beyond her experience. In fact her tone as well as the way she now looked at me suggested she saw something approaching the deviant in it.

"Are you sure he's safe? she asked. "It doesn't seem natural to me."

"We were all against Erik having anything to do with him at first," said Ma before I could say anything in Jakob's defence that might upset my Grandmother. "We were against it," Ma repeated, "but he's ever such a *clever* man. He was a professional opera singer before the war. Erik says all he wants to do is get out of the Camp and fight the Germans. There's ever so many clever people in the Mooragh Camp...musicians, artists, professors...all sorts. And there they are in old shabby clothes digging in the mud on farms and shut away behind barbed wire the rest of the time. It's not right."

"You'd best not say things like that round here," said my Grandmother, plainly shocked at Ma's newfound moral position. "Here they'd have the police knocking on your door if anyone heard you talk like that. Have you seen what the Germans have done to Liverpool never mind every-where else?"

Ma began to argue that to be fair the aliens had nothing to do with the bombing of Liverpool. They may have been born in Austria or Gemany or other places that spoke German but they hated Hitler and the Nazis as much as we did – maybe more. They left Europe because the Nazis drove them out by having people like them killed. They had come to England to be safe and wanted to fight back.

"That's as may be," said my Grandmother, "but folk round here don't see things that way so I'd keep quiet about this chap while you're here if I were you. It'll end in tears if you don't."

"More tea?" Aunty Phyllis interjected thrusting the large pot forward in an attempt to end the sharp turn the conversation had taken so soon after our arrival.

"Jakob's taught me lots of things," I said before Ma could resume her defence of the alien population along the lines of Lilywhite's arguments which, not so long ago when she shared her mother's outlook, would have been unthinkable. "He's told me about the places he's been to, what it's like to be a singer, all the bad things that have happened to hm since he was made a prisoner. If I want to know something I don't under-stand I just ask him and he tells me what I want to know. He knows more than the teachers at my school. Uncle Tom says he's a good farm worker too but I know he doesn't like working on a farm because he'd rather be singing the way he used to before the war. He sang all over the place then."

"I dare say I know more than the teachers at your school too," said Grandma smiling, "and I had to leave when I was twelve."

Thus did she veer away from aliens and Jakob and never mentioned them to me again. She asked me questions about family members which I answered more or less truthfully and then I told her of my fainting in church right in front of the Bishop and went on to describe the riot Carlo's christening had been and one thing led to another until Ma suggested that I wash my hands for dinner, something I was not required to do at home unless my hands were obviously filthy.

Dinner was served up by Aunty Phyllis in her roomy kitchen. The house did have a formal dining room but that was "saved" for special occasions like Christmas and Easter, a funeral or a family birthday. Our arrival didn't seem to have been "special" enough for a fire to be lit and the long mahogany dining table set for meals. The kitchen was cosy, though – more like our living room at home than the formal dining room was. It contained a feature that surprised me when I came back downstairs after perfunctorily rinsing my hands in the upstairs bathroom. The kitchen now contained Uncle Bill, a man of whose existence I was entirely ignorant until Aunty Phyllis introduced me to him.

Ma, who hadn't told me I had an Aunty Phyllis until she proposed this trip, hadn't mentioned Uncle Bill at all. I had assumed that Aunty Phyllis's husband, the father of my poor drowned cousin, must himself have died, maybe so many years ago that Ma had forgotten about him entirely. His name certainly hadn't been mentioned till now. He was a short man, not much taller than Aunty Phyllis. He worked as a plumber in the days when plumbing was a grubby menial trade not the source of instant wealth it has since become. He was like my other uncles in his meek inoffensiveness. Pop would have added him to the list of family "eunuchs" had he ever met him, which, it transpired, he hadn't.

Uncle Bill, in his Lancashire way, said he "wor pleased t'meet me at last," asked a few innocuous questions, made some general observations on the day's weather and the prospects for tomorrow ("not good, lad, there's rain on't way"), sighed deeply, picked up his knife and fork, inspected them minutely as if he'd never seen them or their like before and then put them down in order to stare intently and bleakly at the tablecloth. Ma didn't speak to him; neither did Aunty Phyllis nor Grandma so I began to wonder if he had committed some unspeakable, unforgivable sin. The conversation during dinner was a female affair Uncle Bill remaining silent, focused on his dinner – a well-cooked Lancashire Hotpot. I was content to observe everyone else. Before the meal was properly over Uncle Bill furtively excused himself and said, "Ahm just slippin' down t' t' pub." He left as the three women at the table exchanged enigmatic glances.

"Still at it, then?" Ma asked cryptically.

"E'll never get over it," said Aunty Phyllis dabbing her eyes with a small handkerchief. Ma and my Grandmother both sighed in sympathy.

Later, when I lay in the spare bedroom in my much-washed striped pyjamas in the narrow bed across from Ma's larger one, I asked her about Uncle Bill. I wanted to know why I had never been told about him.

"Nobody thought he was good enough for your Aunty Phyllis," she said. "Your Aunty's a clever woman and could have married above her but she chose Bill, Lord knows why. He's a decent enough chap…wouldn't say *boo* to a goose…but he didn't see much of the inside of a school. He's got a poor job and now he's taken to drink since your cousin drowned. Your cousin was the only child. Phyllis has found the strength to carry on, as people have to do, but Bill can't manage it. He goes down to the pub every night and tries to drown his sorrows in beer. What would the world be like if we all did that? Everybody has some kind of grief in their lives and they just have to put up with it but your Uncle Bill can't…he's weak. Now don't you go repeating what I've just said to anyone."

After Ma had told me this I saw my new-found Uncle in a theatric light. He was much misunderstood. He was a Man of Sorrows and Acquainted with Grief. He took on a kind of tragic stature despite his diminutive size and his pub-going. I made an effort to talk to him and found him diffident at first but he opened up the more we talked. Unlike many of the grown-ups I knew Uncle Bill liked children, perhaps because he was rather child-like himself. After Ma and I had been in his house for a few days he brought me some American comics to read. The daughter of a friend of his at work had been given them by her American Air Force boyfriend. She had passed them on to her younger brother who had now finished with them. They depicted American soldiers invariably winning the battles in which they fought. Every jeep-riding cigar-chomping American in their pages was the image of nonchalance as he mowed down entire platoons of the enemy, "Bammm!!" and "Kazaam!!!" decorating his violent enterprises. For some reason each wore his helmet on the back of his head, the chin-strap unfastened. By contrast buttoned up German soldiers in their coal-bucket helmets goose-stepped their doomed way across the pages to defeat bawling "Jarwohl!!" for no apparent reason. The Japanese were equally comical. They were all about my height, each carrying a rifle twice his size. They all had enormous buck teeth, wore glasses and yelled "Banzai!!!" at intervals. The occasional British soldier, tall and cadaverous, called everyone "old man," never raised his voice and drank a great deal of tea in unlikely places. When I thanked my Uncle for these comics he said that he had enjoyed them too.

"Teks yer mind off things," he said.

Even at that age I thought how sad it must be to rely on beer and American comics to take your mind off the death of your only child and even then I reflected on how inadequate such palliatives must be. When he wasn't talking to me or to someone else Uncle Bill was the very image of inarticulate grief which, perhaps, was why he seemed estranged, isolated from his wife and his mother-in-law who, I recognized as the days went by, was tough-minded and intolerant of what she saw as weakness. My Grandmother believed in soldiering on even when Life's missiles exploded round you, showering you with shrapnel. She regarded those who ran for cover as lacking in moral fibre. So Uncle Bill had to suffer not only the death of his son but lack of respect in his own home. When he died a couple of years later, in his early fifties, I wasn't surprised by the news. Aunty Phyllis lived till she was ninety-five, outlasting two more husbands.

This visit to my Aunty Phyllis and my Grandma had been undertaken without Ma thinking about what I could do to amuse myself in a house full of adults. Ma wanted to talk – at length – with her sister and her mother to make up for lost time. But there was me – a restless child – to consider. The toys my deceased cousin had played with at my age had long been disposed of so I couldn't pass the time in play the way I did in Aunty Doreen's house where everything belonging to Herbert had been lovingly preserved. So what was I to do? My Grandmother thought of an amusement for me on the day after we arrived. She gave me a thick unused notebook and a pencil and told me that if I stood in the bay window of the front sitting room I would see a great many things I wasn't used to on the Island. I could write down in the notebook a brief description of everything passing the house that I thought to be of interest – I would be like a reporter for a newspaper.

At first I thought this a dreary notion. I wanted to play and this wasn't playing – it was more like pointless work. To what end would I be compiling these lists and observations? I would be acting like a clerk in a grocery store making out a bill or an inventory. You can't play with lists; they aren't toys any more than the paper and pencil I would have to use to make them. Did my Grandmother seriously expect me to stand there by the window hour after boring hour simply writing down what I could see? Admittedly there was a great deal more life and action outside of Aunty Phyllis's house than there was outside of ours on the Island but to stand there observing it all from within and reducing it to a series of lists was definitely not my idea of fun.

I didn't think I could tell my Grandmother this so I reluctantly took the notebook and pencil. I was left alone with them in the front sitting room of the house while my aunt and my mother chatted with my Grandmother over pots of tea in the kitchen. I stood by the window listlessly observing the scene outside: women in drab clothes hurrying by holding shopping baskets and handbags; elderly men in cloth caps, some with dogs on leashes (whippets seemed to be a particular favorite) and some without, walking at a more sedate pace with nowhere in particular to go; people on bicycles, horse-drawn carts making deliveries, a cat sitting in the sun on a neighbor's front steps, a passing dog that stopped to stare at the cat causing its back to arch and its fur to stand on end. Was I to stand here all day writing down these mundane sightings? I could see such things at home. I didn't have to come all the way to Lancaster to make lists of them. When my friends at school asked me what I had done on my holiday I could hardly tell them that every day I stood by a window taking note of anonymous people, an offended cat, a peeing dog. They would want to know why I hadn't gone anywhere of interest or done anything remotely exciting.

My Grandmother, however, knew what she was about. I hadn't been standing at the window for long when I heard the sound of engines approaching. Soon, up the street came the first jeep I had ever seen outside of a cinema or a comic. It was followed by a long column of military vehicles: heavy trucks, heavy guns on long low carriers, tanks carried in similar fashion, field guns on wheels towed behind trucks large and small, camouflaged armoured cars – one after another the vehicles of war drove right past my Aunty Phyllis's house. I scribbled fast in my notebook trying to make sure that every vehicle was accounted for. After this column had passed and I thought that the rest of the day would be anti-climactic a second column appeared. Columns of vehicles in fact rolled by my aunt's house all day and by the end of it I was hooked. I wanted to do nothing else but stand there taking note of trucks and armoured cars and long carriers bearing tanks, dis-assembled aircraft. I would like to have asked the soldiers riding in canvas-covered trucks or sitting astride khaki-colored motorbikes where they were going in such numbers. The sheer volume and variety of vehicles overwhelmed me. Hundreds passed my aunt's house on every day of my stay in Lancaster, a vast army heading south for some military purpose as yet undisclosed. I was eager to find something novel, a significant variant of the vehicles rumbling by (a red jeep? a truck with wings?). I was as ardent as the most dedicated train-spotter. Had anyone outside of our household observed me they might have thought a diminutive spy was at work feverishly recording the types and numbers of military vehicles for the Fuehrer. This daily occuption of mine became a kind of craze which my mother observed with some uneasiness.

"Are you sure you're all right standing there by that front window all day?" she asked. "You don't seem to want to stop at meal times."

I tried to explain my excitement about what I was seeing at first hand, something entirely foreign to Island experience, something that might prove to be of historic importance sort of like watching the Roman army, once quartered here in Lancaster, suddenly on the move southwards either to resist or effect an invasion. I described the vehicles I had seen passing the house, the sort of details I had begun to look for. I showed her my notebook now well-filled with penciled descriptions, little sketches.

"Well," said Ma in a dubious tone of voice, "as long as you're keeping yourself amused…"

I suppose she could see that I had been possessed by a sort of fixation. I simply didn't hear when I was called for meals my whole attention absorbed by those passing military convoys. Sometimes they continued to pass the house at intervals all night and then I was sorely tempted to creep downstairs to the sitting room to observe them until I reflected that I wouldn't be able to see much on the blacked-out street. I did tell Uncle Bill about what was passing the house every day before he went off to the pub.

On the third day of my vigil he came home from work early and joined me at my observation window. I don't know whether he had been sent by Aunty Phyllis to find out if I was "all right" (people not "all right" were unbalanced in varying degrees) or came simply to satisfy his own curiosity about what it was that had seized and held my attention so tightly.

"These army lorries and that catch yer curiosity do they?"

"Yes," I said wishing he'd go away and leave me to my note-taking. On this occasion Uncle Bill was not a Man of Sorrows Acquainted With

Grief but a pestering adult prying my attention from the military theater out there on the street.

"What is it about all that as meks yer write it down in a beuk?"

I told him that it was Grandma's idea but that I enjoyed it because it was a kind of game I could play by myself and I emphasized the "by myself" hoping he would take the hint and leave me to it. By this time I had begun to imgine myself as a British spy parachuted into a German city to take note of the enemy's military strength. A spy in such circumstances doesn't want to be visited by his Uncle Bill asking him daft questions, distracting him from the crucial task for which he has trained long and hard. Uncle Bill was going to blow his cover.

"T'Romans lived 'ere once," said Uncle Bill in no hurry to leave the room. "Ay, they did that, lad. 'Appen their soldiers come marching up t'street reet past ooer front door though 'course ooer 'ouse wasna 'ere then. It's old but not that old. T' Castle's reet where t'Roman fort used ter be. Yer should go t'see t' Castle before yer go 'ome. It's fulla 'istory is t' Castle. Goes back 'undreds an' 'undreds o' years it does. Mists o't past, lad, mists o't past." Uncle Bill sighed heavily and coughed as if the mists had got to his lungs.

This brief excursion to the Castle might have been Uncle Bill trying to wrest my attention away from its exclusive focus on the street but perhaps he felt attracted to History and thought I would be interested in the ancient building which had aroused his imagination. He went on to tell me about the Priory too.

"T' monks lived theer long ago," he said. "Yer do know what a monk is don't yer lad?" (I nodded). "T'monk's building…that's the one 'as is called a *Priory*…that building 'as been theer eight 'undred year. Lancaster grew round t' Castle and t' Priory. Mind you t' Romans built 'ere first…before t' Castle and t'Priory…and even before them there were folk as lived in mud 'uts. Yer didn't get t' Romans on t'Isle o'Man did yer? Y' 'ad Vikings and such theer. Big long boats they come in, wi' sails an' oars and shields all down t'sides. Rough lads were t'Vikings. Knock yer flat as soon as look at yer an' knock yer flat again if yer gave them a funny look. They'd tak everythin' y'd got, yer wife included. Wouldn't want ter meet one o' them big bearded buggers on a dark night wi'out a pleeceman."

At last, noting that I was a lot more interested in history-in-the-making outside in the street than past history, no matter how intriguingly violent, Uncle Bill then left me to my observation and frantic notations. It was the following day that he gave me the first batch of American comics, perhaps as a less direct way of breaking my focus on the street. I thought that there must have been discussion with Aunty Phyllis or Ma or both preceding his attempted intervention so Uncle Bill was not as entirely cut off from discussion in his own house as I had imagined after that first dinner there.

The campaign to wean me from the street outside – to counteract the obsession my Grandmother had innocently set in motion – led Ma, my Aunty Phyllis and my Grandmother to propose a visit to Lancaster Castle and Priory. Ignoring my protest that I would rather stay in the house they told me to prepare for an outing.

"A growing lad like you needs fresh air," said my Grandmother. "A growing lad like you should see a bit of history," she added. "I know you've got castles on the Isle-of-Man," she went on, "but every castle's different so we'll take the bus and then we'll walk round the Castle and the Priory so you can soak up a bit of local history. You'll be able to tell your friends at school all about it after you get home. I bet none of them has seen these places."

So off we went, my elders extolling the benefits of fresh air and viewing the monuments of the past and me wanting more than anything to remain in that front room recording the passing military show while pretending to be a spy. Yet in spite of myself the Castle did stir my imagination when we reached it as did the Priory, both Norman in origin. We wandered about looking at the prime features of these ancient buildings my Grandmother reflecting aloud on how cold and comfortless by modern standards life must have been in the Twelfth Century and long after behind all that solid stone.

"Some things," my Grandmother eventually pronounced, "don't change. This Castle was built when people were always at each other fighting, killing, robbing…it was built to protect people from other robbers and invaders. Here we are still at it eight hundred years or more later except that now a castle wouldn't be much use with modern bombers and big guns that would have these walls down flat in no time. These days we have to go underground like frightened rabbits when the siren goes if we want to stay alive."

After my Grandmother said this it occurred to me that I hadn't heard a siren since we had been here. We were more likely to be urged by their loud wailing to take shelter back on the Island than we were here.

"There used to be canons here and lots o' iron railings – they've all been tekken to be melted down for modern guns and such for the war. A lot of other railings in't town 'ave bin tekken too. People 've given up their own garden railings for t' war effort."

This information came from Aunty Phyllis who normally said very little, at least when I was present. Perhaps she wanted to take her mother's mind off those underground shelters she had mentioned her aversion to which was as great as to falling bombs, though as far as I could tell she had yet to experience either.

"Our schoolyard has railings all round it," I said, "but they haven't been taken for the war. Our school's just like a prison," I said.

"But not a prison like this castle," said my Grandmother. "There are cells in there with no windows and the running water is water running down the walls. People were flung into these places once and forgotten about. This gate we're coming up to is called John O'Gaunt's Gate and there were prisoners in olden days that were dragged out of the cells in the Castle and hanged in that gateway for all to see. The bodies were left there swinging at the end of a rope till either the rope rotted or the bodies did and fell off. At least that's what I've heard. Later when they used to cut off the heads of prisoners they were stuck on spikes on the walls of the

Castle to rot or provide a feast for the rooks who'd start by pecking the eyes out."

"Don't go on like that, mother," said Aunty Phyllis, "y'll frighten t'lad o' 'is wits. 'E'll 'ave nightmares and wet the bed."

"You won't will you Eric? You've got beyond that haven't you?" my Grandmother responded.

"'Course," I replied not at all sure about the nightmares. The Castle was a grim gray fortress with a vast square and round towers. I could quite see why anyone dragged inside it to be flung into a cave-like cell would abandon all hope.

The Priory created a different impression. This place could be a refuge from the arbitrary authority of the Dukes of Lancaster. I was interested to learn that it had been begun around the time that the Maughold Church of Carlo's christening had also been started though in a very different style. I wondered what it would be like to sing in the choir in a building as old as this rather than in the plain Victorian St. Paul's, scene of my weekly choral labors.

My Grandmother who, it transpired, disliked churches ("homes for hypo-crites") soon discovered an urgent need for a cup of tea and a rest so we set off down Castle Hill in search of a café. Afterwards we did some shopping in the busy City Center and then took a bus back to Aunty Phyllis's house. With all the walking and standing I was too tired that day to resume my scrutiny of military convoys though one was passing us as we walked up the street from the bus stop.

"They're a blasted nuisance," said one of my aunt's neighbors turning into the house just in front of us. "They never stop with their noise and their smell. Their exhausts fill the air so much with smoke y'canna breathe. The engines are that loud yer canna 'ear yerself think. I dunna know why they 'ave ter drive straight through town. Why can't they go round it? All day an' all night they're at it driving past keepin' us all awake. Someone should complain. There should be a law against it."

"This way's quicker and easier, I suppose," said Aunty Phyllis. "There is a war on," she added reprovingly suggesting to her neighbor that a bit of annoyance was a small price to pay for eventual peace and security.

"Well it upsets Ginger," the neighbor replied as if that were the ultimate argument against convoys.

I asked who Ginger was and my aunt told me he was the neighbor's cat – the one I had seen sunning himself on her doorstep the day I began to chronicle the passing military scene.

"She thinks more of that cat than she does of Dan (her husband) and why she calls it Ginger when it's as black as the ace of spades I don't know. She must be color-blind as well as daft."

"Well, what d'ye think o't Castle now you've seen it? Smashin' in't it?" said Uncle Bill.

"I liked it," I said, "but I wouldn't want to be locked up in it."

"It'd be smashin' though if y'owned t' place and y' lived theer in comfort and were waited on 'and an' foot wi' trumpets like that theer John O'Gaunt."

"But you might hear the prisoners down in the cells under the ground. Grandma says they'd be shouting in pain and screaming for mercy all the time."

"Aye, lad, there's that but yer could just shut all 't winders."

"Did they have windows when the Castle was built?" I asked.

"Well," said Uncle Bill, "if they didn't they should have."

Our time sped by. Soon the ten days of our visit were coming to an end and we faced the prospect of the return journey. By this time my fascination with military convoys was beginning to wane. I was glad we were going home. I felt constrained in my aunt's house where I had to be on my best behavior all the time. I started to think more of those Ma and I had left behind and began to miss them – even Pop and Carlo. I looked forward to telling Jakob all about the journey. I would omit nothing so that even though he couldn't leave the Island in fact he could do so in imagination and wander freely, mentally speaking, in the places I had visited. He'd be interested in the boat journey and especially the corvette sent to guard us. I would tell him about nearly being swept down onto the Liverpool quayside by the press of other passengers leaving Ma frantically looking for me on the ship. I would describe the golden Liver Birds, the crowded train and the obnoxious woman in our carriage who made me stand even though I was tired out. I would describe as much of Lancaster as I had seen but especially the Castle and the Priory. I would of course tell him about the military convoys and how I became caught up in describing them. I would tell him about my sad Uncle Bill. Above all I would tell him how glad I was to be back to talk to him. I would impress upon him my hope that he would never have to leave the Island because I would never be able to find another friend like him. The more I thought about it on the journey home the more crucial it seemed that I must beg Jakob not to leave the Island when he was free. I didn't think to ask myself how, as a professional opera singer, Jakob could make a living. The Island wasn't into opera. Pantomimes at Christmas and minstrel shows in summer were more in its line.

As I saw the Island taking shape in the distance that day we went back home, Ma standing with me this time on the top deck of the ferry, I began to feel more excited even than I had felt as our train pulled out of Lancaster station very early that morning with Aunty Phyllis there on the platform waving her handkerchief in farewell. There is something about being at sea on a sufficiently large and stable ship sailing in calm waters (as long as one forgets the possibility of U-boats) that engenders or reinforces romantic notions. Unhampered by facts and practical considerations I envisioned a time in the not-far-off future when Jakob would be a free man, would take up residence in a cottage in Glen Auldyn or, like Old Pete, at the base of North Barrule not far from the sea. I would be a constant visitor there and we would have long uninterrupted conversations about everything under the sun. Life would be as good as it gets and, of course, the war would be over. By the time we reached *Rosetree Villa* I was in the most sun-lit mood ready to tell Carlo of my adventures and hopes. Carlo, it transpired, was interested neither in my adventure nor my hopes nor anything else. He was still filled with resentment at being left behind. He stood in the living room surly, combative, irate, threatening, like a human moth, to eat everyone's coats.

CHAPTER THIRTY-FIVE

ELECTRIC WITH EXCITEMENT I COULD HARDLY WAIT TO REACH THE farm the Saturday after we returned from Lancaster. I was eager to tell Jakob all about the holiday. I was sure he'd be as thrilled as I had been by the protective corvette, the endless military convoys, the Medieval Castle started by Roger de Poitou son of William the Conqueror – neither of whom I had ever heard of before. I wanted to tell him about the Benedictine Priory, the Liver Birds and Liverpool. I would tell him about everything I had experienced, everyone I had met – my grandmother, my aunt, my tragic uncle, the woman on the train who had taken my seat. There was so much to tell. I prattled about it all to Uncle Tom in a sort of breathless rehearsal as we drove out to the farm but he remained silent. He focused on the road ahead, a cigarette burning in the corner of his mouth, his eyes screwed up because of the smoke, apparently unimpressed by my adventures. But that didn't matter. Jakob would appreciate the wider world to which I had been introduced even if Uncle Tom didn't. He was probably jealous that I had been able to go on holiday to England and he hadn't. I silently forgave him his pettiness. I was in too good a mood not to.

When the truck came to a stop in the farm street I jumped out eager to find Jakob at once. I darted in and out of various buildings looking for him until quite literally I bumped into Liz almost knocking her down.

"Eh, lad, look where you're going!" she said, "you nearly had this bucket o' milk out of my hand. Did they teach you to flatten your elders over there across the water?"

"Where's Jakob?" I asked too excited to apologize or pause to begin telling Liz about my roving adventures. That could wait till later in the day.

"Didn't Tom…? No, I can see he didn't," Liz answered her own half-formed question. "I told him to be sure to tell you so you wouldn't get up here expecting to find him. I might 've known he'd leave it all to me."

"Find who?" I asked misgiving beginning to creep over me like a dank mist from the sea.

"He didn't have the heart to tell you did he? I wanted him to tell you that Jakob's *gone.*"

"Gone? Gone where?" I asked hoping to be told that Jakob's absence was local and temporary. Perhaps Tom had loaned him to another farmer who needed extra help. Perhaps he had to work in the Camp. Maybe he had to sing in a Camp concert and had been allowed to stay there to practice as had happened at odd times in the past.

"He's *gone,*" said Liz with the same emphasis as before. "As in *gone for good.* We've lost him! The government has sent him back to the mainland. He's been set free. The day afer you left for your holiday Tom was told that Jakob was being released to do war work in England. They didn't tell us what sort of war work. We really shouldn't be surprised should we? They've been letting the aliens go for a while now and we were pretty sure they wouldn't keep Jakob here. He's done nothing wrong has he? He always worked hard. We've never had to complain about him…well, not officially anyway though I had to have a word with him about Mary. But he couldn't help falling for her could he? She was such a lovely girl. Now we've lost them both!"

Having said this Liz put down her bucket as the tears started to run down her face. She had taken Mary's loss hard as she had developed motherly feelings for her and she'd always had a soft spot for Jakob. To lose them both was, in a way, like losing a child all over again. She said as much after I too began to cry and need comforting. We stood there holding on to one another grieving our losses, the image of wartime bereavement.

"Well," said Liz wiping her eyes with the back of her hand, "best get on. There's work to do. There's cows to look after and milk to deliver rain or shine whether Jakob's here or not." She picked up her bucket and went off to wherever she was going before I interrupted her.

I couldn't take such a stoic view of the situation so wandered round the farm heavy of heart. I hung despondently over a five-barred gate, stared into the distance and cried again. This was the blow I had feared but hadn't wanted to think about much. I had persuaded myself somehow on the ferry bringing Ma and I home that when Jakob was released he wouldn't leave the Island. As I thought about what Jakob's loss would mean it occurred to me that he would surely have left a message for me of some sort. He would have written a note telling me how he would miss me and letting me know where he was going and how I could get in touch with him. The shock of the news of his leaving had driven such practical considerations out of my head. I went to find Liz to ask about the note she must have forgotten.

She was in the dairy. I asked her what Jakob had told her of his immediate plans and where we could write to contact him.

"He left without getting in touch with us. One day he was here and the next we were told he had gone back to England. He certainly didn't leave us an address to write to…or any message."

"You mean he just went without saying goodbye or telling you anything about where he was off to? Jakob wouldn't do that."

"But that's just what he did," said Liz. "I suppose he didn't want any fuss. And after all he didn't come to the Island of his own free will did he? He's been behind barbed wire for over two years and treated like a criminal just for being who he is. I'm sure he was as keen to leave as he was loathe to come in the first place. Don't forget lad that he was getting out of a prison. He probably couldn't get off this Isle of prisons fast enough. Any road, we'll never know and if you're sensible you won't go thinking about it till it makes you miserable. That won't change the facts. We have to put up with what we can't alter in this life."

"But he was my friend! He's been my friend since I first came here. He told me about all sorts of things. He wouldn't just go away and not leave a message."

"I don't suppose he had any say in the matter," Liz said, "or, come to think of it, any time. He was probably told to have his kit ready sharpish and not allowed to leave messages or get in touch with us. He was probably told that day he didn't come to work to be ready to leave in an hour or two. We were telephoned and told he was leaving but nothing else. He wasn't told where he was going when he was sent here either was he? The police just took him from where he was living and hardly gave him time to collect any of his things before they marched him in front of a committee and on to a train. That's the way the authorities work in wartime. They don't worry about people's feelings. They're not concerned about justice. So don't you go blaming Jakob. The powers-that-be wouldn't be asking him who he'd like to say goodbye to or leave a message for. They wouldn't be asking him what address he'd like notes from anyone here to be sent to. But cheer up. Maybe he will write to us when he's free on the mainland and doing whaever war work he has to do. You'll just have to be patient and wait. You can't blame him for not wanting to stay behind the wire can you? Would you have wanted to stay if you had been in his place?"

Eventually I forced myself to accept this view of things – at least officially. But I was doubtful. I hoped that Jakob would write to me care of the farm since he didn't know my address but I feared that he would try to put his Island experience behind him, the good with the bad. I knew from our talks how deeply angry he was at being treated like a criminal in the country to which he had turned for sanctuary. He would do war work to help defeat the Nazis who had defiled his country and forced him into exile but afterwards he would go back to the opera. In both spheres he would have too much to do and to think about. He would make new friends – probably meet another Mary – and so his old acquaintance would fade from mind. I had seen how he had shut the original Mary out of his thoughts once she had left us even though she hadn't really wanted to go.

So all the fancies I had been indulging of late to deny the inevitability of Jakob's departure vanished before the brutal fact that I had seen him for the last time before I had left for England. He wouldn't get in touch with any of us. He might not be allowed to. He would resume his life from where it had been so arbitrarily interrupted. It was hard that I hadn't been granted an official farewell but when I thought about what such a scene might entail, eventually I was glad I had been spared it. I would have begged him to stay, cried like a little kid – like Carlo – and altered nothing.

Elsie Cottier, seeing my look of misery, couldn't resist rubbing salt into my wounds.

"So, ya pal's been an' gone an' left ya without sayin' *terrar*. Just shows ya what them German f'las is like. He'll be off to help the Nazees now he's on the loose again. They should've kept him locked up for the duration if you ask me."

"No one's asking you. You're as thick as a brick," I told her but she just laughed as she pushed her wheelbarrow into the barn.

I found Rory and Tory more congenial company than Elsie Cottier. They listened sympathetically while I told them how miserable I felt with Jakob gone and then, to cheer me up, they started to dance around inviting me to throw stones for them to chase. I threw a few half-heartedly. As I was doing so Johnny appeared to tell me how he felt about Jakob leaving.

"Baker (Johnny's version of *Jakob*)...Baker's fled (left) to see Yram (Mary)," he explained to me. No doubt this was how Liz had explained Jakob's absence to him. He would have been as upset as I was if he had been told that Jakob wasn't coming back.

"I heard, Liz told me," I replied.

"I kile Yram," said Johnny before going back to the work he had been doing before he saw me with the dogs. I wondered what Tom and Liz would tell him when Jakob didn't reappear eiher by himself or with Mary. His monthly visits to the shepherd would probably help him to get over the loss of people he seemed to regard as members of his extended family. I wished that I had a close friend I could confide in. I could hardly share confidences with my Douglas relatives or with the likes of Bessie or the neighbors and I didn't want to tell the kids at school.

"What's up with you?" Ma asked eventually, a note of concern in her voice. My moodiness made her suspicious. "Have you been in a fight? If you have your father had better not hear of it. You know he won't be having you behaving like some rough kid dragged up in a back street. And I don't want mothers coming up here reading me the riot act because you've been out thumping their lads."

"I don't get into fights except with Ronnie Skillicorn and he always starts them"

"Well what's made you look so miserable? You know your face will stay that way if the wind changes. You'll go through life looking like an under-taker at a funeral. You'll turn the milk sour. You'll frighten babies in their prams and their mothers will tell the police where to look for you."

"I can't help the way I look," I said on the brink of tears. "It's Jakob. He's left the Island. He's gone for good. He went while we were across seeing Grandma and he's not coming back. They let him go and he didn't leave me a note or anything. He just went and now he's forgotten me!"

Having painted this forlorn picture I started to cry. I saw myself as a waif abandoned and the sorrow I had felt when Liz first told me her news welled up once more. Ma was concerned. Like Liz she gave me a hug which I didn't resist the way I would normally have done protesting that I wasn't a little kid any more.

"Are you sure he didn't leave a message for you?" Ma asked.

"He didn't say goodbye. Aunty Liz says he wouldn't have had time to. He was told he was being set free and then taken back to England before he could tell anyone."

"Well, she's probably right," said Ma. "But cheer up. He'll send a letter once he's settled. He'll be so glad to be out from behind all that barbed wire that he'll just be enjoying his freedom for a while. It'll take him time to get used to being in the everyday world again. It doesn't happen overnight, you know, not if you've been a prisoner for a couple of years the way he has. But when he's settled into his new life and he's comfortable he'll write. You were both such good friends."

"No," I said sadly, "he won't write. When Mary left because she had to, he stopped talking about her right away and she was his girlfriend. He'll forget about me. He didn't want to come here to the Island and he won't want to remember anything about the place."

"Well, that's to be seen," said Ma, "but there's no use looking on the black side of things right away. It will only make you unhappy and it won't change the facts. If your Dad and I let ourselves worry about Ronald we'd be worried all the time. It wouldn't help him if we worried about him like that and it won't help you to worry about Jakob. Think of all the times you had together. Remember them and then if he doesn't write to you you'll still have good memories of the two of you on the farm."

This sensible piece of advice seemed too glib to me.

"That's easy for you to say," I retorted, "but Jakob wasn't your friend. You didn't even want me to talk to him at first. If a really good friend of yours had left here while you were away and they weren't going to come back and they didn't say goodbye or tell you where they were going to or even if they'd miss you then you'd feel miserable too."

"Which friend left?" asked Bessie who walked into the room just then, as usual, wading into a conversation not intended for her.

"Erik's friend...the prisoner Jakob at the Camp. He was let go while we were away in Lancaster and Erik's only found out about it today. He's upset because Jakob didn't leave a note with Liz to tell him where he was going."

"They've let that f'la loose? Have them f'las in government got any brains? I've said since them Germans from that ship that put into Douglas in 1936...them f'las that marched along Douglas promenade in their Nazi uniforms with drums and bugles and waving that swastika flag about... I've said since that very day we should round up f'las like that, lock 'em up and keep 'em locked up till they see sense. Now they're lettin' these aliens out to help the Nazis win the war. The government has gone off its rocker."

"The aliens aren't Nazis, Bessy," said Ma. "They want to *fight* the Nazis."

"That's what they might be sayin' ta get out of an internment camp. Ya wouldn't be yellin' *Heil Hitler* in there would ya? Ya wouldn't be stickin' yer arm up in the air and goose-steppin' about and goin' on about the Fatherland. Oh no! Once these f'las is away you'll see what tricks they'll get up to. They'll all be back before long. Erik'll only have to wait a few months and that pal of his will be here again, mark my words. Why he wants to be friends with a Nazi is beyond me. You keep tellin' him that aliens aren't friends of Hitler and you'll only encourage him. That's no way to win a war."

"General Bessie at it again is it?" said Pop who had come into the living room from the back yard while Bessie sang one of her theme songs. "What battle are ya fightin' this time Bessie? Whose army's doin' the wrong thing now?"

Ma explained about Jakob and about Bessie's confusion of aliens with Nazis.

"Well, ya may have a point there, Bessie," said Pop. "The government had its reasons for puttin' these f'las behind the wire."

"And doesn't the fact that the government is letting them out again show that it realizes it made a mistake?" Ma asked.

"Lettin' them out is the mistake," said Pop. "Anyway, it's not lettin' them all out. It knows some a them f'las *are* Nazis."

"If Jakob has been let go that shows he isn't one of them and he never was," I piped up.

"Not necessarily," said Pop. "If the government made mistakes about putting people into the camps they could be makin' mistakes in lettin' some of them out."

Finding discussions like these futile I let the matter drop and went up to my bedroom to indulge in misery. Why did life have to be so full of troubles? Not so long ago my days had been occupied with carefree play when I didn't have to be in school or church. The heaviest crosses I had to bear then were Miss Quirk's eccentric conduct in church, Ronny Skillicorn's insults in the school playground, the Vicar's admonitions before and after church services, Ma or Pop's temporary annoyance at my coming home late for tea and that brief unhappy stay with Aunty Doreen. These were as nothing compared to the loss of Jakob whose permanence on the farm I had allowed myself to take as an article of faith.

A few days after my shock at discovering that Jakob had gone had been blunted I approached Lilywhite. It occurred to me that since she worked as a volunteer librarian at the Mooragh Camp she might know something about the rules concerning prisoners after they had been released. I wanted to know if in fact they were allowed to write to people on the Island – people those who were allowed out of the Camp might have become friendly with.

"I don't know," she said. "At least I'm not at all sure which amounts to the same thing. But I shouldn't think they'd want to after all they've been put through over here. They've really been through a wringer as the Amerian airmen say."

"What about if they had friends…real friends?"

"You're asking because of that chap on the farm aren't you? You've never been into the Camp have you? Believe me if you had to live in it you'd want to forget it. The people in the Camp were put there by force just because they had German names and in many cases German backgrounds. But only a handful of them ever supported Hitler. Most were Jews the Nazis would have killed if they had stayed in Germany so they came to Britain to stay alive and before the war we took them in. Then once the war started we changed our minds and said they could be dangerous to us so the government locked them all up. Think about that. What if the government decided that all Manx people were dangerous and had to be locked up – or all boys with the name Erik? That sounds stupid doesn't it but that's what happened to your friend Jakob Weiss. He had a German name – he was a refugee with a German name and that was enough to get him imprisoned here. He was one of many intelligent creative and professional men who had done nothing to deserve what happened to them but who were all crowded together behind barbed wire having to live four to a room. And don't forget the German women refugees… they're all held in the south of the Island…in Castletown, Port Erin and Port St. Mary. If you've endured two years without your freedom or your family even if you weren't roughly treated by the guards, even if you got out in the week to work on farms, you would still want to get away from here so much that when you were let go you'd want to try to forget the experience had ever happened. You would want to pick up the pieces of the life you left behind. You might not think your friend is being fair to you since you had nothing to do with his being here but you belong to the place where he was so unjustly imprisoned – a place he'll want to forget. Writing to you would bring it all back so it doesn't really matter whether he's allowed to write or not. He won't want to. The best thing you can do is to remember the good times you shared together. Maybe when the war is over and time has passed Jakob *will* come back to see how you are. But who knows how long that will be? Better get on with your life and remember him as the sort of friend most boys your age are never lucky enough to have at all. You really have been very lucky. How many boys or girls at your school have had an international artist to talk to and tell their secrets?"

I hadn't thought of the matter in this way being more concerned about what I had lost than with what I had gained. Jakob had changed me whether he intended to or not. He had made me aware of a world far wider than the Island on which I had grown up. He had talked to me of Europe and its great cities many of which he had visited. He had talked to me of art, especially operatic art – a subject never mentioned in my family or even in my school. He had begun to make me feel that it was important to acquire knowledge, to aspire to something better in life than the mundane concerns of either my family or of the provincial society in which we lived. He had made me feel that it was important to see something of the world when I was old enough and when the war was over. He had in fact given me something of an informal education, one not provided by my school and which I see now, with all the perspective of many decades, helped to push me in the direction of that higher education which has been the business of my entire adult life. Of coure I couldn't take comfort in any of this when I was still a child but I felt that Lilywhite had made a valid point and that I had been lucky to have been Jakob's friend however hard it was to lose him.

I decided not to tell anyone at school about Jakob's leaving the Island. I had kept him a secret from those I mixed with referring to him only obliquely now and then. Many of the children I knew would, like their parents and like Bessie, have unthinkingly called him a Nazi. They would want to know how I could be friendly with a German. I would have told them that Austria wasn't Germany but they would have retorted that Hitler came from Austria so they were all alike. But then there was Colin Fayle.

He was a year younger than me and not one of the children I played with in the woods, or in the churchyard or playground. He wasn't a member of St. Paul's choir and he didn't live anywhere near us. His parents had a small tidy house on the north side of the town on a hill above and beyond the Internment Camp. One day I saw him weeping openly in a corner of the school playground during the morning break. Had things been normal with me I would have written him off as a sissy for resorting to tears like a girl but the wound of Jakob's departure was raw and I knew that all too easily I could cry in public myself if someone said the wrong thing. So I felt sympathetic and went up to him to ask what was the matter.

"Mind your own business," he said not wanting to draw attention to himself yet unable to stop crying either.

"Something must be the matter," I said, "or you wouldn't be out here crying where everyone can see you."

"Go away and leave me alone," he said wiping his runny nose on the sleeve of his jacket.

"Suit yourself," I said and walked off. If he wanted to make himself the center of jeering attention there was nothing I could do about it if he wouldn't let me.

On that occasion he was lucky not to have attracted the unwelcome notice of the playground bullies. Later in the week he was not so fortunate. Then I saw him surrounded by a ring of taunting boys egged on, of course, by Ronnie Skillicorn. He was crying again, quite openly. I pushed my way through the circle to Ronnie to ask him – belligerently – why he was "picking on a little kid younger than you."

"Because he's a sissy," said Ronnie. "He's a mummy's boy out here crying like a little girl."

"And you're brave, are you, picking on kids who can't fight back?"

"What's it to you?" Ronnie was genuinely surprised at the hostility I was showing him over Colin's plight. "Since when have you been a pal of his?"

"I'm not."

"Then bugger off while I teach him a lesson."

"It's time somebody taught *you* a lesson," I said, by now furious. I punched Ronnie on the nose, which caused blood to flow and an expression of complete incredulity to pass across his face. Ronnie wasn't quite sure what had happened. One minute he had been standing there, cock of the walk, master of all he surveyed, and the next he was on his back on the cold playground concrete temporarily confused while I wrung my right hand which had skinned, bleeding, painful knuckles.

But Ronnie wasn't immobile for long. He had been temporarily stunned but soon came round. His first emotional response was amazement that I had both the gall and the strength to knock him out. His second was to promise that after school there would be a re-match and this time he would beat me to a pulp. Before I could utter some taunting response a boy rushed up to tell us that the Headmaster had witnessed the fight from his window and wanted us both in his office right away.

"Brawling in the playground...or anywhere else in the school...is, as you both know all too well, simply not allowed," said the Headmaster wheezing with emotion. "I have had cause to punish both of you before. You don't seem to have taken those occasions seriously. I'll see if I can make a firmer impression this time. Bend down, both of you!"

We did as ordered and the Head whacked our bottoms with his cane, one of us then the other, turn and turn about, until his arm was tired. Both of us wept silent tears of pain and humiliation.

"If I have any more trouble from either of you," he said before dismissing us, "then I'll have your parents in here to tell them what a disgrace to the school you both are."

"You're a couple of hooligans and I'll tell them so. Any more brawling in this school, any more of this ruffianly behavior and I'll expel you both! Is that clear?"

Fearfully we assured him that it was indeed clear and we left his office walking now with pain and difficulty.

"It's all your fault," said Ronnie when we were at a safe distance from the Headmaster's office.

"If you hadn't been bullying that little kid none of this would have happened," I retorted.

We satisfied ourselves with mutual recrimination after Ronnie decided that revenge was a dish best not served at all. I was fearful that Ma and Pop would find out what I had been up to. If she heard about it my conduct would convince Ma that I *was* turning into that rough kid of her imagintion.

I did approach Colin Fayle again. I told him that since I had fought Ronnie on his behalf and had been severely punished for doing so he owed me an explanation of his playground weeping fits. I demanded to know what he had been crying about.

"My Dad," he said. "He's in the army and he's been killed in an accident. A shell went off when it wasn't supposed to and blew him up." It seems he worked in a bomb disposal unit.

I felt immediately guilty for eliciting this information especially since the telling of it made Colin cry all over again. To make up for my insensitivity I told him about Jakob, about our friendship and what it meant to me, about how he had abruptly left so that he seemed as good as dead since he wasn't coming back. I had to face never seeing him again. By the time I had finished this story I was crying too so there we stood, two small victims of war grieving our losses. Colin's was so much greater than mine that I felt ashamed of my emotion.

Days, weeks, months passed and there was no word from Jakob. My mind went back to the day when I saw that Spitfire crash. I now thought of what it must have been like for the pilot's family to be told that he had been killed in Ramsey Bay. His family's loss, like Colin's, was so much more final than mine. After all it was possible that when the war was over and the troops had all returned to civilian life Jakob might walk back into our lives as my elder brother did. The Polish pilot and Colin's father would never return to their families but there was at least a chance that Jakob might turn up one day. That's why, in the decades that followed, whenever I walked through the streets of London or the larger cities of Europe I was on the look-out for him but look as I might, summon what hope I could, I never saw him again.

Acknowledgements

I HAVE RELIED LARGELY ON MEMORY BUT HAVE FOUND USEFUL INFORmation in the following:

"The Manx Experience": <u>A Chronicle of the 20th Century</u>,
Vol. I., 1901–1950, edited by Gordon N. Kniveton.

<u>The Isle of Man</u>, by R. H. Kinvig: Liverpool University Press, 1975.

<u>Island of Barbed Wire:</u> The Remarkable Story of World War Two
Internment on the Isle of Man, by Connery Chappell: London, 1984.

<u>"Collar the Lot":</u> How Britain Interned and Expelled Wartime
Refugees, by Peter and Leni Gillman: London, 1980.

"The Isle of Man" by the Rev. John Quine:
Cambridge County Geographies, 1911.